Praise f[illegible]
Poppy Denby In[illegible]

"Poppy Denby's back doing what sh[illegible]es best, and this time in Newcastle! Cleverly plotted as always, with an exceptional eye for detail and a fabulous amateur sleuth, Veitch Smith carries us back once more to the Golden Age for this delicious murder mystery."

Dr Collins (Dr Noir) founder of Newcastle Noir Crime Festival

"This latest in the Poppy Denby series continues Fiona Veitch Smith's compelling grip over historical story and murder mystery. She throws a spell as she brings together her cast of characters that instills in the reader empathy with them and forms a vivid sense of place (in this case north-east England) and period. Smith's choice of a 1920s setting is inspired, with its deep social and cultural changes which are so vividly captured you could wonder if the author had time-travelled."

Colin Duriez, author of *Dorothy L. Sayers: A Biography: Death, Dante and Lord Peter Wimsey*

"Poppy Denby's latest investigation combines an intriguing cold case mystery with a murder puzzle set in Newcastle in 1924. Complete with map and cast of characters, this is great fun for fans of mysteries set during detection's Golden Age."

Martin Edwards, author of *Mortmain Hall, Gallows Court*

Also by Fiona Veitch Smith

The Poppy Denby Investigates Series

1. *A Front-Page Murder*
2. *Murder at the Old Vic Theatre*
3. *Murder on Lexington Avenue*
4. *Murder at Winterton Hall*
5. *Murder at the Art Gallery*
6. *Murder of an Oxford Scientist*

The Miss Clara Vale Mystery Series

1. *The Picture House Murders*
2. *The Pantomime Murders*
3. *The Pyramid Murders*
4. *The Penford Manor Murders*

Murder at the Art Gallery

Fiona Veitch Smith

embla books

First published in Great Britain in 2025 by

embla books

Bonnier Books UK Limited
HYLO, 5th Floor, 103-105 Bunhill Row, London, EC1Y 8LZ
Owned by Bonnier Books
Sveavägen 56, Stockholm, Sweden

Originally published as *The Art Fiasco* by Lion Fiction in 2020.

A CIP catalogue record for this book is available from the British Library.

ISBN: 9781471417801

This book is typeset using Atomik ePublisher.

Printed and bound in Great Britain by Clays Ltd, Elcograf S.p.A.

Embla Books is an imprint of Bonnier Books UK.
www.bonnierbooks.co.uk

FSC www.fsc.org MIX Paper | Supporting responsible forestry FSC® C018072

1 3 5 7 9 10 8 6 4 2

For my granddad Fred Veitch:
Your art lives on.

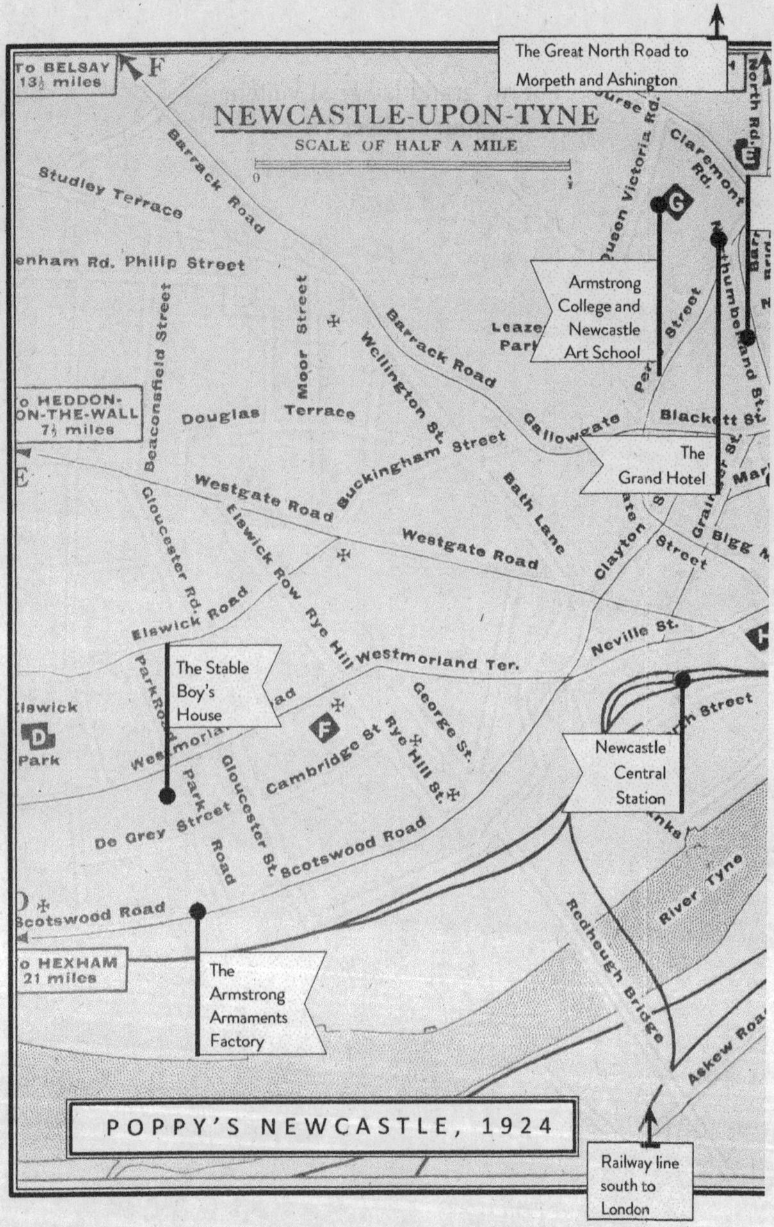
NEWCASTLE-UPON-TYNE
SCALE OF HALF A MILE
To BELSAY 13½ miles
o HEDDON-ON-THE-WALL 7½ miles
o HEXHAM 21 miles
The Great North Road to Morpeth and Ashington
Armstrong College and Newcastle Art School
The Grand Hotel
The Stable Boy's House
Newcastle Central Station
The Armstrong Armaments Factory
Railway line south to London
Barrack Road
Studley Terrace
Philip Street
Beaconsfield Street
Moor Street
Douglas
Terrace
Wellington St.
Buckingham Street
Westgate Road
Gallowgate
Blackett St.
Bath Lane
Clayton Street
Gloucester Rd.
Elswick Row
Elswick Road
Rye Hill
Westmorland Ter.
Neville St.
George St.
Cambridge St
Rye Hill St.
Park Road
De Grey Street
Gloucester St.
Scotswood Road
Redheugh Bridge
River Tyne
Askew Road
Queen Victoria Rd.
Claremont Rd.
Percy Street
Northumberland St.
North Rd.
Leazes Park
Elswick Park
POPPY'S NEWCASTLE, 1924

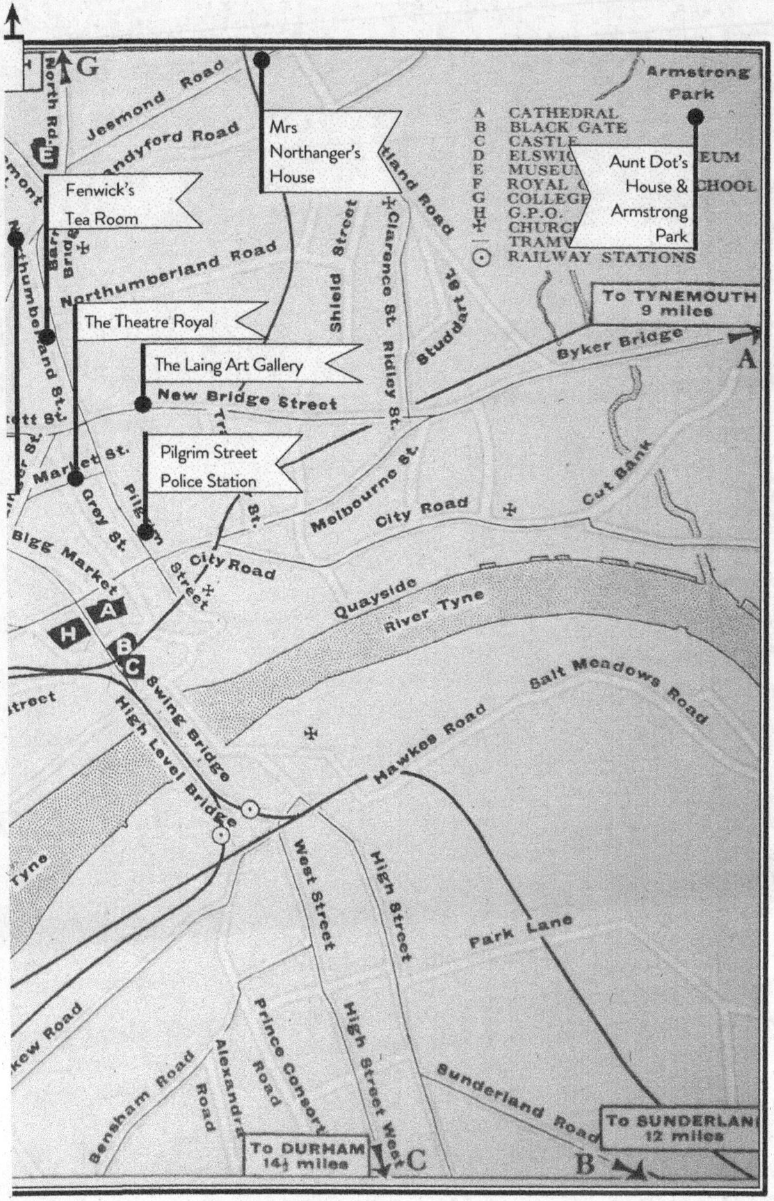

From: *The Dunlop Book: A Motorist's Counsellor and Friend* Ed. J. Burrow & Co. Ltd., London, 1920

Chapter 1

30 September 1897

Ashington Colliery, Northumberland

Agnes Robson hurried into the church hall, smiling an apology at the gentleman in charge, and took her usual place at the easel nearest the window. The other young artists – half a dozen of them, ranging from eight to fourteen – were already busy with their paints and brushes. Agnes lifted the sack off her canvas to reveal a half-finished study in oils. She inhaled the fumes, allowing the familiar smell to settle her quickened breath, picked up a brush and chewed the end while she contemplated the composition.

She had been attending the art class – which was held every Saturday afternoon for the children of pitmen – for four months. Since graduating from watercolour to oils, she had discovered that the paint did not dry completely between each class, and she could still work and manipulate last week's efforts if she needed to. Mr Brownley, the art teacher who came up on the train from Newcastle, had suggested she take the painting home to work on it during the week, but she had declined. Her mam did not like her coming to the classes. She had to leave her job at the laundry an hour early to get here, and Mrs Madsen always paid her a penny less on Saturdays because of it. So, each week she bought a bag of boiled sweets from Mr Storey's shop and bribed her fellow artists so they wouldn't tell on her. As for Mrs Madsen, well, she had come up with a plan to keep her quiet, too.

"That's coming along very nicely, Agnes. What do you think you need to do to improve it?"

Agnes looked up coyly through her dark lashes to see the tall figure of Michael Brownley at her right shoulder. He wore a paint-splattered smock over his smart tweed suit, but splodges of paint daubed his leather shoes. He never bothered to clean them. Obviously he didn't get into trouble like Agnes did. The girl always took her clogs off to paint, and her darned stockings, braving the cold of the wooden floor. As the classes had run through the summer this had not been a problem up until now, but as autumn was approaching, she might have to reconsider her attire.

She curled her toes, then lowered her eyes from the kind, handsome face of her tutor, to contemplate her painting. It was a view from the railway bridge that separated the twin pit villages of Hirst and Ashington. The track sloped gently to the right, leading the eye to the edge of the canvas where it continued in the viewer's imagination. To the left of the track was the blackened brickwork of Mr Storey's general goods shop on Station Road; then, in the distance, silhouetted against a splash of sky, was the giant wheel of the pithead, blocking out the sun. But as the track curved away, the light returned, with the brightest part of the painting in the top right corner.

Agnes contemplated her tutor's question. *How could she improve it?* She took the tip of the brush handle out of her mouth and used it to point to the foliage on the trees, sparsely lining the track. "Can I change the colour, Mr Brownley? Of the trees? They was green when I started it, but now they's orange and yella. I was looking at it on the way ower. The picture's changed ower time."

The tutor smiled at her, his full lips pushing back the whiskers of his moustache and beard. Agnes' heart skipped a beat.

"Of course you can change it. It's your creation. You can do what you like. But why do you want to do it? How do you think it will *improve* your painting? Is it just because the scene you imagined has changed, or is there some other reason?"

He paused, looked deeply into her dark brown eyes, then said: "Perhaps it reflects a change of emotion?"

Agnes felt her cheeks flush. The lad next to her tossed her a curious look, then returned to his charcoal sketch.

"I'm not really sure, Mr Brownley. It's just that it doesn't *feel* right with the green. And . . . and . . ."

"Yes," he said, leaning in, until she could smell the sharp scent of his aftershave cutting through the turpentine miasma. "And what? Don't be scared to say what you feel, Agnes – there is no right and wrong here."

She swallowed hard. "Well, it's because of the sun. Or the lack of it. The pithead blocks it oot. But I want to show that it's still there, in a way, through the natural things. Though the leaves are dyin' they'll be back. They've sucked in the sun. And they'll take it with'em. Where e're they go."

Brownley sucked in his breath. "That's beautiful, Agnes. Beautiful. You have an artist's soul."

Agnes flushed again. "Th-thank you, Mr Brownley."

"You will help me clean up afterwards, won't you?" asked the tutor as he moved on from his prize pupil to give some attention to his other charges.

"Aye. I will."

Agnes pulled on her stockings. Then her bloomers. Michael Brownley ran his finger down the girl's spine.

"I hope it didn't hurt too much," he said. "The last thing I want to do is hurt you, Agnes."

"No. It didn't hurt."

"Then what's the rush?"

"I need to help me mam with the tea. It's getting dark."

Brownley rolled over on the makeshift mattress on the floor and looked through the window, smeared with coal dust. The girl was right; it was getting late. He had been a fool to let time slip by. The hall caretaker would be here soon to lock up.

He sat up and pulled on his trousers and vest while the girl thrust her arms and head through her pinafore and started re-braiding her hair into two pigtails. She looked so young with clothes on. Despite having the body of a woman, Agnes Robson was barely more than a child. A pang of guilt struck him.

He hoisted his braces over each shoulder, then quickly pulled the sack cover over the painting he was working on. It was a nude of Agnes, sitting with her knees pulled up to her chest and her long black hair cascading over her naked white body. It was a very tasteful painting, he thought, with no breasts or genitalia on show. He was glad of that. He did not want to disrespect the girl. In fact, he regretted giving in to his base urges in the first place. He shouldn't have done it today. Nor last week.

He pulled out his wallet and counted out some coins. It was twice as much as he normally gave her for posing. He knew she would use some of it to pay off the woman at the laundry – to keep her quiet about coming to art classes – so it would be money well spent.

"Th-thank you, Mr Brownley."

His hand closed over hers, then he lifted her small white fist to his mouth and kissed her knuckles. "No, thank *you*, Agnes. Thank you."

Agnes hurried up Station Road, trying to beat the last rays of sun as they slipped over the edge of the world. At the building site where they were constructing the new Methodist chapel, she stopped to let a horse and cart pass, then readied herself to run the last few hundred yards to her house at the end of Eleventh Row.

"Is that you, Agnes?" She heard a voice behind her and turned to see a young woman, in her mid-twenties, holding a small boy by the hand.

"It is, Mrs Denby."

The woman clicked a padlock shut on the door of a shack. The corrugated iron structure was the temporary home of Trinity Methodist Chapel, which hosted Sunday School classes and church services for the more religious-minded miners. The Methodists were just one group trying to save the souls of the men who descended into the black bowels of the earth, and they had to share the mission field with Anglicans, Roman Catholics and Salvationists. The art classes were held in a Church of England hall.

"Will we be seeing you at Sunday School tomorrow, Agnes?"

Agnes lowered her eyes, not wanting to meet the probing gaze of the minister's wife. *Can she see I've just sinned?*

"I'll have to ask me mam. She might need me to help with the bairns."

"You can bring the bairns with you, Agnes. We have room for them all." She looked down at her young son huddled next to her.

The young woman smiled as she gestured to the makeshift building. "At least we will when the new chapel's built. But you know we won't turn anyone away, don't you?"

"Aye, Mrs Denby, I know that. But it's still up to me mam."

"Should I come ask her?"

Agnes imagined her mother, peeling tatties, with one bairn hanging to her skirt and another screaming in the crib, while she boiled water on the fire for her da's Saturday night bath. She wouldn't thank Agnes for bringing a God-botherer home with her, not at the busiest time of day. And she wouldn't thank her for being too late to help with the tea, either.

"That's all right, Mrs Denby. Don't worry, I'll ask her meself."

"You do that, Agnes," said the woman, kindly. Then she winced and raised her hand to her swollen belly.

"You all right there, Mrs Denby? Is the bairn kickin?"

"Aye, she is."

"She?"

"We're hoping for a girl, Agnes. A little sister for young Christopher. Aren't we, pet?" The young mother tousled the golden curls of the little boy. He grinned up at Agnes.

"Good night then, Mrs Denby. Will you be getting home all right?"

"I will, thank you Agnes. The reverend's just gone to fetch the cart. I hope to see you tomorrow."

"Aye, Mrs Denby, me too."

Agnes picked up her skirt and hurried across the road, then down the alley that ran alongside the colliery terraces, her clogs clacking on the cobbles. The Robson house was on the very end of Eleventh Row – the street closest to the pit. The pit bell rang, jangling her nerves. Her da would be home soon from his shift. He'd be wanting his bath, then his tea; then he'd head doon the Kickin' Cuddy for a few pints with his mates. Only when their father had left for the pub would the Robson children be able to have their baths. She would have to help wash the littluns first. Then Agnes would have her turn. Then her mam. Her brother, eleven-year-old Jeremy, would have a bath on the morra when he got back from his night shift doon the pit.

She spotted Jeremy's dark head bowing into the pigeon coop at the top of the vegetable allotment backing onto their house. One of his birds had won top prize at the last community gala, coming first in the race from Morpeth to Ashington. It was only five miles, but he was dead proud of it.

Agnes smiled. Jeremy was a clever lad. And a gentle soul. Too good for the pit. But what choice did he have? What choice did any of them have?

She turned the corner into Eleventh Row and startled the neighbour's cat, stalking a rat down the middle of the railway track. Each row of terraces – ninety-six houses per street – was separated by a rail line which, every morning, carried in coal for heating and carried out night soil from the outside toilets, known as netties. There was one netty for every two houses. The Robsons were a family of six. Their neighbours, eight. The cat hissed at Agnes. Agnes hissed back.

She opened the little gate, passed the coal shed and pushed open the kitchen door. And there before her was the scene she had just imagined when talking to Mrs Denby: her mam was peeling potatoes while her four-year-old brother, Frank, clung to her pinny, and the baby – Emma – cried in the crib.

Her mother looked up, her eyes bone weary. "The babby needs a new nappy. Thought you'd never get back. What took you so long?"

Agnes made a point of putting some money into the tea caddy on the shelf then turned to pick up her baby sister. The stench hit her like the whiff of a slop bucket.

"I was talking to Mrs Denby. The reverend's wife."

"The Methodist?"

"Aye. She was askin' if I was coming to Sunday School on the morra."

Mrs Robson sniffed and rubbed her nose with the back of her hand. "I'll need ya at home."

"Aye. That's what I told her."

Agnes put a towel on the proggy mat in front of the fire where the cauldron of water was boiling for her da's bath. The tin tub would be unhooked from its peg on the wall when her da was ready for it. She lay down her wriggling baby sister and unhooked the nappy pins.

The child had produced a good-sized stool. She wiped the bottom clean, rolled up the old nappy to be emptied later into the netty and put a fresh one on. Clean, warm and finally getting some attention, the baby grabbed at Agnes' pigtail that swung tantalisingly across the child's face. Agnes smiled and tickled her tummy, eliciting a delightful giggle from the youngest member of the family. Worried that he would be missing out on the fun, the four-year-old also made his way to the mat and threw his arms around his older sister's neck. "Can we play pit ponies, Aggie?"

"Aye pet, after tea. All reet? I need to help our mam first."

Mrs Robson smiled. "Thanks pet. When ya've finished there, get the bacon oot the larder, will ya?"

"Aye mam."

Mrs Robson suddenly stopped and looked intently at her eldest daughter kneeling on the floor. "What's that on the back of ya pinafore?"

Agnes looked over her shoulder, trying to see what her mother was referring to.

"There on the hem." Her mother put down the potato knife and walked over to the hearth. She bent down and ran her finger along the hem of Agnes' skirt. She stood up straight, her lips pursed, her finger erect and accusing.

Agnes swallowed hard. Her mother's finger was coated in bright ochre oil paint. The same colour she had used to change the foliage on her painting from summer to autumn.

"Have you been gannin behind me back?"

"What? Whatya mean?"

"Don't play coy with me, missy. You've been gannin to that art place instead of workin'. When I told you not to."

"I haven't! I put four shillings in the caddy. Mrs Madsen gave me the full amount. Check for ya self if ya don't believe me!"

Mrs Robson pulled back her hand and slapped her daughter across the face.

"Don't use that tone of voice with me, lass!"

Agnes fought hard to hold back her tears. Then she walked to the caddy and emptied it onto the table, flicking out the four shillings she had just put in. "See, it's all there. Count it ya self if the money's all ya care aboot."

Her mother's face softened and she reached out her hand and

patted her daughter's shoulder. "No pet. The money's not all I care aboot. And I'm sorry I hit ya. But . . . ," she cupped Agnes' chin in her hand and stroked her cheek with her thumb, trying to wipe away the redness of the slap, ". . . I've been hearing things. Aboot that posh bloke who comes up from the Toon. He never tried anything when ya was there, did he?"

Agnes pulled away from her mother, making a show of putting the money back into the caddy. "Whatya mean, try anything?"

"Don't be coy, lass. Ya know."

Agnes sighed and put the lid back on the caddy. Her face was still stinging from her mother's slap. "Aye, I do. But no. He didna try anything when I was there."

"Ya swear?"

"Aye Mam. I swear."

14th October 1897

THE MORPETH HERALD

BODY FOUND IN ASHINGTON PIT

ASHINGTON COLLIERY– the body of a man has been found at the bottom of Ashington Pit. The dead man was discovered last Sunday morning (the 7th) at the change of shift. It is believed his neck was broken.

The man has been identified as Mr Michael Brownley (28) of Newcastle upon Tyne. Mr Brownley, who was a lecturer at the Newcastle School of Art at the University College, ran free art classes for the children of pitmen in Ashington and Hirst. He had been running the classes at St John's Church in Hirst most Saturdays since June 1897.

It is unclear how Mr Brownley came to be near the pit, which is over a mile from the church and not in the vicinity of the railway station. The miners who found the body at the bottom of a shaft, temporarily shut for maintenance, say they smelled alcohol on his breath and that his clothes were muddy and dishevelled.

Police said that Mr Brownley was last seen at the Kicking Cuddy public house having a drink. They speculate that he may have been intoxicated and become disorientated on his way back to the train station.

Police are asking for any witnesses who may have seen Mr Brownley leaving the Kicking Cuddy around eight o'clock to contact them.

Mr Brownley is survived by his widow who is expecting their first child.

Chapter 2

Monday, 30 September 1924

Newcastle upon Tyne

The Flying Scotsman chugged – rather than flew – over the King Edward VII Bridge spanning the River Tyne, slowing to walking pace before jolting to a stop under the Victorian vaults of Newcastle Central Railway Station. Poppy Denby gathered her suitcase from the luggage rack and stepped out onto the smoke-filled platform. The coal dust caught in her throat and she coughed, looking forward to exiting the station onto the sunny expanse of Neville Street. It was an Indian summer in the North East of England and Poppy counted her blessings. London, where she now lived, was usually a few degrees warmer than her native Northumberland and she had packed her warmest winter coat in anticipation. But today she didn't need it, and she cut a smart figure in her red Chanel suit, cloche hat, Mary Jane shoes and swish white silk scarf, tied, most tastefully, in a fashionable knot at her neck.

It had been four and a half years since she had first made the journey in the other direction, from the provincial northern city to the nation's capital. During that time she had launched herself into a rewarding career as a journalist on a leading London tabloid and improved her fashion sense immensely. She had also become one of the city's most famous amateur sleuths, working with the team at *The Daily Globe* to solve murders and scoop the paper's rivals. But up here in Newcastle she hoped to have a break from all that, looking forward to a couple of weeks' holiday visiting family and friends.

It was her father's sixtieth birthday and there was going to be a party up the Great North Road in Morpeth next Saturday. However, at the invitation of her Aunt Dot, she had decided to come up five days early to see her eccentric aunt's latest project, and to support her friend Delilah who was starring in a play at Newcastle's Theatre Royal. Poppy smiled to herself, thinking about the time she and "the gang" had previously been on tour together – to New York! Golly, that had been quite an adventure. She didn't expect anything as dangerous or exciting to happen to her here in Newcastle.

She stepped out of the station's ostentatious portico onto the concourse where motorised and horse-drawn taxis lined up to meet commuters off the London to Edinburgh train. She looked left along Neville Street towards St Mary's Cathedral, then right towards the George Stephenson Monument as a tram trundled past. Then, she spotted what she was looking for: a bright yellow Rolls Royce zipping towards her from the direction of the Mining Institute on Westgate Road. The motor drew appreciative looks from the row of male taxi drivers, which transformed into utter shock as it double-parked alongside them, the window wound down, and a woman in motoring leathers barked out: "In you get, Poppy. I don't want to bother with parking!" Poppy grinned, slipped through the gap between two dull black taxis, opened the back door of the Rolls and tossed in her suitcase. Then she opened the passenger door and climbed in beside her aunt's companion, Grace Wilson.

The fifty-five-year-old gave Poppy a quick nod, then stuck her arm out the window to indicate she was pulling out. She did a deft U-turn, ignoring the hoots of oncoming traffic, and cut across the tramline within a hair's breadth of a jam-packed omnibus.

"Golly, Grace, you're not taking any prisoners!"

"Sorry Poppy," she said as she completed her manoeuvre. "I don't want to leave your aunt alone too long."

"Oh? Why's that? Is something wrong?"

"Not physically, no, but left to her own devices she will spend every last penny we've got! The decorator is due this afternoon and I don't want Dot making decisions without me."

Poppy braced herself as Grace swerved to avoid a man on a bicycle, with a basket of bread tied to the handlebars.

"Damned fool!" shouted Grace.

Golly, thought Poppy, *what's happened to the quiet and mild-mannered bookkeeper?* She gave Grace a furtive glance and noted dark lines under her eyes and an even paler cast than usual to her normally inexpressive face. "Are you all right, Grace?"

Grace let out an exasperated sigh as she was forced to slow down at the pedestrian crossing leading to the Literary and Philosophical Society. Her gloved fingers tapped out an impatient tattoo on the steering wheel.

"Did you know that your aunt has invited Agnes Robson to stay with us for a week?"

Poppy smiled at a little girl, holding tightly to a rag doll as she crossed the road with her mother. "The artist Agnes Robson? The one who has just had the exhibition at the Tate?"

"Yes, that's the one. You covered that exhibition, didn't you?"

"I did, yes. And Aunt Dot came with me to the press showing, if you recall. It's when you were off visiting your mother in Margate."

With the pedestrian crossing clear, Grace let out the clutch and pressed the accelerator, steering the Rolls onto the Georgian grandeur of Collingwood Street. "That's right. Well, apparently Dot told Agnes that she'd inherited the house in Heaton and that we were planning on coming up to renovate it into rooms to rent. Turns out our trip up here coincides with an exhibition Agnes is having at the Laing. And she's gone and invited herself to stay with us."

"Invited herself? I thought you said Aunt Dot invited her." Grace pursed her lips, driving the Rolls through the Grey Street intersection at a snail's pace, as a horse and cart clopped ahead of her. Then she prepared to turn left into Pilgrim Street. "The exact sequence of events is unclear – I believe Dot had had a couple of glasses of bubbly at the time – but someone invited someone and Agnes, apparently, is going to be arriving tomorrow evening."

"Oh dear," said Poppy. "It's going to be a bit of a full house, then, isn't it? If it's a problem I can stay in a hotel . . . or go up early to Morpeth?"

"You will do nothing of the sort! You're family. And so is Delilah . . . well almost."

As the Rolls drove past Shakespeare Street Poppy cast a quick glance towards the rear entrance of the Theatre Royal. "Has she arrived yet?"

"Last week. But we've hardly seen her. Final dress rehearsals are in full swing."

Grace stuck out her hand, indicating a right turn into New Bridge Street, heading towards the Free Library and the Laing Art Gallery. "Don't worry, Poppy, we have plenty of space for you and Delilah – if you don't mind rooming with your old chum – but we haven't got all the rooms sorted yet and somehow we've got to find a place for Agnes."

Poppy gave her honorary aunt a sympathetic smile. She had suspected when she first heard of the plan to renovate the house that it might be a fractious affair. Although Grace and Dot had been friends for fourteen years – and were devoted to one another – they were chalk and cheese in their attitudes towards money. Take for instance the yellow Rolls Royce they were driving. Dot had taken the opportunity to buy it when Grace was in prison (an eighteen-month sentence for withholding information from the police) to replace an old but serviceable Model T Ford. When Grace was released she was heartened that her old friend welcomed her back with no recriminations, but appalled that Dot had been spending money like the Sultan of Zanzibar.

Grace, who had been the bookkeeper for a militant cell of suffragettes before the war, had been managing Dot's financial affairs since they first met. The former doyenne of the West End stage was the first to admit she didn't have a clue about money. So when Dot inherited the house up in Newcastle, Poppy expected the two women to have very different ideas on what to do with it. Grace wanted to renovate the seven-bedroomed home and sell it at an inflated price. However, Dot was reluctant to sell, feeling she owed it to her dearly departed relative to keep it in the family. So they came to the compromise arrangement of renovating the property and then renting out the rooms to ladies of a professional standing – and installing a caretaker for when they went back to London. Apparently they already had a waiting list of women who worked as lecturers at Armstrong College, as well as some teachers and a couple of secretarial assistants. There was not that much respectable supervised accommodation for single ladies of status in the northern city, so Grace and Dot felt they were on to a money-spinner.

The Laing Art Gallery – with its distinctive tower – was coming up on the left. Poppy noted that a sign was already up for the Robson exhibition: "Memories and Mementoes: Agnes Robson, daughter of the North". Poppy nodded to the sign. "Is this the first time Agnes has done an exhibition up here, do you think?"

Grace rolled her eyes behind her driving goggles. "Apparently."

Not much love lost between those two then, thought Poppy. *Is there something Grace isn't telling me?*

But she decided not to interrogate her chauffeur any further. The woman seemed stressed enough. And so they sat in silence as they made their way out of Newcastle proper and over the Byker Bridge, spanning the Ouseburn Valley. Below them the coal barges wound their way towards the Port of Tyne, from where their precious cargo of black gold would be shipped to every corner of the world.

Soon the expensive motor vehicle was powering its way up Shields Road – eliciting appreciative glances from pedestrians on the busy shopping street – and then turning into Heaton Road. As they went over the railway bridge Poppy slapped her forehead. "Golly Grace, I forgot there's a station here. I should have booked my ticket to here and saved you driving into town."

Grace gave a tired smile. "That's all right, Poppy. You weren't to know. Have you ever been to Heaton? It's a very small station and not all the north-bound trains stop here."

Poppy admitted that she had – but only when she was very little – to visit the eccentric Aunt Mabel from whom Dot had inherited the house. "I remember it being very grand compared to our house in Morpeth. And it had a beautiful view of the park. But that's about all I remember. And I'd forgotten that we'd come on the train."

"Yes, Aunt Mabel was very eccentric indeed. Now we know where Dot inherited it from." Grace laughed, and Poppy was relieved to see that her mood had lightened.

They drove past the Baptist church on the right and the ramshackle Heaton Hall on the left before finally pulling up outside a row of genteel white brick terraced villas, overlooking beautiful parkland. And there, in the small front garden, in her wicker wheelchair, was Poppy's Aunt Dot, talking to a man holding a roll of luxurious wallpaper.

"Good Heavens," muttered Grace, "I wonder how much *that's* going to cost?"

"And this, finally, is the attic suite. Just look at that view!" Aunt Dot – a plump woman in her mid-fifties, with spectacularly coiffed blonde curls – wheeled her way over to the recessed window. It had been a bit of an effort getting the wheelchair up the narrow stairs while Dot used the newly installed stairlift, but Grace and Poppy managed it between them. Now comfortably back in her chair, Dot gestured to the sloping treelined paths of Armstrong Park, meandering down the valley to Jesmond Vale. In the foreground was a medieval ruin.

"Isn't that King John's Palace?" asked Poppy. "I remember Christopher and I playing knights and dragons there when we came to visit Aunt Mabel."

Aunt Dot laughed, her bluebell eyes twinkling through heavy make-up. "Yes, that's where you used to play. But it's not a palace and it never belonged to King John."

"Oh really? That's what Aunt Mabel told us."

"It's what it's commonly known as around here. Your Aunt Mabel always enjoyed a good yarn. Did she ever tell you about the time she travelled on camelback from Bucharest to Baghdad?"

Poppy laughed. "She did! Neither Christopher nor I had any idea where Bucharest or Baghdad were."

"Neither did your Aunt Mabel," said Grace drily from the doorway.

"Come now, Grace, that's not entirely true," said Dot. "Aunt Mabel was a real adventurer. Gertrude Bell gets all the publicity, but if you read Mabel's diaries you'd know that she deserved much more credit than she got. She collected everything in this house – from Egyptian stele to Roman amphora."

"And dead badgers and mouldy pheasants," added Grace with a grimace.

Poppy looked around her at the clutter-free attic that was in the process of being converted into an elegant bedroom. "I remember the house was filled with treasures! Where's it all gone?"

"We donated it all to the Hancock Museum. Once they've sorted through it they will probably name a gallery in her honour! Imagine that – 'The Mabel Denby Room.'"

Grace snorted. "Once they've got rid of all the junk they might have enough for a single cabinet." Her voice was chiding but there was a kind twinkle in her eyes.

"I wouldn't have minded an opportunity to look through it," said Poppy wistfully. "There might have been something I would have liked to keep."

Dot looked crestfallen. "Oh Poppy! How selfish of me; I never thought! But you do know, don't you, that the house will be yours in the end? That's why I wouldn't let Grace sell it. It needs to stay in the family."

Poppy was startled. "The house is mine?"

"Of course! But . . .," Grace gave Dot a warning look over Poppy's shoulder, ". . . not yet. It's still in my name. Mabel left it to me. But as I don't have any children, it will pass to you one day as my next of kin. Besides, I think your father should have had half the share. As you know, Aunt Mabel was never happy that Malcolm married a Methodist and gave up his law studies to become a minister."

Of course Poppy knew that. Her father's side of the family never stopped telling her. Malcolm Denby came from a Church of England family who were never that "serious" about religion. But when he met her mother, Alice – an earnest and sincere evangelical Christian – he claimed that he'd "found God" and that the good Lord wanted him to go into the Methodist ministry. His family, including his sister Dot, never quite got over it.

Poppy gave a tight smile, not wanting to give her aunt a chance to take aim at her mother and her puritanical ways, and quickly changed the subject.

"So, when do you think your first lodgers will be able to move in? And do you have a caretaker yet?"

"I think we should be ready in about a month's time," said Grace. "But we don't have a caretaker yet. We are –"

"Oooooh! Forgot to tell you, Grace. When you were out picking Poppy up, Mrs Whatsername from two doors down – the one with the poodles – said she had someone she could recommend. A retired art teacher from Armstrong College. Apparently Mrs Whatsername's son knows her. He's the one – if you remember – who is helping curate Agnes' exhibition." She turned to Poppy. "Golly! I haven't told you yet, Poppy! Guess who's coming to stay with us tomorrow night?"

"Agnes Robson," said Poppy. "Grace told me in the car."

"I know! Isn't it fantastic? Such a famous artist! And she'll be staying here with us! When I saw her at the Tate I just had to extend the offer of hospitality. It's the least I could do. Did I ever tell you –"

"Dorothy!" Grace snapped. "You're digressing. What about this potential caretaker? Did you get her name? References?"

"Er, no. Not yet. But Mrs Whatsit, the poodle lady –"

"Sherman, her name is Mrs Sherman."

"Yes Grace, that's the one. She has all the details. You can ask her."

Grace gave an exasperated sigh. Poppy smiled at her sympathetically.

"So, as I was saying," continued Dot, turning back to her niece, "I was tickled pink when Agnes agreed to stay with us, and –"

The door downstairs opened and slammed shut. A voice trilled up the stairwell. "Cooey! Anyone home? Is that Poppy's suitcase I see?"

"Delilah!" called Poppy, relieved for the interruption and delighted to hear her old chum's voice. "We're up here!"

Chapter 3

Armstrong Park was golden. It was late September and the trees lining the meandering paths, and hemming the busy greens, were glorious in their early autumn foliage. Poppy and Delilah walked arm in arm through the gates of the park and headed towards the old ruin. "It's called King John's Palace, but apparently it was built fifty years after John died! Aunt Dot told me it actually belonged to the Sheriff of Newcastle – a fellow called Adam of Jesmond."

Delilah squeezed her arm. "Adam's a good name, don't you think?"

Poppy looked at her petite brunette friend. "Have you heard from him? *Your* Adam?"

Delilah sighed, stopped, then reached into her handbag for a cigarette. She didn't offer one to her chum, knowing that Poppy didn't smoke. Poppy waited patiently for her friend to light up and take her first drag.

After a long exhale Delilah finally said: "I had a letter from him a few months ago. He's in New York at the moment with Stanislavski. No idea when he'll be back in old Blighty."

Poppy frowned. Adam was the only man who had ever come close to taming the exuberant jazz club singer and actress. Delilah was a thoroughly modern miss who felt no shame in taking on and discarding lovers. But Adam had been different, and Poppy had thought for a while that she might be bridesmaid at their wedding. Delilah had thought that too – until Adam decided to take up a job offer with his idol and mentor, the famous theatre director Konstantin Stanislavski, touring the world's leading theatres.

Poppy empathised. The love of her life – Daniel Rokeby, a former photographer with *The Daily Globe* – had moved to Kimberley in

South Africa two and a half years earlier to live with his children, who had been looked after since the death of their mother by Daniel's sister. There had been talk for a while of Poppy moving there too and getting a job on the local newspaper, but it never happened. She had hoped that Daniel would soon tire of his life in Africa and come home. In fact, all the letters she had received from him during the first year suggested that things were not going well with his sister and her new husband, and she had half expected him to return within six months – but he had decided to stick it out for the sake of the children. Now, more than two years since their tearful farewell in Southampton, Poppy was finally realising that she should get on with her life, personally and professionally.

Delilah exhaled again, wafting the smoke away from Poppy with a kid glove. "And Danny Boy? Any more from him?"

Poppy shook her head and bit her lip, intent on not letting her emotions get the better of her. "Not since Easter."

Delilah pouted and wrinkled up her exquisitely manicured brows. "Men be damned!" Then she laughed and put her arm back through Poppy's. "Come, I'll show you something spiffing!" The two women picked their way carefully down the sloping tinder path, past tennis courts, a bowling green and a croquet lawn, towards a wrought-iron and brick pavilion and colonnade.

Delilah stopped in front of a flight of steps and gestured with a theatrical flourish: "And this, Miss Denby, is the scene of the crime. *This* is the place my mother, your Aunt Dot, Grace and some of the Newcastle suffragettes firebombed back in 1913. They left a note saying 'no peace until women get the vote.'"

"Golly," said Poppy, "I never knew the Chelsea Six were in on that. I thought it was just the Newcastle sisters."

Delilah winked at her. "It was, *officially*, but my mother told me they had come up on the train to support them. I'm not sure if any of the Chelsea cell threw the actual Molotov cocktails, but they were definitely here when it happened. In fact, it wasn't long before the Lord's cricket pavilion bombing that put my mother in jail. No one was injured in either attack. They'd made sure to do it when the venues were empty. But that didn't stop them from being arrested and convicted for the Lord's bombing. Someone ratted on them. And my mother always believed the person who had sent an anonymous note to the police was none other than Agnes Robson."

Poppy's jaw dropped. "By Jove! Are you serious?"

Delilah took a last drag on her cigarette, dropped it and stubbed it out with a swivel of her shoe. "Oh yes. My mother always thought it was her. And so did Grace. But Agnes denied it and your aunt – and the rest of the Chelsea Six – believed her. Grace and Gloria were outnumbered. Besides, they had no proof. Just a hunch. But then my mother died and the cell fell apart and they went their separate ways. The Agnes thing fell by the wayside. But I thought you might just want to know why Grace is in such a foul mood about Agnes coming to visit."

Poppy shook her head, trying to take it all in. "But why is Dot inviting her then?"

Delilah shrugged. "I asked her the very same thing last night. And she said: 'Grace has been forgiven much, Delilah, so she has no right to hold anything against Agnes.'"

"Really?" said Poppy. "She said that? That sounds awfully serious for Aunt Dot."

Delilah chuckled. "Your aunt *can* be serious when she needs to be, Poppy."

Poppy nodded her acquiescence. "Yes, I suppose you're right. And I suppose she's right too. If there's no actual evidence that Agnes did it – and if Agnes herself denies it – then it's time to let bygones be bygones. There's been a lot of water under the bridge since then."

"Quite. I've let it go and moved on. If I can, then Grace should too. And that should be that," said Delilah in a tone that suggested she would rather not discuss it any further.

Poppy didn't blame her. She knew Delilah's mother's death – at the height of the suffragette struggle – still haunted her. She looked up the pavilion steps and the colonnade filled with tea tables. "Shall we share a pot of tea?"

"I think that's a splendid idea," said Delilah, giving her friend a wistful smile.

As they were shown to their seats a woman with two white poodles was paying her bill.

"Hello, Mrs Sherman," said Delilah, catching her attention. "May I introduce my friend Poppy Denby? This is Dot's niece. Poppy, this is Mrs Maddie Sherman who lives two doors down on Jesmond Vale Terrace."

Mrs Sherman was a sturdily built woman in her mid-fifties wearing a sensible tweed skirt and jacket. On her head she sported a matching tweed hat with a partridge feather in the brim. Poppy imagined her out somewhere on a country estate – not in the middle of a city park. The two dogs sniffed enthusiastically at Delilah's shoes.

"Suzie, Charlie, stop that! I'm sorry, Miss Marconi. And Miss Denby, I'm very pleased to meet you. Your aunt has told me all about you. Are you intending to stay long?"

Poppy smiled. "Just a week. I'm going to be attending Delilah's opening night, then heading up to see my parents in Morpeth."

"Will you also be coming to the Agnes Robson opening?"

Poppy shrugged. "I'm not sure. I only heard about it for the first time today. When is it?"

"Thursday evening. The day before Miss Marconi's play, I believe."

The dogs were now sniffing Delilah's knees. She patted them gingerly. "Yes. Opening night's Friday. I've got a dress rehearsal on Thursday so won't be able to go to the exhibition. But I'm sure Dot and Grace will be going. Well –" she gave a knowing look at Poppy, "– Dot will. I believe your son works at the Laing, Mrs Sherman?"

Maddie Sherman looked as proud as Punch. "Oh yes, Dante is curating the exhibition. It's quite an honour. They thought of bringing someone up from London to do it, but the gallery assured Agnes' manager that Dante was the man for the job." She turned to Poppy. "My son has done very well for himself, Miss Denby. But hasn't yet found a wife . . ."

If Poppy were not mistaken, Mrs Sherman was sizing her up. "I'm sure you're very proud," she said, simply.

Delilah, who was now picking white dog hair off her stockings, chipped in: "Shall we have that tea now, Poppy? I'm parched. Oh, waiter! Over here please." Then to the woman in tweed: "I'm sure we'll see you again, Mrs Sherman. Enjoy the rest of your walk."

If Mrs Sherman felt rebuffed she didn't show it. Poppy though felt quite embarrassed. When the woman and her dogs were out of earshot she whispered: "That was a bit rude, Delilah."

Delilah shook out a napkin and placed it on her lap. "Do you think so? Sorry, but if I'd left it any longer those dogs would have been chewing on my thigh bone and you would have been engaged to Dante Sherman." She giggled. "Golly, who would have thought someone as ordinary as Mrs Sherman would choose such an exotic name for her child?"

"Perhaps it was his father."

"Possibly. He's deceased apparently. But he was an icky – ick – fiddlesticks, how do you say it? An ick-thee-olo-gist. There, that's right. Quite exotic, isn't it? Something to do with Greek mythology? The fellow who flew too close to the sun?"

Poppy chuckled. "An ichthyologist is someone who studies fish. And Dante is the name of an Italian poet. But yes, quite exotic. Have you met him?"

"I haven't," said Delilah, as she eyed out the cake trolley.

"Then how do you know he's not good marriage material?" asked Poppy, teasing her.

Delilah batted her eyelids in mock flirtation: "I don't! But as you shall be meeting him first, I shan't stand a chance!"

"Who says I'll be meeting him first?"

"Are you really not going to the exhibition? I should imagine it would be rude not to, particularly as Agnes will be staying with us. I at least have an excuse."

Poppy shrugged. She wasn't really sure why, but she just didn't feel like going. She was here on holiday and she had only recently covered an Agnes Robson exhibition in London. It felt too much like work. "I suppose you're right. It will be rude not to." She sighed.

"Don't be so glum, chum. I'll tell you what, why don't we go to the pictures together this evening? There's not much to do in this town – no decent jazz clubs – but they've got dozens of bioscopes. There's one not far from here. Shall we go see what's on?"

Now, a night out with Delilah at the flicks did *not* sound like work. "Yes," she said, fanning out her napkin, "that sounds like jolly good fun."

***

The Scala Picture Hall on Chillingham Road was in walking distance of Jesmond Vale Terrace. Grace offered to give the girls a lift, but as the evening was clear they decided to take a stroll. Lace curtains twitched as they walked down Rothbury Terrace. Delilah refused to tone down her dress sense for the provincial northern city and wore exactly what she would have done on a night out in London: a brown Van Dyck velvet ankle-length coat with gold embroidered swirls, trimmed at the hem, cuff and collar with poofs of voluminous black sable fur. Wisps of her dress's cream chiffon train peeked out the bottom, swirling around her delicate ankles, and swishing the autumn leaves on the pavement. Both the dress and coat were from the January collection of Paul Poiret, Delilah's latest favourite designer, bought straight off the runway in Paris.

Poppy, on the other hand, wore an older but still stylish coat she'd bought two years ago at a sale at Selfridge's on Oxford Street. It was a Drecoll-inspired (but not original) black Roman crepe with large silver buttons offset to the left, running from collar to hem. A drop-waisted belt with silver buckle, fastening on the right hip, brought balance to the asymmetrical silhouette. A modest trim of grey fox fur at cuff and collar finished off the outfit. Underneath she wore her most recent purchase, for which she'd saved up for six months: a mauve silk Charles Worth with intricate grey embroidered flowers. Delilah would have considered it an afternoon dress. But for Poppy it was more than suitable for a night at the pictures. It was either that or the wine-red Lucien Lelong with train, which she wanted to keep for the exhibition opening – yes, she'd decided she really *should* go. The Lucien Lelong had been a gift from Aunt Dot for her twenty-sixth birthday in April. She had only packed two evening dresses, so she wasn't sure what she would do now for Delilah's post-opening night do.

Poppy and Delilah turned into Chillingham Road and joined the flow of passengers alighting from a tram, making their way to the brightly lit Scala Theatre. The Scala was one of over thirty new cinemas that had been built in Newcastle since the start of the Great War. The industrial northern town was booming with its coal mining, ship building and armaments factories, all given an enormous boost during the years of conflict. Although the boom years were now slowing down, and the region was beset with industrial strikes and rising unemployment, those of middle earnings still had considerable disposable income. The two friends joined a queue of well-dressed Geordies – the ladies in furs and the gents in white tie and tails – as they made their way into the plush art deco foyer, bedecked with marble floor and potted palms. They appeared to be the only two unaccompanied women present, eliciting disapproving glances from the older audience members through clouds of cigarette smoke. Delilah was used to an air of scandal following her wherever she went. Poppy was not quite as comfortable, but she straightened her spine and resolved not to let it bother her.

After they checked their coats into the cloakroom, they bought tickets for the evening's main feature: *The Humming Bird*, starring Gloria Swanson. The girls thoroughly enjoyed the story of the Parisienne pickpocket (played, most charmingly, by the lovely Miss Swanson wearing boys' clothes) who falls in love with a newspaperman who then disappears when he is sent off to war. Poppy and Delilah laughed, cried and cheered with the audience, accompanied by live piano, and wondered at the skill of Miss Swanson in conveying such emotion without using any words. Poppy's heart ached at the scenes where the heroine – Toinette – thought her beau might be dead, surreptitiously wiping away tears and trying to dismiss thoughts of her own lost love. But by the end of the story the lovers were reunited and Poppy and Delilah burst into applause. "Bravo! Bravo!" cried out Delilah, tossing her head at the tuts from a matron sitting behind them.

Leaving the main auditorium, Delilah suggested they get drinks from the bar. Poppy wasn't comfortable with this. She was becoming more aware by the minute of the glances and whispered asides. "Do you mind if we just have a nightcap at home? I'm awfully tired after the journey up. I'm sure Aunt Dot has a well-stocked cocktail cabinet."

"She does," laughed Delilah. Then, *sotto voce*, so the tutting woman behind them was bound to hear: "And there won't be any mother superiors there either."

Poppy stifled a giggle and took Delilah's arm as they made their way onto the street. However, just as they turned back towards Rothbury Terrace, Poppy felt a tug on her shoulder, and before she realised what was happening the strap of her sequinned evening bag was wrenched off her arm. A young lad wearing baggy flannels and a flat cap raced off down the street. "Stop! Thief!" she screamed at the top of her voice.

She started to give chase as best she could in her Cuban heels, but was soon overtaken by a tall, athletic gentleman in a tuxedo. The tuxedoed gent picked up speed and, like a sprinter in the Paris Olympics, rapidly gained ground on the lad. He deftly weaved between motorised vehicles and horse-drawn carts and, despite the boy's efforts to shake him off, had him collared in under a minute. The boy bellowed out a string of profanities for which he received a clip around the ear.

Poppy and Delilah and a gathering crowd waited for the man to drag the thief back to the theatre. As he did, a bobby on a bicycle pulled up and assisted him.

"Righto, DI Hawkes. I'll take him in. Can you ask the lady to come and make a statement in the morning?"

"I will, Sergeant," said the tuxedoed man, then he turned towards Poppy, with her evening bag in his outstretched hand. "I believe this is yours, miss."

Poppy, flushed with excitement and relief, took it from him. "Golly sir, thank you ever so much."

"You are most welcome, miss. Sheer luck that I happened to be coming out of the Scala at the same time. My name is Hawkes. Sandy Hawkes."

"And you're a policeman?" asked Poppy, checking that the contents of her bag were all accounted for.

"I am. I'm a detective inspector with the Newcastle upon Tyne City Police, Criminal Investigation Division. But I'm off duty tonight, accompanying my mother and sister." He nodded to two women huddled under the eaves of the theatre. Poppy's heart sank when she recognised one of them as the tutting woman who'd sat behind them.

"Have you ladies become separated from your escorts?" he asked, looking around for any spare gentlemen that might belong to them.

"We have not," said Delilah, once again taking Poppy's arm. "We're up from London," she said, by way of explanation, "and are staying with relatives. Lucky for us you have the same taste in moving pictures, Inspector Hawkes!"

Hawkes smiled and for the first time Poppy noticed that he was a pleasantly handsome man. He appeared to be in his early thirties, with blond hair, neatly parted, and a smartly trimmed moustache. She could not tell the colour of his eyes, but they seemed friendly and inquisitive.

"Well, thank you ever so much for your help, Inspector. I assume you will have to take my details. My name is Miss Denby. Miss Poppy Denby. And I'm staying with my aunt on Jesmond Vale Terrace."

Hawkes nodded in acknowledgment. "A pleasure to meet you, Miss Denby."

"And I'm Miss Marconi. Miss Delilah Marconi. You might have heard of me? I'm playing Gwendolyn Fairfax in *The Importance of Being Earnest* at the Theatre Royal."

Hawkes smiled politely at Delilah. "I'm afraid I haven't managed to book tickets for that, Miss Marconi."

"Then I shall arrange to get you some! It's the least I can do to thank you for saving us!"

"That is very kind of you, Miss Marconi. Although I was just doing my duty."

"But you're off duty! And you were very, very brave! The scoundrel might have had a weapon!"

Hawkes was beginning to look uncomfortable as Delilah gushed her thanks. Poppy took pity on him and interjected: "So do you need me to make a statement now or later, Inspector? I heard your sergeant say I could come into the station tomorrow. Is that correct?"

Hawkes nodded in agreement. "If you could, Miss Denby, that would be grand. Do you know where the station is on Pilgrim Street?"

"I don't, I'm afraid, but I can find out."

"Oh I do!" said Delilah. "It's not far from the theatre. I'll take you there tomorrow, Poppy. Then we can have a spot of lunch."

"Then that's sorted. May I walk you home? Jesmond Vale Terrace, you said? That's on Heaton Road, isn't it?"

"It is," smiled Poppy. "Thank you for your offer, Inspector, but I don't want to put you out. Besides, your sister and mother appear ready to go home."

Hawkes glanced over at the two women, who were not hiding their impatience. "Won't be long, Mother!" Then to Poppy and Delilah: "Perhaps then we can all share a cab."

It really wasn't a long walk home, but now that the adrenaline of the chase was wearing off, she *was* feeling a little tired. Besides, spending a little more time with the charming police detective was not the worst fate in the world. "Thank you, Inspector Hawkes. That will be most welcome."

Chapter 4

Tuesday, 1 October 1924

Newcastle upon Tyne

Poppy and Delilah got off the bus at the Eldon Square war memorial. Poppy asked Delilah to hold on a moment while she took the flower from her lapel and laid it at the foot of the monument, as St George on his steed looked on. The monument had been unveiled the previous year so this was the first time Poppy had seen it. She said a little prayer in memory of her brother Christopher and the other young men of the region who had died in foreign fields. As often happened when she thought of her brother, tears came to her eyes. But she wiped them away, fixed a smile on her face and turned to her friend who was lighting a cigarette: "Thanks, Delilah. Where to now?"

Delilah put her arm around Poppy's waist and gave her a squeeze. "It's a beautiful statue." Then, brightening: "I just need to pop into the theatre to confirm my rehearsal schedule for this evening, then I'll take you down to the police station. After that, we can go shopping in Fenwick's! It's a fabulous emporium! Who would have thought they would have something like *that* in Newcastle?"

Poppy chuckled. "Why aye," she said in her best Geordie accent, "there's nowt London 'as that we divvint!"

Delilah giggled. "Oh, you're such a card! I can't wait for you to meet my new friend Peter. He's going to be joining us for lunch."

Startled – although she knew she probably shouldn't be – Poppy asked: "New friend? That's quick; you've only been here a week!"

Delilah took her friend's arm, steering her left down Blackett

Street towards Grey's Monument. "He's the arts correspondent from the local newspaper. He interviewed me a few days ago. And well, what can I say, we got on . . . erm . . . awfully well."

She smiled, and Poppy thought she had never seen her more beautiful. Her dusky Mediterranean complexion was offset to perfection by a lilac turban, with the tips of her bobbed black hair brushing her cheeks.

Poppy was once again wearing her red Chanel day suit, which she knew suited her blonde hair and fair skin. Although her wardrobe was nowhere near as extensive as Delilah's – who had managed to pack a dizzying number of outfits for her brief tour north – she knew that each ensemble was carefully chosen for style, quality and durability. Her frugal nature was influenced not so much by her salary (which was actually fairly generous) but by her Methodist upbringing. She had grown up being told time and again that not everyone was as lucky as she. And "waste not want not" was a mantra she had imbibed from the nursery onwards. Since moving to London she had loosened her purse strings considerably – her job required a certain level of presentation – but when she could she bought clothes on sale or even second-hand. If she had had any talent whatsoever as a seamstress she would have sewn her own clothes, but she was a woman who knew her creative limits.

Despite her efforts at living as simply as she could relative to the Bright Young Things with whom she socialised, she knew her mother would still not approve of what she considered "frippery". The Chanel suit would most certainly *not* be worn to her father's sixtieth birthday party on Saturday. But her parents were not here today, and she loved spending time with her stylish friend and would indulge – modestly – in whatever shopping spree Delilah had planned.

She and Delilah turned right at the imposing column of Lord Earl Grey and down the exquisite curve of the street named after him. Architecturally, Poppy thought, it rivalled any street she had seen in London, and she wished people wouldn't only think of coal when they thought of the northern city. It was mid-morning on a Tuesday and the streets were scattered with shoppers and office workers stepping out for a breath of air. Market stalls on the pavement sold everything from fresh fruit to feather dusters, and behind them the formal shops lured in the more well-to-do shoppers. Poppy cast a glance into the regal mosaic-lined Edwardian Central Arcade, and wondered if the music shop – JG Windows – was open. She might pop in there later and buy some sheet music as a present for her mother. She had already bought her father a leather-bound volume of John Wesley sermons that he preached on his tour of Northumberland.

Down the hill one hundred yards or so on the left, past the Lloyds Bank building, was the neo-classical Theatre Royal. Delilah led her past the main entrance with its impressive portico of Dorian columns, and turned left into Shakespeare Street towards the stage door entrance.

"I'll just be a tick!" she said. And she was. Two minutes later she was back outside and slipped her arm through Poppy's. "Right, I'm only on at eight tonight. So that leaves us the whole afternoon and early evening to have some fun!"

"What do you have planned?" asked Poppy.

Delilah chuckled. "Well, that depends on what happens at the police station."

"Oh? It shouldn't take too long. It was only an attempted bag snatching. We should be in and out in half an hour."

"Good golly, Poppy, didn't you notice? That police inspector's eyes were on stalks when he saw you. He could have arranged for the sergeant to take your statement there and then. Why do you think he didn't?"

"Because the sergeant had his hands full with the thief and the detective inspector was off duty, with his sister and mother in tow."

"Fiddlesticks! It was because he wanted to see you again. To give him a chance to speak to you without his millstones there."

Poppy rolled her eyes. "You've been reading too many romance novels, Delilah. It's standard procedure to ask someone to make a statement the following day in non-urgent crimes. Besides, I very much doubt DI Hawkes will take my statement himself. He probably won't even be there."

Delilah winked at her friend. "Oh really? Mark my words, Poppy, mark my words."

Five minutes later Poppy and Delilah walked up the steps of the

Newcastle City Police Station on Pilgrim Street. They approached the uniformed sergeant at the desk, who greeted them with a smart: "Good morning ladies. How may I help you?"

Poppy was pleasantly surprised at the tone of the greeting. Her usual encounters with the police in London – who resented what they saw as press interference in their cases – were not always as friendly. She had, however, earned the grudging respect of the Metropolitan Police's Detective Chief Inspector Jasper Martin for her tenacious pursuit of the truth that had helped him catch more than one slippery villain. But up here in Newcastle, despite it being her home county, she was unknown. And she was very grateful for that.

She smiled at the desk sergeant. "Good morning, Sergeant. My name is Miss Poppy Denby. I'm here to make a statement. Last night in Heaton I was the victim of a bag snatching; however, two of your officers were there to assist me and caught the thief. They asked me to come in today."

The sergeant nodded. "Did you get the officer's name?"

"I'm not sure of the uniformed officer's name – but he was a sergeant, and he was the one who brought the culprit in –"

"It wasn't *him*! It was Detective Inspector Sandy Hawkes!" Delilah chirruped. "He *personally* requested Miss Denby come in and ask for him by name."

The sergeant nodded sagely. If there was a flicker of a smile under his fine moustache he hid it well. "All right ladies, I'll see if DI Hawkes is available. Won't you take a seat please?"

Poppy glowered at Delilah as the sergeant retreated into the station, and whispered: "Really Delilah, did you have to?"

Delilah batted her eyelids innocently. "What, Poppy? Did I have to what?"

Half an hour later Poppy and Delilah came down the steps of the police station and headed towards Fenwick Department Store. Poppy was cringing with embarrassment. "I cannot *believe* you invited him to play tennis with us!"

"And I cannot believe you didn't pack your tennis dress! Really Poppy, you ought to plan these things in advance." Delilah chuckled and steered her reluctant friend up the hill towards Northumberland Street. "Not to worry though, Fenwick's has a charming sporting wear department; we'll get you kitted out in no time!"

The girls nodded politely to two gentlemen who raised their bowler hats in greeting. As soon as they passed, Poppy hissed: "He didn't want to come, Delilah. You painted him into a corner."

"Poppycock! He nearly bit my hand off when I gave him a chance to see you again. Gracious me, Poppy, you really need to have a look in the mirror some time."

Poppy sighed. She was embarrassed, yes, but, she had to admit, she was also secretly pleased. She would never have had the courage to invite the handsome detective to anything herself. And a game of tennis would be a fun way to get to know him better in a decent chaperoned environment. Fortunately, she had taken some tennis lessons in London so she would not make too much of a fool of herself – she hoped.

Poppy and Delilah waited at the side of the court in Armstrong Park, Poppy wearing her new tennis frock. It was a simple but flattering drop-waisted white linen dress with a blue and white pleated skirt and a blue necktie. She had replaced her usual cloche hat with a bandana to keep her curls at bay. Delilah, of course, outshone her with a pink and white Suzanne Lenglen-inspired creation, whose mother-of-pearl buttons held together the wispiest of silks.

Delilah waved as she spotted the confident, striding figure of Peter MacMahon wearing tennis whites and sporting a straw boater. MacMahon was the journalist from the *Newcastle Daily Journal* whom Poppy and Delilah had met earlier in the day for lunch – or "dinner", as they called it in these parts. Although physically MacMahon was not Delilah's usual type of man – he was short, stocky and freckled – after spending an hour in his company Poppy could see exactly why the actress was so taken. The man was funny, intelligent and charming, with a grin to match Billy Bunter's. When Delilah asked him to join them for tennis later in the afternoon, he agreed immediately, then, as an afterthought, asked: "Who will make up the fourth?"

"Detective Inspector Sandy Hawkes," said Delilah triumphantly.

Peter choked on his crumpet. "Good Lord! How did you get that old sourpuss to say yes?"

"You know him?" asked Poppy.

"Doesn't every reporter know their local coppers?" asked Peter.

Poppy admitted that that was the case and realised, very quickly, that MacMahon and Hawkes must have a very similar relationship to her and DCI Martin. *Oh dear*, she thought.

"Oh Sandy! We're over here!" Delilah hailed the police detective as he rounded King John's Palace, heading towards the courts. He was wearing a striped blazer over his tennis whites and carrying a large racquet bag over his shoulder. The sporty attire looked good on him, Poppy thought.

"Good evening ladies. And good evening MacMahon. I didn't know you'd be joining us?"

"Oh, didn't I tell you?" asked Delilah innocently. "Peter agreed to make up the fourth. Now, I've only managed to book the court for an hour, but it should let us get a set in. So, who is going to partner whom?"

Poppy stood for a moment, awkwardly, knowing exactly whom she would like to be partnered with, but not wanting to appear forward. Delilah gave her a little wink.

"Why don't Sandy and Poppy team up and then Peter and I?"

Sandy smiled at Poppy. She smiled shyly back. "You'll have to do the donkey work," she said. "I'm not the best player."

He looked at her with open admiration. "Oh, I'm sure you'll be splendid."

Delilah coughed to bring them all to attention then spun her racquet on the grass. "Rough or smooth, Popsicle?"

"Rough please."

The four players watched as the racquet fell to the ground. "Rough it is."

"Excellent!" said Sandy, then turned his attention to Poppy. "Shall we warm up, first, Miss Denby?"

"Yes," said Poppy, accompanying him to the south side of the court. "I think that would be wise. And please, call me Poppy."

* * *

Poppy had never run so much in her life. She now realised her lessons at the Wimbledon Lawn Tennis and Croquet Club had been the gentlest of introductions to the game. Balls flew past her, over her and, in one embarrassing moment, under her, as she attempted to leap into the air. Peter graciously held back whenever he served or hit a ball in her direction, and Delilah cheered her on, so she didn't feel too crushed when she lost point after point. Sandy, however, played like a demon, doubling his efforts to make up for her failings, particularly when he served to Peter. A few shots slammed into the male journalist's body, but he didn't wince and accepted Sandy's not-too-convincing apologies. In reply, he served a few body blows of his own. Eventually though – and to Poppy's relief – the game came to an end when she missed the most benign of lobs from Delilah. The score was 3–6 and she turned, bit her lip and apologised to Sandy. Despite his obviously competitive nature, he smiled at her sympathetically. "Don't worry, Poppy, it's only a game. And you did splendidly."

She looked up into his blue eyes – yes, in the light of day she could finally see their colour – and felt a little stir in her belly. *Golly, he is a charming man.*

Together they walked to the net to shake hands with their opponents.

"Well done, MacMahon. You've got a strong forehand there."

"And your backhand's not too bad, Hawkes."

The two men laughed and shook hands with begrudging respect.

Delilah clapped her hands. "Good-oh! A truce! Shall we celebrate with drinks? I told Dot we might pop in for some sundowners."

"Dot?" asked Sandy.

"My Aunt Dot. Miss Dorothy Denby. That's who Delilah and I are staying with. Will you gentlemen join us?"

"I would like that very much," said Sandy.

"And I," agreed Peter.

The four young people walked up the hill towards Jesmond Vale Terrace, but soon separated into two couples, as Delilah and Peter tarried behind.

Poppy was strongly aware of Sandy's physical presence beside her. His blazer was stuffed into his racquet bag and his light cotton shirt clung damply to his chest. She looked quickly away. "Thank you for putting up with me," she said. "I hope you still had fun despite being saddled with the runt."

He chuckled. "I wouldn't want to be saddled with anyone else, Poppy. Besides, I have the feeling that what you lack in tennis skills, you more than make up for with other talents. What is it you do in London? I have a suspicion that you may be one of those ladies who works in a profession."

"Would it bother you if I did?"

"Not at all. We live in a modern age and I believe that women are capable of doing remarkable things. So, what do you do down in London?"

Poppy caught her breath. *Oh dear, he doesn't like journalists . . . ah well, better get it over and done with.* "I work for a newspaper."

"Oh really? Are you a secretary or a typesetter?"

Poppy cleared her throat, taking a moment to suppress her irritation at the common misconception she'd heard so many times before. "No, actually – I'm a reporter. My official title is the arts and entertainment editor, but in reality I am the entire arts and entertainment department. I suppose I do the same type of thing as Peter MacMahon. I interview famous artists and cover exhibitions, theatre shows, films and so on."

Sandy nodded. She couldn't tell whether he approved or not.

"Probably not entirely like MacMahon though," he offered, after some thought. "He does the arts malarkey up here, but he also helps on the crime beat when the regular bloke's got too much on his plate. That's where I know him from. And let's just say he should stick to theatre."

"Oh," she said, feeling offended on Peter's behalf – perhaps a little more than she should have. "I don't see why he should just stick to theatre. Sometimes people are good at more than one thing, you know. And besides, it may surprise you that I too sometimes write crime articles. So what do you think about that?"

Sandy stopped and stared at her, a montage of emotions playing on his face. "Well, gosh, what can I say?" Then he grinned. "Well, I did say I suspected you were a woman of many talents. Just as well you don't work here then. Or fireworks might fly!"

Before Poppy could reply, Delilah and Peter caught up with them.

"I could murder a glass of bubbly!" trilled Delilah, just as a taxi pulled up across the road, outside Aunt Dot's house. The driver jumped out and opened the back door, helping an elegant woman in a full-length fur coat out of the vehicle.

"Oh look, Poppy, it's Agnes! Cooey Agnes! Over here!"

Delilah ran across the road and pulled Agnes into a sweaty embrace, nearly flooring the taxi driver with her tennis racquet. Peter MacMahon let out a low whistle. "Is that Agnes Robson? *The* Agnes Robson?"

"It is," said Poppy. "Come on, I'll introduce you."

"But then I could scoop you."

Poppy smiled at him, and then at Sandy. "You go ahead and get the story. I'm on holiday."

Chapter 5

"Chin chin!" Agnes Robson clinked her champagne flute against that of a beaming Dot Denby.

"Thanks again for putting me up, Dot, or I'd be drinking alone in a hotel."

"Perish the thought! What about Gerald? Where's he staying?"

"He's ill. Down with gastroenteritis. So he won't be coming with me this time."

"Is that much of a bother?"

"It is, actually," said Agnes. "I've never been very good with the public side of it all – unlike you – so I've always relied on him. He's been my manager and publicist for ten years now."

"By Jove! That long?"

"Yes, I took him on just as the war was starting. He was with the Bloomsbury Set, if you recall. That seems like a lifetime ago now . . ."

Agnes' voice drifted and she looked over as a peal of laughter emanated from the young people sitting in the alcove of the bay window, all of them still dressed in their tennis togs. The two men – the reporter who had tried, unsuccessfully, to interview her earlier, and the policeman – would most probably have fought in the war. But unlike so many, they had made it back safely. She smiled as she watched the mildly flirtatious behaviour of the two girls, Delilah and Poppy. Delilah looked so much like her mother, Gloria. Although she and Agnes had never been close friends, Agnes had been very saddened to hear of her death when Delilah had only been fourteen years old. And she had been as shocked as everyone else four years ago to learn the true circumstances behind the suffragette's death. Agnes had never been comfortable with the militant methods of the

Chelsea Six – including Dot Denby and Gloria Marconi – but she did not believe they deserved what they got. She turned to Dot, trying to remember what she was like before her legs were crushed by the police horse in 1910. Yes, these women had paid with their lives so people like her could have the vote. And for that she was grateful.

Grace Wilson was standing quietly in the corner, her tall grey presence casting a shadow over the gay gathering. *I must try to put things right with her*, thought Agnes. She knew Grace suspected she had ratted on the sisters when they attacked the Lord's Pavilion in 1913 – resulting in the incarceration of Gloria Marconi and her friend, Elizabeth Dorchester – but she hadn't. Yes, she had publicly criticised the suffragettes' methods – and had even written a letter to *The Times* – but she had most definitely *not* turned them in. In fact, that was one of the reasons she had accepted Dot's invitation to stay with them while she was up in Newcastle: it was time to clear the air between them. Grace cast a cool glance in her direction. Agnes swallowed. *But perhaps not tonight.*

Poppy Denby jumped up and offered around a plate of macaroons. *Always looking after people, just like her mother, although she takes after her father in looks.* Agnes remembered Alice Denby with mixed emotions. She would always be grateful to the minister's wife for helping her during that terrible time after Michael Brownley died and rumours abounded about their affair, but it was a very painful time in her life that she did not wish to dwell on. Seeing Poppy reminded her of it and tonight she knew she would likely have dark dreams. However, it wasn't all bad. After things had settled down, Mrs Denby had helped find her a position in service with a County Durham family called the Moultons. And if it hadn't been for that, she would never have met Claude.

Claude Moulton was the black sheep of his family. He was a Bohemian artist in his mid-thirties and, like Michael Brownley before him, was drawn to Agnes' dark, almost gypsy, looks. He asked her to pose for him – fully clothed – and was charmed when he caught her on her day off doing some sketches of her own. The day before he was to leave he approached her as she was elbow-deep in laundry and asked if she would like to come with him to be his model in

Paris. Agnes, now estranged from her family in Ashington, looked at the raw eczema on her hands and wrists, and agreed immediately. So the next morning, before the Moulton family was up, she and Claude ran off. It was the summer of 1900.

At the end of the long, love-soaked journey from Durham to London to Paris, they arrived at Claude's apartment-cum-studio in the art sector of Montmartre. Ironically, it was in a converted laundry nicknamed *Le Bateau Lavoir* (The Wash House). Claude introduced her to his fellow artists, of whom Agnes had never heard at the time, but who were to become world-famous over the next two decades: Picasso, Matisse, Toulouse-Lautrec; they in turn had taken over the studios from Gauguin, Van Gogh and Cezanne. It was an exciting life for a seventeen-year-old: posing for Claude when the light was good, and drinking and watching cabarets at the Moulin Rouge when the light was bad. Whenever she could she practised her own art, borrowing old canvases and watching the masters at work. Slowly but surely she developed into a fine artist in her own right – but no one, other than Claude, was yet aware of her talent.

She lived with Claude for ten years – posing, cooking and cleaning for him, and, occasionally, avoiding his fists when he'd had too much to drink or been turned down, yet again, for one of Paris' summer Salon exhibitions. During that time she had become pregnant and miscarried twice. In some ways though she was relieved: Montmartre was no place to raise a child. Claude, despite his protestations to the contrary, had no intention of marrying her, and she began to think she should leave him. Despite the free-love ethos of the Bohemians she was at heart a conservative young woman who yearned for respectability. By the spring of 1910, when she was twenty-six years old, she had managed to squirrel away enough money to pay for passage to London. All she needed was the courage to leave. But each time it stirred in her, Claude would confess his love, how much he needed her, how lucky she was to have him and that perhaps this was the summer they might finally get married . . .

Then one night Claude never came home. The next morning a gendarme arrived to tell her he had been killed in a bar fight in an argument about non-payment for a portrait. A few days after the funeral she was visited by Claude's cousin from Durham. He told her he was the executor of the will and with barely veiled disgust announced that she was to inherit Claude's share of the family trust fund. Agnes was amazed. In all the years she'd been with him they had lived hand to mouth from the sale of his paintings or her modelling for other artists. She had no idea that he was actually the beneficiary of £1,000 a year. And now, her feckless lover and mentor had left it all to her. Finally, what she had always yearned for – respectability – was in her grasp. She might be the daughter of a coal miner and an artist's mistress, but with money like that she could start a new life in London as Agnes Robson, Post-Impressionist painter, fluent in French and an independently wealthy woman.

Poppy Denby approached her with a smile on her pretty face. "Macaroon, Agnes? They're delicious!"

Agnes smiled back. "Thank you, Poppy, I will." She picked a sweet confection off the plate and then, on the spur of the moment, said: "Poppy, I'm going to Ashington tomorrow. There's a community hall opening which I've donated money to and they're putting up a plaque with my name on it. I believe the press will be there. Would you mind awfully coming with me and filling in for Gerald? He normally handles my publicity, but the poor fellow's poorly and couldn't come up."

The smile vanished from Poppy's face and was replaced with a sympathetic but reluctant look. "I'm sorry Agnes, but I'm on holiday, I'd rather not..."

"I can pay you."

"No, that doesn't matter. It's just I was hoping to have a bit of a rest."

"Please, Poppy. I'm in a panic about it. I haven't been home in years and I'll have enough to contend with managing my family. I need someone to shield me from the press." Agnes paused and took a deep breath before continuing. "You see, there's a bit of a story I'm worried might be dug up. And if it is, it could distract from the exhibition."

Poppy suddenly looked curious. "A story? What kind of story?"

Agnes looked over at the reporter from the *Newcastle Daily Journal* then lowered her voice. "It happened many years ago. When I was barely more than a child. But someone died under mysterious circumstances, and to this day there are people in Ashington who believe I did it – that I am guilty of murder."

Poppy's blue eyes were like saucers. "Good heavens, Agnes, really?"

"Yes really. So will you help me? Please? I just need someone to field questions and keep the reporters focused on the opening of the hall and the exhibition. Can you do that?"

Poppy nodded. "Yes, I can, but I need to know what the story is in order to know how to spot a question about it."

Agnes let out a sigh of relief. "Thank you, Poppy. Come to my room later and I'll tell you all about it."

Poppy waved goodbye to the charming Sandy Hawkes and Peter MacMahon who said they would escort Delilah to her rehearsal in town. Sandy had wondered whether Poppy might accompany them, suggesting perhaps they could have a spot of supper, but she declined. She had enjoyed the policeman's company very much, but she had just spent the last four hours with him – and unlike Delilah, did not want to appear too eager. Besides, she was intrigued to hear what Agnes had to tell her. So after a light supper with Grace and Dot, she and Agnes left them to bicker over wallpaper swatches, and retired to Agnes' room. She had been given the newly painted attic suite, and the bay window was open to let out the sharp smell of emulsion. Poppy mentioned the smell to Agnes, but the older woman laughed, saying she'd spent her life breathing in paint fumes and had barely noticed it.

The two women positioned themselves on the window seat in the alcove and Agnes told Poppy her tale, stopping to pour them both a sherry when she finished the part about inheriting the money from Claude.

Poppy looked at her with new-found respect. "My word, Agnes, I never knew you'd had such a struggle. But what good fortune to have received that money. Did things get much better for you when you came to London?"

"It took a little while, but yes. Largely thanks to your aunt. I went to see a play one night at the theatre and I saw your aunt's name on the programme. I had never known her when I was in Ashington, but

I had heard talk that the Methodist minister's sister was an actress, and I recognised her name. I introduced myself to her afterwards, and your aunt, being your aunt, immediately pulled me under her wing. She'd heard that I was an artist – fresh from Paris – and she introduced me to some friends of hers in the Bloomsbury Set. You've heard of the Bloomsbury Set, haven't you?"

Poppy nodded. She had interviewed a number of former and current Bloomsbury associates in her time as arts and entertainment editor at *The Daily Globe*, including the author Virginia Woolf and her sister, the artist Vanessa Bell. She had also met the influential art critic Roger Fry who was known to make or break careers. "I assume that Roger Fry must have liked your work."

Agnes gave her a shrewd look. "Fortunately, yes. When your aunt introduced me to him he was just preparing to give the first of his famous Post-Impressionism exhibitions. Seeing I knew many of the French artists in person, he asked me to be his assistant. He said he couldn't afford to pay me but instead said I could hang a few of my own pieces. And I did! So the London art world began to associate me with the big names. Let's just say it didn't do me any harm."

"Not half!" said Poppy, remembering that Agnes had exhibited in some of the world's top galleries. And now, here she was in Newcastle as a "northern lass made good". Poppy noted that Agnes had lost most of her regional accent in the twenty-five years she'd been away, but, just occasionally, the odd flattened vowel slipped through. She wondered how the people of Ashington would take to this coal miner's daughter coming home. Would they warmly embrace her or think she was lording it over them?

"So," she said, "tell me about the event in Ashington. Who organised it and why do you think the question of the art teacher's death will be raised? What was his name again? Brownley?"

Agnes sipped her sherry and Poppy noticed a slight quiver to her hand. Poppy didn't think Agnes was a particularly heavy drinker, so was the tremor an emotional one?

"That's right," said Agnes. "Michael Brownley. He was a lecturer at what is now Armstrong College. He ran courses for the children of miners. The event tomorrow is connected to that. The college runs all sorts of community classes there now and has had a new hall built. Because that's where I got my start all those years ago – and linked in I suppose to the exhibition at the Laing – they have decided to call the hall after me. I'm sure I don't have to tell you that it's more to do with them piggybacking on my fame and getting press coverage for it, than anything to do with being grateful for the money I gave them."

It was a cynical but accurate observation. Poppy acknowledged that that was probably the case and that the local press would not be as keen to cover the event without the "big name" association. "So, why do you think they will rake up Brownley's death? It was twenty-five years ago."

"Twenty-seven, actually. October 1897. It was just something that your friend from the *Journal* said. Mr MacMahon. He said he'd be at the event tomorrow and that he'd been doing some research and came across a clipping about Brownley's death years before. He wanted to know if I had any comment."

"And did you?"

"No, I didn't. I shut the interview down then. Quickly but politely. He was charming and let it go. I think he just wanted to get back to Delilah. But he did say he'd ask me again tomorrow."

Poppy nodded and took a sip of her own sherry. "Yes, he probably will. I certainly would if I were in his shoes."

"Do you think he's the only one who will know about it?" Agnes asked.

"You say he said he found the clipping during his research?"

"Yes, that's what he said."

Poppy smiled at Agnes sympathetically. "Then I'm afraid not. All newspapers keep archives of old stories linked to famous people. At my paper they're called the Jazz Files. They're probably called something different at Peter's paper, but they'll do the same thing. So that'll be him from the *Newcastle Daily Journal*, then probably someone from the *Chronicle*, the *Northern Echo* and the *Morpeth Herald* too. All the regional papers should be there, and if he knows about the Brownley thing, they probably will too. Tell me again what happened to him?"

Agnes leaned back and rested her cheek on the windowpane.

It reminded Poppy of a Vanessa Bell painting.

"His body was found at the bottom of the main Ashington Pit shaft. Not far from me mam and dad's house."

Poppy noted the slight slip into regional dialect; just the odd word, but it was there.

"He'd been on the sauce – had had a couple of pints at the Kickin' Cuddy – and was heading back to the station. But he never got there, apparently. His body was found by the morning shift. My brother Jeremy was there when they came on him. His neck was broken. No one saw him after he left the pub. The police could find no witnesses and came to the conclusion that he fell down the shaft drunk."

Poppy absorbed this, then recalled the layout of the mining village from the time she'd helped her parents there with the winter soup kitchen. "But the shaft is not on the route from the Kicking Cuddy to the station."

Agnes looked at her, her brown eyes a pool of pain. "Aye, that's the problem. The police think he might have been coming to see me."

"And why would they think that, Agnes?" Poppy asked, already suspecting she knew the answer after the artist's confessions of her "living in sin" in Paris.

Agnes turned away and looked out the window. The sun had already set and the park below was in shadow. "Because, Poppy, he seduced me. He asked me to pose for him, then after that to – to – well, to have intercourse with him. I was only fourteen and completely starstruck. I thought no one else knew, but when he died some of the other children told their parents that I was his "bit on the side". So that's why the police came asking. Because me mam and dad lived so close to the pit, they reckoned he had come by our house. But he hadn't. None of us had seen him. The police talked to the neighbours and none of them had seen him either. So there was no evidence one way or the other. He might have come looking for me – he'd been told I couldn't come to class anymore because me mam had found out – but he never got to the house. He'd never been before. It was dark. Raining. He was probably drunk. He could easily have got lost and wandered over to the pit. He might even have gone to ask directions. We'll never know. But you see Poppy, there's some nasty people in Ashington, and nasty rumours got about. Some of them said I did it."

"Did Peter MacMahon say that? That he'd heard rumours that you'd done it?"

Agnes shook her head. "No, he didn't. He just said he believed my first art teacher had been tragically killed in Ashington. He wanted to know how I felt about it all these years later."

Poppy chewed on her lip as she normally did when she was thinking. It didn't sound, to be honest, like Peter was out to dig up dirt on Agnes. The artist was filtering his question through her own complicated feelings of sadness and shame. And, perhaps, anger too. Poppy didn't think she would have to field any questions about Agnes' possible link to Brownley's death – that was just village gossip, and if there'd been any evidence an arrest would have been made – but Agnes seemed certain there would be some.

She reached out and took Agnes' hand. "Listen Agnes, I really don't think there's anything to worry about. If I had read that report I would have asked you about it too. But without actually seeing what it said, I reckon it would have just been a factual account of the finding of the body or the declaration of accidental death, rather than rumours of your involvement. When Peter saw you he seemed delighted to have an opportunity to get a scoop on interviewing a world-famous artist, not a suspected murderer. And," she laughed gently, "I would know as I've interviewed both. But don't worry. I *will* come with you tomorrow. And I'll have a word with Peter when I'm there to find out what it was he actually read. It'll all be fine. You just focus on the opening. I'll handle the rest."

Agnes squeezed the young reporter's hand. "Thank you, Poppy. Thank you very, very much." Then, to Poppy's dismay, Agnes burst into tears. After a few awkward moments of Poppy giving her a handkerchief and patting her shoulder, Agnes pulled herself together. "I'm sorry. It's just – well – it's all a bit emotional. The last time I was back here was me dad's funeral in 1916. And that didn't go well. I'm hoping things will be better this time."

Poppy smiled at her encouragingly. "I'm sure they will, Agnes. People's feelings are always frayed at funerals. It'll be better this time.

And you're here for your job. Just focus on that. You're a wonderful artist and that's what people want to acknowledge."

Agnes dabbed her eyes and sighed. "I hope you're right, Poppy. I really do."

Chapter 6

Wednesday, 2 October 1924, Ashington Colliery, Northumberland

It had been twenty-seven years since Agnes had first painted the curve of railway line leaving Ashington. It was a motif that recurred time and again in her work: roads, rivers, railways – leaving somewhere and petering off to somewhere else. It had become one of her signatures; that and her brazen use of colour. Her first tentative experiments with it under the overly watchful eye of Michael Brownley had become bolder over the years. Influenced by Gauguin, Matisse and Van Gogh, she had learned to push her palette to extremes. Solid blocks of colour approximated trees and buildings that demanded the viewer either embrace it or look away. It was the colour – that splash of ochre on her hem – that had given the game away to her mother. She had personally gone to see Brownley the following week and told him in no uncertain terms to stay away from her daughter. It turned out that was his last ever lesson. He was to die later that night.

Memories of her time with Michael had not surfaced for many years – not until that reporter yesterday had mentioned it. The last time she was here – in 1916 – the village was in mourning for the thirteen lives lost in the mine explosion that had killed her father. And she was focused on seeing her family again for the first time in seventeen years. It hadn't gone well. If she had expected the warm embrace of her mother, she didn't get it. There was no overt animosity, just indifference. Her mother shook hands with her – yes, she *shook* her hand – as if she was just one of the few dozen well-wishers, and then moved on down the line. Her brother, Jeremy, had been a little warmer. But as the new head of the family, trying to save his mother from eviction from the mine house she now lived in alone, he didn't have time to catch up with his estranged older sister. But he did at least say she "looked well" and that something good must have come from her running off. And then, before he went to talk to Reverend Denby, he had said: "Give Mam time. She's missed ya. It's just all mixed now with her missing Da."

So she had given it time. For three days she wandered like an unwanted house guest around her family home. She helped with the cooking and cleaning and hanging out washing, but none of these tasks penetrated through her mother's defences. On the fourth day, at breakfast, she asked her mother if she would like to get away for a while. She said she could take her back with her to London for a bit. Her mother dropped her porridge spoon, splashing milky oats onto the green checked tablecloth. "Why would I want to do that? So you can show me off to your posh friends? I don't think so, lass. But I do think it's time you went back yaself." And so Agnes packed her bag, gave her mother a kiss on her cold cheek and got the first train back out of there.

Now, eight years later, she was returning again. And this time, worries about how her mother would receive her were vying for head space with Michael Brownley. She had not loved Michael. She had slept with him more out of not knowing how to say no to someone so important, rather than out of any uncontrolled adolescent desire. He had not forced her. He had asked her if she wanted to and she had said yes, simply because she didn't know how to say no. He had been kind and gentle, but he was no great lover. Not that she had anything to compare it with then, but even so, she had felt that it was all just a bit messy and silly. But if that's what Mr Brownley wanted, who was she to say no?

If she had, where would she be today? Married to a miner with a brood of kids? Still working at the village laundry? She might have been "decent" but would she have been happy? Would she have been able to continue with her art? She very much doubted it. And even though she wished she hadn't lost children and lovers, or been estranged from her family, she did not wish she'd never become an artist. She did not wish she had never lived and worked in Paris and London. But it had come at a cost. She looked at the young blonde woman beside her: Malcolm and Alice Denby's daughter. She too had left home and was following her dream. But she had had more opportunities than Agnes. She had connections and class behind her. Yes, her family were not rich, but they had had enough to give their daughter a start. Unlike Agnes, whose only chance at "a start" was to become someone's mistress, Miss Poppy Denby had more respectable options open to her.

Agnes recalled that Alice Denby had been pregnant with Poppy when Michael Brownley died. And that her little boy, the cherubic Christopher, had later died in the war. Yes, she too had suffered loss. Agnes did not for one minute think Poppy had a silver spoon in her mouth and she was grateful the young journalist had agreed to accompany her today. Just as she had been grateful Poppy's mother had accompanied her away from Ashington all those years ago. She had wondered how much Alice had told her daughter about what happened at the time, but after a few conversations with the honest and open young woman, Agnes came to the conclusion that Mrs Denby had been true to her word and not told anyone about her shame.

The train shuddered to a stop at the station, and there on the platform was a delegation from Armstrong College and the Ashington Miners' Institute waiting to greet her. She smoothed down her exquisite mink coat, put a regal smile on her face, and said: "Are you ready, Poppy?"

Poppy was pleased to see such a good crowd waiting outside the Agnes Robson Community Hall to greet her new "client". Poppy appraised them, wondering for a moment whether a new career lay ahead of her in public relations or arts management. No, she thought, it wasn't for her. She was happy to help out today, chatting to reporters on behalf of Agnes, but it wasn't what she was cut out for. She eyed up the press corps: two reporters and two photographers. In the end only the *Morpeth Herald* and the *Newcastle Daily Journal* were there, the latter represented by the grinning Peter MacMahon who raised his bowler hat to her and Agnes as they arrived. The gentleman from the *Morpeth Herald* was someone she knew attended her parents' church.

When they had first got married, Malcolm and Alice had worked for a Methodist Mission here in Ashington, but when Poppy was a few years old they had taken up an appointment in the more well-to-do market town of Morpeth, just a few miles up the road. They had never lost touch with the mining village though and continued to be involved with the local Methodist circuit, sharing resources and preachers.

The reporter, a bearded man in his early sixties called Walter Foster, raised his hat when he saw Poppy. "Miss Denby! What a pleasure to see you! I was hoping to have a word with you at your father's birthday party on Saturday. You will still be coming, won't you?"

Poppy smiled. "Good day to you, Mr Foster. Yes I will. That's why I'm here, actually. I just stopped off in Newcastle for a few days to see some friends and relations. But I shall definitely be there on Saturday. I'll look forward to catching up with you then."

Foster nodded to his rival from the Newcastle newspaper. "Have you met young MacMahon, yet?"

"I have. I had the pleasure of making Mr MacMahon's acquaintance yesterday."

MacMahon winked, cheekily, at Foster. "Indeed we did. And I had the pleasure of getting an advance interview with Agnes Robson. Isn't that right, Miss Denby?"

"Well, she told me the two of you had a little chat, which reminds me..." Poppy readied herself to probe what the reporters knew about the Brownley death, when suddenly they were all called to attention by an elderly gentleman in a brown suit, who had been introduced to Poppy earlier as Professor Reid of the art school.

"Ladies and gentlemen, thank you all for coming today to open this marvellous facility. And thanks also to..."

The professor droned on for fifteen minutes. In his speech he thanked the serious-looking gentlemen from the Miners' Institute, wearing their best cheap suits and collars, starched within an inch of their lives; and he thanked the "good people of Ashington and Hirst", represented by a group of mothers and their children, who had been scrubbed until they shone. The children were learning to paint and draw and an exhibition of their work was hung inside the hall. Professor Reid told the children, very solemnly, that they were honoured to have a world-renowned artist here to judge the competition and went on to give an overview of Miss Robson's illustrious career. He mentioned that she had first tried her hand at painting right here in Ashington. That she, like the children, was the daughter of a miner, and if they worked very, very hard, they too might have work hung in the world's leading galleries. The children looked at Agnes in awe. The mothers, if Poppy were not mistaken, appeared to suppress a collective smirk. Or had she just imagined it?

Professor Reid did not mention the death of Michael Brownley or Agnes' years of exile. He summed up her difficult years in one simple sentence: "Although from humble beginnings, Miss Robson had the good fortune to learn from the great masters in Paris before being discovered by the famous art critic Roger Fry in London." No mention of her running off to Paris with an older man and living in sin. No mention of failed pregnancies. No mention of a scandalous Bohemian lifestyle. Instead, he spoke of her as one of the country's best-loved avant-garde artists. She was a leading light in British Post-Impressionism. Her work was challenging, and at times controversial, always pushing the boundaries of conventional form and palette. He was proud, although she had not studied at Armstrong College proper, to consider her an alumna of their community outreach programme and honoured that she had agreed to lend her name (and money) to their ongoing work here in Ashington.

As his hagiography came to a close he was rewarded with polite applause and camera flashes. He looked quietly pleased with himself, thought Poppy, and she wondered what Agnes made of it all. The artist seemed politely appreciative of the plaudits but, Poppy noted, kept her gaze turned away from the women and children. It was then the turn of Agnes to say a few words. The reporters' pencils were poised expectantly, but her comments were few, and her accent decidedly middle English.

"Thank you Professor Reid; you are too kind. It is the ongoing work of the Newcastle Art School at Armstrong College that is to be applauded, not my humble contribution. Gentlemen of the Miners' Institute, thank you for the honour of allowing me to lend my name to this hall. I hope it serves the people of Ashington and Hirst well. And now, children, I think it's time you showed me your paintings."

"It should've been called Brownley Hall!" a woman from the back of the crowd shouted out.

"What is that, madame?" asked Professor Reid. He was met by a wall of silence from the mothers and quizzical looks from the children. A number of gentlemen from the Miners' Institute cleared their throats awkwardly.

Agnes flashed a terrified glance at Poppy. Poppy stepped forward. "I think the lady said it should be called Brownley Hall. That, I believe, is a reference to Miss Robson's first art teacher. In fact, she was just telling me about him on the train ride coming up, isn't that right Miss Robson?"

Agnes looked like a deer in the headlights. Poppy willed her to calm down. They had spoken about this eventuality over breakfast: what to do if Brownley's name was brought up. She had urged Agnes to not skirt away from it but to mention her gratitude to him and all the other teachers she had had in her life. That way he would be just one of many. But would she?

Poppy caught a glimpse of Peter MacMahon out of the corner of her eye. He was raising his finger to ask a question. *Come on, Agnes...*

And then, just as Poppy thought she would have to intervene again, Agnes spoke. Her voice, thankfully, was calm and clear. "The naming of the hall was not my decision. But I'm sure Armstrong College meant no disrespect to Mr Brownley. Yes, he was their first teacher here, but there were many more who came after him; each of them made their own contribution to this community and we should be grateful to them all. And now, I think it's time to see what these wonderful children have been doing."

With that she turned on her heel and walked into the hall. "What do you remember of Michael Brownley, Miss Robson?" Peter MacMahon's voice called out after her.

Poppy stood beside a confused-looking professor who appeared unsure as to whether to follow Agnes inside.

"And you, Professor Reid!" shouted Walter Foster from the *Morpeth Herald*. "Do you recall Michael Brownley's death? Should his name be on the hall too?"

Reid took on a glazed look and turned to Poppy.

She took a step forward. "I think Miss Robson has said all that needs to be said today. Michael Brownley was the first of the teachers here, and she and the community will always be grateful to him. Isn't that right, Professor Reid?"

"Er, yes, we are. And to answer your question, Mr Foster, no we did not think his name should be on the hall. Michael Brownley, and I remember him from when I too was a young lecturer, did an excellent job getting this project started. But it wasn't his only project. He worked elsewhere too. In fact, we have a commemorative plaque in his name in the department along with others of our colleagues who died while working for us. Granted, most of them were during the Great War, but he and one or two others, who died outside of combat – by illness or accident – are remembered too. So I can assure you, he has in no way been snubbed. If you would like to come to the college I can show you the plaque."

Oh dear, thought Poppy, *if only he had not added that last sentence . . .*

"I'll take you up on that, Professor," said Peter MacMahon before the older reporter could answer.

"And so will I," said Foster, stepping in front of MacMahon. "It'll make an interesting side article."

Poppy groaned inwardly. *Oh dear; this press liaison malarkey is turning into a fiasco.*

Inside the hall Agnes enjoyed her time with the children. She was surprisingly at ease with them, slipping, without realising it, back into her native dialect. She was introduced to the children's teacher: a young man in his late twenties, around the age Michael Brownley had been when she'd first met him. She looked at the older girls in the group and wondered if any of them had the same type of relationship with their teacher as she'd had. She hoped not. One of the girls – a red-headed young beauty, around twelve years old, who said her name was Edna – looked like she might be a prime candidate. Agnes took extra time with her. Her work was good: a watercolour of a pit head silhouette with an orange poppy growing through the cracks in a paving stone in the foreground. It was a little cliched in subject, but the technique was strong and it showed an understanding of emotional narrative.

"That's very good, Edna."

"Ta, miss."

"D'ya like paintin'?"

"Aye miss, I do."

Agnes looked over at the art teacher who was in conversation with one of the men from the Miners' Institute, then lowered her voice. "And d'ya ever stay after class to help Mr Simons?"

Edna screwed up her nose, making her look very young. "Nah miss. Me mam needs uz back home. I go straight back, I do."

Agnes nodded her approval. "That's good Edna, that's very good. And what do you want to do when you grow up?"

Edna looked across at the group of mothers sipping tea and munching on egg sandwiches. "I don't know, miss. Get married? Have bairns of me own?"

Agnes pursed her lips. "Have ya not thought of doing something with ya art? Ya very good, ya know."

"Like you, miss?"

"Aye Edna, like me." But even as she said it she realised Edna's chances of becoming a professional artist – or in fact anything other than a wife and mother – were very slim. It was then that an idea began to form in her mind. What if she were to set up a bursary scheme? To help gifted female artists to go to a good school? There were a couple of well-respected girls' schools in the area, but not for the likes of young Edna. She could speak to Dot Denby about it. That would be just the sort of thing Dot might want to get involved in. And perhaps Grace too. Grace, a bookkeeper, was very good at administration. Not Agnes' or Dot's strength. She would give it some more thought.

She had three rosettes in her hands. She selected a boy of around eight for third place, a girl about the same age for second, but reserved the first for Edna. The girl looked tickled pink and blushed like a beetroot when Professor Reid congratulated her, before she ran over to the group of mothers calling: "Mam! Mam! I won!"

Her mother came over to have a look. "Eeee pet, well done!" Agnes stepped forward and reached out her hand. The woman looked at it curiously for a moment, then reached out her own. It was limp and quickly withdrawn. "Hello, I'm Agnes Robson. You have a very talented daughter, Mrs . . . ?"

"Storey. Mrs Storey."

"Storey? Are you related to Mr Storey from the general goods shop? I used to get sweets there when I was little."

Mrs Storey's eyes narrowed. "Aye, I remember."

Agnes stiffened. Mrs Storey was in her late thirties. Storey would be her married name. Had Agnes known her as a child? Under a different name? She would have been one of the younger children in the group . . . Agnes couldn't remember, and didn't want to open a hornet's nest by asking.

Agnes forced herself to continue making small talk, then moved on to the parents of the second- and third-placed children. Then something caught her eye. A man had entered the hall, standing in the doorway, cap in hand. He was tall and slim, stooped slightly at the shoulders. His greying hair made him look older than his thirty-nine years. It was Jeremy, Agnes' brother.

He caught her eye and smiled. She made her apologies to the group she was with and walked over to him. She wanted to fling open her arms and embrace him, but she didn't. She knew that might be considered acceptable to her arty middle-class friends in London, but it would not be in working-class Ashington. Not even with her brother.

"Jemmy, I was wonderin' if you'd come. I'm glad ya did."

She looked over his shoulder, hoping to see any other family members. Hoping to see her mam.

"Anyone else with ya?"

"No, Aggy. They wouldna come."

Agnes struggled to hide her disappointment.

Jeremy looked over to the gossiping mothers eyeing him and his sister with disapproval. “Because of them’uns.”

Agnes glowered at the women. Challenged, they turned away. “Aye, I could have done without them’uns today too.”

“But she’s asked uz to ask ya if ya’ll come home for tea. She’s put a spread on.”

Agnes’ heart jumped into her mouth. “She has? Really?”

“Aye, she has. Will ya come, Aggy?”

Tears welled in her eyes. “Aye Jemmy, I will.”

He smiled. “That’s grand. And ya can meet me wife. And the bairns. I’ve told them all aboot their Auntie Aggie.”

Suddenly, they were joined by Poppy Denby. Poppy had been valiantly keeping the journalists away from Agnes. But she looked frustrated.

“I’m sorry to interrupt, Agnes,” she smiled at the tall, stooped miner, “but I really think you need to say a few words to the reporters.” She turned to the man, then said: “Hello, there. I’m Poppy Denby.”

“Oh, I’m sorry,” said Agnes, instinctively reverting back to her middle-English accent, “this is my brother, Jeremy Robson. Jeremy, this is Miss Poppy Denby, the Reverend and Mrs Denby’s daughter.”

Jeremy reached up and pulled his forelock. “Pleasure to meet ya, miss. Ya mam and dad are good folks.”

Poppy smiled and thanked him. “Yes they are. It’s my dad’s sixtieth birthday coming up.”

“Aye, so I’ve heard.”

“Listen,” said Poppy, turning to Agnes, “I don’t want to keep you from your family, but the reporters are – they’re, well – digging a bit. And I think we need to give them something to distract them from . . . ,” she cast a quick look at Jeremy, “. . . from you know what. And the best way to do that is to get them interested in another story. I was wondering, do you have any ‘scoops’ you can give them? Something about your upcoming work or anything like that?”

Agnes thought for a moment, then said: “Actually Poppy, I think I might. What do you think of the Agnes Robson Bursary for Artistic Young Ladies?”

Poppy's face lit up. "I think that sounds splendid! Have you spoken to any other reporters about it?"

"No, not a soul."

"Then that's perfect. Would you be prepared to talk to them about it now?"

Agnes looked over at the reporters, then at her brother, waiting patiently for her. "Actually Poppy, do you think you could put them off a bit? Give them enough to keep them interested but then delay the actual interview? I need to give it a bit more thought first, and . . ." she smiled at Jeremy, ". . . me mam's waiting for uz."

Poppy nodded her understanding. "Yes, I can do that. But we can't leave them too long."

"Not too long, Poppy, I promise. Just not today, please. Not today."

Chapter 7

Thursday, 3 October 1924

Laing Art Gallery, Newcastle

The Indian summer in Newcastle was finally showing its heels. A pair of horses that were being led into the public stables adjoining the gallery clomped their way through a light carpet of oak leaves and acorns, and the lad who told them to "hey up" had a woollen scarf tucked into his collar. Poppy, wearing her best but flimsiest evening gown, pulled her coat collar up against the biting breeze. She was waiting on the steps of the gallery for the arrival of the press, watching a horse-drawn cart pull up to the nearby "lying-in hospital" for pregnant married women of limited means. She watched as one of the ladies in question was helped out of the cart and guided into the hospital. *Only married women*, she noted. She thought of the unmarried Agnes and her two miscarriages. Where did women like her go if they carried to full term? A sister ushered the woman in and closed the door.

Poppy turned her attention back to the gallery. She had arranged for Peter MacMahon from the *Journal* and Walter Foster from the *Herald* to get to the exhibition an hour earlier than the public to take photographs of the artwork, and to talk to Agnes about her idea for bursaries for female artists. She had had some difficulty yesterday convincing the reporters that they had nothing to gain by printing rumours about Agnes' involvement in a decades-old death, but finally managed to persuade them that if they did they would lose all access to the artist and the inside track on the bursary fund. "This isn't a rumour; it's fact. But if you'd rather we gave the story to the *Northern Echo* . . ."

The men had reluctantly agreed. Poppy knew that everything depended on how well Agnes did in her interview with them today. She had spent some time earlier that morning coaching the artist in the best way to answer questions and hoped that she had taken at least some of it on board. Poppy was a little bit annoyed with how much time this "press liaison" role was taking up. Hadn't she just agreed to go to Ashington? But now here she was at the gallery too. Perhaps she should take Agnes up on her offer of payment; she was supposed to be on holiday, after all. Yet somehow she felt she needed to see Agnes through this. She was surprised at how vulnerable the older woman seemed up here in the North. When Poppy had interviewed her in London she was the epitome of the confident, sophisticated artist. But here – well, here she was just the daughter of a coal miner whose community showed her scant respect. And, up until yesterday, her family had rejected her too.

There was something in that that pulled at Poppy's heartstrings. Perhaps it was because she too had difficulties with her family. Neither of her parents were thrilled with her choice of career. And if her mother had her way, she would have no career at all. Granted, they had not turned their backs on her as Agnes' family had done for many years, and they were not at all estranged, but there was still tension between them. Poppy's mother feared her insistence on working would rule her out of the marriage stakes, and, Poppy had to admit, she might be right. After all, it was partly due to her job that she had declined Daniel's offer to go with him to South Africa.

A brown-suited man turned the corner from New Bridge Street, near the lying-in hospital, into Higham Place. It was Walter Foster carrying a camera case and tripod. He waved to Poppy.

"Good evening, Mr Foster. No photographer?"

Foster shook his head. "No, just me. Budget cuts. Is MacMahon here yet?"

"Not yet."

"Good-oh. Then perhaps I can see Miss Robson first."

Poppy chuckled. "Don't worry, Mr Foster, you can both have a turn. I've arranged for each of you to speak to her for fifteen minutes."

"Only fifteen minutes?"

"I'm afraid so. Miss Robson has a lot to do this evening. But if you don't get all you need tonight you can forward some written questions to me in the morning and I'll see that Miss Robson answers them for you. Ah, here's Mr MacMahon."

A black cab pulled up and let Peter MacMahon and his photographer out. Poppy repeated the arrangements that she had just explained to Foster and MacMahon echoed the other journalist's complaint.

"I'm sorry Peter; that's all I can do for now. But there should be lots you can do at the exhibition opening tonight. Don't forget there will be friends, family and dignitaries you can speak to too." Poppy was slightly perturbed that she had to tell the men how to do their jobs. If the shoe were on the other foot she would know exactly how to go about getting a story, even with the restrictions imposed on them.

Poppy ushered the men into the gallery and through the Marble Hall with its hanging baskets of evergreen plants. She checked in her coat at the ladies' cloakroom while the reporters and cameraman did the same at the gentlemen's facility.

Poppy ducked into the powder room to check her outfit – the spaghetti-strapped, wine-red Lucien Lelong with train Aunt Dot had given her – then touched up her lipstick and checked that her marcelled waves were behaving themselves under the diamanté headband. Happy with the results, she emerged from the cloakroom to appreciative glances from the press posse.

"Golly, you look splendid, Miss Denby!"

"Thank you, Mr MacMahon," said Poppy, quietly pleased with the response.

Lifting her train, she led the way up the granite staircase – past its distinctive arts and crafts stained-glass window – to the landing of the first floor. Around a rotunda with a broad granite balustrade, caterers were setting up drinks and food tables, while in the corner between the entrances to galleries A and D, a string quartet were tuning up. Way above them, the last of the afternoon sun wept through the glass ceiling of the oculus. Poppy looked over the balustrade to see her aunt's neighbour Mrs Sherman – without her two poodles – cross the hall of the atrium below. Poppy wondered for a moment what she was doing here, then remembered that she was the curator Dante Sherman's mother. In fact, she was about to meet Mr Sherman now. Agnes had told her that he was insisting on accompanying the reporters around the exhibition to ensure that they "behaved". Poppy sighed to herself; it always disappointed her what a poor reputation journalists had with the general public.

Memories and Mementoes: Agnes Robson, daughter of the North had been hung in Gallery A – on the far side of the rotunda. To the right of the double doors was the largest painting in the Laing: *Holy Motherhood*, a renaissance nouveau homage to fifteenth-century religious iconography, by contemporary artist Thomas Cooper Gotch. It had first been exhibited for the gallery's opening in 1902. Frozen forever in a bronzed gilt frame, four women, playing instruments or reading books, flanked the "holy mother" who sat, indifferent to the naked infant lying on her lap. The painting had always disturbed Poppy as there wasn't an ounce of maternal love in any of the characters. She remembered as a child contemplating the painting, feeling sorry for the poor, cold baby, who was supposed to grow up to be the saviour of the world.

Standing in front of the painting was the dandy figure of Dante Sherman, with a clipboard and pen. He wore a conventional tuxedo and tails, but peeking out of his jacket were flouncy Byronic cuffs, worthy of Oscar Wilde, and a velvet collar. Instead of a plain white bow tie, he wore an elaborate cravat of white silk with gold embroidery. As Poppy and the journalists approached, he allowed his gold-framed monocle to drop out of his eye socket and dangle down the front of his jacket.

"Ah, Miss Denby and the gentlemen from the press." He checked his pocket watch. "You are five minutes late."

"Our apologies, Mr Sherman. Agnes said you would be willing to show Mr MacMahon and Mr Foster the collection, is that correct?"

Sherman pursed his lips and checked his pocket watch again. "It is – briefly. So shall we get started? Miss Robson is waiting in Gallery B, which we are currently using as a green room. Follow me please."

Sherman turned on his well-polished heel, pushed open the door to Gallery A and led the journalists through it. He pointed to the door of Gallery B. "Miss Robson is in there. One of you can get started with her and I'll take the other one around the exhibition. We will swap over in exactly fifteen minutes. Any questions?"

"Er yes," said an amused-looking Peter MacMahon, winking at his photographer. "Who's going first? Should we toss a coin, Foster?"

"I, well I –"

Sherman snapped his fingers in front of MacMahon's face. "Decide. Now. Time is ticking."

"Well," said Poppy, annoyed by Sherman's manner, but at the same time realising time was not on their side. "Perhaps Mr Foster would like to go first with Agnes. He has come the farthest. Then we'll swap over. Is that all right?" Her tone, and challenging stare at Peter MacMahon, brooked no disagreement.

"That's fine and dandy," said MacMahon, a Cheshire cat grin still on his face. "All right, Bob?" he asked his photographer.

"All right, Pete," the man replied, and started unpacking his tripod.

Poppy smiled her thanks at the man, appreciating his no-fuss attitude – so like Daniel's – and then gestured for Walter Foster to accompany her through the gallery to the makeshift green room. As Foster pushed open the door she heard Dante Sherman drawl, "So, here we have a fine example of Miss Robson's work from her early years in Paris. You see the use of primary colour and the marked influence of Gauguin –"

The door swung shut behind her and Foster, and they stepped into a screened-off section of the long vaulted Gallery B. In front of her, lying on a Chippendale *chaise longue*, was Agnes. Her neck was resting on the arm of the furniture and her eyes were closed. One hand was resting on her forehead.

"Agnes? Are you all right?"

Agnes opened her eyes and turned her head towards Poppy; a tired smile gently emerged.

"Sorry Poppy – yes, I'm fine. I was just having a little rest before everyone arrives. And . . . oh, it's the gentleman from the press; I had almost forgotten."

She sat up and dropped her legs to the floor, smoothing down her green velvet gown. Poppy noted how beautiful she looked. Her hair – which she still wore unfashionably long – was pinned on one side with a diamond-encrusted comb and then swept down over the other shoulder in a cascade of ebony waves.

"Good evening, Miss Robson. If you don't mind, would you stay just where you are? The light is just right. And I apologise, but I will have to ask you questions as I set up the camera, as I am on my own."

Poppy, realising Foster would not have time to do a proper interview in the allocated slot if he had to take snaps too, decided to offer her help. Daniel had taught her some basic camera technique and she had started taking photographs as a hobby since he left. In some ways, it kept his memory more alive.

Walter Foster looked relieved and settled down on a chair opposite Agnes as Poppy stepped into the photographer's shoes. She took an old Kodak Brownie from Foster's bag. She gave it a quick once-over, estimating that it was a mid-war variety, much like the one with which Daniel would originally have learned his craft.

"There's film in the front pouch of the bag," Walter Foster told her. "Do you mind if I just get on?"

"No, you go ahead. I know what I'm doing."

Poppy kept one ear on the interview as she clicked open the back of the Brownie box and pulled out the film shuttle, loaded a roll of 120 film, then fed it around the box and inserted it back into the leather casing. Foster's questions to Agnes seemed to be focused on how and when she had got the idea for the bursary. Poppy relaxed a little as Agnes gave him a full and informed answer. The more Agnes fed the reporter, the less chance he would be hungry for something that wasn't on the menu.

Poppy wound the film until she saw a number "1" in the counter window. Then she checked through the viewfinder and adjusted the aperture. Agnes looked relaxed and was well lit from the skylight above. It was getting a little dim, however, so Poppy decided to use a flash. She dug around in Foster's bag until she found what she was looking for, checked the bulb was intact and then clicked it onto the Brownie.

The interview was going well and Poppy took a shot. Agnes, as a celebrity artist, was used to having her photograph taken and managed to pose and speak at the same time, and wasn't in the least startled by the flash. Poppy advanced the film and, when the flash had cooled enough to replace the bulb, took another shot, then – eventually – two more. As there were only twelve exposures on the 120 film, she decided to leave it there, unsure how much film Foster would need to photograph some of the paintings. As she wrapped things up, she heard Foster say: "One final question . . ."

Good, perfect timing, thought Poppy.

"How much did your experience of losing your first teacher – Michael Brownley – influence your decision to help young girls from poorer backgrounds? And do you ever wonder how exactly he died?"

A stone dropped to the bottom of Poppy's stomach.

"I, well I . . ." she heard Agnes start, before she stepped forward and tapped her wrist.

"I think our fifteen minutes are up here, Mr Foster; time to move into the gallery. Thank you so much for your time, Agnes. I think we've got all we need here."

Foster glowered at her for a moment, but then with a tight smile, nodded briefly and said: "Of course, Miss Denby. And thank you Miss Robson, you've been very, how should I say, *informative*."

Before Poppy could challenge him any further, the door flew open and the cheeky face of Peter MacMahon appeared. "Is it my turn yet?"

Relieved, Poppy fixed a smile on her face and said: "Yes, it is. Mr Foster has just finished."

Agnes, still looking tired, waved Poppy over.

"Poppy, would you mind awfully keeping an eye open for my brother? He said he might be bringing my mam. If they do come I doubt they'll feel comfortable in a place like this. It would be nice if they could see a friendly face first."

Another job . . . thought Poppy with a sinking heart, but it would be churlish of her to refuse. And yes, she could imagine that the miner and his mother *would* feel uncomfortable in a place like this. She smiled at Agnes as Peter MacMahon took the seat Walter Foster had just vacated.

"Of course; I'll see if I can find them. I also believe that that young lass – Edna – might be coming with her mother too. Wasn't it part of her prize?"

"It was. But they should be with the art teacher. My family will be on their own."

"Understood," said Poppy and followed Foster out of the room. She quickly facilitated the handover of the journalist to the curator, Dante Sherman, who tapped his pocket watch and said: "You're late. Now we've only got ten minutes. I hope you're a fast study, Mr Foster . . ."

Poppy was tempted for a moment to offer to do his photography for him, but she stopped herself. *No, Poppy, you are not responsible for him. It's time to draw a line.*

Chapter 8

The landing on the second floor of the Laing Art Gallery was beginning to fill up around the rotunda, and through the aperture, Poppy could see more people arriving below. The string quartet had started playing and around a dozen ladies and gentlemen in evening gowns and tuxedoes milled around sipping glasses of complimentary wine or champagne. A quick perusal told her Agnes' brother was not yet there. She had not met Mrs Robson, but she doubted she'd be there on her own. And – she thought, sympathetically – she doubted she would be wearing one of the very expensive gowns on display. However, there was someone she did recognise. She made a beeline across the landing and with immense relief greeted a large, pasty-faced man in his sixties and his young male companion. "Gerald! What are you doing here? Agnes said you were ill and couldn't make it up."

The large man's face lit up with recognition. "Poppy Denby! I thought I might see you here. Rollo told me you were up this way. Yes, I wasn't well – ghastly tummy bug – but Gus here convinced me to push through. We caught the train up this morning. We're staying at the Grand. Have you met? This is Gus North, Miss Robson's studio assistant. Gus, this is Poppy Denby from *The Daily Globe*, in London. She covered the exhibition at the Tate. I don't think you were there that night . . ."

As Gerald spoke he turned to face the younger man directly, and articulated his words clearly, accompanied by some hand gestures.

Gus North nodded his understanding, smiled and turned to Poppy. When he spoke, his softened consonants and flattened tone suggested someone who had been born deaf. And then, to confirm, he said, "I am very pleased to meet you, Miss Denby. I hope you don't mind me staring at your face, I do not intend to be rude – although you are lovely to behold – however, I am deaf and need to read your lips."

Poppy smiled in return. "Not at all, Mr North. Do tell me if I am speaking too quickly. I can slow down if you like."

"No need for that," said Gerald. "Gus is a dab hand at it. And as you can see, he has even taught me a little of the sign language the deaf folks use."

Gus laughed, his dark brown eyes twinkling with mirth. "Although you have just signed 'the singing the donkey legs use.'"

Poppy and Gerald joined in the laughter. Gerald grinned, showing donkey-like teeth above a stack of double chins. "Obviously I've still got some way to go then."

Gus reached out his hand and squeezed Gerald's forearm. "Just glad you've given it a go, old man."

"It's the least I can do, old sport." Then Gerald looked around at the growing number of guests. "Have you seen Agnes, Poppy? She doesn't seem to be here."

"Oh, she's through there," said Poppy, pointing to the still-closed doors of Gallery B. "She's speaking to a reporter from the *Newcastle Daily Journal*. Actually, I'm so glad you are finally here. She asked me to fill in for you, helping to liaise with the press, but I must admit I'm not enjoying switching from poacher to gamekeeper. Do you think you could take the job off my hands now?"

"Goodness, yes," said Gerald. "And thank you for all your efforts. Is there anything I need to know?"

"Well, actually, there is. You see, there have been some questions about –"

But before Poppy could finish, the doors swung open to reveal Agnes, in her figure-hugging green velvet gown, accompanied by Dante Sherman.

Her eyes swept the room. "Gerald! Gus!" cried the artist, rushing forward to greet her publicist and assistant.

As she did, Poppy spotted the tall, stooped frame of Agnes' brother in the atrium below. He was accompanied by an older version of Agnes in a much more modest dress. She turned to tell Agnes that her family had arrived, but the woman had launched into an animated conversation with her two employees and the gallery curator, so Poppy decided to slip away and meet Jeremy Robson and his mother on her own.

She headed towards the stairs, where she was met by Maddie Sherman and Grace Wilson, directing two gentlemen who were clearly under strain as they carried Aunt Dot and her wheelchair up the stairs.

"Just put me down here, boys," said Dot, "and then get yourself a drink. You deserve it."

Poppy thanked the two sweating gentlemen, thinking to herself that they might have reconsidered their chivalrous offer after they discovered how heavy Aunt Dot really was. However, what was a lady in a wheelchair to do? Dot had installed stairlifts in her homes, but most public buildings, with fewer than four floors, didn't have elevators. The Laing did have galleries on the ground floor, but most of its best work was held in the four interconnected galleries on the first floor.

Poppy greeted her aunt, Grace, and Mrs Sherman but then immediately excused herself, saying she needed to escort Agnes' family upstairs.

"Her family are here?" asked Mrs Sherman.

"Yes, I just saw them through the rotunda."

"How lovely for Agnes," said Dot. "Don't you think, Grace?"

Grace nodded, casting a glance across to the famous artist.

"Yes, I'm pleased for her."

Poppy noted that there was no sarcasm in her voice, and wondered if the women had finally managed to lay aside their differences. Agnes had broached the subject of the art bursaries with them last night at dinner and both Dot and Grace had instantly warmed to the idea.

Poppy left them as Dot directed Grace to get them all some drinks. "Are you having anything, Mrs Sherman?"

"Please, call me Maddie," said the curator's mother.

Poppy waved a brief goodbye to the three older ladies as she picked up her train and made her way down the stairs, just as the string quartet broke into Stravinsky's "The Rite of Spring". She hummed to herself as she stopped at the bottom and perused the Marble Hall and the arriving guests. Finally, behind a hanging basket, she spotted the tall figure of Jeremy Robson, looking stiff in his starched collar and smart suit. It was a day suit, not a tuxedo, and he stood with narrowed eyes, watching the other men, who looked like posh penguins, smoking and chatting with ease.

Poppy felt desperately sorry for him and hated the perceived snobbery that made men like him feel they didn't belong in a place like this. But change was in the air. The country had its first socialist Labour government under Prime Minister Ramsay MacDonald, voted for by men like Jeremy Robson – and, Poppy knew, her father Malcolm Denby. Poppy herself – at twenty-six – was still too young to vote, as only women over thirty who owned property were able to do so. Poppy and her suffragist friends all hoped that Mr MacDonald would change that and extend universal voting rights to all.

"Good evening Mr Robson. Mrs Robson." Poppy smiled a warm welcome to the miner and his mother. Closer up, she looked even more like Agnes, but with sixty years of wear on her face. Her hair, originally as dark as her daughter's, was now streaked with grey. But it was tastefully styled into a chignon and Poppy noticed a smart string of pearls at the open neck of a dated, but elegant, black coat. Poppy imagined that it would have been the same coat she wore to her husband's funeral back in 1916. The coat was unbuttoned and it revealed a mauve silk dress, flatteringly, but not indecently, cut. If she were to look closer Poppy suspected she would see the telltale signs of a handmade garment.

Jeremy looked relieved to see a familiar face and doffed his fedora hat. "Miss Denby. I'm pleased to see you. This is my mother, Mrs Sadie Robson."

Mrs Robson gave a tense but polite: "Evening Miss Denby. You look a bit like your father, you do. The reverend. Is he here?"

"He's not, I'm afraid. Neither is my mother." She gave a wry, conspiratorial smile. "Not their sort of thing, if you know what I mean. A few too many airs and graces, my mother would say."

Mrs Robson gave a nervous laugh, but appeared to relax a little.

"My aunt is though. Dot Denby. Did you ever meet her? She's

originally from Newcastle but would sometimes visit us when I was growing up in Morpeth. And I think she may even have come to the chapel in Ashington once or twice."

"I never attended chapel much," said Mrs Robson with no note of apology in her voice. "I let the bairns go sometimes though. They had a Sunday School. Isn't that right, Jemmy?"

"Aye, it is, Mam. Agnes sometimes would take us – me and the little 'uns. I send my lot now," he said, "every week." His eyes sought Poppy's approval.

As someone who didn't attend chapel very much herself anymore, she wasn't in a position to judge. But nonetheless, just to make him feel more comfortable, and as her parents' representative, she said: "That's very good to hear. It certainly won't do them any harm."

"Aye, that's what I believe too."

Just then, young Edna Storey, with her flame-red hair tamed into two neat plaits, arrived with her mother – looking just as unimpressed as she had at the community hall – Professor Reid and the young art teacher from Ashington. The two groups greeted one another. Edna could not contain her excitement.

"Are we late? Have we missed it?"

Poppy chuckled. "Not at all. Would you like to come upstairs? Miss Robson is there already and I think the event is about to start?"

"Oh yes!" said Edna and sped off towards the staircase.

"Hold your horses, missy!" called out her mother, shrill and authoritative. Edna stopped instantly. The adults caught up with her and headed up the stairs together.

Half an hour later, Agnes and Dante Sherman had finished their speeches and the doors to Gallery A were flung open for the guests to admire the art at their leisure. Poppy was just about to follow Mrs Robson and Jeremy into the room when she caught a glimpse of a young woman in a buttoned-up Victorian day dress, stepping onto the landing. She was short of breath and holding her skirt to reveal unflattering ankle boots.

"Good heavens, Delilah, what *are* you wearing?" asked Poppy, excusing herself from Agnes' family for a moment to greet her friend.

Delilah looked rueful. "Not exactly the height of Paris fashion, is it? According to my director this is what Gwendolyn would have worn in *The Importance of Being Earnest.* Personally I think Gwendolyn would have had much better taste. Anyway, I'm not needed for the next hour while they work on some lighting issues – why are there always these 'issues' the night before opening? So I thought I'd stop by and support Agnes." She looked around at the near-empty landing. "Oh. Have I missed it?"

"No. Just the speeches. Everyone's gone through to the gallery to look at the paintings now. Do you want to come?"

Delilah grinned. "Not before I've had a drink." She headed over to the drinks table and asked for a glass of champers. "Would you like one, Poppy?"

Poppy, who would not have drunk anything if she'd been working, reminded herself that now that Gerald the publicist was here, she was off the hook.

"Oh go on then," she said.

Delilah picked up two glasses and gave one to Poppy. "Chin chin, old bean."

"Chin chin."

Two small glasses of champers later (yes, Poppy had to admit Delilah *was* a bad influence), the two women joined the rest of the guests in the gallery.

"So where's Agnes?" asked Delilah, who had already told Poppy that she needed to get back to the theatre shortly.

Poppy noticed that the doors to Gallery B were now open and the guests were freely wandering between Agnes' exhibition – past the cordoned-off area of the "green room" – and the permanent exhibition halls of Gallery B and the intersecting galleries C and D.

"Perhaps she's through there," said Poppy. But after a quick perusal of the long, galley-shaped vaulted exhibition halls, Poppy and Delilah could not find the artist. Nor was she in the small cordoned-off "green room".

Poppy asked a few of the guests, including Aunt Dot, if they had seen Agnes. None of them had for the last while. Suddenly, Poppy noticed a door at the back of the green room section that was slightly ajar. She had seen it when she was taking photographs for Walter Foster and had wondered where it led to. She decided to check it out.

But just as she and Delilah headed towards it, the actress said: "Oh spiffing! There's Peter. Do you mind if I just say hello? If you find Agnes, tell her I'll be with her in a tick." Then she flounced off, as coquettishly as she possibly could in her frumpy costume, to chat to the young journalist.

Poppy smiled at the enthusiasm of the two young lovers as she pushed open the door to see where it led. She soon realised she was "backstage" at the gallery. The polished wood floors and rich wallpapered walls were replaced with stark, cold concrete and stone, and a wrought-iron handrail – that looked like it needed a lick of paint – leading down into the bowels of the building and up towards the roof.

As the door to the gallery closed, the hubbub of the chattering guests and the distant sound of the string quartet were replaced by the snuffle and stomp of horses. Poppy looked down the stairs, sniffed and realised they were just above the stables that she had earlier noticed, adjacent to the gallery entrance on Higham Place. *Has Agnes gone down to the stables?* But just as she was about to go down, preparing herself to call out the artist's name, something on the steps above her caught her eye. It was Agnes' bejewelled hair comb. Poppy scuttled up half a dozen steps to retrieve it, then noticed that a door at the top of the short flight of steps was open. A chill wind hit her and she shivered in her sleeveless evening gown. *Has Agnes gone to get some fresh air?*

Poppy ascended the stairs, pushed open the door fully and stepped out onto a catwalk. There was enough light from the moon and the streetlights below to show that the narrow pathway circumvented the roof of the gallery, leading towards the tower on the far side. As far as Poppy knew, the tower – with its arched cupola, covering what could have been a belfry, but it had no bells – was merely a folly, with no access from the main building, apart from the roof. The catwalk appeared to have been installed for workmen to maintain the roof tiles and gutters. There was a ladder of around ten feet in height leading up the side of the tower from the far side of the catwalk.

"Agnes!" Poppy called into the cool autumn night. "Are you out here?"

There was no answer, but then a light – possibly a match – flashed briefly under the cupola of the tower. *She's having a cigarette. Silly place to have one . . .*

Poppy, who was feeling a little unstable after her two glasses of champagne, decided not to try to negotiate the catwalk, high above the city streets, and resolved to go back inside. She reminded herself that Agnes was not her responsibility. If the woman was trying to avoid the publicity of the exhibition then that was Gerald's job to deal with, not hers. And if she just wanted some time alone after, perhaps, an emotional encounter with her mother, Poppy felt she should just leave her. She understood how difficult mother-daughter relationships could be.

Poppy slipped Agnes' comb into her little evening bag and reminded herself to give it back to her later.

But just as she clasped the door handle, she heard the sound of raised voices behind her. One voice was clearly recognisable as Agnes'. And it sounded terrified. "Leave me alone! Leave me, I tell you!" The other voice retorted but was lower, quieter and less distinct. Poppy could not place it. Nor whether it was male or female. But one thing she was sure of – Agnes was very upset.

"Agnes! Agnes! Are you all right?"

Poppy threw caution to the wind, lifted up her dress train and picked her way along the narrow catwalk, grateful for the railing running along the side of the roof. Still, it was a low barrier, the walkway was damp and her dress and shoes were not designed for clambering around on rooftops. But Agnes needed her. The shouting had turned to screams and Poppy could now see the silhouette of two people struggling under the cupola of the tower. Agnes, her long hair loose and flailing, was blocking Poppy's view of her assailant. Poppy called out again: "Stop! Stop it! Leave her alone!"

But then her foot caught in her hem and she stumbled. She threw out her arms and grabbed the railing, arresting her fall. For one awful moment she caught sight of the cobbled street and pavement of Higham Place below her, imagining herself lying there, broken on a blanket of fallen oak leaves. She took deep breaths to steady herself, then looked up to the tower, just in time to see Agnes clutch her throat, step backwards and fall over the railing. There was no sound until the body hit the pavement below with a sickening thud. Poppy screamed.

Chapter 9

"Does anyone have any brandy?"

Aunt Dot took a hip flask from a helpful gentleman and held it to Poppy's lips. Poppy was shaking uncontrollably, despite three layers of jackets placed over her shoulders.

Walter Foster, Peter MacMahon and his photographer came through the door to the back stairwell, shaking their heads. "Whoever was there isn't there now, Poppy, but . . ." Peter looked anxiously at Delilah and Dot, hovering over Poppy, ". . . you're right. Someone has fallen off the tower."

A gasp went around the green room, which was quickly filling up as guests, on hearing that something terrible had happened, made their way back from the various exhibition halls.

Poppy saw, once again, in her mind's eye, Agnes falling, her hair billowing around her like a black cloak. Poppy remembered how she'd got up and immediately ran towards the tower. But then she'd stumbled again, tripping over her train. This time she fell towards the roof and her head slammed against the tiles. Everything went dark. In retrospect, she couldn't say how long she had lain there. Had it been seconds? Minutes? Or longer? Whatever it was, it was long enough for Agnes' assailant to slip past her and back into the gallery. Had he gone down into the stables and out onto the street, slipping away into the maze of streets and alleys in this part of Newcastle? Or perhaps he – if it were a he – had come back inside. Poppy looked around her at the anxious faces of Agnes' guests. There was Gerald and Gus . . . and Delilah and Grace . . . and there was the young girl Edna, crying in heaving sobs. Dante Sherman was in earnest conversation with the three journalists who had just been out on the roof.

"I'm calling the police!" he announced and stalked off.

"Wh-where are Agnes' brother and mother?" asked Poppy.

Dot looked around her. "I can't see them. Anyone?"

Maddie Sherman, Dante's mother, stepped forward. "They ran out as soon as the fellows came in and said someone has fallen off the roof. Oh dear God, you don't think . . ."

She looked at those huddled around her, as the realisation dawned on all of them, that if it were Agnes who had fallen, her family were about to see her dead body.

"But – but –" said Poppy, clutching at straws, "what if she's just injured? It was a long fall, over three storeys, but people have survived worse, haven't they?" Poppy thrust the flask back at Dot, tossed off two of the three jackets, got up and ran towards the rotunda landing, followed by the rest of the guests. At the top of the stairwell she was overtaken by Peter MacMahon, Gus North and some of the younger men, who sprinted down the stairs two at a time.

By the time Poppy and the rest of the guests got downstairs, through the Marble Hall and out of the front door onto Higham Place, there was already a small group of people gathered at the foot of the tower. On her knees, with her daughter's head on her lap, was Mrs Robson. She was sobbing and repeating the same phrase, over and over again: "Oh me bairn, me poor bonny bairn."

A devastated Jeremy Robson stood behind her, wringing his hat in his hands. Also on her knees was a nursing sister, in uniform. Poppy looked beyond her to the lying-in hospital where a group of pregnant women and their attendants had gathered in the doorway.

A huffing, out-of-breath Gerald Farmer appeared at Poppy's right shoulder. "Is she dead?"

"I – I – think so," said Poppy. "If she wasn't I – I – think they'd be rushing her off to hospital. There's a nurse with her, but she doesn't look like she's treating her."

"Oh God."

Just then, Gus North emerged from the huddle and walked towards them, tears streaming down his cheeks. He was signing something. He appeared too distraught to speak.

"Are you sure?" asked Gerald, his voice incredulous.

"What is it?" asked Poppy.

"I think –" said Gerald, swallowing hard before continuing, "I think Gus just said Agnes' throat has been cut. But I could be wrong. Am I wrong, Gus?"

Gus shook his head slowly and sadly, then ran his finger along his throat.

The string quartet had packed up and the caterers cleared the detritus of the evening's refreshments by the time the witnesses to Agnes' death returned to the building. It hadn't taken long for the police to arrive from the station on Pilgrim Street, in the form of DI Sandy Hawkes, his sergeant (a fellow called Jones) and four constables. Poppy watched as Sandy took control of the scene, asking the nurse to bring a sheet from the hospital and to take Mrs Robson and her son back with her, under her care. After the immediate family and the nurse left the scene, Sergeant Jones set about creating a cordon around the body, positioning the four constables at compass points, and barking at the photographer from the *Journal* to "have some respect for the dead".

Sandy turned to the crowd and asked who had found the body. "Technically that would be Agnes' mother and brother, and I think the nurse," said Peter MacMahon, for once his face devoid of its cheeky smile. "But Foster and I spotted her from the roof and –" he cast a glance over his shoulder to the ashen-faced Poppy, "Miss Denby believes she saw her fall."

Sandy locked eyes with Poppy. The charming tennis partner was no longer. In his place was a steely, professional police officer. "Is that right, Miss Denby?"

"It is," said Poppy. "I saw Agnes arguing with someone and – although I can't be sure – I think she was pushed."

Everyone from inside the gallery had already heard this, yet could not restrain themselves from letting out another gasp of horror. That, coupled with the quickly circulated news that Agnes' throat had been cut, meant there was no doubt in any of their minds that they were at the scene of a murder. The air was charged with ghoulish curiosity and abject sorrow, depending on how close in life the onlookers had been to the deceased.

Sandy's eyes narrowed. "Right, then I'll need to speak to MacMahon, Foster and Miss Denby. Did anyone else see Miss Robson go into the tower? Or know that she intended to?"

Gerald Farmer raised a nervous hand. "Farmer, Gerald Farmer. I am – was – Agnes' manager. I think I might have been one of the last to see her. I was chatting to her, then she said she needed to go to powder her nose. I never saw her again after that until – until – Miss Denby here came in in a state, telling us she'd seen Agnes fall..."

He started to choke up, and Gus put a calming arm around his shoulder.

There was a shuffling silence from the crowd as they waited for the inspector to respond.

"All right. Then for now – and I mean just for now – the rest of you are free to go."

"Er – excuse me, Sandy – I mean, DI Hawkes – do you need me?"

"No, Miss Marconi. You may leave. But first, please give your name and address to Sergeant Jones. And that goes for the rest of you too. We will be in touch with each of you over the next few days. Do any of you intend to leave town?"

Again there was silence but then a quivering female voice said: "S-sorry Inspector, we – me and the lass – need to go home to Ashington. Is that all right?"

Mrs Storey had her arm around a quivering, sobbing Edna. Poppy was glad to see Sandy's face soften as he looked towards the mother and child. "Aye, that's fine. Ashington isn't too far. Now take the girl home. I'm sorry she had to see all this."

Mrs Storey nodded, caught the eye of the art teacher and asked: "Will you take us home?"

The young man said he would. After the Ashington folk left, the rest of the crowd formed a makeshift queue to give the sergeant their details. Then Sandy indicated, with his finger, that the self-identified witnesses should follow him. "Oh, and Mr Sherman, will you come too please? I will need someone from the gallery to show me around."

"We'll wait for you, Poppy," said Aunt Dot, with Grace behind her holding the handles of her wheelchair.

"No need for that, Miss Denby, I will give Miss Denby – Miss *Poppy* Denby, that is – a lift home. I shall visit you and Mrs Wilson tomorrow. And you too, Mrs Sherman; I believe you live nearby?"

"I do," said Maddie Sherman, hovering at her son's shoulder. "Number six. Just two doors down. Shall I come to Miss Denby's house?"

"If you could, that would be very helpful."

"And what time will that be?"

"Whenever I am able to, madame," said DI Hawkes and he turned on his heel. Aunt Dot, Grace, Maddie and Professor Reid from the art school huddled together and waited for Sergeant Jones to take their details as Poppy, Gerald, Gus, Dante Sherman and the two journalists accompanied the inspector back into the gallery.

"Right," said Sandy, "talk me through it. Mr Farmer, is it?"

"It is."

"So where were you when you were speaking to Miss Robson?"

"In the main exhibition hall," said Gerald, leading the group from the rotunda landing into Gallery A where Agnes' paintings lined the walls. Poppy realised she still hadn't actually had a chance to look at the exhibition. She felt a lump form in her throat. *Dear God, poor Agnes. Please, help us to find out who did this to her.*

"And I was standing right here, I think, in front of this still life of *Lilies in a Vase*. And Gus was over there in front of *The Railway Family*. Isn't that right, Gus?"

Gus nodded.

"What were you talking about?"

"Oh, this and that. She was asking how I was feeling – I'd had a gippy stomach – and thanked me – thanked us – for coming up anyway. She'd told me that she'd had some tricky interviews with some journalists . . ."

Sandy cast a glance at Peter MacMahon and Walter Foster. "We did nothing more than our jobs, Hawkes," said Peter.

Sandy raised his hand to silence him. "You can tell me about it later, MacMahon. And you too, Foster. For now I want to follow Miss Robson's last movements. Carry on, Mr Farmer."

"Well, that was the main thrust of it really. Oh, that and her idea about the bursary for artistic girls. She wanted me to action that straight away. She said she had spoken to Dot Denby and Grace Wilson about it and they were keen to get involved."

Gus pulled at Gerald's sleeve and began signing. Gerald, with a deep look of concentration on his face, translated. "Gus says – I think – that he was shocked – no, not shocked, surprised – that Mrs Wilson would be interested in helping Agnes."

"Oh, and why's that?" asked Sandy.

"Well, because Grace Wilson and Agnes have a bit of history. Going back to their suffragette days. You see, it's all about –"

"It's all been cleared up now," said Poppy, anxious not to let Grace be dragged into a murder investigation without her being there to defend herself. "I can tell you about it later," she added, when Sandy gave her an interrogative stare.

"All right then. I look forward to hearing about it. So . . . what else did Miss Robson say before she left you?"

"Well, that was it to me. She then spoke briefly to Gus, but I didn't see that. Mr MacMahon was asking me to clarify some things for his article. Gus, what did she say to you?"

Gus spoke briefly with his hands.

Gerald nodded. "She just asked him if he was enjoying himself."

"And that's all?" asked Hawkes, looking at Gus.

Gus nodded.

"Did she seem upset when she left?"

"Not at all," said Gerald. "She seemed relieved that we were here and was beginning to relax. She said she'd see us later. Isn't that right Gus?"

Gus nodded.

"And which way did she go to powder her nose after she spoke to you, Mr North?" asked Hawkes.

Gus pointed down the gallery. "That way."

"So," said Sandy, wandering in the direction Gus had pointed. "Where does this lead?"

"Not to the ladies' cloakroom," said Dante Sherman. "We only have facilities on the ground floor. That door leads to Gallery B. Part of it is blocked off to make a temporary green room – for the artist and her entourage to relax in – but the rest of it is still part of our permanent exhibition."

Sandy pushed open the door to Gallery B and took in the screened-off area in the right-hand corner and the rest of the gallery to the left. "What's over there?" he asked, pointing down the length of the gallery to double doors at the end.

"That leads to Gallery C and then beyond that Gallery D. Have you not been to the Laing, Inspector?" Dante asked.

"I have not. Shall we get back to the business at hand? Right, so we've just been in Gallery A; this is Gallery B, which interconnects with two further galleries. Am I correct?"

"You are, Inspector. The four galleries form an interconnecting square. The entrances to galleries A and D are on the rotunda."

Peter looked back over his shoulder. "So, Miss Robson could have been taking a roundabout route to get to the landing and then down the stairs to the cloakroom?"

"She could have," said Dante, "or perhaps she just didn't know where she was going."

"Or perhaps she just got lost," chipped in Poppy. "It's a complicated layout."

Dante glowered at her as if she had just personally insulted him.

Sandy gave her a flicker of a smile which was instantly replaced by his professional facade.

"And where were you while Mr Farmer and Mr North were in conversation with Miss Robson, Miss Denby?"

"I was on the rotunda. With Delilah. Having a drink."

Poppy wondered if she should mention that it had actually been two drinks – albeit two small ones – but she decided not to, just in case the policeman might question her ability to recollect events. She was quite sober, but she did not want to have to justify herself to that effect.

"And did you see Miss Robson emerge from – what was it now – Gallery D?"

"No I didn't. Agnes came out of neither of the doors – to galleries A or D."

Sandy nodded, taking it all in. "All right then, how did you get from here to when you saw Agnes in the tower?"

"I was – er – I went looking for her and ended up on the roof."

Golly, just as well I didn't mention the second drink. I sound as though I was squiffy!

Sandy gave her a curious look. "And how – and why – did you end up on the roof?"

Poppy explained how she and Delilah were looking for Agnes and then she'd spotted the door at the back of the temporary green room open. She led the inspector and the rest of the witnesses to the door in question.

"Is this door always open?" Sandy asked Dante Sherman.

"No. It's usually locked. The staff have keys though."

Sandy nodded. "Will you be able to give me a list of all the staff members with keys?"

"I can."

Sandy asked Poppy to lead them on the route she followed when looking for Agnes. She told him that she had considered that Agnes might have gone down to the stables until she spotted the comb on the steps above her, leading to the roof.

"And the door to the roof? Is that usually locked too?" Sandy asked Dante.

"I'm not entirely sure, I never come up this way myself; it's purely for maintenance access. You see, there is no actual way into the tower from the building. It's a folly – an architectural excess – with no functional purpose."

"But one *can* actually get to the tower over the roof? And access it?"

"I believe so, yes. But it might be better if you spoke to the gallery caretaker. I can put you in touch with him tomorrow. He isn't here this evening."

Sandy climbed the steps and appraised the door. "It looks like it has a bolt from the inside. So perhaps no key is needed for here. Which of you touched the handle?"

"I did," said Poppy. "And I."

"And I."

The voices came from the two journalists who stood on either side of Poppy, just a step below her.

"Remind me again why you two went onto the roof?" asked Sandy.

"It was when Poppy came back into the gallery. She was crying and shaking and in a state of shock, saying she'd seen Agnes fall from the tower. So I decided to come and have a look," said Peter.

"And so did I," Walter added.

"Scared MacMahon would scoop you?" smirked Sandy.

"No," said Walter, pulling himself up to his full height, which made him a couple of inches taller than his *Journal* rival. "I was worried about whoever had fallen. MacMahon and I just happened to be near one another when Miss Denby came in."

"Hmmm," said Sandy, putting on a pair of gloves and opening the door. "Come with me, Miss Denby, and show me where you were when you saw what you saw. MacMahon and Foster, wait here; I'll call you when I'm ready for you. The rest of you can go back into the gallery. There's no need for us all to be up there trampling over evidence."

Poppy and Sandy stepped out onto the roof, the cold air taking them both by surprise. Sandy inhaled quickly and said: "Are you warm enough? You're not really dressed for the occasion."

Poppy pulled the gentleman's jacket closed over her evening gown. She wasn't sure whom the jacket belonged to but she was grateful for it. "I'll be all right, thank you."

"Are you sure? Here, take my coat – I'm wearing a warm jacket underneath." Sandy's voice had lost the edge of aloof professionalism, and Poppy detected a touch of the charming man she had spent time with earlier in the week.

"Thank you," she said, allowing him to drape the lambswool Ulster overcoat over her shoulders.

"It's quite a view from up here," he said, taking in the twinkling electric and gas-lit streets sloping down the hill towards the River Tyne, like strings of Christmas lights. During the day, Poppy imagined, they might be able to see the Castle and the quayside to the south, Grainger Town with its genteel Georgian buildings to the west and the Town Moor with its resident cows to the east. Their view to the north would be blocked by the building behind them. But looming just fifty yards in front of them was the tower where a woman had just died.

"That's where it happened," said Poppy, pointing to the oblong structure with its arched cupola on top. "I wasn't sure at first whether she was out here, but then I saw a match – I think – light up. I assumed she'd gone to the tower to have a cigarette."

"A funny place to go for a smoke," observed Sandy.

"That's what I thought."

"What did you see?"

"Well, it was lighter than it is now. It wasn't entirely dark yet and there were no clouds obscuring the moon. I saw a woman, who I thought looked like Agnes. She was talking to someone, but standing in front of him."

"Him?"

Poppy thought for a moment, pursing her lips. "I honestly don't know. It could have been a man or a woman. I didn't see the person."

"How did you know there was someone else there?"

"I heard two voices. One was definitely Agnes'. The other I couldn't make out, but it was lower and more muffled."

"Lower like a man's?"

"Possibly. But I honestly couldn't say for certain."

"All right," said Sandy, "could you make out anything that they said?"

Poppy closed her eyes and returned to the terrifying few moments before Agnes fell – or was pushed – to her death. "I could hear them arguing – more from the tone than the words – then I heard Agnes say, 'Leave me alone, I tell you, leave me alone.' She sounded terrified. I called out then, asking if she was all right, but there was no answer. So I started towards the tower. I walked along here –" she pointed to the narrow catwalk, "and when I was a few yards along, I saw them starting to fight."

"I thought you said you didn't see the other person."

"I didn't, at first, but when they started fighting – physically wrestling with each other – I saw their silhouettes. Agnes' hair was loose and blowing. I couldn't see the other person properly, only that there *was* another person. Does that make any sense?"

"Yes it does. What happened then?" His voice was low and gentle; lulling almost. Poppy wondered if this was his practised "keep the witness calm" voice. He was standing very close to her, but not touching. Poppy could smell pipe tobacco on his coat collar. Silence fell between them like dew. Then, after a few moments, she closed her eyes again and relived the last horrible moments of Agnes Robson's life.

"Like I said, they were scuffling. Agnes' hair was flying everywhere. So I ran towards them. But I tripped on my dress." She opened her eyes again and pointed to the approximate place she fell. "When I regained my footing and looked up again, Agnes was stepping back towards the arches, clutching her throat."

Sandy took her by the shoulders – firmly but gently – and turned her towards him. Then he looked deeply into her eyes. *Is this how he interviews all his witnesses?*

"She was clutching her throat? Did you see the other person slash at her?"

Poppy shook her head. "No, I didn't. Like I said, I'd tripped. It must have happened then. In fact I didn't see the other person again. All I saw was Agnes stepping backwards, clutching her throat, then – then –" Poppy's voice caught with emotion, "then I saw her fall. And she didn't scream. There was just all this hair, billowing around her like a witch's cloak. But she didn't scream and I didn't know why. But now I do. Someone had cut her throat. Oh God, Sandy! Someone cut her throat!"

Then, to her frustration, she started to cry. She tried to stop but couldn't. And before she knew it she was in Sandy's arms and he was holding her close, stroking her back and resting his chin on her head.

After a few moments she steadied herself and pulled back, wiping at her eyes with the back of her hand. "I'm so sorry, I – I –" She thrust her hands into the coat pocket, then remembered it wasn't her own. "Do you have a hanky?"

He smiled at her, his face awash with sympathy, then reached into his lapel pocket and produced a handkerchief. "Here," he said.

She took it and dabbed at her damp eyes and runny nose, embarrassed by her show of emotion. She had investigated murders before but none of them had ever affected her like this. Sandy, however, took her emotional display in his stride. "Don't worry; it was a very upsetting thing to witness, Poppy. But I need you to tell me *everything* that happened after that. Take your time and try not to leave anything out." He reached again into his jacket pocket and this time took out a metal case. "Cigarette?"

Chapter 10

That night Poppy lay awake listening to the rain that set in around midnight. The bed next to her – Delilah's – was empty. It was not unusual for her friend to stay out until the early hours of the morning, but tonight, of all nights, she wished she were not alone. Downstairs she heard sobbing – either Dot or Grace, but probably Dot. When Sandy had finally dropped her off, she had filled Dot and Grace in on what had happened. Both women, who had been waiting up for her, had been crying. Even Grace. "Who do you think could have done it?" she asked.

"I don't know, Grace; I honestly don't. Hopefully DI Hawkes is good at his job and will get to the bottom of it soon. He'll be interviewing everyone who was in the building."

"What if the person wasn't in the building though?" asked Grace. "Didn't you say that you thought you heard someone down in the stables?"

"No, I didn't say that. I said I wondered if Agnes had *gone down* to the stables."

"Yes, but someone *could* have come up, couldn't they? What if they had got through the stable doors from the street? And then slipped back out the same way?"

Poppy honestly hadn't thought of that. But Grace had a point. She would mention it to Sandy in the morning.

It was after two o'clock when Poppy finally tumbled into a fitful sleep, tortured by dreams of Agnes falling from the tower while she and Sandy kissed, wrapped in swathes of Agnes' black hair.

Friday, 4 October 1924

Newcastle upon Tyne

The next morning over breakfast, Poppy, Dot,and Grace, all red-eyed, sat in silence. The temporary maid – usually a chatty young lass – ferried plates and cups from the table, looking pale and confused. Poppy wasn't sure what time Delilah had got in, but she was sound asleep in the bed next to her when Poppy jerked into consciousness around seven o'clock. There was a place set for the young actress, and another, Poppy assumed, for Agnes.

Eventually Dot spoke. "It's Delilah's opening night tonight, isn't it?"

Poppy thought for a moment and said: "Golly, you're right! And we're all supposed to be going."

"I just don't think I can watch a comedy," said Grace.

Dot, usually so ebullient, nodded her agreement. "Neither can I. I'm sure Delilah will understand. We can go next week when things have settled down. Inspector Hawkes said he would be around later and they would need to search Agnes' things. Someone will need to be here for that."

"That will more than likely be later this morning, Aunt Dot. They'll be gone by this evening, and I do think Delilah still needs our support."

"I just can't, Poppy . . ." said Grace, her grey eyes haunted and harrowed.

Grace is taking this hard, Poppy thought. *Not surprisingly, I suppose.* Grace had been through a dreadful time over the last few years. She had been to prison for her role in the unintentional death of a suffragette – Delilah's mother – and its subsequent cover-up. However, both Dot and Delilah had eventually forgiven her, accepting that she had not intended her actions to have such a tragic end. The courts, however, had not been as forgiving, and Grace had been sent to prison for two years. Fortunately, Yasmin Reece-Lansdale, the wife of Poppy's editor Rollo Rolandson, was a leading barrister and friend of Aunt Dot and Grace. Yasmin had managed to get Grace released on probation after eighteen months. The terms of the probation were now up and Grace was a free woman. But, Poppy knew, she was still imprisoned in her heart and mind, unable to let go of the horrors of the past. Poppy wondered if that was one of the reasons Agnes' visit had upset her so much – the artist had been a reminder of the terrible time when Gloria died.

Dot reached out and squeezed her friend's hand. "Don't worry; I'll stay home with you, darling. But Poppy's right, someone needs to support Delilah. She's worked so hard to get this role, and I'm sure she'll be marvellous. So you go, Poppy. And maybe you can give our tickets to someone else."

"I'm not sure who."

"How about that handsome policeman? He seemed fond of you."

"DI Hawkes?" Poppy shook her head firmly. "No, I think he'll be far too busy working on the case."

Dot cocked her head to the side, her curiosity piqued. "But you would like to, wouldn't you? I detect a little flush, don't you, Grace?"

Grace stared ahead and did not answer.

Dot gave her friend a sympathetic look then turned back to her niece. "Are you sure he'll be too busy? He won't be working *all* day and night, surely?"

Poppy pursed her lips, annoyed that she had allowed Dot to sense that she was attracted to Sandy. But was she? If her dreams from last night were anything to go by, then she most certainly was.

She forced a tight smile and said: "I'll see. I'll definitely go though. Delilah will need me. And don't forget, it's also Father's birthday party tomorrow. Do you think you can make that, Grace?"

Again Grace stared straight ahead.

Dot sighed, then put on a happy face. "I'm sure Grace will be feeling better by then, won't you, darling? But if not, not to worry. Poppy and I can just get the train up to Morpeth on our own and let you have some time alone here." She once again patted her friend's hand.

Just then the doorbell rang. The maid stuck her head into the dining room and asked: "Should I get it, Miss Dot?"

"Yes please, Betty." Dot cupped her hands and bounced up her curls. "I wonder who it is? Probably your handsome inspector, Poppy."

To her annoyance, Poppy's heart skipped a beat. *Golly girl, pull yourself together! This is not the time or place for romance.* Aunt Dot gave her a knowing look.

Betty the maid returned a few moments later and said: "It's Mrs Sherman from two doors down. The lady with the dogs, Miss Dot. Should I bring her in?"

Poppy let out a relieved sigh. Good. She was not quite ready to see the handsome policeman this morning. She was barely out of her dressing gown.

Dot smiled at the maid. "Of course, Betty. She can join us for breakfast if she likes. Do we have enough eggs?"

"We do, miss."

"Jolly good; then invite the lady in please."

Maddie Sherman clomped her way down the hall wearing a pair of muddy boots. Grace roused herself long enough from her malaise to ask her to take them off.

"We've just had new carpets laid," she said tersely.

Maddie looked taken aback, but then complied, adding quietly: "Sorry, I didn't realise I'd picked up any muck in the park. Bit boggy down there I suppose after last night's rain."

Grace did not respond, but Dot swooped in with her usual charm. "Oh that's all right, Maddie; it's no bother at all. Easily done. Would you like anything to eat? We have eggs."

Maddie smiled gratefully at Dot as she took off her boots. "I've had some breakfast, thank you, but a cup of tea would be lovely. Where should I put these?"

"In the hall," said Grace. "Like I asked you to do yesterday when you came to visit, remember?"

Maddie, chastened, lowered her head and scurried out. She returned a minute later in her stockinged feet, and sat in the place where Agnes should have been.

"I'm sorry. I should have remembered about my boots. It's not like me to have to be told twice. It's just – well – my mind is taken up by other things. Like all of us, I should imagine." She smiled at

Grace, hoping for a truce. Grace softened slightly. Maddie relaxed. "Have the police been around yet?"

"Not yet," said Dot. "We thought for a minute you might be them. How did you sleep? We barely slept a wink, did we?" Dot took in Grace and Poppy, her large blue eyes perfectly made up despite the early hour.

"No, we didn't," said Poppy.

Maddie shook her head and let out a long sigh. "Terrible business. Who could have done such a thing? That poor woman. And poor Dante."

Dot looked startled. "Dante? Why? Has something happened to him too?"

Maddie's hand flew to her mouth. "Goodness no! Not like that. I can't even bring myself to think about it. But," she said, recovering her composure, "this will be a terrible blow for him, professionally. It was his first major exhibition that he has solely curated. And such a big name too: Agnes Robson. He has been working on it for over a year, in discussions with Agnes and Gerald Farmer. As well as the Tate. He's borrowed some of their paintings, and they don't just lend them to *anyone*, you know. But Dante has an impeccable reputation and came to them with top-notch references. He's done remarkably well for himself, for a young man of his age."

Grace turned her grey stare on Maddie and said: "A woman has died."

An awkward silence fell upon the table, broken only when Betty came in with a fresh pot of tea. Dot played mother and poured the tea.

After a few minutes, emboldened by the strong tea, Maddie turned to Grace and said: "I apologise, Mrs Wilson. I know it's not the level of tragedy that Agnes' family will have to endure, but a mother must think of her own child too. Isn't that true?"

"I have no children," said Grace.

"Oh. That's a shame," said Maddie.

This is getting very frosty, thought Poppy. "So, Mrs Sherman, you say Dante had been working on the exhibition for over a year. Whose idea was it to bring Agnes up here? Hers or his? Or someone else's?"

Maddie turned to Poppy, visibly relieved to not have to engage with Grace any further. "Oh, it was Dante's. He'd read in the newspaper that there was going to be a community hall opening in Ashington with a donation from Agnes. He contacted the journalist who wrote the story – that fellow Walter Foster from Morpeth who was there last night – and asked him for more information. He was then put in touch with the Ashington Miners' Institute, who put him in touch with the art department at Armstrong College. However, Professor Reid is already an old friend of the family – my late husband, Dr Sherman, and he were in the same battalion together during the Boer War. It was Simon Reid, I believe, who knew Agnes' manager and publicist – that fellow Gerald Farmer – and he was the one who put Dante in touch with them. Dante suggested Agnes have an exhibition at the Laing to coincide with her trip up to open the community hall. It took a bit of persuading, apparently, but she finally agreed. It was quite a coup for a young curator, I must say. I'm very proud of him. And now, oh dear, I'm not sure what's going to happen about the exhibition . . ."

"Surely they'll keep it up in her honour, don't you think?" offered Dot.

"I would hope so," said Poppy, "but for now the whole building will be closed as it's a crime scene."

Maddie's hand again went to her mouth. "Goodness, Poppy, when you put it like that . . ."

Maddie recovered, then finished her tea. As soon as the cup hit the saucer Grace said: "Well it's been lovely seeing you, Mrs Sherman, but we must get on. We have someone coming to wallpaper the drawing room today. I'll send Betty along as soon as the police arrive. Although I don't know why they can't see you in your own house."

Maddie stiffened. "Well, Mrs Wilson, if *that's* the way you feel about it . . ."

Dot flashed a warning look at Grace, then turned her warm smile on Maddie. "Don't be silly; of course it's not. Grace – like the rest of us – has just had a shock, that's all. She's not quite herself. She doesn't mean to be rude. Of course you're welcome here, Maddie.

Any time. I'm just sorry it's in such horrible circumstances, that's all."

Maddie's face dropped. "Yes, horrible circumstances," she echoed. "Quite horrible circumstances."

Armstrong Park was full of puddles. Poppy – who had borrowed a pair of wellington boots from Grace – was picking her way down the path towards Jesmond Vale burn. She went past the waterlogged bowling green as two men in mackintoshes were attempting to slough off the excess water with sackcloth and brooms, then the pavilion where just the other day she and Delilah had enjoyed tea. The chairs were stacked on tables, as a waitress mopped the patio. She was swilling water into a gutter that Poppy could see was already clogged with sodden leaves. Although it had stopped raining, fat droplets fell from the trees above, and Poppy put up her umbrella as she walked under the overhanging canopy on her way down towards the burn.

Poppy needed some air to clear her head. After Maddie Sherman had left, Grace had pulled herself together enough to supervise the decorators who had arrived shortly after breakfast. Aunt Dot was in the courtyard garden where, after the breakfast dishes were sorted, she directed Betty to clear the pots and flowerbeds of weeds. Great Aunt Mabel had never been much of a gardener, but Dot thought the area between the back door and the garage could be put to better use than just as a place to string a washing line. She was mulling over hiring a professional garden designer, but had not yet been able to convince Grace to allocate a budget to it.

Poppy herself enjoyed gardening, and had grown up helping her parents tend the cottage garden attached to the vicarage in Morpeth. But she had declined Dot's suggestion that she help out, saying she needed to be alone for a while. Dot did not take offence.

So here she was, all alone, apart from dog walkers and a couple of optimistic nursemaids hoping the weather would soon clear so they could give their charges full rein.

Poppy was going over the events of the previous night, trying, in her mind's eye, to see which guests were where when she'd left through the green room back door. It seemed a logical assumption that whoever was there could not also have been on the roof with Agnes. However, she was also aware that since the four interlocking galleries had been open – and the guests free to roam between them – she would not be able to know the whereabouts of each of them, even if she could bring to mind the fifty or so people in attendance. And then, of course, there was the catering and gallery staff as well as the musicians. It was not a verifiable fact that it was a guest who had killed Agnes. There was also the chance – as Grace had pointed out – that the killer might have come in from off the street, through the stables, and not been part of the exhibition at all.

There were so many variables, but Poppy felt she needed to at least start to cross some people off her list. *Her list . . .* Why was it *her* list? She was here on holiday. She should not be working as a journalist or press liaison lady, or moonlighting as an amateur sleuth. She had got the impression last night that DI Sandy Hawkes was a very competent detective, having worked with a number of them over the years. She had no doubt that he and his men would be going over the crime scene with a fine-tooth comb as soon as it was light enough to do so. And, as Sandy had made clear last night, everyone who was there (or at least who was known to be there) would be interviewed.

Somehow, though, she doubted that they would be interviewed in quite the way she had been last night. Her heart did a little pirouette. She stopped on a wooden footbridge over the burn, pulled down her umbrella and hooked it over the rail. Then she leaned on it with her forearms and watched the choppy grey water, swollen by last night's downpour, surge below. *Ah Sandy*, she thought, and then allowed herself to fantasise. *Sandy put his hands on her shoulders . . . Sandy stared into her eyes . . . Sandy lowered his head and pressed his lips to hers.* She imagined the tickle of his moustache on her nose and the tip of his tongue as it explored her mouth . . . *Good golly girl!* Poppy pulled herself up. What on earth was she thinking? Was she really contemplating allowing herself to be swept along on a stream of romance? After what had happened with Daniel, she was reluctant to expose her heart to more pain. Besides, she was only going to be here for a few more days. She was due back in London – at work – next Tuesday. She was only really here to see the house Aunt Dot and Grace were renovating, attend Delilah's opening night and then to celebrate her father's sixtieth birthday party.

How had she got dragged into this whole art fiasco? And now, here she was, starting to think about investigating a murder. It just wasn't her place. No sirree, as her American editor would say. But then she brought to mind the beautiful, sad Agnes Robson as they had sat together in the attic bedroom, telling her tale of abuse, loss and then her journey to art world success. She remembered the vulnerable woman, so desperate for her mother's approval, and the tears of happiness she had shed when she heard her family would attend her exhibition. Agnes, dear Agnes, was on the verge of finding peace in her troubled life. She was reconciling with her family and returning to lay to rest the ghosts of her past. *The ghosts of her past . . .* Had it been one of them that had slit her throat and pushed her from the tower? Again Poppy turned her attention to the galleries before she'd gone out the back door. Of the people she knew, she recalled seeing Aunt Dot chatting to a group of four men and women. She didn't know any of them. Then she pictured Delilah and Peter MacMahon. Peter's photographer was packing his kit away in the far corner. But where was Walter Foster? She couldn't recall seeing him. She had, however, seen young Edna, munching on a sausage roll and standing in front of one of Agnes' paintings of a family picnic on a lawn. Had her mother been with her? Poppy couldn't quite recall . . . but, yes, her art teacher had been. He had been talking to Professor Reid from the art school. Good, she could cross them off her list. And Gus and Gerald? Where were they? Gerald had said last night that they had been talking to Agnes before she went to "powder her nose". They said they were in Gallery A. But Poppy had walked through Gallery A and hadn't seen them. Perhaps they had moved on to Gallery B by the time she got there, or perhaps . . .

"Poppy! Poppy! Oh, come quickly!" Poppy looked up to see Delilah, wearing a blue and white polka-dot mackintosh, running towards her, panic-stricken.

"Good heavens, Delilah, what is it? What's wrong?"

"Oh Poppy," gasped Delilah, doubling over and leaning her hands on her knees to catch her breath. "Come quickly! The police are at the house and they're arresting Grace!"

Chapter 11

Delilah double-parked the yellow Rolls outside the Pilgrim Street police station and helped Poppy get Aunt Dot out of the car and into her wheelchair. Dot was far too worried to be her usual genial self, and chided the two younger women to hurry their horses. They ignored the police constable who demanded they move the motor car "at once" and carried Dot, with a great deal of effort, up the steps. The constable repeated his demand from behind them, threatening to confiscate the vehicle.

"Young man," said Dot, when Poppy and Delilah had finally managed to get the wheelchair onto an even keel, "if you had just taken the trouble to help us instead of being such a jobsworth, we could have got this done much earlier. You, sir, are not a gentleman!"

"No, you're not," said Delilah, flouncing past him and climbing into the vehicle. "I'll be back in two ticks!" she called out to the two women at the top of the steps and then started the engine.

Poppy pushed Dot into the police station and approached the front desk. Dot made up for her low vantage point by calling out in a loud voice: "I demand to see Grace Wilson!"

The desk sergeant looked first to Poppy, then down at Dot. "You demand what, madam?"

"I demand to see Grace Wilson. She was falsely arrested about an hour ago. I was told they were going to bring her here to be charged."

The sergeant scratched his head with the end of a pencil. "Falsely arrested, was she? Then she won't be here, madam; we only do things by the book."

Poppy stepped forward, exuding her most conciliatory air. "Of course you do, Sergeant. My aunt is a little upset. Please, accept our apologies. However, we *would* like to see Mrs Wilson. Mrs Grace Wilson. DI Hawkes brought her in, I believe."

The sergeant narrowed his eyes and appraised Poppy. "Weren't you in here earlier this week to see DI Hawkes? About an attempted mugging?"

Poppy smiled. "Yes, that was me. And DI Hawkes was very helpful. Is he here?"

The sergeant shook his head. "He isn't, miss. He brought in the prisoner – Mrs Wilson, that is – and left her to be processed. He's out again interviewing other witnesses."

"The – the – *prisoner*?" spouted Dot.

Poppy shushed her with a firm hand on her shoulder. "Ah, I see. May we see Mrs Wilson then, please? We will need to help her arrange legal counsel."

The sergeant poked at the same spot on his head with the nub of the pencil. "I could let one of you in. Just one."

"Then it should be me!" Dot insisted.

The sergeant leaned over and assessed Dot's wheelchair. "Don't think that'll get down the stairs, madam. The holding cells are in the basement. Best the young lady goes."

"Yes, but –"

"It's fine, Aunt Dot. I'll go. I'll pass on your love to Grace. Look, here's Delilah; she can sit with you." Poppy caught Delilah's eye as she stepped into the charge office. "Over here, Delilah. They're letting me see Grace. But only one of us can go. Can you and Dot stay here?"

"Of course, Pops, I'll stay as long as you need."

Grace was as pale as a grave shroud. She sat, unshackled, on a rickety chair in an interview room. She had not, yet, been taken to a cell, but the police sergeant standing outside the door said she would be as soon as Poppy left. The women were told they had fifteen minutes to talk – and not a moment longer. Poppy sat down on the chair opposite with a scarred and grime-streaked table between them. The room was airless, with no window, lit only by a bare electric lightbulb that gave off a crackly hum and was reflected in a large mirror.

Poppy took Grace's cold, bony hands in hers. "Oh Grace, I'm so sorry. Dot is here, but they wouldn't let her down. Delilah is with her. They both send their love."

Grace nodded.

"Look," said Poppy, "we don't have long. Have you called anyone yet? A lawyer? The sergeant said if you can't get anyone yourself they can arrange one for you. You don't have a solicitor up here, do you?"

Grace shook her head.

"What about the fellow who dealt with Aunt Mabel's estate?

He could put you in touch with someone, couldn't he?" Grace considered this for a moment and said, very quietly, "I don't think he'd be much help. He was as old as Marley. What I really need is someone like Yasmin. I wonder if she knows someone up here? Do you think you can call her, Poppy?"

"Of course!" said Poppy. "I'll do it as soon as I leave you. If anyone can help, it will be Yasmin. Don't worry, Grace – I'm sure she'll get you the very best counsel possible. Can I tell her what the actual charge is?"

Grace looked towards the door where the burly sergeant was waiting and lowered her voice. "Murder, Poppy: they're actually charging me with murder."

Even though Poppy had suspected this was the case, the words fell like bricks between them. "Oh Grace, that's dreadful. On what grounds? Have they told you?"

Grace nodded. "Yes, some of it. Apparently there was a witness."

"But there couldn't have been! You didn't do it!"

Grace squeezed Poppy's hands. "Of course I didn't. But they have a witness who saw me in the stables around the time Agnes died."

Poppy shook her head in confusion. "But Agnes didn't die in the stables. So how can that be?"

"Because I lied, Poppy. They caught me in a lie."

"Why? How?"

"I told DI Hawkes that I was in one of the other galleries: Gallery C. But I wasn't. I was in the stables."

"B-but – why? Why did you say that?"

Grace shrugged, her bony shoulders jutting through her grey felt jacket. "Because – ironically – I thought that if I'd told them where

I really was they would have suspected me of being involved." She gave a hollow, little laugh, which failed to light up her eyes. "How very, very, silly of me."

Poppy scrunched up her forehead, trying to understand Grace's motivation. "But why?"

"Because, Poppy, I am probably the only person there last night with a criminal conviction, who has previously been the suspect in a murder."

"But you were cleared of that!"

"Of murder, yes, but we all know that my actions contributed to Gloria's death, don't we? I was worried if DI Hawkes found out about that – which, apparently he has – I would be top of his list of suspects. So I decided to pretend I was just one of the crowd in the gallery. There were so many people, I thought it would be difficult for him to prove that I wasn't. But, I hadn't realised someone had actually seen me in the stables. I was convinced that – apart from the horses – I was alone."

Poppy checked her watch; they had five minutes left. She needed to get as much information from Grace to give to Yasmin as possible. "Why were you in the stables? Briefly, we don't have much time."

Grace nodded and straightened up, adopting her familiar no-nonsense demeanour. "Because I don't like crowds. You know that. And even though Agnes and I were in the process of burying the hatchet, we weren't quite there yet. I just needed to get away for a bit. So when I noticed the door at the back of the gallery was open a touch, I went out."

"Did you not consider going up to the roof?"

"No, not at all. I wanted to see the horses."

Poppy nodded. "All right, that makes sense. So, really, all Sandy – DI Hawkes – has on you is that you lied about where you were and that you were in the stables. He hasn't placed you on the roof at all. Good, I'm sure that's enough for whoever Yasmin suggests to represent you, to work on. In my experience of murder cases, that is all very circumstantial. He'll need a lot more than that."

Grace pursed her lips and looked away.

"What?" said Poppy. "Is there more?"

Grace let out a long, painful sigh. "Yes. Firstly, Hawkes knows that Agnes and I had some history together –"

Poppy tensed. Yes, and she had been the one to tell Sandy . . . Well, to clarify, after Gus and Gerald mentioned it.

"But beyond that, he claims that he has found the murder weapon, in the stables, and that it belongs to me."

"What the deuce?"

But before Grace could answer, the sergeant marched up to the table and announced in a no-arguments-will-be-tolerated voice: "That's it ladies, time is up."

"B-but Mrs Wilson hasn't finished telling me –"

The sergeant gripped Poppy's arm firmly. "She can tell it to her barrister."

While Aunt Dot and Delilah waited for her in the car, Poppy went to the post office and put in a call to Yasmin's office in London. Fortunately the barrister was in and listened, intently, to Poppy's story about Agnes' murder and Grace's arrest. Yasmin was an art collector and owned some of Agnes' paintings. She was shocked to hear of the artist's death, but less so about Grace's suspected involvement. "Unfortunately, she has form with this sort of thing, Poppy. I would have been surprised if the Newcastle police *didn't* think she were a suspect. But what's this about the murder weapon? Do you know what it is?"

Poppy said she didn't. "So, can you recommend anyone up here?"

"I could make some calls. But actually, I think it will be best if I come up. What's the time to Newcastle on the Scotsman? Six hours?"

"Five to six, depending. But you'll come? Yourself?"

"Yes, I will. Grace is a good friend, as you know. And I'm already familiar with her past record, seeing as I represented her in her former bail hearing."

"Oh, that's wonderful! Thank you Yasmin. Will you send a telegram to Dot's to confirm when you've managed to get a ticket?" She gave Dot's address.

"Got it. And I will. I'll try to get there for tomorrow afternoon. In the meantime, I'll get a recommendation for a local lawyer to cover for me until I arrive. I'll do that immediately. You say she's still at the police station?"

"She is, yes. Pilgrim Street."

"Jolly good. Someone should be there by the end of today. But until then, Poppy, I need you to get as much information for me as possible on Agnes, her associates, her family, who was at the exhibition and so forth. Can you do that for me without getting yourself arrested for interfering in a murder investigation?"

Poppy grinned. "I shall do my best, Yasmin."

Both Dot and Delilah were immensely relieved that Yasmin had offered to come up to represent Grace. "If anyone can get Grace out, Yasmin can," said Dot, who agreed with Poppy's suggestion that she go back to the town house to await further developments. Delilah said she would drop her home and then get to the theatre. The young actress was delighted to hear that Poppy still intended to come to the opening night show. "And so will I!" announced Dot. "I need something to take my mind off all this. And nothing can be done until Yasmin arrives here tomorrow."

"Well, not entirely nothing," said Poppy, who told her friends that she was going to do a bit of investigating on Yasmin's behalf. After waving off the yellow Rolls, Poppy went into the Fenwick's tearoom, ordered a pot of Earl Grey and a currant scone, and took out her notebook. With pencil poised she planned out her strategy to find out as much information as possible before Yasmin's arrival. This was not her first murder case, but it was the first one she was investigating that was *not* linked to a journalistic story she was working on. In the past her investigations were always tied into the editorial needs of the newspaper and this both inhibited and enabled her. The inhibition came with needing to assess the information received for newsworthiness and not being able to devote as much time as she would like to leads that would not provide column inches.

Yes, her primary motivation was always to find the ultimate truth and for justice to be done, but that always had to be coupled with the need to produce copy that would sell newspapers. However, the benefit of always being on the payroll of a paper was that she had a certain authority – and protections – as a representative of the press that would enable her to ask questions and gain entry to places which might otherwise be closed to her. Like the police press conference, for instance. Which got her thinking . . . She made her first note:

> 1. *Go see Peter MacMahon at the* Journal *and find out what he knows. Can he help in any way? NB let him know I'm not there as a rival journalist, just a concerned friend.*

> 2. *Ditto Walter Foster in* Morpeth.

Drat! Morpeth! It's Father's birthday tomorrow! And Yasmin's coming! But she won't be here until late afternoon. I could still get to Morpeth and back before she arrives. Father is having a lunch. Mother won't be happy that I'm rushing off early, but that can't be helped. Surely she'll understand when I tell her the circumstances. If I get up to Morpeth early morning I can get to see Walter Foster before the birthday party . . . Actually, didn't he say he was going to be at the lunch?

Poppy made another note beside point 2 and circled it: *ring Morpeth Herald and arrange meeting with W.F.*

She poured herself another cup of tea and looked up to see Gus North and Gerald Farmer arrive in the doorway. The room was busy and every table was occupied. She tried to wave them over, but they didn't see her and turned around and left. Ah well, never mind, she'd try to see them later. She made another note:

> 3. *Arrange interview with Gus and Gerald – staying at the Grand. Initial chat to find out more about Agnes' business in London and how the exhibition was set up. NB Yasmin will want to speak to them too.*

> 4. *Get guest list of who was at exhibition, plus, if possible, a staff list. Go to Laing . . . speak to*

Dante Sherman . . . tell him I am acting on behalf of Grace's legal counsel . . . might get me more access . . .

5. Arrange to speak to Agnes' family in Ashington – will it be best to wait for Yasmin?

Poppy put a question mark in a circle next to this one. Then finally, after picking the last currant from her tea plate and popping it into her mouth, she wrote:

6. Find out about so-called murder weapon and who the witness was who saw Grace.

Poppy rolled her pencil between thumb and forefinger. How was she to get that information? She quickly wrote "Sandy" and underlined the name three times.

Chapter 12

The Laing Art Gallery huddled on the corner of New Bridge Street and Higham Place like a gargoyle in a graveyard. A small group of curious onlookers watched from across the road as a man in a brown work coat and flat cap ran a mop over the bloodstained paving stones at the base of the tower. Two policemen watched him, and one of them greeted Poppy as she approached.

"Good afternoon, miss. The gallery is closed today. You'll have to come back tomorrow."

"Oh, I'm not here to visit the gallery. I'm here to see the curator, Mr Sherman. I am . . ." – she paused for a moment, unsure how to phrase it – ". . . I am here on behalf of one of the lawyers representing a suspect in the case."

The constable's eyes narrowed. "You're a lawyer? Didn't know they had lady solicitors. And I'd be very surprised if they have lady barristers. It's a proper man's job that."

Poppy bit her tongue, willing herself not to be riled. After a moment she said, feigning nonchalance, "Oh, I'm not a barrister. I am – well, I'm temporarily working for one – who is, in fact, a lady. She's from London. They have a few lady lawyers in London, you know. She'll be arriving tomorrow. In the meantime she has asked me to gather some information for her. So I need to get into the gallery please."

The policeman hooked his thumbs into his belt. "I've never heard of no lady lawyer. They might have them in London – with all their newfangled ways – but they *don't* have them here. Have you ever heard of such a thing, Constable Brown?"

"I haven't, Constable Stewart. You'd better be on your way, miss."

Poppy sighed inwardly, but managed to not allow her annoyance to show on her face. "All right then, you will have to go inside and ask Mr Sherman to come out here to meet me. Can you do that, please?"

"Mr who?"

"Sherman. Dante Sherman. He's the curator."

The two policemen looked down at Poppy with disapproving menace. Then, suddenly, a kind voice piped up from behind them: "Mr Sherman is in his office, miss, I can take you to him if you like." It was the man in the brown overall coat with the mop. The water in the bucket had turned blood red, and a dark smudge marked the spot where Agnes' body had smashed into the pavement.

"No one is allowed in the gallery," asserted Constable Brown, folding his arms and pursing his lips under a scraggly moustache.

Poppy sighed again, this time not entirely managing to hide her annoyance. It was time to up-rank the fellow. "Then I shall just have to tell DI Hawkes that you wouldn't let me do my job."

"You know DI Hawkes?"

"Actually, I do. We have recently become tennis partners."

"Tennis? I didn't know the governor played tennis?"

"Very well, actually. Is he here? Can you get him?"

The two constables looked at one another, not knowing what to do. Eventually Constable Stewart answered. "He's not here. He was, but not anymore. He's at the post-mortem."

"The post-mortem? Oh. Where's that?"

"That's Latin for when they examine the body after death. But I'd expect a lady lawyer to know that. Are you sure you're a lawyer?"

Poppy tapped her foot. "I never said I was a lawyer. And I asked, 'Where's that?' not 'What's that?' So now, tell me, where is the post-mortem being held? I shall find DI Hawkes myself and let him know how unhelpful you have both been."

"Ooooh, hoity toity, aren't ya?" mocked Stewart, accompanying his words with an affected flap of his hands.

Poppy slammed her shoe onto the pavement. "*And* . . . after I have told him that, I shall arrange for my associate – who *is* a lawyer – to apply for a court order. Or a *subpoena*, as they sometimes call it. That's a Latin word too."

At that, Constable Stewart laughed. "Oh go on. Let her in, Brown. It'll be easier than bothering the DI when he's busy. And I doubt a young lass like her could do much trouble. Can you take her in, Helsdon?"

Helsdon – the elderly caretaker – doffed his cap to the constable. "Aye, sir, I can. This way, miss."

Helsdon picked up the bucket and mop and led the way into the gallery. Poppy felt two sets of eyes boring into her back. She let out a sigh of relief when the doors of the gallery swung shut and she and the caretaker stood alone in the sepulchral silence of the Marble Hall.

Poppy turned to the stooped gentleman carrying the bucket. "Thank you for accompanying me, Mr Helsdon. And thank you for cleaning that up outside. Not a pleasant job for anyone."

Helsdon peered at her from under his cap, his eyes pale blue and red-rimmed. His skin hung in loose waves from his cheekbones. He had the look of a man who had once carried some weight but had lost his fullness. But there was a kindness there and Poppy warmed to it. She remembered something Dante Sherman had said last night to DI Hawkes: that the caretaker was the one who knew who had keys for the back door of the gallery.

"Mr Helsdon," she said, as he led her across the hall, under the rotunda and to a room labelled "caretaker" tucked under the stairs. "I don't know if you know but I was here last night and saw Miss Robson fall from the roof."

"Oh miss, that must have been a dreadful thing to see."

"It was," said Poppy quietly, Agnes' final ghastly moments etched forever in her mind. "And Miss Robson was a friend. So you see, apart from what I said to the policemen outside about temporarily working for a lawyer – which is entirely true – I have personal reasons for wanting to find out what happened last night. I thought it only fair to tell you."

As Poppy had expected, the personal confession endeared her to the kindly looking old man. He opened the door of the caretaker's room and put the bucket and mop inside, then closed the door again. He rubbed his hands down the sides of his overall coat. "Well, thank you for sharing that confidence with me, miss. And I'm very sorry about the loss of your friend. But I'm confused. I heard you say that you worked for the lawyer of one of the accused. I heard they arrested a lady. Do you know her?"

Poppy nodded. "I do. She too is a friend. But I know for a fact she didn't do it."

"Oh aye? Who did then?"

Poppy opened her hands wide. "I don't know, Mr Helsdon, but I intend to find out. For both my friends' sakes – the one who died and the one who has been falsely accused."

"I heard they have evidence."

"Oh yes? And have you heard what that evidence is?"

"The stable lad found a knife in the straw. I heard it belonged to the lady who has been arrested."

"And who did you hear that from?"

"The stable lad. He heard the inspector – that DI Hawkes – tell Mr Sherman."

"Hmmm, and was it the lad who saw Mrs Wilson – the lady they've arrested – in the stable last night?"

"Aye, it was. He saw her last night before he went home. Then he found the knife this morning and told Mr Sherman about it."

"I see," said Poppy, wondering how she might get to speak to the stable lad. One witness at a time though. "Thank you. That's very useful. However, there's something else you might be able to help me with. I imagine someone like you knows all the ins and outs here at the gallery. And Mr Sherman mentioned last night that you would know who had keys to the back door and whether or not it was left open last night."

Helsdon turned to Poppy with a guarded expression. "I'm sorry, miss. Like I told the polis, I was sure the back door was locked before the exhibition started. We had brought up the last of the paintings earlier in the day. The ones that got here late."

"Oh? Which were they?"

"Two came up in a separate delivery from the rest. One was of a mammy and bairn walking along a railway track, and the other one was of some flowers. I can't remember what they were. Mr Sherman was very relieved when they arrived and he asked me to make sure everything was locked up afterwards."

"So you locked the door then?"

Mr Helsdon stiffened. "Aye, I did, miss. But . . ."

"But what?"

The elderly caretaker looked over his shoulder and lowered his voice. "But not all the keys are accounted for." He pulled a large ring of keys from his pocket. "I keep these with me, but there's spares in me room downstairs. When the polis asked me to show them all the keys I went to get them and it wasn't there."

"The second key for the back door was missing?"

"Aye miss, it was. And it still is. But it's not my fault. I swear by me granny's grave. It was there when I went home last night."

Poppy smiled gently at the worried man. "I believe you, Mr Helsdon, and I'm sure the police will too."

He nodded. "I hope you're right, miss. I don't want it on me conscience that that poor woman died because of my mistake."

Poppy bit her lip. She knew exactly how he felt. If she only hadn't tripped on the roof last night she might have got to Agnes in time . . .

"It wasn't your fault. Whoever pushed Miss Robson from the roof was to blame. And that wasn't you or me. And if killing her had been their intention from the start, then they would have found a way to do it even if they hadn't been able to get a key to the door. Which reminds me: the door to the roof – does it have a key?"

Helsdon shook his head. "No miss, not anymore. It did, years ago, but it got lost. Now we just use the bolt. It locks and opens from the inside."

"Thank you, that's very helpful."

They walked through a gallery of contemporary British art, past a five-by-three-foot oil painting of children playing on a beach, by Laura Knight. Poppy had seen it a couple of years earlier when it was on loan to the Tate. She would have loved to have taken it in again, but she had more important things to do today. Eventually they came to a door with "curator" written on it. Helsdon knocked and waited for a reply.

"Enter!"

Helsdon opened the door and put his head round. "Mr Sherman, sir, there's a lady to see you. A miss – oh I'm sorry miss, I didn't catch your name."

Poppy smiled at him. "That's all right, Mr Helsdon. My name is Miss Denby. May I come in, Mr Sherman?"

Poppy pushed open the door to reveal the young curator sitting behind an oak-wood desk.

"Miss Denby! How did you get in here?" Sherman looked vaguely annoyed. But then, from what Poppy had seen of him over the last couple of days, vague to outright annoyance was the curator's default expression. Poppy was used to dealing with recalcitrant interviewees in her line of work, so she adopted her usual air of polite professionalism.

"The policemen said I could see you. I hope that's all right. I need to speak to you."

"This lady knows the lady who was killed last night. And the other one what done it," said the caretaker, cap in hand.

Poppy stiffened. Dante Sherman's eyes narrowed. "Thank you Helsdon, that will be all. Come in, Miss Denby. Do sit down."

Mr Helsdon cast a quick look at Poppy. She smiled at him.

Reassured, he retreated, closing the door behind him. The curator gestured again for Poppy to take a seat, but did not rush out from behind his desk to pull out a chair for her. As Poppy sat she noticed that Dante had eschewed his flamboyant Oscar Wilde look from the night before for a more conventional day suit. His only nod to Bohemia was a pink silk handkerchief and rose quartz cufflinks. He had replaced his monocle with a pair of ordinary spectacles over which he peered at his guest.

"So, Miss Denby," he said, closing a file – but not before Poppy had a quick glimpse of the contents. It was a letter from the British National Gallery – otherwise known as the Tate – with the subject line: "Authentication query of Agnes Robson's *The Railway Family*." *The Railway Family . . . Could that be the painting Mr Helsdon referred to?* Poppy filed the question and the information away in a mental folder entitled "must follow up".

"Now, how may I help you?" asked Dante, his fingers templing protectively over the closed file.

"Well, Mr Sherman, as you probably know already, my aunt's companion, Mrs Wilson, has been arrested for Agnes' murder. She is, of course, innocent."

"So you believe."

"Indeed. As does anyone who knows her."

"Not quite everyone . . ."

"What do you mean?"

Dante picked a loose thread from his jacket cuff. "Well, I overheard Gerald Farmer tell DI Hawkes that Gus North said there was some history between Agnes and Mrs Wilson. Some kind of bad blood."

Poppy smarted. "It is no secret that Grace and Agnes had a falling out some years ago. But I can assure you that they were in the process of laying that to rest. And even if they weren't, Grace would never murder anyone!"

"Oh really? Wasn't she involved in the death of that suffragette back in –"

Poppy slapped her hand onto Dante's desk. "Mr Sherman, I am *not* here to dredge up ancient history."

"No?" said Dante, cocking his head to the side then straightening his glasses with his finger. "Well, someone seems to be. And DI Hawkes thinks there's enough evidence to arrest her. Have you heard about the knife in the stables?"

"I have. But I have not heard what evidence connects it to Grace? Have you?"

"I have not."

"Well then. Best not jump to conclusions. The last I heard we are still subject to impartial justice in this country and are innocent until proven guilty. Which, I have no doubt, Grace will be. And to that end, I would like your help . . . please."

Poppy willed herself to calm down. Getting into an argument with Dante Sherman would not help her get what she had come here for.

Dante leaned back in his chair and interlaced his fingers over his stomach. "Oh really?" he drawled. "And how may I be of help, Miss Denby?"

"I am here on behalf of Mrs Yasmin Rolandson, KC. Formerly known as Yasmin Reece-Lansdale, KC. Have you heard of her?"

"I have indeed. I read about her in the papers when she became the first woman to be admitted to the bar at the Old Bailey. That was a few years ago, wasn't it?"

"It was. Anyway, she has agreed to represent Grace and will be arriving from London tomorrow. In the meantime, she has asked me to gather some evidence on her behalf. Do you have a copy of the guest list from last night as well as the names of all the members of staff present – including the catering staff and the musicians? Oh, and I will also need the name of the stable boy, please."

Dante picked up a pen and twirled it between thumb and forefinger. "I have already given that list to DI Hawkes."

"I'm sure you have, but the defence is legally required to have access to the same information."

"Then ask DI Hawkes for it. It is he who is legally required to provide it, not me, I wager."

Poppy pressed her fingernails into her hand. "Mrs Rolandson will furnish you with a court order . . ."

"Then let her do it." Dante stood up, clearly indicating the meeting was over. "If that is all, Miss Denby, I have a lot of work to do."

Poppy stood too. "Well, thank you for your time, Mr Sherman. No doubt Mrs Rolandson will be in touch soon – with that court order."

"I look forward to receiving it," he said, his voice dripping with sarcasm.

Poppy turned and left, not waiting for the curator to open the door for her. As she pulled the door closed, she caught a glimpse of him staring at her with undisguised animosity. *So much for his mother's intentions of "matching us up"*, thought Poppy. She shuddered at the idea. Then, with the door as a firm barrier between them, she looked to left and right. There was no one there. *Good*, she thought, then quickly worked her way back to the Marble Hall, up the stairs and to the galleries above. As she passed the rotunda she heard Sherman call out: "Helsdon! Did you see Miss Denby leave?"

"No sir, I didn't, but I was in my room here, sir . . ."

"Go and check with those police officers out there. And if she's not gone, come and tell me. If she has, do *not* under any circumstances allow her back into the gallery. Is that clear?"

"Yes, sir."

Poppy crouched down behind the balustrade. She did not want to be seen if either Helsdon or Dante looked up. What was she to do? Should she make her presence known? No, she would not. She would go into the Agnes Robson exhibition as originally intended – consequences be damned!

Poppy slipped into Gallery A and closed the door behind her. She knew she didn't have much time before Dante or the police officers found her. She quickly perused the walls and located the paintings she assumed were the two that had arrived late: *The Railway Family* and *Lilies in a Vase*. She wished she had a camera with her to capture the images, but she did the best she could to imprint them on her mind. She would check with Peter MacMahon and Walter Foster to see if either of them had taken photographs of the two works last night. Also, there was the catalogue listing of the exhibition. She was sure she had seen it at Aunt Dot's house . . .

She stared at the haunting image of *The Railway Family*. The woman, hunched up and carrying a heavy sack – perhaps filled with belongings – was trudging along a railway track. Poppy thought she recognised it . . . wasn't that the curve of line leaving Ashington Station? The woman was holding a child's hand – it was hard to tell if it was a boy or a girl as the mite was wrapped up in a ragged coat that poorer children of either gender would wear, its head and neck wrapped in a scarf. A dirty, stain-streaked face looked back at the viewer. There was no doubt this was a child in distress. Poppy, who was no expert, assessed that it was oil on board. It had the characteristic Robsonesque blocks of colour, but it seemed different from other Robson paintings she had seen, different from the others hanging in this gallery – it was more narrative than expressionistic. Granted, Agnes often had roads or railway lines in her paintings, but they rarely had people, and certainly not people who were telling a story.

She cocked her head to listen: no one, as yet, was approaching. She then turned to the second painting: the still life of lilies in a vase. This was more typical Robson, she felt. Again, it was oil on board, but – if she were not mistaken – it was not quite dry. How could that be? She dabbed at it tentatively with her finger. Yes, it was slightly tacky. Had this literally come off Agnes' easel? Was this why it was late – because Agnes was waiting for it to dry? Or was there another reason? Poppy really had no idea whether or not the paintings held any clues or were connected in any way to Agnes' death, but so far they were the only thing – apart from the missing key – that had stood out as unusual. And then there was that letter from the Tate she had glimpsed on Dante's desk . . .

"Check in there!" she heard, and saw the door to Gallery A start to open. She ran towards the connecting door to Gallery B.

"Oi! Miss! Come back here now!" It was the voice of one of the police officers.

She was very tempted to run but she knew it would make things worse. She stopped – her hand on the door – and turned around. One of the policemen came in, closely followed by an embarrassed-looking caretaker.

"Is anything wrong, Constable?"

The policeman strode purposefully towards her. Poppy held her ground.

"You shouldn't be in here. It's a crime scene."

"Oh? I'm sorry. No one said I wasn't able to walk around the gallery when I was invited in."

"Mr Sherman said he asked you not to," said the policeman.

The caretaker lowered his eyes.

"Actually, he did nothing of the sort. I took my leave of him and decided to pop in here to have a look at Agnes' paintings. No one said I couldn't."

"Well, I'm telling you now. Come with me please." The constable reached out as if to take hold of her. Poppy stepped aside.

"I am quite capable of leaving under my own steam, Constable. Good day to you. And good day to you too, Mr Helsdon."

Poppy willed herself to channel Delilah as she swished past the men, her head held high.

"And y're not to come back," growled the policeman.

Poppy's eyes narrowed. *Oh, just try to stop me.*

Chapter 13

Poppy and Aunt Dot spent the evening at the theatre. For a few frivolous hours, Poppy pushed the mystery of who killed Agnes Robson into the wings, as the escapades of Algernon, Gwendolyn, Cecily and Jack – and the revelation of an abandoned baby in a handbag – took centre stage. Delilah was – as expected – delightful as the love-struck Gwendolyn, and Poppy chortled along with the Newcastle audience at the shamelessly snobbish put-downs of her mother, the ghastly Lady Bracknell. After the final curtain, Poppy accompanied an usher who pushed Aunt Dot towards the bar in the foyer, as the former actress mimicked the most memorable line of the play: "To lose one parent, Mr Worthing, may be regarded as a misfortune; to lose both looks like carelessness."

She said it with such aplomb that she received a round of applause as she entered the bar. Once the word got out that this was *the* Dot Denby from the West End who had herself played Lady Bracknell in a London production back in the day, she was soon surrounded by admirers.

Poppy was pushed further and further back from her aunt until she bumped into someone. She turned around to apologise and realized it was Peter MacMahon.

"Poppy! I'm very sorry."

"No Peter; it is I who is sorry. However, I am very glad to see you. I was hoping to speak to you. In a professional capacity."

The journalist cocked his head to the side and said teasingly:

"Professionally? Oh that's a pity." Poppy raised an eyebrow in mock disapproval. "Well, seeing as you're already spoken for by this evening's leading lady, what choice do I have?" And then, feeling slightly uncomfortable playing the coquette, she added: "Seriously, Peter, I *do* need to speak to you. About Agnes' murder and the investigation. You do know that our friend Grace Wilson has been arrested, don't you?"

Peter nodded sympathetically. "I do, and I'm sorry to hear it. Do you think she did it?"

Poppy was startled and took a step away from the journalist. "I do not!"

Peter raised his hands placatingly. "All right, all right. You know I had to ask. Would you – er – be up for an interview to give Grace's side of the story?"

Poppy didn't like being on the receiving end of a journalist's questions. She'd discovered that much during her short stint as Agnes' press liaison. But she was glad of the experience; she felt she now had new insight into how her interviewees might feel. On the other hand, she recognised a kindred professional spirit in Peter MacMahon. She too would have used her closeness to the subjects in a murder investigation to get a scoop if she could. But if she played it carefully, she could use this to her advantage.

"Well, Peter, I would have to ask both Grace and Dot for their permission. It is their lives, really, that will be the most impacted by any publicity. However, I could encourage them to do so if it is worth their while . . ."

Peter looked at her quizzically. "What are you suggesting, Poppy? The *Journal* does not have the budget to pay sources! I'm surprised you even asked, to be honest."

Poppy flushed, suddenly realising how her comment must have sounded. "Oh no, Peter, nothing like that! I just need your help in accessing certain information. As I'm not officially representing a newspaper, I have limited opportunity to question people. Grace's barrister – who will be arriving here tomorrow – has asked me to dig around a bit for her. But again, it's not in an official capacity."

Peter leaned back on his heels and hooked his thumbs into his red satin cummerbund. "What sort of information?"

Poppy looked around to see if Dot was still occupied with her "fans". She was. Good. She leaned into Peter. "All sorts. Firstly, I would like to speak to the stable lad who allegedly found the so-called murder weapon. Also, I was wondering if you had any sources inside the police here who might give you the heads-up on any developments – such as results of a post-mortem, lists of witnesses and so forth."

Peter raised a sardonic brow. "Surely you're not suggesting that we might have a bent copper on the payroll."

Poppy raised an equally sardonic – although better manicured – eyebrow. "I know how newspapers operate, Peter. I doubt you're paying anyone – if you did, there'd be corruption charges to be faced if it ever came out – but it wouldn't surprise me if you had a mutually beneficial relationship with someone on the police. They feed you information in exchange for keeping certain things out of the public eye, or delaying publication, or bumping something above or below the fold."

Peter shrugged. "I couldn't possibly say."

"I would never expect you to. But I would like to know if you will tell me anything you can about the investigation. And in exchange I can arrange an interview with Dot and – if it can be arranged – Grace herself, after she's been cleared."

"Only after?"

"Yes," said Poppy firmly. "Only after."

Peter rocked back and forth on his heels, mulling over the offer. Finally he said: "Agreed. But it must be an exclusive. Foster will want the same, I've no doubt."

No doubt he would. Poppy weighed this up for a moment. What might she need from Walter Foster that Peter MacMahon couldn't give her? Possibly information about Agnes' background. The *Morpeth Herald* was better placed than the *Newcastle Daily Journal* for that. But the *Journal* was right here in the middle of Newcastle where the current investigation was taking place. Hmmm, she would have to think of another way of dealing with Foster if she needed to . . . She pulled herself up, suddenly. Since when had she become a wheeling-dealing newspaper hack? What happened to an honest answer for an honest question and pure human decency? She gave herself a mental shake. Then she reached out her hand.

"Deal. Do you think you could find out who the witness is who said they saw Grace in the stables? Or do you know already?"

"I don't, no. All I know is that the stable lad told the curator – that Sherman fellow – that he'd seen a lady in the stables, who it turned out matched Grace's description. And then Sherman told Hawkes."

"What did Sherman tell Hawkes?" came a voice from behind her. A chill went down Poppy's spine as she recognised the voice of Sandy Hawkes. She turned around to see the police inspector looking dashingly handsome in a tuxedo.

"DI Hawkes. Good evening. I didn't know you were at the show."

Sandy nodded at Poppy, his face inscrutable. "Delilah arranged some tickets for me."

"I thought you might have been too busy with the investigation . . ."

"I have a team of Tyneside's best investigators working for me, Miss Denby; they can hold the fort for a few hours. Besides, I was hoping to see you here, rather than going around to your aunt's. It's less . . . well, it's less formal." He gave a little smile.

Poppy's heart did the funny little pirouette it had started to do whenever she thought of the detective. She willingly calmed herself. Surely now that her aunt's companion had been arrested for murder, there was absolutely no hope for any budding romance between them.

But Hawkes did not seem put off. "May I get you a drink, Poppy?"

Poppy. He had called her Poppy . . .

"Er, yes please."

"MacMahon?"

"No thanks, Hawkes. I'm going to meet Delilah backstage. I said I'd head out with the cast for drinks afterwards. Are you coming with us, Poppy?"

Poppy shook her head. "I would have, but apparently Gerald and Gus are coming around tonight to pick up Agnes' things. Assuming, DI Hawkes, the police have finished with them?"

"We have taken what we need. They can take the rest. Unless her next of kin want it?"

"I think Gerald is going to arrange to have everything returned to Agnes' mother. That's what Dot said. Anyway, no Peter, I shan't be joining the cast. I've already told Delilah. But shall I see you tomorrow so we can continue our conversation? I'm off to Morpeth for my father's birthday party, but I should be back early evening."

"I'll call by then. Good evening to you. And to you, Hawkes."

Sandy waited until Peter had left then said: "Right. Drinks. What will it be?"

Poppy again looked to see if Dot was nearly ready to go. But the former doyenne was still deep in conversation.

"A glass of white, please."

Sandy returned with two glasses of white wine. "So," said Poppy, after taking her first sip, "why did you arrest Grace?"

Sandy peered at her over the rim of his glass, took a sip, then lowered it. "Because we had sufficient evidence to charge her."

"Such as?"

"Such as what I will be showing to her barrister when she arrives. I believe you have secured the services of a famous lady lawyer from London."

"We have," said Poppy. "She is a personal friend of the family."

"And the one who got Mrs Wilson out of prison early last time."

Poppy cast a glance towards Aunt Dot. She looked like she might be wrapping things up.

"That's right. I see you've been doing your research."

Sandy chuckled. "What else did you expect? I'm not just a dumb copper from a northern toon."

"I never said you were. I'm sure you are very good at your job. But in this case, I believe you have got it wrong. Grace did not do it."

"Then who did?"

It was Poppy's turn to chuckle. "Surely a clever copper like you should be able to find out."

Sandy was suddenly serious. "Oh I will, Poppy, I will. But there is enough to hold Mrs Wilson on for now. I will continue to look for evidence to strengthen the case against her – or to release her. And I would appreciate it if you didn't interfere. I heard you were impersonating a lawyer at the gallery earlier today."

Poppy choked on her wine. "I did nothing of the sort! Mrs Rolandson – the former Miss Reece-Lansdale, KC – asked me to try to get some information for her in advance of her arriving tomorrow.

I told the constables on guard there that that was what I was doing and that is what I attempted to do. There was nothing underhanded about it."

"So is that why you were sneaking around the gallery?"

"I was *not* sneaking! Now listen here . . ."

"Is everything all right?" Aunt Dot approached them in her chair.

Sandy straightened up. "It is, Miss Denby, yes. I was just laying down some boundaries for your niece. Just like in tennis she seems to struggle to keep within the lines." He made the last comment with a playful twinkle in his eye.

But Poppy was in no mood for games. She thrust her glass back at Sandy, then said: "Are you ready Aunt Dot? I think we need to get home."

"I am, yes. Gerald and Gus will be waiting for us."

"Would you like a lift?" asked Sandy, holding two half-empty glasses.

"No thank you," said Poppy. "I think we both know where those lines are now, DI Hawkes. My aunt and I shall get a taxi." Poppy took hold of Aunt Dot's chair and spun her round, then marched them both out of the theatre.

Gerald and Gus were waiting for them on the porch when Poppy and Aunt Dot pulled up in the taxi. "So sorry we're late," said Dot. "I hope you haven't been waiting long."

"Just a few minutes," said Gerald.

Poppy opened the door while Gus pushed Aunt Dot's chair up and over the front step. Grace and Dot had not yet got around to putting in a ramp to the front door. Gerald was at Poppy's shoulder and said quietly to her: "Look Poppy, I'm sorry we said anything about Grace and Agnes' feud. I hope that's not what got her into trouble."

Poppy pushed the door open and removed her hat. "I don't think so, Gerald. Besides, I also told DI Hawkes about it – after you mentioned it – so in that case we are both to blame. But no, he said they have more evidence against her."

"Like what?"

"Apparently there's a knife linked to her. But I haven't found out yet how it is linked and why they assume it's hers."

"It's utterly ridiculous! Grace wouldn't hurt a fly – everyone knows that." Dot took her hat off and passed it to Poppy. "And she certainly isn't the type of woman to carry around a knife."

"Did they speak to you about the knife, Aunt Dot, when they questioned you this morning?"

"They did. They asked me if any knives were missing from the house. I said I had absolutely no idea – I'm not the keeper of the cutlery."

"So you didn't corroborate it then. I wonder who did?" asked Poppy, hanging Gus' bowler hat on the hatstand.

"Don't worry, Poppy," soothed Dot. "Yasmin will get to the bottom of it. She sent a telegram, by the way. She'll be arriving at three o'clock. Will you be able to meet her?"

"I don't think we'll be back from Morpeth by then. I'll ask Delilah if she can pick her up. Do you think she can use the Rolls?"

"Of course! She knows where the keys are kept. Right, Poppy, will you take the gentlemen upstairs to Agnes' room? I'll get us some drinks for when you get back down. Shouldn't take you too long. Sherry, everyone?"

Gus, Gerald and Poppy all said yes to a nightcap and then went upstairs. Agnes' attic bedroom was not as neat as she'd left it. Clothes and personal items were scattered across the bed and the floor after the police had searched them earlier in the day. Poppy hadn't been there when it happened so wasn't sure what they had taken. There wasn't much anyway – just the contents of a large suitcase that Agnes had brought with her. Her fur coat was still at the Laing, and of course the beautiful green velvet gown she had worn to the reception was with her at the mortuary. Poppy and the two men wordlessly started gathering and folding, placing everything back in the suitcase. Poppy came across the catalogue for the Robson exhibition at the Laing under a discarded silk stocking. She matched the stocking with its mate on the bed and then paged through the catalogue. She could not find the two paintings she had seen earlier that day.

"Er Gus, Gerald . . ." she said.

Gerald tapped Gus' arm and turned him towards Poppy so he could see that she was speaking to them.

"Gentlemen, when I was at the gallery this afternoon the caretaker told me that he had last opened the back door in order to bring in two paintings that arrived late. Do you know anything about them? They're not in this catalogue, so I'm wondering if they were intended to be at the exhibition in the first place, or were just afterthoughts."

Gus and Gerald looked at one another. Gus nodded to Gerald to speak on their behalf.

"Er, yes. We brought them up with us on the train."

"So you brought them in with you when you arrived at the exhibition?"

"No, we brought them around earlier. We came straight from the station, dropped off the paintings and then went to the hotel for an early supper before we came to the exhibition proper."

"Oh," said Poppy. "All right. That makes sense. So you dropped them at the back entrance?"

Gerald nodded. "Yes. All paintings get received there. Out of the public view. Sherman sent us instructions in a telegram."

"Mr Sherman was in contact with you?"

"Of course. Agnes never dealt with these sorts of arrangements. That's why she hired a manager. I set the whole exhibition up with Sherman. Which was why it was such bad luck when I fell ill. Poor Agnes had to come on her own."

"Why didn't Gus come with her?"

Gerald looked at Gus. Gus replied. It was the first time she had heard him speak since the previous evening. "Agnes and I would have struggled without Gerald."

"But you are – were – her assistant."

"Her studio assistant. I helped her keep her paints in order. Primed her canvases. Framed her paintings. We got on very well. But socially . . . she struggled with me being deaf. She was shy and needed someone to talk for her sometimes. I couldn't do that easily. Gerald could. So . . ." He spread his hands and shrugged. Poppy waited for him to say more. He didn't.

"So," she continued, feeling she still hadn't got to the bottom of the paintings, "why did you bring them up separately? Gerald?"

"Sherman asked for them. Agnes hadn't put them forward for display – as you can see from the original catalogue – but Sherman had seen them on a visit to Agnes' studio and specifically asked for them."

"How strange," said Poppy. "Why didn't Agnes put them forward? Do you know?"

Gerald looked at Gus who, after pausing to formulate his words, said: "Agnes had decided to rework *Lilies in a Vase*. She had never been happy with it. She didn't think it was ready to show."

"So, that's why the paint wasn't quite dry . . . How strange, though, that you brought it even though it was wet."

Gus shrugged. "Oil paints can take many weeks to dry properly. Sherman wanted it and we saw no need not to bring it."

"No need? What about that Agnes didn't want it shown?"

Gerald and Gus looked at one another. Gus nodded to Gerald, who took over the conversation. "Agnes could be . . . well . . . she could be erratic. What she said one day wasn't always what she said the next. So we took the chance that she wouldn't mind. And besides, Dante Sherman can be very persuasive."

"Oh? How's that?"

Gerald cleared his throat. "He's, well, very influential. For a man of his age. He has got one of the top jobs in the region. And he has friends at other galleries. If he took offence to something, it might influence other galleries."

Poppy was surprised. She had always been under the impression that it was famous artists that called the shots, not gallery curators. But, she had to admit, she didn't know that much about it. Might be worth doing a feature article on it when she got back to London . . . She brought herself back to the present.

"So had Agnes changed her mind? When she saw the paintings had arrived?"

Gerald shrugged. "I'm not sure. She didn't say."

Poppy nodded. From what she had gathered so far, that was very much like Agnes. She would often bottle things up – not say exactly what she felt. "I see. Oh – and the railway one – why didn't she want that one to be exhibited?"

This time it was Gus who spoke, slowly and carefully. "That I don't know. She just didn't put it forward. She never gave a reason."

"But it's been seen before, hasn't it? By the Tate?"

Gus shook his head. "No, it wasn't at the Tate exhibition."

"And why's that?"

Again Gus shrugged. Poppy frowned. She had not yet mentioned the letter she had seen from the Tate about authentication. But why had neither Gus nor Gerald mentioned it? Clearly the Tate *had* seen it, even if it hadn't been exhibited. Was there some question over its authenticity? Poppy felt she needed to talk to Yasmin about it and decided not to press Agnes' colleagues further now.

"All right, thanks."

"Why do you ask?" asked Gerald. "Do you think this has something to do with her death?"

"I honestly don't know, Gerald. It's just something that struck me as out of the ordinary. Those are the first things I look for when I'm investigating."

Gerald opened his eyes wide in surprise. "You're investigating?"

Poppy picked up a skirt and folded it along the waistband. "Not officially, no, but Yasmin has asked me to do a bit of digging. And as you probably know, I've done this sort of thing before."

Gerald grinned. "Yes, your sleuthing exploits are well known, Miss Denby."

Poppy smiled and continued folding. As she did, a photograph slipped out of the pocket of the skirt. She bent down and picked it up. It was a photograph of a painting of a young woman – not much older than a girl – with long black hair. The girl was naked, sitting with her arms wrapped around her knees. The nudity was obvious but no breasts or genitalia were shown. It was, Poppy supposed, what would be considered a "tasteful" nude. The girl looked out of the painting, her dark eyes innocent, not seductive. Who was she? She was vaguely familiar . . . Poppy turned the photo over and saw some handwriting: *Stay away.*

She held the photo up for Gerald and Gus to see. "Do either of you know what this is? Is it one of Agnes' paintings?"

Gerald took it and examined it. "No, not as far as I know. It's not her style, is it, Gus?" Gus was looking at the photograph, his face visibly paling. Then he shook his head firmly. "No, I've never seen it. Excuse me." The young man turned on his heel and left.

Gerald called after him: "Gus! Are you all right?" Then he muttered an expletive, apologised to Poppy and said: "He can't hear me. I'm sorry Poppy, I need to see if he's all right. This business with Agnes has hit him very hard. Can you finish here on your own?"

"I can," said Poppy and watched sympathetically as the manager went to comfort his friend. However, she couldn't shake the feeling that Gus actually *had* recognised the painting.

She slipped the photograph into her own skirt pocket then finished packing Agnes' suitcase.

Chapter 14

Saturday, 5 October 1924
Morpeth, Northumberland

At ten o'clock on Saturday morning a train pulled into Morpeth Station. Waiting for it was a tall, grey-blond man of sixty, wearing a black suit and a clerical collar. The Reverend Malcolm Denby was as lean and wiry as he had been when he was twenty-five years old and left his law studies at Durham University to marry an earnest Methodist girl whom he had met handing out free cups of soup to the poor of Newcastle. Malcolm, on his weekends home from Durham, started attending Brunswick Methodist Chapel in the centre of the city, rather than the high Church of England St George's, in well-to-do Jesmond, which his family had attended for four generations. Alice Drew, the girl who had first caught his attention on a freezing cold morning on Northumberland Street, was a greengrocer's daughter. Her father had a stall in Newcastle's Grainger Market, and her mother, like all decent women, stayed home and looked after the house and their six children. Alice was the youngest child and had not had any formal education other than that offered on Sundays by Brunswick Methodist. But what she lacked in intellectual learning, she made up for in goodness, kindness, gentleness, faithfulness and self-control. She spoke to him often about the Fruit of the Spirit and how she felt called to help those less fortunate than herself – all in the name of her beautiful saviour, Jesus Christ. As he came from a family that was far more fortunate than hers, and had, after all, been baptised in the name of the same beautiful saviour, he felt stirred to do the same.

Despite his family not considering Alice a good match, he married her anyway, in 1894, and changed his course from law to theology. A few years later he became an ordained Methodist minister, and he and Alice, and their two-year-old son Christopher, took up one of the mission's more challenging posts in the twin mining villages of Ashington and Hirst, in Northumberland.

The post was a hard slog. The miners were glad of the practical support of the mission – the Sunday School for the children and the access to spiritual services for baptisms, weddings and funerals – but the expectation that they were to give up their one free day a week, where they didn't have to go underground and could spend time in the fresh air and sun, was too much to ask for some. Beyond that, the mine itself provided leisure activities for its workers and their families – including galas, fairs, brass bands and an array of educational courses held through the Miners' Institute. Ashington was considered a model mining community by industry standards, and even boasted a state-of-the-art sports ground. Over the years Ashington had produced some fine sportsmen, including cricketers, rugby players and footballers, some of whom were to eventually play for regional and national teams. Add to all that the lure of dog racing and fighting, as well as the all-consuming passion of pigeon rearing and racing, and the Methodist Mission – and indeed all of the other church groups trying to save souls in the town – were hard pressed to offer anything other than spiritual succour; and for many they found that at the Kicking Cuddy, anyway. Eventually, though, Malcolm and Alice's hard work bore fruit, and a small, but thriving congregation took root, justifying the building of a fine stone chapel.

They spent five years there, including their time overseeing the building project, and despite the many challenges, they were some of the happiest of their lives. It was there that young Christopher grew from a toddler to a child. And it was there that beautiful Poppy was born. But Malcolm knew it was also a hard time for his wife, Alice. He spent most of his time preparing sermons and officiating at services, but it was Alice who took the brunt of the day-to-day troubles of the miners and their families.

Only this morning, after reading Walter Foster's article in the

Morpeth Herald about the murder of Agnes Robson, had he been reminded of the time when Alice had tried to help the unfortunate woman when she was a young girl, and all the rigmarole around it. It was that, he recalled, that had eventually prompted them to apply for the position at the more well-to-do Morpeth Methodist. Alice could no longer take the hatred and vitriol thrown at the Robson family and their supporters after the death of the art teacher and the revelation that the young girl had been having conjugal relations with him, while the children of the miners innocently painted in the next room. To this day, Malcolm still shook his head at how the townsfolk saw the Robson girl as a willingly fallen woman, not a victim of a seducer who took advantage of his position of power.

But now she was dead. He had been shocked to read that his very own Poppy had witnessed the death, and that his sister's friend Grace had been arrested. He had hidden the newspaper from Alice over breakfast. He knew how she felt about their daughter's wild escapades as a reporter and sleuth in London, which despite Poppy's best efforts to play them down, sometimes still made it into the regional press up north. He too was worried about her, but unlike his wife, had grown proud of their only daughter, and begrudgingly come to respect her choice of career. Alice, he knew, did not think she should even *have* a career; she thought that paid work was not something a Christian woman should aspire to – unless it was as the wife of a clergyman (with a two-for-the-price-of-one stipend) or, at a push, a teacher or a nurse. However, even those jobs should be given up to serve husband and family when the time came. And the pursuit of a husband and family – after pursuit of a relationship with God – should be their daughter's primary goal.

Malcolm, as a good Christian man himself, paid lip service to these views. Yet, secretly, he admired women who made a go of things. His Aunt Mabel had been a marvellous traveller and adventurer. His own sister, Dot, had moved to London back in the early 1900s and made a name for herself as one of the leading actresses of her day. And then, of course, she had become one of the famous Chelsea Six suffragettes and helped pave the way for women to get the vote. As a political socialist, Malcolm quietly welcomed the extension of suffrage, but his wife, he knew, did not. And despite now qualifying herself to vote, he knew she had not yet acted upon it.

Malcolm sighed inwardly. He had hoped that today, on the celebration of his sixtieth birthday, the Denbys would be able to have a rigmarole-free family get-together, with some friends and congregants from the church. But with the death of Agnes, and the supposed involvement of Grace Wilson (what in heaven's name was going on there?), it would be far from it. Nonetheless, as the door of the train carriage opened and he saw his sister and daughter waiting to disembark, his heart leapt with happiness. He loved these two women, no matter what shenanigans they got up to.

He waved at them: "Dot! Poppy! Over here!"

A quarter of an hour later – with the help of station porters – Dot was disembarked from the train and into an awaiting taxi, her wheelchair strapped to the back. Malcolm got in the back with Poppy while Dot took the front seat. He directed the driver to take them to St Mary's churchyard. "Your mother is there."

Poppy nodded. Her brother, Christopher, had died two days before her father's birthday. It was the ninth anniversary of his death today.

"Actually, Daddy, could you drop me at the graveyard? I wouldn't mind going to visit Christopher too. I shall see if Mother wants to walk back with me. Or we can catch a bus. Is that all right?"

Her father, his shoulder pressed against hers in the snug confines of the taxi, squeezed her hand. "Actually, I think that's a good idea, pet. Your mother will be pleased to spend some time alone with you before everyone starts arriving for the buffet lunch. Your aunt and I can catch up, too."

"Splendid idea!" said Dot, turning around and beaming at her brother.

Poppy smiled to herself. Dot was never good at hiding her true feelings. What she really meant was: *What a relief that I don't have to spend as much time with my sister-in-law as I first feared.*

The taxi driver pulled up outside the cemetery and let Poppy out.

"We'll see you in about an hour," said her father, and waved to her as they pulled off.

Poppy climbed the stone steps and skirted around the six-hundred-year-old church of St Mary the Virgin. She picked her way through fallen grave markers – some nearly as old as the church itself – and made her way towards her brother's grave in the more modern part of the cemetery. Under a spreading yew, burgeoning with red berries, she came across the family burial plot of the Davison family. She stopped for a few moments to pay her respects. Buried along with other family members was Emily Wilding Davison, the suffragette who died protesting in favour of women's suffrage at the Derby back in 1913.

It was two years before her brother died and a year before the Great War started. She had been fourteen and her brother seventeen. They had joined a crowd of thousands lining the streets to honour the return of Emily's body. Aunt Dot, Grace and the four other members of the Chelsea Six had come north to attend the memorial. Soon afterwards, two of their members would be imprisoned for arson, when they returned to London. But for now, they were all together and she, Christopher and both her parents had come to pay their respects. Poppy's mother – although not a supporter of women's suffrage – came out of respect for a fellow Christian woman and Methodist.

Poppy wished she had some flowers to place on the grave, but all she had were her warm thoughts and prayers. She thanked God for Emily's life and for the brave women – like her aunt and friends – who were inspired by her. She prayed too for Emily's family, who, eleven years later, would still be feeling the loss of their loved one. And then she turned left towards where her own loved one lay.

Hunched over the neat plot, edged with stones and decorated with a single vase of orange chrysanthemums, was her mother. Alice's brown hair, painted now with streaks of grey, was pulled back into a tight bun. Her hat lay beside her handbag on the grassy bank. As Poppy approached a gust of wind picked up the brown felt with a swirl of dry leaves. Poppy skipped forward and caught it as Alice turned towards the commotion. She smiled gently as she saw her daughter, but her brown eyes were still pooled with sadness.

"Hello pet," she said.

"Hello Mam," said Poppy, and sat down on the grass beside her mother's handbag.

"Is the taxi here?"

"Aye, it is. But I've sent Daddy and Dot home in it. I thought you and I could walk or catch the bus." She paused and looked at the gravestone. "After we've spent some time with Christopher."

Christopher's body had only been returned to them three years ago. They thought it had been buried in a mass grave in Flanders, but in 1921 a farmer had come across a skeleton when clearing some land. It was of a young British soldier. His tags identified him as Private Christopher Edward Denby. A post-mortem showed he had died of a single gunshot wound to the heart.

However, this grave plot had been here since his death in 1915, and his mother, Alice, had tended it in anticipation of his eventual return. Now here he was, resting forever.

The wind was picking up even further and now large drops of rain fell on the two women. Alice looked up at the sky and said: "God is weeping with us."

Poppy, who in the past had often wondered why, if God did weep with us, he didn't do anything to stop the cause of the weeping in the first place, just nodded her agreement. She and God currently had a temporary truce. It was not that she no longer questioned him, but she no longer worried as much that her questioning meant she had lost her faith.

She put up her umbrella and stepped forward to cover her mother.

"Thanks pet. I suppose we should be getting back then. Lots to do before folk start coming for your father's party."

"Is there anything I can do?"

"Aye, there might be – putting out and clearing up. The church ladies are helping, so that's something."

"Aye," said Poppy, noting that, as she usually did with her mother, she had slipped into her old Northumbrian dialect. "Well we'd better get going then." She checked her watch. "There should be a bus coming in about fifteen minutes, if they still come past this way."

"Aye, they do."

Alice stood up, dusted down her skirt and put on her hat. She didn't have an umbrella so stayed close to Poppy. To her daughter's surprise, she linked arms – a physical intimacy quite out of character. Poppy's mother had never been demonstrably affectionate, yet Poppy did not doubt that she loved her. It was just . . . what was the word? . . . *difficult* to receive that love at times. Alice's love seemed to come with conditions. She had very set ideas about how a Christian – and particularly a Christian woman – should behave. Poppy, unfortunately, rarely lived up to those standards, at least not since she'd moved to London. In Alice's eyes, Poppy's fashion choices were frivolous, her make-up inappropriate, her consumption of alcohol dangerous and her career choice quite unsuitable. On previous visits home Poppy had pointed out that Alice herself worked, as she served the church, ran a charity shop and organised soup kitchens.

"But that's God's work," her mother had said. For a few years Poppy had thought she was right – and felt guilty for her life choices – but she had recently come to realise that her job as a reporter, seeking the truth and keeping the public entertained and informed, was just as much "God's work" as her mother's. Did her mother not read newspapers? Of course she did. Then why should someone who chose to produce them be considered lower in God's pecking order of acceptable work? And as for her side-line in detection, well, just ask the families of the victims whether or not Poppy's work had any value.

However, this was not a discussion Poppy wanted to get into today and she hoped her mother didn't either. The two women walked arm in arm under the umbrella to the bus stop.

"Is it only Dot who is with you?" asked Alice.

"It is. Grace is . . . busy."

Alice sniffed. "I read the paper this morning, Poppy, even though your father tried to hide it from me. I know what happened."

"Oh. I see." Poppy braced herself for another one of her mother's pet complaints: how that Wilson woman has brought shame to Dot. And why, oh why, does Dot put up with it?

But that's not what Alice said. Instead, in a voice heavy with unshed tears, she said: "Poor, poor Agnes. She didn't deserve to die like that.

I pray that the good Lord will have mercy on her. I don't know if she repented of her wild life – I've heard the stories of what happened in Paris – but she didn't have the best start, you know. And she was a lovely lass. She really was."

Poppy pushed open the gate at the bottom of the steps and the two women exited the graveyard onto Castle Bank and walked down the hill towards the bus stop.

"Yes, she told me all about it."

"Really? Oh, I'm glad she got it all off her chest. What did she tell you?"

Surprised and heartened by her mother's sympathetic tone, Poppy went on to tell her mother everything that Agnes had told her, and what had happened in Newcastle over the last few days. Well, nearly everything; she decided to leave out the frisson of romance between her and DI Sandy Hawkes. Poppy's lack of suitable marriage prospects was another topic she always tried to avoid with her mother.

Alice listened quietly, and as they took their place at the bus stop, she said: "So you're doing some detective work then."

Poppy tensed. *Oh dear, here we go . . .* "Well, sort of, but not properly. It's just until Yazzie gets here – I mean Mrs Rolandson, the barrister."

"Your editor's new wife?"

"Yes, that's her. She is a top-notch lawyer."

"And she's still working now that she has a family?"

Poppy's fist tightened around the umbrella handle. "She is. She and Rollo are quite well off, you know, and can afford domestic help."

"How nice for them."

"Yes it is," said Poppy, more snappily than she intended.

They were both silent for a while, looking up the road, hoping the bus would come soon. Eventually Alice spoke. Her voice was quiet and uncertain, something Poppy had rarely heard. "Don't stop investigating, Poppy," she said. "You need to find out who did this to Agnes. Her family deserve to know."

Well, you could have knocked Poppy down with a feather. Was

her mother actually *encouraging* her in what she once described as her "scurrilous hobby"?

"I'll do my best," said Poppy. "Between me, Yasmin and the Newcastle police – despite them thinking for now that Grace did it – I'm sure we'll get to the bottom of it."

"I pray that you will. Her poor mother must be beside herself. I shall see if I can visit her."

"I'm sure she'll appreciate that. Do you think I could come with you? Me and Yazzie? I'm sure she'll want to talk to the family and it would help if the introduction could be made by someone Mrs Robson knows and trusts."

The bus summited the hill. Alice opened her handbag and took out her purse. "All right. I'll see what I can arrange. Will Monday be too late for you?"

"Monday should be fine. Aunt Dot has a telephone in the house now. I'll give you the number when we get home. Can you ring when you know what's happening?"

Alice said she would. And then, as the bus pulled up, she said, to Poppy's utter astonishment: "I wonder if this has something to do with Agnes' baby."

"What baby?" Poppy whispered as the two women stepped on to the bus and paid their fare.

Alice gave her daughter a knowing look, then led the way to a seat halfway down the aisle. She nodded to other passengers and waved to a woman further back. Then she sat and lowered her head towards her daughter. "The baby I swore never to talk about," she said in hushed tones. "But if it might help to find Agnes' killer, I think you need to know."

It was half past three when the last of the platters, teacups and saucers were returned to the kitchen of the church hall. Half a dozen ladies – all of whom Poppy had known since she was a baby – got their fill of news about Poppy's life in London, and passed on their own about which of Poppy's peers had just got married or had a baby. Somehow word of Poppy's photographer beau had made it up to Morpeth and the ladies commiserated with her that he had abandoned her for a life in the colonies. Mrs Green – the convener of the prayer group – gently patted her on the arm and declared that perhaps it was for the best, as she had heard the young man was not a believer in the good Lord. "Thou should not be unevenly yoked, Poppy," she said.

Poppy was saved from having to choose between swallowing her tongue or giving Mrs Green a piece of her mind by the Reverend Denby appearing in the doorway. "Do you ladies mind if I steal my daughter for a few minutes?"

Relieved, Poppy slipped into the curve of her father's protective arm and left the ladies to a discussion of the relative merits of cleanliness and godliness.

"Thanks Daddy," she said, resting her head on his shoulder for a moment.

Malcolm kissed her on the forehead. "Thank you for coming all this way to see me."

"Oh Daddy, of course I'd come to see you! I'm so sorry that it's all been marred by the awfulness with Agnes. You know I was planning on staying with you and Mother until Monday. But I'm sorry; I think I need to go back to Newcastle."

Malcolm looked at his daughter with pride. "I know you do. Your mother has told me. And she's right. You need to go. Just promise me you'll come up for a longer visit soon."

"I promise Daddy, I will. How about Christmas?"

"That will be lovely, my flower."

Her mother came up to them. "Thank you for your help, pet. I've rung for the taxi and it will be here shortly. Dot's already outside, talking to Walter Foster."

Oh dear, thought Poppy. *What information is Dot passing on to him? It's definitely not about Agnes' baby* . . . Poppy was sure after what she'd heard on the bus that her mother had not told anyone else, other than her husband, about that. However, Poppy could not wait to tell Yasmin about it when she got home as she, like her mother, believed it might very well have something to do with Agnes' death.

Poppy hurried outside to find Walter and Dot chuckling away about something. Whatever it was, it surely wasn't the serious business of Agnes' death.

"Oh Poppy! Walter and I were just remembering a show I did at the Theatre Royal. When was it, Walter – back in 1908?"

Walter chortled. "It must have been. I was covering the arts and entertainment beat, Poppy, just like you. In those days we had a budget that allowed me to travel down to Newcastle to do reviews of London shows on tour. Your aunt was up doing an Ibsen. The leading man – Ralph Rudolph – was a notorious soak. He kept fluffing his lines, but your aunt covered for him marvellously!"

"Oh yes! Do you remember the time –"

"Sorry, Aunt Dot, do you mind if I interrupt for a moment? I need to speak to Mr Foster."

Walter took Dot's hand and kissed it. Dot giggled. Alice Denby shook her head in mild disapproval. Malcom Denby smiled benignly.

"Of course, Poppy," said Walter, standing up from the garden bench to join Poppy.

"A fine article in the paper this morning, Mr Foster. My father showed it to me. I was just wondering, though, about the last paragraph you wrote. The one about the tragedy 'stirring up memories of the unsolved death of Michael Brownley twenty-seven years ago'. What did you mean by that and what was your source?"

Walter tensed as Poppy knew he would. She wouldn't like it if her professional practice was questioned either. "I meant, Poppy, that there were parallels between the two deaths. Both, of course, involved Agnes, but both also involved someone being pushed to their deaths from a height."

"But as far as I know Brownley wasn't pushed to his death. Wasn't it declared an accident? Or do you have further information on that?"

The older journalist cleared his throat. "Nothing official, no. But it was widely speculated upon at the time. It was before you were even born, young lady. But I was working on the paper. *I* remember. *I* am the source."

Before Poppy could offer her observation that she was of the opinion that it was not a journalist's job to speculate and fan the flames of gossip, the taxi arrived and she and Dot were bustled into the vehicle and waved off by her parents and a glowering Walter Foster.

"What did Walter have to say, darling?"

"I'll tell you about it on the train home," said Poppy, quietly fuming.

Chapter 15

It was five o'clock when Aunt Dot and Poppy arrived back at Jesmond Vale Terrace. The taxi from Heaton Station pulled up behind the yellow Rolls.

"Nice motor," said the driver.

"Thank you!" said Dot. "It's mine, but my driver is – well, she's a little poorly at the moment."

"A lady driver?"

"Of course!"

Poppy had no doubt that the exorbitant fare charged was a direct result of that comment. Dot, as usual when it came to money, didn't blink an eyelid; while Poppy had to literally scrape the bottom of her bag to find sufficient money to cover it.

The driver did at least help Poppy get Aunt Dot out of the taxi, into her chair and onto the front veranda, before leaving with a covetous backwards glance at the luxury car.

Poppy fumbled for her key but didn't have to use it as the door was flung open. They were greeted by a harangued-looking Delilah. "Poppy! Dot! Thank heavens you're here. I have to get to the theatre. Dot, do you mind if I take the Rolls again?"

"Not at all, darling!"

Delilah bent down and gave her a kiss, then grabbed her hat, coat and a vivacious silk scarf, just as an unearthly wail emerged from the front parlour.

"Good Lord," said Dot. "Is that who I think it is?"

"Yes," said Delilah as she skipped out the door, like a deer escaping a hunt. "Yazzie brought Rollo and the twins!"

* * *

Rollo Rolandson, the owner and senior editor of *The Daily Globe*, was a New York dwarf who had won the London tabloid in a poker game back in 1916, when he was over in Europe as a war correspondent for the *New York Times*. In 1920 he had given Poppy her first paying job, first as an editorial assistant, and then, after she'd helped finish a story by the paper's recently deceased senior reporter, he'd promoted her to journalist. She officially filled the post of arts and entertainment editor, but he felt just as confident to assign her to tough crime stories.

His wife, Yasmin Reece-Lansdale, was the daughter of a British major and an Egyptian socialite. She was born and raised in England, went to the best schools and then on to Oxford where she was one of the first women to take a degree in law. More recently, she had taken the bar exams, and was one of only two female King's Counsels working at the Old Bailey. Prior to that she had worked as a solicitor in the City of London, representing mainly foreign clients in property and arts acquisitions, while on the side doing pro bono work for the Women's Suffrage and Political Union. It was there that she had first met Dot Denby, Grace Wilson, Delilah's mother Gloria and the rest of the Chelsea Six. She had also been friends with Agnes Robson whose work she had bought on behalf of some of her clients. She and Rollo had been friends and unashamed lovers for years and everyone had thought that's what they would remain: the free-spirited bachelor and the ardent feminist, pointedly Bohemian in their personal relations, shrewdly capitalist in their business pursuits. But then, two years ago, they had stunned their family and friends by announcing that they were finally going to get married. Then, six months after that, they confounded the whole of London society by declaring that Yasmin was pregnant – at forty-five.

Roland Junior (known as RJ) and Cleopatra (known as Cleo) were now fourteen months old. They were currently clambering onto Aunt Dot's knee. "Sorry Dot, they're a pair of monkeys," said Rollo as he retrieved his son, a mini version of himself with a shock of red hair. The lad immediately started crying, reaching out his podgy little hand to his darker-haired sister, who was claiming the prize of playing with Aunt Dot's beads.

"That's all right, Rollo, they're a joy!"

"Tell me that after twenty-four hours," said Rollo, with a lopsided grin.

Rollo looked tired, Poppy thought. It was a long trip up on the train with two energetic toddlers, both on the verge of walking. Their nanny – a warm, motherly woman called Ivy – accompanied them, but she was now in the kitchen helping young Betty clean up the dinner dishes. With Grace in gaol, Dot had asked Betty to sleep over for a few days to help her with personal things. Poppy had said that she would be more than willing to help, but Dot had said no. "You need to devote all your attention to finding who killed Agnes, darling. I've asked Betty to get another girl to help with the char work; she should be arriving tomorrow. And I'll pay Betty more for the extra responsibilities. She's a good girl. And it might help her get a permanent position as a ladies' maid after we've gone back down to London."

"Right," said Yasmin, standing up and brushing some of her children's discarded food from a pair of stylish culottes. "It's time to get to work. Poppy, I think we should stay here in the dining room – we'll need the table. Rollo, can you and Dot take the children into the parlour until Ivy is ready to give them their bath?"

"Aye aye captain!" Rollo looked up at his wife and gave her a mock salute, accompanied by a grin. "I'll come back in when the monsters are gone. I might be able to help. There's more to me than just being a house husband, you know." It was said jovially, but Poppy knew Rollo meant it. He was a man who was happy for his wife to work – and actively encouraged it – but he was not prepared to have the traditional roles inverted. Poppy looked at the couple – she the tall, dusky Anglo-Egyptian lawyer, he the short, red-headed American editor – and wondered what dynamic might exist if they could not afford domestic help. Would Yazzie be prepared to stop work to look after the children while Rollo carried on with business as usual? She doubted it. But she could be wrong.

Yasmin gave each of her offspring a kiss and a cuddle, warning them to be good for Daddy and Auntie Dotty, before depositing both on Dot's knee. "All aboard!" cried Dot, while Rollo made choo-choo noises, as he pushed Dot's chair out of the dining room, to the accompaniment of squeals of delight from the children.

Yasmin shut the door behind them with an audible sigh, then opened her briefcase and took out a document folder, a sheaf of notepaper and a pen. The two women settled down at the table.

"First up," said Yasmin, "as I mentioned to Dot yesterday in the telegram, I have managed to secure the services of a local solicitor. He went to see Grace yesterday and has set the ball in motion to have her released on police bail. Unfortunately, by the time he had met with her and filled in the requisite paperwork it was after four o'clock on Friday. The local magistrate does not sit over the weekend so I'm afraid the earliest we can get a hearing is nine o'clock on Monday. However, the solicitor has agreed to meet with me tomorrow morning – apparently he is not a churchgoing man, and I offered to pay double his usual fee – and I hope that he can arrange to get me in to see Grace then. If not," Yasmin gave a wan smile, "I don't think we should worry too much. Grace, unfortunately, has experience with the justice system so will be able to handle a couple of days in the slammer."

Poppy bit her lip, remembering how resigned Grace looked when she left her on Friday morning. "I hope you're right. Do you think she'll remain in the police holding cells for the weekend, or will they have taken her somewhere else?"

"The local solicitor – Wylie's his name – said they'd be keeping her there. Was the place all right?"

Poppy, who had also seen a few holding cells in her time – but not as a prisoner – said that it was.

"Good. So, what do we know? Wylie has only been given access to the bare minimum so far. They have a witness who saw Grace in the stables soon before Agnes' death, when she said she was in the gallery. Being caught out in a blatant lie hasn't helped her cause. He also tells me they have found a weapon and the medical examiner has confirmed that it was the one used to slash Agnes' throat. However, and this is interesting, apparently the laceration to the throat did not go deep enough to kill her. In other words, if she hadn't fallen – or been pushed – off the tower, she might very well have survived."

Poppy's mind was once again assailed with the horrific image of Agnes falling to her death. "If only I hadn't tripped I might have got to the tower and saved her . . ."

Yasmin gave Poppy a sympathetic smile. "Don't do this to yourself, Poppy. From what Wylie tells me about the distance between the door to the roof and the tower, I doubt you would have made it there in time. I will, of course, have to see it for myself, and Wylie tells me he hasn't personally been up there, but judging from what he could see from street level, he says it would have been impossible. So stop beating yourself with that rod. You are not doing Agnes any favours by dwelling on a false sense of guilt."

Poppy nodded, grateful for Yasmin's attempts to soothe her conscience. But she still felt bad. Nonetheless, she knew Yasmin was right and she wasn't helping Agnes or Grace by allowing herself to be crippled by it.

"Did Wylie say how they have linked the knife to Grace?"

Yasmin nodded and flipped a page in the folder and read through some notes. "Yes. Apparently it was a Stanley knife – those ones with a triangular blade used by decorators to cut wallpaper. That's why the wound was so shallow. A longer blade would have done more damage. It's unclear – as yet – whether the killer realised that or not. If so, then there may be a question of whether or not there was genuine intent to kill. Which might prove useful if – God forbid – they ever get Grace to trial."

"But she didn't do it!"

Yasmin frowned. "Getting emotional about this is not helping, Poppy. Legally, I will do all I can to get the charges against Grace dropped before it ever goes to trial, but if I don't succeed, well, then I need to be prepared to try to at least have the charge reduced from murder to manslaughter. I would be remiss in my duties if I did not start preparing for various possible outcomes, even at this early stage."

Poppy knew Yasmin was right. "I'm sorry."

Yasmin nodded. "Right, so as I was saying, Wylie said it was a Stanley knife. The police, apparently, interviewed Grace and Dot's decorator . . ."

Poppy remembered the man with the roll of wallpaper who had been here when she arrived last Monday.

". . . who said that he had accidentally left his Stanley knife here on Wednesday, the day before the murder. He said he'd left it on the hall table."

"Why did the police interview him? Surely that's a big leap to make."

"His name was engraved on the knife's handle."

"Ah. Then why haven't they arrested him for the murder?"

"Because his story was plausible – he'd left the knife here. Plus he was not, to anyone's knowledge, at the exhibition. Grace was. The police's case so far is that Grace found the knife and brought it with her to the exhibition. On Friday morning when DI . . . whatsisname," she looked at her notes, "DI Hawkes came to interview Grace and Dot at the house, I believe you weren't here, is that correct?"

"It is. Unfortunately. I was taking a walk in the park."

"Well, apparently Hawkes asked Grace if she had found a Stanley knife. She said she had seen it on the hall table and assumed it was the decorator's. Hawkes asked her to get it. When she couldn't find it, he arrested her."

"Good heavens! Surely it's a set-up!"

Yasmin nodded. "Yes, that's the theory I'm working on too. But I need to prove it. I will have to interview the decorator, of course."

"And the witness who saw Grace in the stables," added Poppy. "She admitted that she was there but said she hadn't seen anyone. The caretaker – I think he'd be worth interviewing – told me it was the stable boy who had seen Grace. The stable boy then told the curator – I'll tell you about him in a minute – and the curator told the police. The caretaker was actually very helpful. He told me that there was a key missing to the back door."

"Oh really? That is interesting," Yasmin made a note. "Did he say who had access to the key?"

"He did. He said officially it was him and Mr Sherman. But he also said that it was kept on a hook in his downstairs storeroom. I accompanied him when he put a mop and bucket back, and he didn't unlock or lock it. I don't know if that would be different after hours, but it wasn't locked while he was there. So anyone could have got their hands on it if they knew where to look."

Yasmin pursed her lips as she wrote. "All true. But still, that does narrow it down to people who knew where the key was kept. Which means someone with inside knowledge – or at least access to inside knowledge – of the workings of the Laing."

"Yes, I suppose it does."

"Did you manage to get a list of who was at the exhibition? Staff and guests?"

Poppy frowned. "Unfortunately not. Dante Sherman – the curator – refused to give it to me."

"Oh really?" asked Yasmin, raising a perfectly manicured eyebrow above her striking Egyptian nose. "Let's see how long he refuses after I get a court order."

Poppy grinned. "That's what I told him. But here," she tore a couple of pages out of her notebook and passed it over the table, "these are the names of the people I've remembered who were there. I've made a note against each one of what I can remember – or what I've found out – about their whereabouts at the time of Agnes' death. I'm sorry it's not more exhaustive." Yasmin perused the notes then nodded her thanks. "It's a good start, Poppy. It will get me going until I've managed to secure the full list from the police or the prosecution." She ran her finger down the list until she came to the name of Dante Sherman. "You said you had something to tell me about the curator. This Sherman fellow?"

Poppy nodded eagerly. "Oh yes. I'm sure he's hiding something, Yasmin, I really am."

"Oh?"

"Definitely." Poppy went on to tell Yasmin exactly what had happened in the curator's office, how defensive and antagonistic he had been, as well as what she had spotted about the Tate gallery and the letter about the authentication of *The Railway Family* painting. It was at this point that Rollo entered the room and joined the women at the table. He listened to Poppy's explanation with interest.

"So, you say those two paintings came late? That they were not in the exhibition catalogue?" asked Rollo.

"That's right."

"Do you have any photographs of the paintings?"

"I don't, but I think the reporter from the *Newcastle Daily Journal* might. Why?"

Rollo took a sheet of paper from the pile in front of his wife and started writing. "Because I can send them to Ike Garfield in London and ask him to drop by the Tate to find out what they know about them. I'll get him to do it anyway, with or without the photographs. I think you're right in focusing on them as something out of the ordinary. Don't you agree, darling?"

Yasmin said she did and that getting *The Daily Globe*'s senior reporter on it was an excellent idea. "You say there were two paintings?"

"Yes. *The Railway Family* was one and another called *Lilies in a Vase*. The lilies one was still a little tacky. I wondered why they had been brought up separately. Apparently they came up with Gerald Farmer and Gus North." She went on to tell Yasmin and Rollo about what Gus and Gerald had said about the paintings. Yasmin was making furious notes. "Interesting. Very interesting. So they said Sherman had insisted they bring them up with them? That he had wanted them here and they felt unable to say no?"

"That's right. They said he was an influential man and that they didn't want to get on the wrong side of him. They said he could make things difficult for them with other galleries."

"How strange," said Yasmin. "I thought Sherman was a young fellow. And that this was his first big exhibition. Why do they think he has such power?"

Poppy shrugged. "I don't know. I thought it odd too. He certainly has an imposing personality, but I would have thought that Gerald had dealt with far more influential people than him in his time. He is, after all, just a curator of a regional gallery. Sure, the Laing is the biggest gallery in the area, but it's not exactly the Louvre or the New

York Met, is it? Agnes has been exhibited worldwide; why would they be worried about him bad-mouthing them to a few northern galleries?"

Rollo was folding a discarded linen napkin into a swan as if the children were still needing to be entertained. "Perhaps," he said, without taking his eyes off his creation, "Sherman is blackmailing them. Or has some other hold on them – something personal. Nothing to do with the art business after all."

Yasmin tapped her lip with her pen. "Yes, that is a possibility. But it does seem most likely that it has something to do with art. The letter Poppy saw from the Tate, for instance . . ."

"As I said, I'll get Ike on to that. But," he tapped his nose with the side of his finger, "my newshound nose is twitching. How about you, Poppy?"

Poppy gave a playful twitch of her own nose, which brought a smile to Rollo's face. "Well, actually, there are a couple of other things I haven't told you about yet. Which might back up your theory, Rollo – at least partially."

She pulled a photograph out from the back of her notebook. It was the one she had found in Agnes' room of the painting of the naked girl. She explained where she had found it and that both Gus and Gerald said they had never seen it before. She also told them that Gus had left the room very upset afterwards.

"Gerald said it was just that he was upset by Agnes' death. But I think it was more. I think we should try to speak to Gus about it again."

Yasmin nodded. "Yes, about that and the other two paintings. Also, Rollo, would you be able to ask Ike if he can do a search of Agnes' studio and flat in London? I will arrange to get a court order to allow entry."

"Good idea," he said. "Actually, let me do it now. Where's the telephone, Poppy?"

"It's in the hall. But before you go, there's something else I need to show you. Look here." She flipped over the photograph and pointed to the handwritten note: Stay away. "That's what seemed to upset Gus. And now, look at this." Also from the back of the notebook she removed an envelope, addressed to *Mrs Malcolm*

Denby, The Manse, Morpeth Methodist Church. There was no return address, but it was postmarked Leeds, three weeks earlier. She opened the envelope and extracted a single sheet of paper. She read it out loud:

Dear Mrs Denby,

It has come to my knowledge that you knew the artist Agnes Robson when she was a girl in Ashington and that you helped her get rid of a baby. I believe you have kept this secret for twenty-seven years. May I suggest you keep it for twenty-seven more? As you know abortion is illegal, not to mention a mortal sin in the eyes of God. This is just a friendly warning for you to keep your mouth shut lest your husband's employer hears about it and he loses his job.

Most sincerely,

A concerned Christian.

For the first time in the four years Poppy had known him, Rollo Rolandson was dumbstruck.

"As you can see," said Poppy, laying the threatening note and the back of the photograph side by side, "it's the same handwriting."

"I see that," said Yasmin, her intelligent eyes taking it all in. "When did you get this letter?"

"Just this afternoon. My mother gave it to me at my father's birthday party. Incredibly, she actually wants me to do some sleuthing."

"What did she say about the letter?"

Poppy pursed her lips. "She said it arrived in the post last week. She was shocked to read it, but didn't show it to anyone at the time, because she said she had sworn to Agnes and her mother never to talk about what actually happened."

"Which was?"

"She wouldn't say."

"Good God, what game is your mother playing?"

Poppy bristled. "She is *not* playing a game. She gave me this letter because of what happened to Agnes. She said it suggested that something from her past might have contributed to her death. And I think she's right."

"But she won't tell you what *did* happen?"

"She said she needs to ask Mrs Robson's permission first. Surely that's fair enough."

Yasmin didn't look convinced but nodded brusquely. "All right. When will she do that?"

"Monday. She's going to try to arrange for you and me to meet with Mrs Robson. She will telephone us when she has something set up."

"All right, fair enough."

"Can I get you ladies something to drink?" asked Rollo.

Yasmin asked for a whisky – if there was any – and Poppy, wanting to keep a clear head, asked Rollo to ask Betty to make some tea. The editor quickly withdrew to get the drinks.

Yasmin picked up the photograph again and read the writing on the back. "You say this was in Agnes' things?"

"Yes, I found it in a skirt pocket."

"Was there anything else? A letter? An envelope?"

Poppy shook her head. "No. Nothing. But the police had searched the room earlier that day and taken things away. They might have found something else but missed this."

Yasmin made a note. "I'll check. When do you think your mother will call about the meeting? What time on Monday?"

Poppy shrugged. "I doubt it will be before lunch. Mrs Robson is not likely to have a telephone so Mother will have to go to Ashington herself to speak to her. Then she will have to telephone us from the post office. She knows it's important for us to speak to her, but she will still want to be respectful of Mrs Robson's grief. Hopefully though we can get up there on Monday afternoon."

"All right, that's fine. I'll be at the arraignment hearing in the morning anyway. And while I'm doing that, do you think you might be able to question Gus again about the photograph?"

"I'll try," said Poppy. "I also might try to see if I can get someone else to identify it."

"Oh, who's that?"

"There's an art professor I met the other day. He opened the community hall in Ashington with poor Agnes. He seemed to be an expert on her work..."

Before Poppy could finish her explanation about Professor Reid, the telephone rang. She heard Aunt Dot call out: "Poppy! Can you get that?"

Poppy jumped up. "Excuse me a minute, Yazzie." She went into the hall and picked up the receiver, just as Rollo exited the parlour carrying two tumblers of whisky.

"Good evening, the Denby residence."

"Poppy? Is that you?"

"It is. Who's this?"

"It's Peter MacMahon from the *Newcastle Daily Journal*. I'm sorry I haven't been able to come around as promised – something has come up at work – but I thought I'd give you a ring to tell you that I've found out where the stable boy from the gallery lives. Would you like to come and see him with me tomorrow morning?"

"Oh, yes please, Peter! Thank you. Where will I meet you?"

"Don't worry, I'll pick you up. Is nine o'clock too early?"

"No, that's perfect. Oh, and Peter," Poppy watched Rollo push open the dining room door with his foot, "would you mind if I brought someone with me?"

"Who's that?"

"My editor, Rollo Rolandson. He's just arrived in Newcastle."

"*The* Rollo Rolandson? The Yankee Dwarf?"

Poppy turned her shoulder and hunched over the receiver, lowering her voice. "That's right. Mr Rolandson – the *American* gentleman."

"Why's he here? Is he trying to get a scoop?"

"No," said Poppy, annoyed at MacMahon's apparent pettiness. "He's accompanying his wife who is Mrs Wilson's legal representative. He's here in a private capacity. Besides, even if he does write something about it, *The Daily Globe* is hardly your rival, is it Peter?"

MacMahon was quiet for a moment, then said: "No, I suppose it's not. All right. He can come along. See you at nine tomorrow."

Poppy rang off then turned around to see Rollo standing there.

He grinned. "Of course the Yankee Dwarf will be writing about it. Why else do you think I'm here, Poppy?"

Poppy felt herself flush, as if she were a small child caught doing something silly. "Er, to support your wife?"

"Well, yes, but in case you'd forgotten, Miz Denby, Agnes Robson is an internationally renowned artist. Her murder will be making headlines worldwide. You should've known that I'd be here for the story." He laughed and took a sip of his whisky. "No ma'am, hell and high water wouldn't have kept me in London once I'd heard about it."

"But I just told Peter –"

"I heard what you told him, but you were wrong." He grinned. "Despite rumours to the contrary, I have *not* become domesticated, Miz Denby. Your leave is cancelled. As of now we're both back on the job. So when you're finished with Yazzie, you and I need to start drafting some articles. And before you ask, yes, I have brought my typewriter with me. Oh, and I'll also need that phone."

Poppy sighed ruefully. *So, my holiday's officially over.*

Chapter 16

Sunday, 6 October 1924

Newcastle upon Tyne

The River Tyne was a thick, watery artery that wound its way from the life-giving forests of Kielder in Northumberland to the wide sandy beaches of Tynemouth on the North East coast. It had long been a strategic boundary, marking the edge of Roman Britain from the barbarians in the north, before the invaders pushed a few miles further on and built a wall. By 1924, Hadrian's Wall had long been abandoned as the boundary between Scotland and England, and the Tyne and its bridges were no longer militarily strategic. However, they were still the industrial lifeblood of the region, ferrying goods and resources to the ships that took them across the North Sea.

Peter MacMahon took on the role of tour guide to Poppy and her American editor as he drove them on a roundabout route from well-to-do Heaton to the shipyards of Wallsend, and then past the Newcastle Quayside, in the shadow of the "new" castle – built by the son of William the Conqueror. Here cheek-by-jowl warehouses, ferry ports and mills still looked like something out of a Dickens novel despite it being the third decade of the twentieth century. From there they passed under the railway bridge that had brought Poppy into Newcastle only six days earlier and then continued westwards, past the armaments factories and tanneries that spewed their effluent into the river. Driving along Scotswood Road, made famous by a song that every North East child learned in infant school, Peter pointed out the steep rows of Victorian tenements, built in the 1880s for the factory and dock workers, which had, within a generation, already become slums.

This, Poppy thought, was what most people imagined when they thought of Newcastle, not the genteel architecture of Grainger Town, or the leafy parks of Heaton and Jesmond. This, and of course, coal. But as long as the majority of the people in the city lived in places like this, she reminded herself, that reputation would be hard to shake.

"That's Elswick. It's where the stable boy lives. His mam and dad both work at Armstrongs, I'm told, building tanks."

"What makes you think he'll talk to us?" asked Poppy, as Peter turned up one of the impossibly steep cobbled roads, driving slowly so as to avoid children and dogs. "It's highly likely Sherman will have told him not to, don't you think?"

"He doesn't work for Sherman or the Laing. The stables are attached to the gallery, but not part of it. They were there before the Laing was built. It's owned by the Council and services the businesses and private houses in and around that part of Grainger Town. I know all about it because I recently did a story about the Council thinking of closing down the stables – horsepower's on the way out, as you know – and offering the property to the gallery for them to convert into storage facilities. Nothing's been agreed yet though, so the stable employees are not answerable to the gallery management."

That could be useful, thought Poppy. Then she added: "The lad – what did you say his name was again – Jimmy?"

"That's right. Jimmy Jackson."

"Well, Jimmy apparently reported what he'd seen to Sherman at the gallery. And handed the knife in to him."

"Yes he did," answered Peter. "But only, it seems, because his boss told him to. By the time the knife was found, everyone knew about the murder, so the lad was advised to take it straight to Sherman – who then, so my source in the police tells me, handed it to DI Hawkes. However, and this could work for your friend Grace, it seems that in the process any prints that were there might have been had been smudged."

"Well, it certainly weakens the prosecution's case," observed Rollo.

Peter pulled up outside a two-up two-down terraced house with a line of nappies strung across the yard. Outside on the road sat a grimy little girl of around eight pushing a battered and torn pram back and forth.

Peter got out of the car and approached her. "Is Jimmy in, petal?"

The girl stared at him with suspicious eyes but didn't say a word. He reached into his pocket and took out a coin. The girl snatched it and ran into the yard behind her, leaving the pram unattended. Poppy got out of the car too, and noticed, just in time, a rivulet of sewage leaking from under a drain cover. She gingerly stepped over it and approached the pram, resuming the rhythmic pushing to and fro. She looked under the hood and saw, to her relief, that the occupant was still asleep, its lips pulsing around a dummy.

A few moments later the girl returned with a teenage boy in tow. The lad eyed up Peter, Poppy, then Rollo, who had remained in Peter's car with the window rolled down, and said: "What canna do for ya mister?"

"Are you Jimmy Jackson?" Peter asked.

"I am. Who's askin'?"

"Peter MacMahon from the *Newcastle Daily Journal.* And this is Miss Poppy Denby from – well, she's just visiting Newcastle. We were both at the Laing the other night when that lady was killed."

"I've already telled the police all I know."

"I know you have. And you've done a grand job. But we were hoping you might tell us too."

Jimmy lowered his eyes to the rivulet of sewage inches from Poppy's suede Mary Jane shoes, then raised them again. "I might."

Peter reached into his pocket again and took out a crown, holding it between thumb and forefinger. He rolled the coin back and forth as he spoke. Jimmy watched it as if hypnotised.

"Good. So, can you tell us what time it was when you found the knife?"

"Must've been a bit after eight. I'd heard the church bells ringing a bit before that. I was ganning in to muck oot the bay mare that belongs to the fella who owns the jewellery shop doon the road. And me fork hit metal. I bent doon and foond the knife. I'd heard what'd happened the night afore so I went straight to the gaffer. He called Mr Sherman from the gallery and I gave it to him."

"Right," said Poppy. "Thank you Jimmy. And was that when you told him about the lady you saw the night before?"

"Aye it was, miss."

"And what did you tell him? What did you see?"

"Well, I was finished for the night and I'd locked up. The gaffer sometimes lets me do it. He's training me up to be an assistant manager, ya kna?"

Poppy nodded, looking suitably impressed. "So what happened then?"

"Well I realised I'd left me bait box behind. Me mam'll have had me guts for garters if I'd forgot it. So I went back. I was already roond the corner and heading along New Bridge when I remembered."

"And what time was that?"

"Just after nine at night."

Poppy was surprised. "You work twelve-hour shifts?"

Jimmy straightened up, obviously proud of his own work ethic. "Fourteen hours that day, miss. We'd had a lot on with the do at the gallery. Folk had been comin' and goin' all day. The gaffer asked me to stay on."

"All right, so you returned to the stable and you saw . . ."

"A lady comin' doon the stairs from the gallery."

"And what did the lady look like?"

"Tall, thin, short grey hair. Posh lookin'. She was wearing a blue frock."

Poppy looked at Peter and nodded. Yes, that described Grace. "Did you see where she went?"

"I didn't. Just that she was comin' doon the stairs. Me bait box was on a shelf near the door so I just got it and left."

"You didn't speak to the lady?"

"I had no need to, miss. She wasn't doing no wrong."

"Do a lot of people come down the stairs from the gallery? It must make it a bit difficult to work with them disturbing the horses all the time."

Jimmy shook his head. "Not a lot, miss. It's locked most of the time. But sometimes I'll see Mr Sherman and Mr Helsdon. He's the caretaker."

"So not many ladies?" asked Peter.

"No. She's the only one I've seen."

"Who else did you see that day?" asked Poppy. "You said people had been coming and going all day."

"Aye, they were. Because of the do they was havin'. But not so much up and doon the stairs, but in and oot the doors. But now that I think of it there was a bit of up and doon this week too, with all the paintings comin'."

"Do the paintings always come in through the stables?" asked Peter.

Jimmy nodded, his eyes turning once again to the rolling coin. "Aye, sir, they do. Cos their back door comes through our place. Daft setup, but there you gan."

Poppy smiled. "Aye, it does seem a little daft."

Jimmy grinned at Poppy's slip into dialect.

"So who else was coming and going?" prompted Peter.

"Mr Helsdon came and went a lot that day."

"And Mr Sherman?"

"I just saw him the once."

"When was that?"

"When those two dandy toffs arrived."

"Dandy toffs? Can you describe them?" asked Poppy.

"Aye, I noticed them cos they was different from the usual delivery blokes what bring the paintings. They're just workin' fellas loading and offloading. But these fellas were posh." He looked Peter up and down. "Posher lookin' than even you, mister."

Peter grinned and shrugged. "So what did they look like, Jimmy lad?"

"One was old and fat, lots of chins. Mebbe sixty years or so. The young'un was thin and good-lookin'. Mid-twenties. Mebbe thirty. Thick black hair. Gypsy eyes. He talked funny too. Like he was deaf or summit."

Poppy and Peter's eyes met: Gus and Gerald. This wasn't news to Poppy, however, as they had already told her that they had delivered the two paintings through the back door before the exhibition started. But it was still good to have it corroborated.

"So you saw Mr Sherman meet these two 'toffs'?"

"Aye, I did, miss."

"Did you hear anything that was said?"

Jimmy eyed the crown.

Poppy reached into her bag and took out a half-crown. "I'll add this to what Mr MacMahon has there, Jimmy. You've been a grand help so far."

She gave Jimmy the coin and he took it gratefully. "Much obliged, miss."

She smiled at him encouragingly. "You're welcome. Now, please carry on. What happened when the toffs met Mr Sherman?"

Jimmy looked over at the car and frowned. Rollo had climbed out and was picking his way gingerly towards them.

"What the hell is that?"

"That is Mr Rolandson, and I expect you to keep a civil tongue in your mouth, lad!" Peter snapped.

Jimmy mumbled an apology.

"Sorry," said Rollo, "I was struggling to hear. But now I can tell it's the accent not the distance. Geordie, is it?"

Jimmy looked down at Rollo, his mouth agape both at the size of the man and the way he spoke.

"Eeee, he's just like them little fellas in the gangsta films! Me gaffer takes me and the other lad to the pictures as a treat sometimes. Nice fella, me gaffer."

"Jimmy!" said Poppy chastisingly. "Can you concentrate please?"

"Aye miss, I'm sorry. As I was sayin', the young toff talked funny. Funnier than him. Like he was deaf and couldn't talk proper or summit."

"Yes, you said. But what did he actually say?" prompted Poppy.

"Well he was arguin' with Mr Sherman. Real angry he was."

"Angry? Tell me why. What did he say?"

"He was gannin' on aboot Mr Sherman breaking his word. He said summit about Mr Sherman promising him summit and not giving it. Then he said: 'They shouldna be hangin' in there.' But he said it posher – and funnier."

"What 'shouldna be hangin'?" asked Rollo.

"I divvint kna. He didna say. But I think it was the paintings they brought. There was two of them."

"Did you see what they looked like?"

"I didn't miss. They was wrapped up. But there was a bigun – aboot the height of the little fella there, and then a littlun, about yay big." He gestured with his hands a shape about a foot by a foot and a half. Poppy noted that the sizes matched the two paintings that Gus and Gerald had told her they had brought.

Rollo spoke again: "Did the deaf fella say why they shouldn't be hanging?"

Jimmy looked down at him and answered: "No. He didna say. But Mr Sherman said: 'They're going inside. I need her to see them. I need her to know I mean business.'"

"What did he mean, 'I need her to know I mean business'?" asked Peter.

Jimmy shrugged. "I divvint kna sir."

"What happened then?" asked Poppy.

"Well, the fat bloke tried to calm the young'un doon and said they should leave. He said they can talk aboot it back at the hotel."

"And what did the young fella say?"

"I divvint kna, cos he stopped talking with his mooth and started with his hands."

"And what did Sherman do?" asked Rollo.

Jimmy took in all three of them with a glance from shortest to tallest. "Aye, that was a funny thing. He laughed. A real nasty laugh he had too. Never heard him like that afore, I haven't. And then Mr Helsdon came and Mr Sherman told him to take the paintings in and hang 'em."

"And what did the two men do?"

Jimmy shrugged. "Nowt. They just left. But I could tell, the young'un was still seethin'."

"Thank you, Jimmy, that's very helpful. Did you see anything else after that? Did Mr Sherman say or do anything more?" asked Poppy.

"Nowt funny, no. He just followed Mr Helsdon back up the stairs."

"Did you see him lock the door behind him?"

"I didna see it, but I heard it. I heard the key turn in the lock. That's what they a'ways do. So we canna get in and nick the paintings." He grinned.

Poppy smiled at him again. And then, just as a last thought: "Oh, one more thing: did you see anyone go up the stairs to the roof that day?"

Jimmy lowered his head and started scuffing the cobbles with the toe of his shoe.

"Jimmy?"

"Aye, I did miss. I saw Mr Sherman."

"When was that? Before or after you saw the lady come down the stairs?"

"Before. But long before. Before the do in the gallery started. Around five o'clock. I sometimes go up there for a tab."

"A tab?" asked Rollo.

"A cigarette," said Peter.

"Aye, a cigarette. I went up there to have a quick'un and I saw Mr Sherman."

"What was he doing?"

Jimmy shrugged. "Nowt. He was just lookin."

"Looking?" prompted Poppy.

"Aye miss, he was looking from the tower doon to the road below."

Poppy, Rollo and Peter shared a startled look.

"Did you tell the police this, son?" asked Rollo.

Jimmy shook his head.

"Why not?"

"Cos they never asked. Not like yous'uns did. If you hadna asked I wouldna said."

"Why not?" asked Poppy, trying to keep any tone of censure out of her voice.

"Cos I'm not supposed to be up there. It's not allowed. Too dangerous. Only Mr Helsdon is when he lets the workmen up to fix the tiles or clear the gutters." Jimmy then raised his head and looked at Poppy with an air of self-justification: "Daft buggers should put a proper lock on it though if they don't want folk gannin. Pardon me language, miss."

"That's all right, Jimmy; you're right. They should put a proper lock on it. Thank you for telling us. However, we will have to tell the police what you told us."

"Oh miss, please divvint!" Then, as if to ensure she really understood him, he tried again in as posh an accent as he could muster: "No miss, don't. Please *don't*."

Poppy reached out and touched his shoulder. "Don't worry, we'll make sure you don't get into trouble. There are far greater crimes afoot than a young lad sneaking a tab, I can assure you."

But Jimmy didn't look assured.

Peter stepped in. "Miss Denby is right, lad. You won't get into trouble. In fact the opposite. If what you've told us helps to catch whoever killed Miss Robson then you'll be a hero. Here." He tossed the crown in the air and Jimmy caught it. "You deserve it."

Chapter 17

Peter dropped Poppy and Rollo on Percy Street, outside the Grand Hotel, before heading back to his office to type up his latest article on the Robson murder. On the drive back into the centre of Newcastle, they had come to the conclusion that Gus and Gerald would be unlikely to talk in front of someone who was only there in the capacity of a reporter. Gerald, of course, knew Poppy and Rollo from London and was friends with both Aunt Dot and Yasmin. Rollo and Poppy considered waiting for Yasmin before they went to see the two men, but neither knew for how long Yasmin would be busy with the solicitor. Also, Yasmin was going to try to get in to see Grace at the police station; that would also take time. No, decided the two London journalists, they would strike while the iron was hot. After what young Jimmy had told them about the argument between Gus and Dante Sherman, they were convinced that Agnes' staff knew more than they had originally told Poppy.

Poppy announced their presence at the desk and asked if Mr Farmer and Mr North were there. The concierge checked his key rack and told them Mr North was out but Mr Farmer was in. Would the lady and gentleman like to see him? Poppy said they would and they were directed to the hotel lounge to wait. Ten minutes later, an exhausted-looking Gerald, wearing a crumpled white suit, filled the lounge door with his bulk. Poppy waved to him and smiled. He struggled to summon a smile in return.

Rollo approached him, hand outstretched. "Gerald, old sport, you look like you've been run over by a coach and horses. My condolences about Agnes."

Gerald shook Rollo's hand. "Good to see you, Rollo. Is Yasmin here too?"

"She is, but she's already on the job, trying to get Grace out. Got meetings this morning with a local solicitor and the Old Bill. So Poppy and I thought we'd stop by to see how you were doing. Should we order some tea?"

Gerald nodded his assent then settled into an armchair near the window. His darkly shadowed eyes peered out, scanning the quiet Sunday morning street. Across the road a congregation was worshipping at St Thomas' church, but beyond that there were only a couple of pedestrians and the occasional motor vehicle to be seen.

"Is Gus not here?" asked Poppy.

Gerald shook his head morosely. "No. We had a row and he's gone out."

"I'm sorry to hear that. Gus seemed very upset when he left Dot's house on Friday night. Was the argument about that?"

Gerald nodded, setting off his double chins. "He's very upset about Agnes."

"We all are," said Poppy.

Gerald looked at Poppy, his eyes a pool of pain. "Yes, but not like Gus."

"And why is that?" asked Rollo.

Gerald shrugged. "I don't know. He's taken it very, very badly." He looked around as if checking to see if anyone was listening, then added: "He didn't come back to the hotel with me on Friday night. When the taxi dropped us off after we'd collected Agnes' things from your aunt's house, Poppy, he stalked off on his own. I tried to catch up with him, but," he gestured to his large frame, "he's a lot fitter than I am. So I came back. I waited up for him all night. He finally came back around lunchtime yesterday. And –" He bit his lip and shook his head.

"And what?" asked Poppy gently.

"And it looked like he'd been in a fight. He had a black eye and a cut lip. I asked him what had happened, but he refused to talk. He spent the rest of the day in his room. And then went out again last night. He – he – hasn't been back since."

"Oh Gerald, I'm so sorry. That must be such a worry for you."

"It is. I thought about going to the police, but I'm worried that they might think he's run away because he's somehow involved in Agnes' death."

Poppy nodded solemnly. "I'm afraid you're right, Gerald. It doesn't look good that Gus has run off like this. Where do you think he's gone?"

Gerald looked out the window again. "I don't know. But I know it's not because he's involved in any way. This is just how Gus is. He's done it before – in London – when he's upset about something. He takes himself off for a few days. Goes drinking. Fighting sometimes, I think. I don't know. He never tells me what he's done when he returns. But he always returns, Poppy, always. And he will again this time. It's just how he is. But the police won't understand that, will they? They'll think it's because he's guilty of something."

"Is he guilty of something?" asked Rollo.

Gerald's eyes widened with shock. "Good heavens, man! Of course not!" Gerald pressed his hands onto the arms of his chair, as if about to lever himself up.

Poppy jumped in, trying to placate him. "Of course Rollo didn't mean he killed Agnes. It's just that we've spoken to the stable boy who overheard Gus and Dante Sherman arguing on Thursday afternoon, before the exhibition."

Gerald's hands relaxed and he sank back into the chair. "Oh. That."

The three of them sat back in their armchairs as the waiter arrived and placed a tea tray on the table. Poppy poured for them all. Gerald's hands were shaking as he took the cup and saucer from her. He put it down with a clatter, spilling tea over his sugar cubes.

"So . . ." prompted Rollo. "Can you explain to us what the stable boy overheard?"

"I – I – don't think I should be talking to the press about this."

Rollo frowned. "It's too late for that, old sport. The reporter from the local rag is already on it. He was the one who introduced us to the stable boy. But, you know us, and you know that we – and particularly Poppy here – will do more than just write a story.

We'll try to get to the truth. And if what you say is correct – that Gus had nothing to do with it – then we can help clear his name. Just like we're trying to clear Grace's. So come on old bean, tell us what you know."

Gerald had steadied his hand enough to pop the sugar cubes in his tea and stir. Then he looked up first at Rollo, then Poppy. "I don't know where to start. It's just such a horrendous mess."

Poppy smiled encouragingly. "That's all right; take your time. Perhaps you can tell us what you remember about the argument with Sherman. What happened when you arrived at the stable door with the paintings?"

"All right," said Gerald. "That's a good place to begin. A man was there to meet us – the stable manager, I think. He sent the lad around the front of the gallery to get Sherman. Sherman and an old fellow – I think the caretaker – arrived about five minutes later at the door at the top of the stairs, the one Agnes apparently went out of later. Then they came down the stairs and greeted us."

"What was his mood like – Sherman's?" asked Rollo.

Gerald thought about this a moment and said: "Cheerful. Quite cheerful. He seemed pleased to see us. Or at least pleased to see the paintings."

"Did he look at them?"

"He slit open the brown paper to check that they were the right ones, but he didn't fully unwrap them, no."

"What happened then?" asked Poppy.

"He instructed the caretaker to take them inside and hang them in the allocated space in the Robson exhibition. It was then that Gus kicked off."

"Kicked off? How?" Rollo took a sip of his tea, grimaced and then added some more milk.

"He said that wasn't what he and Sherman had agreed. That the paintings weren't supposed to be hung with the rest of the exhibition. That they were just for Sherman's personal collection."

"Personal collection? Do you know what he meant by that?" asked Poppy.

Gerald nodded. "Yes. Sherman had actually bought these two

paintings out of his own pocket. The rest of the paintings for the exhibition were either on loan from other galleries – including the Tate – or on loan from Agnes herself. But these two paintings were different."

"Interesting," said Poppy. "Were you aware that he had bought them?"

"Yes."

"And was Agnes?"

"Well, no."

"And why's that?"

"Agnes is a prolific artist. She *was* a prolific artist. She hired me to deal with the business side of things. That includes the sale of paintings. There is a stash of artworks I can draw on to sell whenever I find a buyer. I don't have to check with her first. But it's up to Agnes which paintings she puts into the pool and which she withholds. Some paintings she considers more precious than others and she wants to know who is buying them and where they're going. Others are more run of the mill and she doesn't really care."

"And these were of the 'run of the mill' variety?" asked Poppy.

"Apparently."

"Apparently? What do you mean?" asked Rollo.

Gerald flashed a glance out of the window, still hoping to see Gus return. "Apparently, because that's what Gus told me. Agnes never gave me these paintings. Gus did. He told me about them when we decided to come up for the exhibition. He said Sherman had seen them when he had been down in London a month or so ago. Apparently he'd dropped by to see Agnes. I didn't know about it. But Gus said Sherman saw these and asked to buy them. Agnes asked Gus to pass them on to me."

"Did he? As soon as Agnes asked him?" asked Poppy.

Gerald shook his head. "No, he claims to have forgotten. He said he only just remembered the day before we planned to come up."

"Claims?" asked Rollo. "Sounds like you don't believe him, old sport."

Gerald exhaled slowly, his mouth sagging into his fleshy jowls. "I'm afraid I don't. As Poppy here pointed out the other evening, the paint on one of them was still slightly tacky. It hadn't been finished that long. Agnes has never passed on a painting for sale that wasn't even dry yet. But, when I asked Gus about it, he just shrugged and said it had been her decision and that's that. I was still feeling green about the gills after my tummy trouble so I didn't argue. We just packed up the paintings and brought them here."

"And the other one?" asked Poppy. "The one with the mother and child on the railway track?"

"That one is dry."

"Had you seen it before?"

"No. But that's not unusual. As I said, Agnes is – was – prolific. I don't monitor her work that closely. Her studio is piled high with paintings. I only visit occasionally and when I do we usually spend time looking at accounts and contracts, or press releases if I'm wearing my publicist's hat."

"Hmmm," said Poppy, taking a sip of her tea. "The thing is, I'm not an expert on her work – or art in general – but I've seen enough of it exhibited to get the impression that that painting is not her usual style. The railway line, yes, I've seen that before. And roads. She often has those, but not with people."

"Oh, there are sometimes people," observed Gerald.

"Yes, but more in the background, as part of the landscape. Not like that one. In that painting they're *characters.* Like the painting's actually about them and not the landscape. And that, as far as I can tell from what I've seen of her other paintings, is unusual. But as I say I'm no expert."

"Then what are you saying, Poppy?"

Poppy bit her lip. "I don't know, Gerald. I'm just mulling, that's all. In these sorts of investigations I've learned –" she cast a glance at Rollo and smiled, "– I've learned to focus on the unusual. If you pick at the thread it sometimes comes loose. Sometimes it doesn't. So at the moment I'm still picking."

Gerald nodded. "All right. I understand. But I honestly can't tell you any more about the paintings."

"Actually, I think you can. Bear with me, if you don't mind. There's something else that's been troubling me – another loose thread. You said the other evening in Agnes' bedroom that Sherman had insisted you bring the paintings up with you. And that it would have been hard to say no to him because he's a very influential man. But why should it have been a problem to bring them if they were already his property?"

Gerald sighed. "Because, for some reason, Sherman had insisted that the purchase remain secret. I don't know why. But that's why when you asked Gus and me about them the other night we didn't mention that he'd bought them."

Poppy nodded. "Well, I'm glad you've mentioned that, because that was my next question. You gave the impression then that Agnes wouldn't have wanted them in the exhibition. Why did you do that?"

"Because she didn't know about the sale. She didn't mind her least favourite paintings being sold to private collectors, but she wouldn't want them in an exhibition. She handpicked the paintings for this exhibition. Paintings she was proud of."

"Yes, that makes sense – that some paintings didn't matter as much to her and she was happy to put them into the 'slush pile' for want of a better phrase. However, wasn't it too soon to put this painting into that pile? *Lilies in a Vase* had barely even been finished. It sounds like it was a current piece."

Gerald shrugged. "Sometimes she knew quite quickly that she didn't like a piece. Sometimes she even abandoned paintings that weren't finished. It's quite common for artists, you know."

"I suppose it is," said Poppy. "But what I'm trying to get at is how could Sherman have seen it a month or two ago if the paint is not quite dry? That suggests a fairly recent work. When exactly did Sherman visit the studio?"

Gerald looked puzzled. "I don't know. Perhaps you could ask Gus when he comes back. As I said, the whole business is a little odd. I shouldn't have misled you the other night – I'm sorry about that, Poppy – but Gus was quite keen to honour Sherman's request not to make his purchase public."

"Why's that?" asked Poppy.

Gerald spread his hands. "I honestly haven't a clue. As I said,

I was feeling green about the gills, so I didn't really take much notice. It wasn't until – well, until what happened to Agnes – that I began to reflect on the whole affair as slightly peculiar."

Rollo raised his hand, indicating to the waiter that they would like a fresh pot of tea. "Yes, it is a little peculiar," he chipped in. "And I'm struggling to get my head around it. I'm a little late to the game, old sport, so forgive me if I ask something Poppy has covered with you already before today."

"No problem. Fire away."

"All right. Tell me then, if you didn't know about the sale to Sherman, who would have handled the paperwork. Who, for instance, would have taken payment and where and how would it have been recorded. Because that's your job, isn't it Gerald?"

Gerald lowered his gaze. "It is. I normally handle sales."

"But not this time."

"No," said Gerald.

Rollo pressed on. "Did he buy the paintings there and then?"

"No. Gus said he sent him a telegram a few weeks ago and asked him to bring them up."

Rollo nodded, absorbing the information, then continued. "Well, that is very peculiar, isn't it?" He looked at Poppy. Poppy nodded, encouraging him to continue. "So why do you think he telegraphed Gus when you handle all the business, Gerald, and while you and he had been working together on the exhibition for months already?"

Gerald's eyes flicked to the window and then back to Rollo.

He looked desperately weary, thought Poppy, in body and in heart.

"I don't know. Gus said Sherman would pay me when we arrived."

"And did he?" pressed Poppy.

"He hasn't yet, no. But I didn't want to push him, what with everything that's going on. I'll sort it all out when everything settles down. Now's not really the time for business."

"Business. Yes, that reminds me," continued Rollo. "When Gus and Sherman were having the row, what do you think Sherman meant when he said, 'They have to be hung inside; she needs to know I mean business'?"

Gerald looked at Rollo, startled. "I didn't tell you that."

"The stable boy did. He said that's what Sherman said to Gus when Gus said that he hadn't agreed for them to be exhibited. And I'm still trying to understand why."

Gerald looked out the window again, pondering. "I don't know. I found it odd too."

"Did you ask Gus?"

"I did. There and then with my limited hand signing."

"And what did he say?"

"It was too fast for me to understand properly, but he said something to the effect that I would have to ask her – Agnes. That there was something going on between Sherman and Agnes and he'd promised not to say anything."

"Promised Agnes or promised Sherman?" asked Rollo.

Gerald shrugged. "He didn't say. But I decided I would ask Agnes. I was already a bit puzzled about why the two paintings had come to be there the way they had."

"And did you ask her?"

Gerald shook his head, sadly. "I didn't have a chance before she died."

The three of them fell into silence as the waiter brought a second pot. After he had left and Rollo poured for them all, Poppy asked: "How long have you known Gus, Gerald?"

"Four, nearly five, years. It was 1919. Agnes had decided that she needed a studio assistant. Gus was without a doubt the best candidate."

"Why's that?"

"Well, apart from his own artistic talent, and his willingness to learn from a woman – you know that's quite a rare thing, Poppy – he and Agnes hit it off straight away. They just – I don't know – connected. In private, anyway. Publicly they didn't do quite so well. Both of them were too introverted. But beyond that, they had a similar view of the world. An artist's view. Agnes could be difficult at times, moody, but Gus didn't let it bother him."

"Sounds like Gus could be moody too," observed Rollo. "Oh, without a doubt! But he is a beautiful soul under it all. We – well – I'm sure it's no secret – but he and I have become very close too." Gerald's eyes misted up.

Poppy nodded sympathetically. "Yes, it's obvious that you have a lovely friendship. It's very special. But tell me, Gerald, what do you know about his background? You said you met in 1919. Was he in the war?"

"He was a non-combatant due to his deafness. He worked in an armaments factory, I think, assembling weaponry. He hated it. So when he heard about the job – for an artist's assistant – he jumped at it. He'd had no formal art training, but he is a very talented amateur artist and wanted to take it further."

"Where did he hear about the job? And where did he come from? Have you met his family?" asked Poppy.

Gerald's eyes narrowed. "Why do you want to know all this? I've told you all I know about the paintings and Sherman's row with Gus. And I agree with you that something peculiar is going on there, but beyond that, I don't think Gus is involved in any way. Perhaps you should interrogate Sherman instead."

"We're not interrogating you, Gerald; we're just trying to get to the bottom of what happened," said Poppy, trying to smooth things over with one of her smiles.

It didn't work. "Well," sniffed Gerald, "I believe I've given you more than enough to go on for now, don't you think? So if you don't mind – Poppy, Rollo – I'm going out to try to find Gus. Good day to you."

Gerald heaved himself out of his chair, picked up a panama hat and without further ado, shuffled out of the lounge.

"Where does he think he's going to find him?" asked Rollo.

Poppy shook her head in despair. "I don't know, Rollo, but if I were him I'd be out there too. Do you think we should tell the police that Gus is missing?"

Rollo downed the last of his tea. "No. As Gerald said, they might think it's an admission of guilt from Gus. They've already arrested one person on flimsy evidence –"

"Well, not *that* flimsy," admitted Poppy. "But what the stable boy said about seeing Dante Sherman in the tower looking down onto the street is surely worth telling them about."

"Yes it is. But let's run it all past Yasmin first."

"Agreed," said Poppy, and she pulled on her gloves.

It was then that she saw Gerald lumber past the hotel window. And if she were not mistaken, there were tears in his eyes.

Chapter 18

That evening, after the nanny had taken the children to bed, Poppy, Rollo, Yasmin and Dot gathered around the dining room table to report back on the day. Yasmin, it seemed, had been able to get in to see Grace and to arrange a short visit for Dot.

"How was she, Aunt Dot?" asked Poppy.

"Oh, you know, as well as can be expected. I managed to take her a few home comforts, so that's something."

"How did you get down the stairs?" asked Poppy.

"I didn't. Yazzie demanded they bring her up."

"Well done my love!" said Rollo, blowing a kiss at his wife.

"Thank you my munchkin," said Yasmin, blowing a melodramatic kiss in return.

Poppy chuckled at the ironically sweet endearments from two of the least lovey-dovey people she knew.

"So, is she in good spirits?" asked Poppy.

"Well, good spirits is a high bar for Grace under ordinary circumstances, but yes, she is holding up. She is greatly encouraged that Yasmin has come up north. As are we all, Yazzie, thank you."

"You're most welcome, Dot. Now, if you don't mind, can we compare notes? I'll start. I went to see Mr Wylie this morning. He passed on everything he has managed to procure so far. I shall be preparing my case for the bail hearing this evening. I don't see why it shouldn't be granted. The evidence against Grace is tenuous at best."

"Is it really?" asked Poppy. "What about the knife?"

"Well, it certainly justified her arrest, but it will not in itself justify a conviction. The prosecution will need more than a decorator's lost knife and a history of animosity."

"Really?" asked Dot.

"Well, in an ideal world, yes. But I will still need to work hard to cast doubt on the link between Grace and the knife. I will have to suggest that the decorator, any of his assistants, or even any of his other clients could have found and used the knife."

"But were any of those people at the Laing Art Gallery?" asked Poppy.

Yasmin sighed. "No. But it certainly gives me scope to argue that it is still circumstantial at best. There were no fingerprints on the knife. And no one saw Grace with the knife. Nonetheless, we need more to bolster Grace's case. It would certainly help if we could cast the eye of suspicion onto other people, to let the jury see that there were other people with motive and opportunity . . ."

"Or we could show definitively that someone else did it," said Poppy, her blue eyes steely with determination.

Yasmin chuckled. "Well, yes, that would be ideal. Do you have any ideas who that might be?"

So Poppy, with help from Rollo, proceeded to tell Yasmin and Dot what they had learned from both the stable boy and Gerald.

The lawyer rolled a pen between her thumb and forefinger. "Interesting, very interesting. So, from what you've told me, there are two potential suspects in the picture: Dante Sherman and Gus North. Both have been acting in a peculiar manner and appear to be hiding something relating to the procurement of those paintings."

"But surely you can't really think that sweet boy Gus did it?" chipped in Dot, as she helped herself to a chocolate truffle.

"I'm afraid he has to be considered a suspect, Dot. Obviously we all hope it's *not* him, but if it is, he must be brought to justice. So, what I propose is that Rollo, you ask Ike in London to do a bit of digging into Gus' life. Have you already asked him to go to the Tate to ask about the letter of authentication?"

"I have, my love. But, darn it, Poppy and I forgot to ask Gerald about that this morning."

"You're right; we didn't," said Poppy.

"Not to worry," said Yasmin, making a note on her legal pad. "I shall ask him about it when I formally depose him. I will be lining up my interviewees as soon as Grace's bail hearing is finished, tomorrow. And Gus, Gerald and Dante Sherman will be top of my list. Has anyone found out anything more about the missing key?"

"Well we haven't, have we Poppy? The stable lad only mentioned that Sherman and the caretaker came through the back door at the top of the stairs. Which doesn't add to anything we know. Both Sherman and the caretaker admitted they used the key. So the question is, who might have seen a need to take the spare one?" replied Rollo.

"Anyone who was at the gallery that day – or that night," observed Aunt Dot. "And, from all the comings and goings on the night – including you, Poppy – I think it's clear that the door was unlocked for the duration of the exhibition." Dot, who was rarely asked her serious opinion on things, looked as proud as Punch to have contributed to the conversation.

"Yes," agreed Poppy, nodding her affirmation. "I think that's the case. But that means someone unlocked it and *left* it unlocked during the exhibition. The caretaker told me that it was always locked after it was used. So why wasn't it this time? Or did someone deliberately open it and leave it unlocked, knowing they would be slipping out sometime during the evening? And if that's the case, we will need to narrow down our suspect list to people who: a, knew that the door was there and where it led, and b, knew where to find a key to unlock it."

"Agreed," said Yasmin. "I shall be demanding a list of everyone who works at the gallery – they are the most likely people to know about the key."

"Or volunteers," added Dot, warming to her new role.

"Volunteers?" asked Yasmin.

"Yes, lots of galleries and museums have an army of volunteers who help with fundraising and so on and sometimes do stewarding work. Grace and I are both 'Friends of the Victoria and Albert Museum', for instance."

"Good idea," said Yasmin. "I will get a list of Friends of the Laing and cross-reference it against the guest list for the evening. Which, by the way, I will be getting a copy of from DI Hawkes tomorrow, Poppy. So Sherman's stonewalling won't get him very far. However, it certainly is telling. Why would he be so objectionable as not to share this sort of information? Surely he would want Agnes' killer to be found and brought to justice as soon as possible."

"Yes, that's what surprised me too when I spoke to him," said Poppy. "There are two possible reasons, as far as I can tell: either he is the killer himself – and let's not forget his very strange behaviour looking down at the street from the tower earlier in the afternoon – or he is trying to hide something else that he fears might be dug up in the murder investigation."

"Or both," chipped in Rollo.

"Or both," agreed Poppy.

"So where do we go from here?" asked Dot.

"Well, I will obviously interview Sherman myself and see what I can shake loose," said Yasmin. "I will also suggest DI Hawkes does the same. Didn't the boy say he hadn't mentioned seeing Sherman in the tower to the police?"

"That's right," said Rollo. "He said he was scared his boss would find out he'd been out for a 'tab' on the roof." He grinned, obviously pleased with himself for using a new word.

"Good, then I'll pass it on to Hawkes tomorrow."

"While you're at it, can you arrange to get a writing sample from Sherman?" asked Poppy.

The other three looked at her curiously. She smiled. "The letter to my mother, of course. Don't forget it's the same handwriting as the note on the back of the photograph I found in Agnes' things."

"Of course." Yasmin jotted it down.

"What will you do, Poppy?" asked Aunt Dot.

Poppy thought about it, paging through her own notes that she'd been making. "I think I will still go to see Professor Reid at the art school. I want to show him the photograph, but also ask him about the two late paintings. He's bound to have seen them at the exhibition. I want to get his take on them."

"What are you thinking, Poppy?" asked Yasmin.

"I'm not really sure, but there's definitely something strange about them. Perhaps Professor Reid has heard some gossip in the art world about it, or can identify something that is technically different about the paintings. I'm also not sure the story about Sherman seeing them 'months ago' holds water, particularly because one of them is still tacky. Actually, on that note, is it in your power to demand to see Sherman's diary, Yasmin? Can we confirm that he actually was in London at the time?"

"At this stage it might be considered overreach. He's not a formal suspect yet. But I'll see what I can do. Right, what else do we have to do tomorrow? Are we still on to visit Agnes' family?"

"Hopefully, yes," said Poppy, "if my mother can arrange it."

Yasmin nodded. "All right. But if she can't, we need to go through on Tuesday morning at the latest, with or without your mother – although I agree having your mother there will be preferable. It's always good for the interviewee to have a sympathetic presence. Also, we need to hear the story behind that threatening letter. I think there might be something very important in that, but we need to know more before we pass on any information to the police. So, that's it then. Tonight I'll prepare for the bail hearing; tomorrow I'll be in court at nine o'clock –"

"Can I come too?" asked Dot.

"Yes, you can. Delilah has already asked the same thing. However, Poppy, I think it's best if you go to see the professor during that time. Is that all right?"

"It is."

"All right, my love, I'll leave you to it," said Rollo, standing up and giving his wife a kiss on the cheek. "I'll hit the old typewriter upstairs. I want to get a story off to Ike tonight. Poppy, will you help me?"

"Of course." Poppy closed her notebook and got up to leave with Rollo and Dot.

"Actually, Poppy, would you mind staying on a minute? There's just one more thing I want to check with you. And Dot," said Yasmin, "would you mind awfully asking Betty to make me a strong pot of tea?"

Dot agreed and left with Rollo. Poppy remained behind, feeling oddly like a pupil called to the headmistress's office, even though she was quite a nice headmistress.

Yasmin smiled at her. "Don't look so nervous, Poppy! Do sit

down. There's just something I wanted to tell you that I think you would prefer was done privately."

"Oh," said Poppy, returning to her seat and folding, then unfolding, her hands in front of her.

"Yes," said Yasmin, checking that no one was about to burst through the door. "DI Hawkes sends his regards. He asked if you minded dropping in to see him at your convenience. He seemed rather concerned that he'd upset you the last time the two of you had spoken. What was that all about?"

Poppy straightened up, recalling the last explosive conversation she'd had with the detective inspector at the Theatre Royal. She explained what had happened, and how Hawkes had accused her of pretending to be a lawyer and interfering in the case, but left out the subplot of the kindling of a possible romance.

But Yasmin was no fool. Her eyes narrowed as she appraised the younger woman. "You're not telling me everything, Poppy. And that's your right. But I thought I should also let you know that Delilah has told me all about the handsome detective saving you from the mugger and your tennis match the following day. She seemed to think the two of you might be soft on one another . . ."

Poppy flinched. Delilah really could be annoying sometimes. She let out a slow, controlled breath. "Well, we're not. And if we were, we certainly wouldn't be any more. I think DI Hawkes has well and truly drawn a line in the sand. He was very rude to me, you know. And I believe any attempts to offer an olive branch are simply motivated by him wanting to get more information out of me to use against Grace." Poppy remembered the way he had questioned her on the roof of the gallery. The very intimate way he had questioned her . . . She flushed.

Yasmin noticed but didn't say anything. Instead she just nodded. "Yes, you're right to be wary of him – professionally. But I wouldn't be so sure that his motivation is entirely dastardly. I read people well, Poppy; it's my job. And while I can see that DI Hawkes will always put the investigation first, I think he is genuinely endeared towards you."

"Well, I am not endeared towards him!"

Yasmin smiled gently. "All right. That's up to you. But may I ask if it's just because you felt he tricked you into giving him information and accused you of interfering in the investigation, or is there something else?"

"Like what?"

"Oh, I don't know, like Daniel?"

Poppy felt her stomach clench at the mention of her former beau's name.

"I – well – I haven't heard from Daniel since Easter, Yasmin. That's six months. I know it takes a while for letters to travel back and forth from Africa, but that's just too long. He's obviously moved on, even if he hasn't had the courage to tell me. Our relationship – in person and in pen – is clearly over." Poppy's eyes began to well up. She bit her lip.

Yasmin reached out her hand and took hold of Poppy's. "Oh, my sweet girl. I'm so sorry. I really thought the two of you would end up married. I know you and he had different ideas about you working rather than looking after his children, but I thought that he was finally coming around to a more enlightened way of seeing things."

Poppy sniffed and wiped at her eyes with the back of her hand. "He was. I do believe that if we'd got married we could have employed a nanny like you and Rollo have. And of course the children are now at school. But, his sister getting married and taking them to Africa with her was not foreseen. And I can't blame Daniel for wanting to be with them."

Yasmin reached into the pocket of her Chanel suit jacket and retrieved a handkerchief, which she passed to Poppy.

"Didn't he ask you to go with him?"

Poppy dabbed at her wet cheeks. "He did. But it would have meant leaving my family, friends and job behind here. I was hoping that he'd come back after a couple of years. And for a while – from the content of his letters – that's what I thought he would do. But," she shrugged and put on a brave smile, "it was not to be. He obviously loves his children more than he loves me. And I don't blame him for it."

"No," said Yasmin, frowning. "But I do blame his sister. The children are not pet poodles. She may have helped raise them but they are not hers. And now she's married, she could start her own family."

"She has," said Poppy.

"Oh?"

"Yes, she had a baby in January. That's the last I heard from Daniel. It's a little boy. Anyway . . ."

"Anyway," said Yasmin, drawing the younger woman into an embrace.

Poppy was surprised. This was not the Yasmin Reece-Lansdale she knew. Marriage and motherhood seemed to have brought out a more demonstrative side to her. And Poppy was grateful.

After a few moments, Poppy pulled away. "Thanks Yasmin. I'm all right. And if you don't mind being the go-between, would you mind telling DI Hawkes that if he would like to apologise to me in person he is welcome to pay me a call?"

Yasmin chuckled. "Good girl. Keep it on your terms."

Suddenly the door opened and the strains of Al Jolson's "Swanee" could be heard emanating from the parlour. Aunt Dot was playing her gramophone records. Rollo stood in the doorway, appraising the two women. "Are you two finished?"

"We are," said his wife.

"Good, then if you don't mind, my darling, I would like my star reporter back. I recall the first time you met her you tried to lure her away to work for you, do you remember?"

Poppy and Yasmin shared a knowing look. "I do. But don't worry, my love, she's all yours."

"Very glad to hear it. Hope you've got your typing fingers warmed up, Poppy; we've gotta lot of work to do!"

Chapter 19

Monday, 7 October 1924

Newcastle upon Tyne

The Newcastle Art School – otherwise known as the King Edward VII School of Art – was part of Armstrong College, a remote campus of Durham University in the heart of Newcastle city centre. The building had been commandeered as a sanatorium during the war, but now, in 1924, was back to its original purpose: housing the Hatton Gallery and the school of fine art. Back in 1897, when the school decided to do an outreach programme to the children of miners in Ashington, it had employed the now-deceased Michael Brownley and, if Poppy understood it correctly, Professor Reid. It was Professor Reid whom she hoped to speak to today.

She got off the bus at the Haymarket bus station, opposite the Grand Hotel on Percy Street, and made her way up King's Walk and through the twin arches that marked the entrance to Armstrong College. She stepped into a beautifully manicured garden where students sat on the lawn enjoying the autumn sunshine, some of them reclining on their book bags, indulging in a pre-lecture cigarette. She asked one of them the way to the art school and was pointed in the right direction.

Inside the building she was pleased to be informed that Professor Reid would be happy to see her. Five minutes later she was sitting in an armchair in a sunlit bay window being offered a cup of coffee by the professor. Out in the quadrangle the smoking students were stubbing out their cigarettes, picking up their book bags and sauntering off to their next lectures. Reid looked on with a mild air of disapproval. "Fortunately, they're architecture students, not ours."

Poppy smiled and accepted the cup and saucer from the professor. It was her third cup of the morning and she hoped she would make it through the meeting without needing to go to the lavatory. However, she really needed the boost. It had been a late night, churning out copy with Rollo and telephoning it through to the long-suffering Ike Garfield back in London. She took a sip of the coffee and allowed the rejuvenating brew to do its job.

Then, for the next couple of minutes Poppy and the professor exchanged the now familiar condolences and expressions of shock: "terrible business", "poor Agnes", "who would have thought?" Poppy then explained that she was working with Grace Wilson's lawyer – because of course Mrs Wilson didn't do it – to prove Grace's innocence and find Agnes' real killer.

"Goodness, do you think he might still be on the loose?"

"He or she," corrected Poppy. "And yes, we believe the police have the wrong person in custody and that means there is still a murderer in our midst."

"My word, Miss Denby, do you think he – or she – might strike again?"

Poppy shrugged. "I honestly don't know, professor. That will depend, really, on the killer's motivation. I have worked on cases where there was only one murder, which in the killer's mind was entirely justified, and that was it. I have worked on others where there were a number of victims – all linked in some way and targeted by the killer. I'm afraid there are cases where the killer will kill again to cover his or her tracks – or to silence witnesses."

Professor Reid ran a finger along the inside of his collar. "To silence witnesses?"

Poppy smiled reassuringly, regretting having alarmed the elderly man. "Don't worry, Professor Reid; I'm sure this isn't one of those cases. It has been over three days since Agnes' death and no one else has been hurt."

Professor Reid nodded, putting on a brave face. But his hand trembled as he sipped his coffee. "Well then," he said, "the sooner we get the real killer behind bars the better. How may I help?"

Poppy reached into her bag and retrieved three photographs. She laid two of them on the small round coffee table and kept the third upside down on her lap. Peter MacMahon had given the photographs to Delilah to pass on to Poppy when the young actress rolled in in the wee hours of the morning. Poppy gestured to the two prints. "Do you recognise these paintings, professor?"

"I do indeed. I saw them on Thursday night at Agnes' exhibition."

"That's right. And, by any chance, is there anything unusual or distinctive about them?"

Reid leaned forward and picked up the photographs, one in each hand. "It's funny you should ask that, Miss Denby. There is something most curious about them indeed. In fact, I asked Agnes about it that night, before she . . . well, before . . . you know . . ." Reid's voice trailed off.

"Really? What is it?"

"Well," said Reid, putting down the lilies picture and then pointing to the bottom right-hand corner of the railway painting with his index finger, "there is no signature. And Agnes always signed her paintings."

"May I?" Poppy took the photo from him and examined the place where Reid indicated the signature should have been. And the art professor was right. There was no signature. "Goodness, I never noticed. And *Lilies in a Vase*?"

Reid passed that photo to her too. "No signature either."

Poppy held up both photographs and looked from left to right, right to left. "And you say you spoke to Agnes about it? What did she say?"

Reid shrugged, pursing his lips. "Well, that was even more curious. She seemed as if she were bottling up some anger when I brought it to her attention. I said, 'Why haven't you signed these, Agnes?' and she answered – rather curtly if I might add, and that's not Agnes, at least not with me; we've always got on well – but she said, 'Well I wouldn't, would I?' And then she flounced off."

"Flounced?"

"Well, I suppose it was more of a stomp. But that would not be very gentlemanly of me to say so, would it?"

Poppy tried to keep the smile out of her voice. "All right, so she 'flounced' off. In a bit of a huff or in anger?"

"Hmm, let me think..." Reid took out his pipe, bashed out the old tobacco into an ashtray, then stuffed some fresh baccie into the bowl.

Poppy's forefinger started tapping the way it did when she was losing patience. She told herself to relax and allow the gentleman to tell his story in his own way, in his own time. It's what Rollo had always taught her.

"I think it was more annoyance. Yes, I would say she was annoyed."

"Then where did she go? When she flounced off in annoyance."

"To corner Gerald and Gus. She seemed quite cross about something. I didn't hear what she said but her body language was quite animated."

"Hmmm, interesting. And could you describe Gerald's and Gus' body language?"

Reid took out a match, struck it and lit the pipe, taking a good few sucks on it. Eventually he pulled it out and said: "Well, Gus seemed angry too. He stood up to her, face to face. And Gerald appeared to be trying to placate them both – mediate perhaps, I don't know. As I say I didn't hear what was said, but that's what it looked like to me."

Poppy nodded, filing this information in the ever-growing folder of "it certainly looks like Gus and Gerald are not telling us the full story".

"Thank you, Professor Reid; that could prove very useful. I shall pass on the information to Mrs Rolandson, the barrister."

"*Mrs* Rolandson. A lady barrister?"

"Yes."

"Gracious me, we never had lady barristers in *my* day. Not that it's a problem of course, but it is unusual, wouldn't you agree? We have a lady professor here at the college too. Not in this department, over in the science building; it's very unusual, very unusual indeed."

"It is," said Poppy, her voice devoid of any encouragement for the professor to continue down this track. "So, what happened after you saw Agnes speaking to Gus and Gerald? Where did she go then?"

"Then? Well, she went out of the room with your Mrs Wilson."

Poppy was not expecting that. "She what?"

"Yes, they left together. I told the police that."

"Are you sure?"

"Quite sure."

"Left for where?"

"I don't know. They just went through a door together. The door into Gallery B. That's where the back door onto the roof is, isn't it?"

"It is. But as far as we know Grace and Agnes did not go out that door together. Grace would have said if they had."

"Well, I can't say for certain where they went. But they did leave Gallery A together, whatever Mrs Wilson has told you." Reid drew again on his pipe, rolling the smoke from cheek to cheek.

Poppy made a note, wondering if this was something Yasmin was aware of. "All right, thank you. So, to clarify, you noticed that these two paintings had not been signed by Agnes. And when you asked her why, she gave an ambiguous answer questioning why she would even do so. But, you also told me that Agnes usually signs her paintings. Why do you think she didn't in this case?"

Reid shrugged, cupping the bowl of his pipe in his palm. "I have no idea. Not all artists sign their work. And some do so inconsistently. But Agnes, to the best of my knowledge – and I've been studying her work for nearly ten years now – was not one of them."

"Are you aware that the two paintings in question only arrived at the gallery a few hours before the exhibition?"

"I wasn't, no. But I was surprised to see them, as they weren't in the pre-published catalogue."

"That's right, they weren't. But were you aware of their existence? Did you know that Agnes had painted them?"

Reid shook his head. "I have seen similar paintings to the *Lilies* – she seemed to like them as a subject matter. But not that specific one. The *Lilies in a Vase* currently hanging in the Laing was only painted a few weeks ago."

"How do you know that?"

"The paint was still tacky."

"Yes, I noticed that too. And *The Railway Family*?"

Reid raised the pipe to his lips, then changed his mind and lowered it again, jabbing it towards Poppy to punctuate his point. "Now that's an interesting one. I first saw it at a private viewing before the big Robson show at the Tate. I believe you covered that show, Miss Denby."

"I did. Around five months ago. But I don't remember seeing *that* painting."

"That's because it had been withdrawn from the exhibition. The Tate – after receiving a few complaints from art experts who viewed it in advance – decided it was too controversial and withdrew it from the main show."

"I don't remember *that* happening!"

"You wouldn't. It wasn't made public and everyone who was there agreed not to mention it to the press."

"And why's that?"

"Because they didn't want the Tate's or Agnes' reputation to be sullied – on a mere suggestion."

"And what was that suggestion?"

Reid leaned forward and jabbed the pipe in Poppy's direction. "Am I speaking to you, Miss Denby, as a journalist, an investigator for a defence barrister, or as a friend of the victim? Or for that matter, a friend of the person accused of murdering the victim?"

Poppy let out a sigh. It was a fair question. "The honest answer, Professor Reid, is that I am all of those things. And you're right to be wary. But I can assure you that my primary motivation is to seek the truth: to find out who killed Agnes and to bring that person to justice. I understand that my role in this is a bit – what's the word – murky, but I can assure you my reasons for speaking to you today are not. If there's anything you can tell me that will help me – us – discover who killed Agnes and why, you will have done the right thing. So please sir, tell me what you know."

Reid leaned back in his chair and rocked his head from side to side, as though loosening a stiff neck. Then he looked directly at Poppy. "All right, I'll tell you. It's nothing you wouldn't find out yourself if you asked the Tate, anyway."

Poppy thought of Ike, who was going to be heading to the Tate this morning. She wondered if he was in the process of hearing the very same information as she was now. "Thank you, Professor. Yes, we are sending someone to the Tate, but it would still be helpful if you tell us what you know."

"Well, in that case, I will tell you that there was some question about the authenticity of the painting. One of the learned gentlemen present queried whether it was, in fact, an Agnes Robson."

"Because of the lack of a signature?"

"No, because of the style and subject matter. You see, Agnes is known for her Post-Impressionistic style and often prosaic subject matter. *Lilies in a Vase* is classic Robson. But this one – even though she has in the past painted roads and railway lines – was more, now what's the word . . . ?"

"Narrative?"

Reid's eyes lit up under his sparse grey brows. "That's it exactly! The two figures seem to be telling some kind of story. That's not what Agnes usually did."

Poppy looked at the photograph of the painting and studied the woman and child. They appeared to be leaving somewhere, with the young woman, her long black hair caught in a plait, carrying a heavy sack. The child looked back at the viewer, its face fraught with emotion. Was it fear? Grief? It was hard to tell.

But the child definitely appeared distressed. Who were they? Where were they going? Where had they come from? Why did they feel the need to leave?

"So," said Poppy, "it was just that it was not the usual subject for Agnes to paint. Surely an artist is able to experiment and change? Perhaps this was something new she was trying."

Reid nodded. "Well yes, of course. But I'm afraid that's not all, Miss Denby. You see, one of the other learned gentlemen, and I must admit I supported him in this, also suggested that the figures had been painted after the fact. That the way the paint was applied implied that the railway line had been originally painted some time ago. But the mother and child were only recently added."

Poppy looked again at the photograph. It was not something she could judge from a black and white image. Nor, she admitted, would she have the skill or knowledge to judge it from the original painting. "All right," she said, "so Agnes added them later."

There was a pained expression on Reid's face. "Oh no, Miss Denby. You see, that's the problem. It was suggested that the figures were *not* painted by Agnes at all. That they were added by another artist entirely."

Poppy's blue eyes widened in shock. "Are you saying it's a forgery?"

Reid shook his head vigorously. "No, of course not. The background – the railway line and the landscape – are believed to be an authentic Robson. But the figures – we think – were added by someone else."

"Good heavens."

"Good heavens indeed."

"Did you – or the Tate – ask her about it?"

Reid nodded and leaned back again in his chair. He took another suck on his pipe and then exhaled, surrounding them both in a cloud of smoke. "We did. Mr Smythe, the head curator at the Tate, requested a meeting with Agnes. She, according to Smythe, was apparently shocked at the accusation."

"Did she deny it?"

"Of course. But she agreed to withdraw the painting from the exhibition, in order to avoid any controversy. And as far as I knew, that was the end of it. That is, until that very same painting appeared at the Laing last Thursday night."

Poppy paged back in her notes and jabbed her pencil at a particular sentence. "You said, Professor Reid, that you asked Agnes why she hadn't signed it. Didn't you ask her why she had decided to exhibit it again when its authenticity had been called into question?"

Reid's eyes widened in surprise. "Goodness no! That would have been very rude. There was no formal declaration that the artwork was a composite; it was just a suggestion. I had just assumed that, as it was now hanging in her latest exhibition, the Laing had taken her at her word and decided that it was in fact all her own. That was good enough for me. I was just wondering if that were the case, why she hadn't then gone ahead and signed it. And it was then that she gave me that curious answer of 'Well I wouldn't, would I?'"

"Yes," agreed Poppy, "that is curious. And perhaps – and I might be wrong – perhaps it suggests that she did not after all believe it was her own."

Reid nodded. "Exactly my thoughts, Miss Denby."

Poppy picked up the photograph again. And then the one of the lilies. "Has no one suggested the lilies is a – how did you put it – a composite?"

Reid shook his head. "No, not at all. It wasn't at the Tate exhibition. And from what I've seen of it, it definitely looks as though it is the work of one artistic hand."

Poppy slipped the photographs into the back of her notebook. "Thank you, Professor Reid; you've been most helpful. I shall pass on all this information to Mrs Rolandson – and the police."

The old man nodded seriously. "Well, I don't know what any of this has to do with who killed Agnes."

"Neither do I. But I'm sure all the pieces of the puzzle will eventually fit together."

"Well, it's been a pleasure seeing you, Miss Denby." Professor Reid readied himself to stand.

"Actually," said Poppy, turning over the third photograph that had been on her lap during the whole conversation, "there is one more thing I would like you to look at." She placed it face up on the table.

Reid leaned forward and took in the nude of the young girl, with her hair falling over her crouched limbs. He looked up at Poppy and gasped. "Good gracious! Where did you get that?"

"I found it in Agnes' things on Friday night. I wonder if you've ever seen it before?"

The elderly art professor had visibly paled. He picked up the photograph, his hands shaking, then said: "Oh my dear Miss Denby. I think you'd better come with me. There's something you need to see."

Chapter 20

Professor Reid led Poppy out of his office and through the corridors of the art department at a rapid clip for a man of his years. They went through the school's gallery, lined with paintings and sculptures by students and alumni, and past a lecture hall where undergraduates were scribbling down the words of a young lecturer. Eventually they came to a flight of steps, which led down into a basement. It was only here that Professor Reid showed his age, clearly favouring his right leg as he clung to the banister on the way down.

"Watch your step, Miss Denby, it's steep."

Poppy was tempted to ask where they were going, but she held her tongue, allowing Reid to tell her – and show her – in his own time, in his own way.

At the bottom of the stairs he opened a door, pulled a light cord and ushered Poppy in. They appeared to be in some kind of storeroom with an assortment of furniture piled high, stacks of paintings covered in sackcloth and the odd – and in some cases *very* odd – piece of sculpture.

He started searching through the painting stacks – peeking under coverings, grunting, then covering them back up again. Eventually he started talking.

"Do you recall last Wednesday, Miss Denby, when Agnes and I opened the memorial hall in Ashington?"

"I do indeed," said Poppy, relieved that his train of thought was going in the direction she hoped it would.

"Well, if you remember, there were some embarrassing shouts from the crowd about Michael Brownley and Agnes' supposed involvement in his death."

"Yes, I remember."

"Then you will also recall how I brushed it aside, saying something along the lines of he was remembered well by the college, or words to that effect. The truth is, however, I lied." He faced Poppy while holding an unframed painting against his body. "You see, Michael Brownley is not remembered fondly here at all. Twenty-seven years ago I was his supervisor. I remember receiving a telegram from a policeman asking me to come through to Ashington. I met him at the hall we were then using to run our community art classes. The policeman told me that Brownley's body had been found in a mine shaft. He had apparently stumbled into the pit intoxicated. The coroner returned a verdict of 'death by misadventure', as there was no conclusive evidence to suggest whether it was an accident or suicide. Or, as you no doubt heard on Wednesday, whether someone else had caused his death.

"But at that stage the policeman did not know any of that. What he did know was that he had found some troubling paintings in a cupboard at the hall. A key had been found on Brownley and it unlocked the cupboard. It held art supplies, as expected, but, at the back, were half a dozen canvases of naked children. He asked me if I knew anything about them. I of course didn't. But I recognised Brownley's style. To cut a long story short, the policeman and I came to the conclusion that Brownley had been using his young pupils as models – without their parents knowing. I begged the policeman not to say anything about the paintings. I convinced him that it would destroy Brownley's reputation and that his family should be protected from that."

Poppy was eyeing the canvas in Reid's hands, wishing he would reveal what it was – although she suspected she already knew. "Just his family's reputation? Or the art school's too?"

Reid nodded, his face awash with shame. "Yes, the school's too. But I can assure you, Miss Denby, if the paintings had been found before he died I would have put a stop to it immediately and allowed him to face the consequences – legal or otherwise. But he was gone. No one would benefit from the paintings coming to light. So, I arranged for a payment to be made to the police benevolent fund, and another to the Miners' Institute, and I whisked the paintings away. I have barely thought of them for the last twenty-seven years, until you showed me that photograph today."

Finally, he turned the painting around to reveal the original oil canvas of the naked girl in the photograph. "If you haven't realised already, Miss Denby, this is Agnes Robson as a fourteen-year-old."

Poppy looked at the eyes, dark hair and dusky complexion, finally recognising in it a youthful version of the woman she had known. "Yes, so it is. But you said there were half a dozen others. Of different children?"

The professor nodded his assent.

"Where are the rest of them?"

Reid looked sheepish. "I destroyed them. In a bonfire."

"Why not this one?"

Reid shrugged. "I don't really know. There was something different about it. The others were – well, without putting too fine a point on it – more explicit, bordering at times on obscene. But this one is quite tastefully done. She is no different from the young muses often used by artists. There is a tenderness to it, a beauty. I – well – I suppose I wanted to keep something of Michael alive. Something positive. He was my student. I struggled to accept that all he had been in life was a pervert. This showed something – well – slightly nobler."

"She was only fourteen," said Poppy accusingly.

Professor Reid nodded, avoiding Poppy's eye. "Yes, she was. But as I said, young models are not unknown. And for that matter, neither are nudes of young children. But, well, it's the *way* they are depicted that's the problem. And the others, in my opinion, crossed that line. This one, I believe, does not."

Poppy suppressed an urge to further shame the professor for his dubious judgment. She needed to keep him onside. "Fair enough," she said, "as far as the painting goes. But are you aware that Brownley entered into sexual relations with Agnes?"

The old professor flushed and turned away. "Yes. I heard the rumours," he said quietly.

"Well, it's true. Agnes told me all about it the evening before we came through to Ashington. So while that painting itself may not be completely improper, it does reflect something more troubling."

Reid nodded. "I quite agree, which is one of the reasons I hid it away. Perhaps I didn't hide it well enough."

Poppy looked around, noting the mish-mash of objects, the door with no lock and the very public nature of the building they were in, and thought to herself, *well, that's an understatement.* However, instead of voicing her disapproval, she held up the photograph and said: "Perhaps you're right, as it does look like someone has found it and taken the time to photograph it. Who has access to this storeroom?"

Reid thought a moment. "Anyone in the building, really. As you can see it's used for general storage."

"And that would be anyone for the past twenty-seven years?"

Reid nodded.

"Well, as it turns out, I think we can narrow it down to a shorter period than that. I'm a bit of an amateur photographer myself – no expert, you understand – but I know enough to tell that this is a fairly recent print, no more than a couple of years old. I could get it dated more accurately than that by a professional, but let's go with that for the moment. And then there's this . . ." Poppy flipped over the photograph and pointed to the note on the back: Stay away. "Do you recognise that handwriting?"

Reid took it from her, adjusted the spectacles on his nose and peered at the message. "I'm afraid I don't."

"All right. It isn't much of a writing sample, I agree. But we are hoping to match it to someone very soon. Could you tell me if anyone connected with the Agnes Robson exhibition at the Laing might have visited the art school in the last year or so?"

Reid shrugged. "Goodness, quite a few, I should imagine. There is a lot of professional interchange between us and the Laing. Also, our own gallery – the Hatton – is open to the public and much the same clientele visit us both. But I can't imagine a casual visitor to the gallery would wander down into the basement . . ."

Poppy agreed that that was unlikely. "But professionally though, would, say, Dante Sherman visit here at all?"

"Sherman? Yes of course. He's a graduate of the school. And since he got the job at the Laing we have worked on a number of projects together. However . . ." Reid looked at the painting which he had now propped against a stack of chairs, ". . . it would be rather unfortunate if it had been him."

"And why's that?"

Reid ran his finger along the inside of his collar in the same way he had done when Poppy had first told him her purpose for visiting. "Well, because of who his father is."

Poppy cocked her head, remembering what Delilah had told her about Dante's father when they had first met Maddie Sherman walking her dogs in the park. "He was an ichthyologist, I've heard. He passed away, didn't he?"

"His stepfather, yes. Oh, Miss Denby, I thought you knew. Dante Sherman is Michael Brownley's son."

Poppy got off the bus on Heaton Road and walked to Jesmond Vale Terrace. Aunt Dot's yellow Rolls was not parked outside, indicating that she, Delilah and Yasmin – and hopefully Grace, if she were granted bail – were not yet back from court. She could, however, hear the squeals of the twins through the open parlour window and the roar of Rollo pretending to be a bear. She smiled to herself and decided to leave her editor to play for a bit longer with his children. So instead of going inside, she went two houses down, pushed open the neat garden gate and knocked on the door. She was met by the furious barking of two little dogs.

A few moments later, the door opened to reveal Maddie Sherman, dressed as if to go out.

"Poppy! How lovely to see you. But you've come just as I was taking the pups out. I'm dreadfully sorry, but they won't settle until they've had their walk."

The fluffy white pooches were skipping around on their back legs like poodles in a circus.

"Perhaps I could come with you? I wouldn't mind a walk in the park myself. Is that all right?"

Maddie beamed. "Of course! We'd love the company, wouldn't we Susie and Charlie?"

Susie and Charlie yapped their approval. A few minutes later, with both dogs on the lead, Maddie and Poppy crossed the road and entered the park. They took a similar route to the one Poppy and Delilah had taken the other day: down the hill, past the tennis courts and then the bowling green and around the back of the pavilion. As they walked they shared a little small talk: the weather, how beautiful the trees were in autumn, the very loud children who had just moved into Dot Denby's house . . .

Poppy laughed. "They're my editor's children. He came up with them to accompany his wife, who is acting as Grace's barrister."

Maddie gave a sympathetic tut. "Goodness yes. I heard that the police arrested poor Mrs Wilson on Friday. Has she been in prison all weekend?"

"The police holding cells, not prison. Unfortunately the magistrate would not sit until this morning. Hopefully, she'll be coming home soon. Yasmin is busy applying for bail now."

Maddie shook her head, making the feather in her tweed hat quiver. "My goodness, it's all so terribly scandalous, isn't it? It's normally such a respectable neighbourhood."

Poppy bristled at the implied criticism of Grace. "Yes, I'm sure it is a little embarrassing for the neighbours, but imagine how poor Grace feels. I think embarrassment is the least of her worries. Not to mention Agnes' family, don't you think?"

Maddie stopped as her male dog cocked his leg against a park bench. "Oh Poppy, I'm sorry. I didn't mean it like that. I often don't think before I speak. Please accept my apologies." She accompanied her olive branch with a gentle touch to Poppy's shoulder.

Poppy relaxed, her bristles soothed. "That's all right, Maddie. I know we all respond to shock in different ways."

Maddie looked grateful to be let off the hook. They carried on walking.

"So," asked Poppy, after a few moments of awkward silence. "How is your son holding up? It's a terrible thing that happened on his watch. And having the police all over the gallery must be very distressing for him."

"Oh it was! It is! And thank you for asking. I know – of course – that

Agnes' family will have suffered the most from this – and of course Mrs Wilson – but you are the first person to remember dear Dante. The poor boy really does not deserve this."

Poppy nodded, trying to exude sympathy she did not feel. Correction: she did not feel for Dante Sherman. But she did for his mother. She would tap into that.

"Yes, it must be hard for you as a mother to see him in difficulties like this. Actually, I was at your son's alma mater today . . ."

"The art school?"

"Yes, I popped in there to talk to Professor Reid. He – he – mentioned your son very fondly." This of course was not entirely true. But what was she supposed to say: we talked about your son as someone potentially connected to Agnes' murder?

Maddie appeared pleased. "Oh, that's very kind of him. Yes, Dante was one of his star pupils. Professor Reid, and the whole department, were very proud when he got the position at the Laing."

Poppy smiled encouragingly. She was on safer ground here in terms of verisimilitude. "Yes, he said so. He said they had worked together a lot since. He also said he was your late husband's – your first late husband's – supervisor . . ."

Maddie stopped, turned and stared at Poppy. "He said that? Why on earth would he mention that?"

Poppy was taken aback. Why would Maddie be so put out about it? "Well, why not? He was saying he was proud of Dante, just like he'd been proud of his father."

"Really?" Maddie sounded incredulous.

Oh dear; Poppy was getting herself into a muddle here. She looked for a way out of it. Eventually she decided to veer a little closer to the truth. "Well, I can't remember his exact words, but he did say he enjoyed Michael's painting style and was very sad that his talent was cut short."

Maddie nodded, but her usual amiable face looked troubled. "Yes, it was cut short. Did he tell you that I was pregnant with Dante at the time?"

"He did. And I'm very sorry. That must have been a terrible time for you."

Maddie let her dogs off the lead and sat down on a park bench. The dogs ran off – but not far – snuffling and romping in a pile of autumn leaves. Maddie patted the bench beside her. Poppy sat down.

"It was," said Maddie. "A terrible time. But thank you for your kindness in thinking of me. I must say, having Agnes in town and all of the hoo-hah around the exhibition has raked up a few memories."

Poppy wondered if Maddie had heard the rumours about Michael and Agnes' relationship, but wasn't quite sure how to raise it. However, to her surprise, Maddie brought it up herself. "It's not true, you know – what they said about Michael and Agnes. Michael would never have done such a thing. What happened to him was a dreadful accident, but one that could have been avoided if he'd cut back on the drink. Unfortunately, Poppy, my late husband enjoyed the sauce a bit too much. I was hoping – with the baby coming – that he would have reined himself in a bit. And he tried, I'll grant you that, but in the end he was just – well, he was just too weak. Michael was a drunk, Poppy, but he was *not* a pervert."

Poppy didn't quite know what to say. She watched the dogs chasing each other round in circles. Then, eventually, said: "It must have been difficult for you though, knowing about the old rumours, when your son became involved with Agnes Robson and the exhibition."

Maddie nodded. "Yes, it was, on one hand, but on the other, it finally assured me that Dante had laid his anger about it all to rest. He treated Agnes like any other artist. And of course, she is – was – internationally renowned. He would have been very silly to allow personal issues to get in the way of such a career-advancing relationship."

"His anger?" prompted Poppy.

"Oh yes. It was terrible for a time. All-consuming. But perhaps I need to go back a bit to explain . . . I married my second husband, you see, when Dante was around two. The dear man legally adopted the baby and gave him his surname. We never went out of our way to hide the fact that he was not Dante's real father, but we never thought there was a need to remind the boy of it either. Michael's parents were both dead so there was no family from his side to visit and muddy things.

"But when Dante was about twelve, he was playing in the loft and found boxes of Michael's old things. He questioned me about it and I told him they belonged to his other father, the one who died before he was born. Dante went mad. He flew into a rage, accusing me of deceiving him and lying to him all these years. Well, let's just say we had some very difficult years with him. But," she turned to Poppy and smiled gently, "then he went off to war. I know your brother died there Poppy, and I'm so sorry for your loss, but for our family it was different. He came back a changed boy – actually, he came back a man. Whatever rage he had about his father was gone. He then went on to study art and, as you know, got himself a very good job. We – his late stepfather and I – were very proud of him. And I still am."

The dogs were growing tired of their game and came and sat at Maddie's feet. Poppy stroked the one nearer to her. "Yes, that much is very clear. He's very lucky to have a mother who is so supportive of him. And a loving stepfather too."

"Isn't that what mothers are supposed to do?"

Poppy thought of her own mother and the tension between them over her life choices. *Is it simply because I'm not a boy?* But she soon shook off her self-pity and turned her attention back to Maddie. She wanted to ask about the painting of Agnes and whether or not she knew if Dante had seen it, but then she remembered that Professor Reid had said that the reason he had confiscated and hidden it in the first place was that he didn't want Michael's family to be distressed. Besides, it wasn't certain that it *was* Dante who had photographed the painting – although she was expecting the handwriting on the back to match Dante's, so it would be surprising if he hadn't taken the photograph too. She wondered if Yasmin had made any progress in getting writing samples . . . If it was his hand, then that meant he had written the threatening letter to her mother about the abortion Agnes was supposed to have had. How had he found out about that? And what on earth was her mother doing facilitating an abortion? She knew her mother to be strongly against such things. Had she had different views when she was a young woman?

The dogs suddenly tore off in a frenzy of excitement. "Susie! Charlie! Come here you naughty dogs!"

They were jumping up at a tree. "Squirrel," said Maddie, chuckling.

Poppy chuckled too. But on the inside she was churning. How would poor Maddie take it if it was revealed that her golden boy was in fact a murderer?

Chapter 21

This time when Poppy returned to Aunt Dot's house, the yellow Rolls was outside. She said goodbye to Maddie – who asked her to pass on her regards to Grace if she were there – and hurried up the path to the front door. She was greeted by Rollo holding the hands of the twins, who were waddling down the hall.

"Poppy! Howdy doody? How about you taking RJ and Cleo for a while? The nanny is helping cook lunch, Yazzie is sorting some paperwork for the case and Delilah claims she's allergic to children."

Poppy chuckled. She could just imagine Delilah saying that. She reached out her hand and took each of the twins. "No problem."

"Good oh!" said Rollo. "I'll give Ike a ring to find out what he's unearthed in London."

"Is Grace home?"

Rollo nodded, looking suddenly serious. "She is. She's having a lie down though, not surprisingly; a weekend in the slammer has taken it out of her. Dot is sitting with her. She's asked us to call them when lunch is ready."

"Is that Poppy?" A call from the dining room.

"Yes it's me, Yazzie. I'm just going to play with the babies for a while."

"Righteo! I won't be long. Just finishing something off here. See you shortly!"

Poppy walked slowly, leading the twins back up the hall and into the parlour as their father clambered onto a chair next to the telephone table and picked up the receiver. As she pushed open the parlour door with her foot, she heard Rollo requesting that the operator connect him to a London number.

Inside the parlour Poppy found a blanket laid out on the floor with a selection of baby toys: blocks, a doll, a metal fire engine and some paper and coloured wax crayons. Poppy sat down on the blanket and smiled at the twins who flopped down onto their bottoms, cushioned by their (fortunately dry) nappies.

"Well, you two little tinkers, what shall we do?"

RJ immediately reached for a crayon and shoved it in his mouth.

"Oh no you don't, young man."

Poppy prised it from his sticky fingers and pushed the rest of the crayons out of reach. The boy scrunched up his face, building up to an almighty scream. Not to be outdone, his sister too started to whimper, her lip trembling. Poppy acted quickly, grabbing the rag doll and making it dance around while she sang "What shall we do with a drunken sailor?", which on the spur of the moment, and with her limited musical talent, was all she could think of. But it did the trick. The children's emotional equilibrium was restored and soon they were attempting to place one block on top of another, as demonstrated by their babysitter.

Ten minutes later, the parlour door opened to reveal Yasmin, smiling down at them. Cleo threw up her arms and squealed. Yasmin laughed and picked her daughter up, swinging her around and up onto her hip. Then RJ demanded the same treatment. Poppy looked on, amazed at the ease at which the formidable barrister appeared to switch from professional to domestic – no doubt made easier by knowing she could call on the nanny when things got out of hand, thought Poppy.

Nonetheless, she was impressed. She wondered if she would be able to juggle her job and her children if that time ever came.

"So," said Yasmin, sitting down on the blanket and encouraging Cleo to push around the fire engine, while RJ remained on her lap, playing with her chunky bead necklace. "The bail hearing was fairly straightforward. Grace is out but can't leave town. No trial date has yet been set, as it was clear from the police's submission that the investigation is far from over."

"Oh?"

"Yes. The prosecution admitted that the evidence against Grace was at this stage just circumstantial and not – as yet – enough to bring before the courts."

"Oh good. And did they say that they were investigating other suspects?"

"Not in so many words, but they did say they were still following various lines of inquiry. That is sometimes shorthand for 'we might have someone else in our sights', but it also might just mean that they have more evidence to gather against Grace."

Poppy nodded, then winced, as Cleo rammed the metal toy engine into her knee.

"Otherwise, I've managed to get hold of a list of volunteers for the gallery and I've asked Dot to cross-check it with the guest list of the exhibition."

"Dot?"

"Yes, she said she wanted to help in the investigation by doing more than just holding Grace's hand. Your aunt may give the impression of being an airhead at times, but she's far from it, you know."

"Oh, you don't have to tell me that," said Poppy. "And Delilah's the same."

"Actresses!" said Yasmin, and they both laughed.

After a few moments of responding to the demands of the children, Poppy continued: "What about the writing sample from Dante Sherman?"

"I've requested one, but – and listen to this – I've been blocked from getting it without a court order."

"By whom?"

"Sherman's solicitor."

"Why would he need a solicitor for this? If he's innocent surely he should just hand over the sample to eliminate himself from inquiries."

"Exactly my thoughts, Poppy. But the solicitor said that the request implied that his client was under suspicion and that would sully his reputation. Complying with it, he said, would be encouraging a – and these were his exact words – libellous line of inquiry."

"Balderdash!"

Yasmin grinned. "I couldn't have put it better myself. In fact, I may just use that very word in my application for a court order." She winked at Poppy, then intercepted her daughter before she rammed the fire engine into the journalist's knee for a second time. By now RJ was beginning to grizzle and Yasmin put him down so he could crawl around too.

"I think we're on borrowed time here, Poppy. I'll ask Ivy to get them something to eat." She picked up her children – ignoring their protests – and carried them out. A few moments later she came back in. Poppy had used the time to tidy up a little and was now sitting on a settee. Yasmin, adjusting her beads, sat down beside her. "So, tell me what you found out this morning with the professor."

Poppy opened her eyes wide. "I thought you'd never ask. Now listen to this . . ."

When Poppy finished, Yasmin was nodding with satisfaction.

"Excellent work, Poppy. It's still very circumstantial – and no one yet has been found holding the smoking gun, or knife as the case may be – however, it does strongly suggest that Agnes' death is tied to what happened twenty-seven years ago. Surely it's far too much of a coincidence that the photograph – and the letter to your mother – were sent so soon before Agnes arrived in Newcastle. And seeing as Grace had absolutely nothing to do with the events in Ashington, and was not connected in any way to either Brownley or Agnes at the time, the case against her is weakening. But not entirely . . . we still need to do some more digging."

"And what do you think about what Professor Reid said about the paintings? That one of them might not be all Agnes' work? And that Sherman went ahead and bought it – and was prepared to exhibit it – despite knowing that its authenticity had been brought into question?"

"Do we know that he knew that?"

Poppy nodded. "I think there's a strong possibility that he did." She reminded Yasmin of the letter from the Tate she'd seen on Sherman's desk.

"But you didn't see what it said, did you? It could just as easily have said that they had investigated the painting and that it was authentic."

"They could have . . ." Poppy began.

"But they didn't." Rollo entered the room and joined them. "I've just spoken to Ike. He's been to the Tate and they are utterly shocked at Agnes' death. It'll make great copy." He grinned.

Poppy frowned at him. Yasmin raised her eyebrows in disapproval.

"Sorry ladies, but it will. Ike has done a stonking interview. And he also found out that the Tate – on Sherman's request – had convened an authentication committee and come to the conclusion that the background of the painting was indeed an Agnes Robson, but the figures were by a different hand."

"Did they say whose hand?" asked Yasmin.

"They said they don't know. And that's what they wrote to tell Sherman."

Poppy tapped her index finger against her lips. "So Sherman *did* know that it was fake. Why did he go through with the purchase, and beyond that, exhibit it as one of Robson's originals?"

"To show Agnes he meant business. That's what the boy said yesterday, wasn't it? That's what he overheard," said Rollo.

"That's right," said Poppy. "I know fingers seem to be pointing at Sherman here due to his strange behaviour – and the fact that he's Michael Brownley's son –"

Rollo raised his eyebrow at this, as it was the first time he'd heard it. "Really?"

"Really," continued Poppy, and she went on to tell Rollo about what Professor Reid had told her as well as her conversation with Maddie Sherman.

"However," she concluded, "that all said, I don't think Gus and Gerald are entirely off the hook. They seem to know more than they're telling."

"I quite agree," said Yasmin, "so I will set up an interview with them."

"That's assuming Gus hasn't done a runner," said Rollo.

Yasmin nodded. "Yes, I'm afraid if he doesn't turn up to the interview I will have to inform the police."

Poppy very much hoped that would not be the case.

"Oh," said Rollo. "Your mother rang when you were all out. She said she hadn't been able to organise a meeting for this afternoon, but had done for tomorrow morning. She said she will meet you off the train in Ashington at ten o'clock. Is that doable?"

"Yes, it should be. Yasmin?"

"Fine by me."

Just then there was a knock on the door and young Betty stuck her head around. "Dinner's ready, Master and Missus."

"Dinner?" asked Rollo. "Have we been talking that long?" Betty looked confused.

"She means lunch," explained Poppy. "Dinner is what we call it up here. Don't worry, Betty; we'll be there in a moment. And thank you. I'll go tell Mrs Wilson and Miss Denby."

Poppy got up and headed towards the stairs. But as she did, the doorbell rang. She waited a moment, her foot poised on the bottom step, but no one rushed to the door. She sighed, turned and walked down the hall. She opened it, and to her surprise came face to face with Detective Inspector Sandy Hawkes.

Pauline's Kitchen on Heaton Road was busy serving its Monday Dinner Special when Sandy and Poppy arrived and requested a table. The establishment – adorned with brass kettles and frying pans – was hosted by a jolly woman with a Northern Irish accent. She recommended the corned beef hotpot which both Sandy and Poppy agreed to. She placed them at a table near the window, repositioning the vase housing a fresh rose, and raising a knowing eyebrow at Poppy.

Golly, thought Poppy, *can't a lady and gentleman have lunch without people imposing all sorts of romantic motives upon them?* Although, she had to admit to herself, when she opened the door to find Sandy, her first thought was: *is this a personal or professional visit?* And she still wasn't clear. He had asked if he could speak to her privately. She had pulled the door closed behind her, not wanting Grace to hear his voice, and told him: "Now isn't a good time. Grace has just got home and we're all about to have dinner." But he'd persisted, suggesting that he could take her out for a bite to eat instead. She had agreed, rushing back into the house to retrieve her hat and coat, and whispering a quick explanation to Yasmin. The barrister gave a curious smile and said: "I hope you get something useful out of the meeting, Poppy."

And now here she was, waiting for the hotpot to arrive while sipping on a glass of homemade lemonade.

"So," said Sandy. "Thank you for coming here with me, Poppy. May I still call you Poppy?"

"You may."

The inspector smiled nervously. Poppy had never seen him looking so unsure.

"Good. Thank you. Well, as I said to Mrs Rolandson the other day, I would like to apologise for what happened at the theatre. I should not have said the things I said and you were right to be upset with me. However, I can assure you," he cast a glance around the room, as if making sure no one was listening in, "I did not try to use you to get information about Mrs Wilson. My motivation for . . . well, for wanting to spend time with you . . . was personal, in the first instance, but, inevitably, I suppose, it became muddied when we were both thrust into this unpleasant business. And that's the truth."

He looked at her, his eyes almost beseeching. She didn't quite know what to say.

When a reply was not immediately forthcoming, he filled the gap. "Because, as you know, we met before any of this happened. And I was – if it does not embarrass you too much for me to say so – delighted when I first saw you. I found you – and still do find you – utterly charming. Even if you are not the best tennis player I have ever encountered." He looked, suddenly, like a little boy.

She laughed. She really couldn't help herself. "Well, I admit, Suzanne Lenglen I am not."

"Oh no; you're far more attractive than Miss Lenglen!" he blurted, then grinned.

Poppy felt herself blush. "Well, thank you. Although Mademoiselle Lenglen is a very interesting woman. Very talented. I've met her, you know?"

"Have you really?"

"I have." Poppy then went on to tell Sandy about the time she interviewed the famous tennis player who smoked and sipped brandy between sets, as well as some of the other famous sports and cultural icons she'd had the pleasure of meeting in her line of work.

"So is that where you first met Agnes Robson? In London?"

"Yes, I covered her exhibition at the Tate. Although Rollo – my editor – and his wife, Yasmin – whom you've met – are personal friends of Agnes. Were personal friends." The conversation lost its sheen of frivolity as she corrected herself.

Sandy nodded. "Yes, Mrs Rolandson mentioned that. Look Poppy, I don't want there to be any misunderstanding between us – now that we've just cleared the air – but, may I be frank?"

Poppy nodded.

"Well, the fact is, whether we like it or not, we are both involved in a murder inquiry. And my professional duty is to always put that first. But on the other hand, I don't want you to think I'm priming you for information. However, if there is anything you can tell me that could help me catch the killer, I'd be greatly obliged if you did so."

"I thought you thought you'd already arrested the killer. Isn't that why Grace just spent the weekend in custody?"

Sandy arranged his features into a serious but non-threatening visage and Poppy couldn't quite shirk the idea that he was still trying to "manage" her.

"You need to understand, Poppy, that I would have been professionally remiss if I had not arrested Mrs Wilson on the evidence at hand. But that doesn't mean that I think she is definitely the culprit – that's not for me to decide; it's for the Director of Public Prosecutions and then the courts – but there was enough evidence for a warrant to be issued and a charge to be laid. However, if you have evidence that exonerates her, or implicates someone else, you should tell me. I believe you have quite a lot of experience in – how should I put it? – helping the police in their inquiries."

He cocked his head to one side and smiled.

She smiled too. "You wanted to say, 'sticking my nose into police business', didn't you?"

He shrugged charmingly. "Well, I'm too much of a gentleman to say so, aren't I?"

Poppy pursed her lips and said: "Hmmmm." Then she sat back to allow Pauline to place two bowls of hotpot and a plate of Irish soda bread on the table.

After the hostess withdrew, Sandy asked: "Shall I say grace?"

Poppy was surprised, but pleased. Her former beau, Daniel, had lost his faith, and she had always just quietly given thanks herself when they ate together. But now she nodded and bowed her head as the inspector prayed a brief prayer for them both.

Prayers said, they both tucked into the food, spearing chunks of potato, leek, carrot and corned beef. After a few minutes, Poppy asked: "How did you know that I have investigated murders before?"

Sandy grinned. "Your reputation precedes you, Miss Denby!"

"You read about it in the press?"

"No, but the press – as in Peter MacMahon – told me about it. And then I contacted Detective Chief Inspector Jasper Martin at the Met in London."

"You were checking up on me?"

Sandy put down his fork and looked honestly and openly at Poppy. "To be frank, yes. After I heard you had been doing some investigating at the gallery the other day, I sent him a telegram requesting a telephone call. We spoke – at length – about you and your editor Mr Rolandson."

Poppy grimaced. "Well, I can assure you that DCI Martin's view of me is quite coloured."

Sandy nodded. "It is – coloured with respect."

"I beg your pardon?"

"Oh yes. Martin had a lot to say about you, Miss Denby, and actually credited you with helping him in a number of investigations. He doesn't have much time for Rolandson – I shan't repeat what he said about him – but he did say, and I quote, 'You can trust that Denby girl, Hawkes. She has a nose for finding the truth.'"

Poppy was flabbergasted. Never in a million years would she have thought that the crusty chief inspector whom she had come into conflict with so many times would have had a good word to say about her. And that, it was now clear, was why Sandy Hawkes could consider her an ally rather than an adversary.

However, there was still a small voice at the back of her head telling her to be wary. So she went ahead and told Sandy what she had found out so far. But she didn't tell him everything. She didn't mention the letter her mother had received – the accusation of an abortion or her mother's involvement in it. She wanted to hear all about that herself, before she decided how much – if anything – to share with the police.

Chapter 22

Tuesday, 8 October 1924

Ashington Colliery, Northumberland

Yasmin and Poppy readied themselves to get off the train at Ashington Station. Poppy wore her plainest skirt and jacket, pleased to see that Yasmin, without being asked, had also played down her usual glamorous looks. Delilah had offered to drive them through in the Rolls but Poppy and Yasmin had declined, sharing an understanding that three well-heeled women swanning into the mining village in a swanky car would not endear them with the locals.

Alice Denby met them at the station and politely shook hands with the barrister, her neutral expression showing neither disdain nor approval for this paragon of women's advancement. She asked after Grace and was told that the bookkeeper was showing signs of melancholia.

"I'm sorry to hear that. I shall continue to remember her in my prayers."

"I think the best thing we can do for her, Mrs Denby, is get to the truth of what really happened to Agnes," said Yasmin as she and Poppy followed Alice out of the station. A few moments later they were crossing the railway bridge into the village. Poppy stopped and looked down the track. She reached into her satchel and took out the photograph of the painting she had received from Peter MacMahon, comparing the two views.

"That's definitely here, isn't it?" Poppy went on to tell her mother what they had found out about two different artists and the later "addition".

"Do you recognise the woman and child, Mother?"

"No. Should I?"

"I don't suppose so. I'm just speculating, that's all. I wonder if they are real people, who really lived and walked down this very track, or if they are the figment of the second artist's imagination. In other words, is this a memory of something that actually happened, or just a whimsy?"

"Or perhaps wishful thinking, of something that might have been . . ." mused Alice.

"What do you mean, Mrs Denby?"

"You will understand once we've spoken to Agnes' mother, Mrs Rolandson."

The women continued over the bridge and passed the Storey Sweet Shop. "Does that belong to the family of the young girl who won the art competition?" asked Poppy.

"It does, yes. Young Edna's grandfather started the shop. Her mother – I think you met her at the exhibition – now runs it. Her husband died during the war."

"Yes, she was there with Edna. She was at the opening of the community hall too. She seemed very – what's the word – judgmental of Agnes."

Alice nodded. "She is. So are most of the people who live here who knew Agnes back then. It's been tough for her mother all these years. Agnes left, but her mother had to deal with it. All the gossip and innuendo."

"What kind of gossip, Mrs Denby?"

Alice turned to Yasmin, her lips pursed. "Well, Mrs Rolandson, I don't normally repeat such things – it is not a Christian way to behave – but under the circumstances I think I could tell you."

Yasmin nodded. "I'd be grateful if you would. Under the circumstances, you might be helping us find a murderer. And I should imagine God would very much approve of that."

Poppy flinched. Despite her best efforts, Yasmin – who like her husband was not religious – had not quite managed to remove the barb from her voice.

But Poppy's mother had heard far worse in her life and chose to let it go. "Well, I'm not sure how much Agnes told Poppy about it, but the gist of it is this: Agnes and a group of children from Ashington and Hirst attended art lessons over the summer of 1897. I remember it was 1897, because I was pregnant with Poppy. The lecturer – Michael Brownley – came from the art school in Newcastle. Agnes' mam became worried that Brownley might have been 'trying his luck' with Agnes and banned her from going. But also because the art class was on the day that Agnes was supposed to work at the laundry. It brought in extra money for the family. But it turned out Agnes snuck away and attended the classes anyway."

"Why did Agnes' mother believe Brownley was 'trying his luck'?"

"She'd heard rumours. Some of the other children had told their parents that Agnes was his 'favourite' and sometimes used to stay behind to clear up after they'd left."

"Did they say any other children might have been involved or attracted his attention?" asked Poppy.

"I don't think so," said Alice.

"Well, that is interesting," said Poppy, and she went on to tell her mother what Professor Reid had told her the previous day about the nude paintings of various children.

Alice stopped. By now they were outside the Methodist chapel opposite Pit Row. All blood appeared to drain from her face. "And the professor never told anyone?"

"No. He wanted to protect Brownley's reputation. For the sake of his family and of the art school."

Alice shook her head from side to side. "I never knew. I never knew."

"Do you think the parents of the children might have found out?" asked Yasmin.

"I don't know. I suppose it's possible. But what's more likely is that the children cast all the blame onto Agnes in order to deflect attention away from themselves. It's classic scapegoating. Unfortunately, in my line of work, Mrs Rolandson, I see that sort of covering up of sin all too often."

"And in mine, Mrs Denby. So you think it's possible the rest of the children conspired – or made some kind of pact – to tar Agnes?"

Alice nodded as she gestured for Poppy and Yasmin to cross the road with her. "Yes, I do, particularly when it got out that Agnes might have been pregnant."

"So you admit she was pregnant then? The threatening letter was right about that?" asked Yasmin.

"It was," said Alice, her tone giving nothing more away.

"Was the pregnancy discovered before or after Brownley died?" asked Yasmin.

"Afterwards, I think. And the village only started speculating about it after Agnes left."

"Speculating that she was pregnant or that she had killed Brownley?" asked Poppy.

Her mother looked at her daughter curiously. "Did Agnes tell you they blamed her for his death?"

"Yes, she did. But she didn't tell me she was pregnant. She did tell me about two pregnancies – and miscarriages – she'd had in Paris. But not the first one."

Alice's shoulders sagged. "Oh no. I didn't know she'd become pregnant again. How very, very sad. Those poor babies. And poor Agnes."

"So," said Yasmin, getting the conversation back on track as they passed a rag and bone man and his cart. "How did you know she was pregnant the first time? Did the family tell you?"

"No, Agnes did. She came to me for help. She didn't want her mam and dad to know. But I said we had to tell them. Her father went mad. They were going to throw her out the house. So I took her in."

"I didn't know that!" said Poppy.

"You weren't born yet, pet. And it was only supposed to be until I was able to get her a position in service down in Durham through friends in the Methodist circuit there."

"She went into service when she was pregnant?" asked Yasmin. "Or was that after you arranged the abortion for her?"

Alice stopped. She pulled back her shoulders and looked up at the glamorous barrister who was half a foot taller than her. "I can assure you, Mrs Rolandson, I would *never* have done any such thing. Abortion is murder."

"But the letter . . ." started Yasmin.

"That has nothing to do with me. However, I'm afraid I cannot tell you any more without Sadie Robson's permission." Alice turned and pushed open a low gate leading to a pit cottage. "So I think you'd better ask her yourself."

Sadie Robson was not used to having such posh visitors. After the grandchildren had all left for school, and her daughter-in-law had gone down to the Kicking Cuddy to do her cleaning job, Sadie had scrubbed the kitchen table, swept the range and put a flagon of bleach down the outside netty, just in case any of the ladies needed to use the "facilities". She had asked her son, Jeremy, to get down the best china from the box at the top of her wardrobe. It had only ever been used at weddings, christenings and funerals – the last being the sending off of her Arthur, killed in the pit disaster of 1916. She hadn't even brought it out for Agnes when she came for tea the other day after the opening of the community centre. Oh, but she wished she had; dear God, she wished she had.

And she wished she'd never let her Arthur send the lass away when she was pregnant. And she wished she'd given a different answer when she got a letter from Agnes asking to come home from that big house in Durham. And she wished she had begged and borrowed and even stole to go all the way to France to bring her bairn back from that lecher. But more than anything, she wished she'd never let her out of her sight at the gallery the other night. If she hadn't, mebbe Agnes wouldn't be dead. And she wouldn't have to be using the best china today.

She filled the teapot with boiling water from the brass kettle on the range, stuck a tea cosy on it and carried it over to the table where the three ladies were sitting. Mrs Denby she knew. She was a good woman, if a bit overeager in the Bible-bashing department. But Sadie would always be grateful for the help she'd given when they found out Agnes was pregnant. And her daughter, Miss Denby, she'd met at the gallery. She seemed like a canny lass. Looked a lot like her father. But the other woman – the foreign-looking one – made Sadie more nervous than she should have been. Even though her clothes were plain, you could tell they were expensive. The woman reeked of wealth and class. She spoke kindly enough, but Sadie still worried that she was being looked down on. Her in her best day frock and cleanest pinny.

"So," said Yasmin, once condolences and pleasantries had been exchanged, "you know why we are here, today, Mrs Robson."

"Aye. Mrs Denby here says you're trying to help find out who killed our Agnes. That you don't believe the woman the police have got is the real killer."

"That's right. We don't believe there is sufficient evidence against Mrs Wilson and we do believe that there are other suspects the police should be looking at too. And one of them is the person who wrote this letter and sent it to Mrs Denby. Do you recognise the handwriting?"

Yasmin spread the letter out flat on the kitchen table between the cups and saucers.

Sadie picked it up and read the letter, her hand going to her throat. "Eeeee, the lying bastard!"

"Who is lying? Do you know who this is?" asked Poppy.

Sadie shook her head. "I don't. No. But I know whoever it is is lying. Our Agnes never had an abortion. Never. Did she, Mrs Denby?"

Alice took the letter from Sadie's shaking hands, then held them in her own. "No, she didn't. But as I promised you all those years ago, I have never said a word about what happened. But I think the truth needs to come out now, Sadie. Will you give me permission to tell my daughter and Mrs Rolandson what actually happened?"

Sadie let out a long sigh. "Aye. All right. If it'll help catch our Agnes' killer, all right. Say what needs to be said."

Alice let go of Sadie's hands and turned to Yasmin and Poppy. "Agnes never had an abortion. I already told you I would never be involved in something like that, and that's the truth. But she was pregnant. As I said, I took her in, but I led you to believe that she went straight from our house to service in Durham. That was not the case. She spent the last five months of her pregnancy at a home for unwed mothers in Newcastle, called St Hilda's. We – her mother and I – felt it was best she moved out of the area before she started showing. Because, as you've already discovered, the folk around here weren't the kindest to her. Particularly after Brownley's death."

"What happened with that?" asked Yasmin. "Why did the people here believe Agnes killed him?"

Alice looked at Sadie. Sadie nodded.

"Because the night he died, Agnes went missing. Mrs Robson told me that she had beaten Agnes when she discovered she'd disobeyed her and gone back to the art classes when she'd been forbidden to."

Poppy cast a quick glance at Sadie, whose lip quivered slightly as Alice told the tale. Poppy's mother continued.

"You see, she'd lied to her mother – again. She'd said she had been working at the laundry when she hadn't. So Mrs Robson gave her a good hiding and sent her to bed without her supper."

"Aye, I did," said Sadie softly. Then nodded for Alice to continue.

"Well, it seems she snuck out. And she didn't come back until after the police found Brownley's body down the shaft. So the rumour got started that Agnes had gone to meet Brownley at the pit – after he'd left the pub, drunk – and she'd pushed him down the shaft."

"Why would she have done that?" asked Yasmin.

"She didn't! My bairn would never do such a thing!" said Sadie, her eyes flashing at the foreign woman.

Yasmin smiled tightly. "No parent likes to think that, Mrs Robson, but may I ask what evidence you have that she didn't?"

"I don't need no evidence, Mrs Rolandson. I know me own daughter and I know she'd never do that!"

Yasmin's tight smile didn't waver. "All right, we'll leave that for now then. But would you mind finishing the story of Agnes' pregnancy? Mrs Denby said she went to a home for unwed mothers in Newcastle."

"Aye, she did. And she had the baby. It was a little lad."

"And what happened to him – the baby?"

Sadie lowered her head. "The nuns took him away. To be adopted. I never had a chance to see him."

"I see. That must have been hard for you. And Agnes," said Yasmin.

"Aye, it was. But it was for the best – for the lad and for Agnes. She was too young to have a bairn of her own."

"Did Agnes feel the same way?" asked Poppy. "Did she want to give the baby up?"

"No Poppy, she didn't," said Alice. "But as Mrs Robson says, it was for the best. She wasn't married."

"Did you consider bringing the baby back here and raising it?" asked Yasmin.

Sadie flashed another angry look at the well-to-do barrister. "No, miss, I did not. I had four young'uns of me own to raise – and another bairn on the way. And as you can see, there isn't room to swing a cat in this house."

Yasmin lowered her eyes. Without being told, Poppy knew Yasmin expected her to take over the questioning.

"I understand, Mrs Robson," Poppy said gently. "So the baby was put up for adoption. Do you know where it went?"

"I don't, no."

"And you, Mother?"

Alice folded and unfolded her hands, a gesture Poppy knew her mother did when she was nervous. Eventually she answered: "No. But one of the nuns at the home for unwed mothers – unfortunately Agnes was not the first young girl I knew to have need of their services – told me she'd heard the little lad had died young. Measles, I think. Which is very, very sad. I just hope he had a happy home until then." She looked at Sadie, one mother to another. "I'm sorry to have to tell you like this. It was a few years after Agnes left for Paris that I heard and I didn't think it would be worth scraping open an old wound."

Sadie nodded her understanding, but her lower lip quivered.

Poppy picked up the letter and read it again. "So this isn't true then."

"Well, it *is* true that I helped Agnes. But not that there was an abortion. So whoever wrote this letter threatening me did not know the full story. He – or she – did know, however, that I was involved in some way. And as I said before – and this is the reason I showed it to you, Poppy – it does seem telling that this arrived the week before Agnes was due to arrive in Newcastle for the exhibition. And then, of course, after what happened there, I thought it might somehow be evidence of something."

Yasmin drained her teacup and put it down with a clink. "You did the right thing, Mrs Denby. I do think it's evidence, although I'm not sure yet of what. We are currently following some leads about who might have written it – we have put in a request for a writing sample from someone –"

"Who?"

"I'm afraid I can't say. If the sample doesn't match, we don't want to be blamed for sullying the name of an innocent man. I hope you understand that."

"But it's definitely a man?" asked Sadie Robson.

"Not definitely, no. But we suspect that it is. We'll know for certain soon. Now, is there anything else you want to tell us about your daughter, Mrs Robson? Anything about what happened in '97? Or since?"

Sadie picked at the tablecloth with her fingernail. "No," she said finally. "There's nothing else."

Chapter 23

"I don't believe her," said Yasmin, as they left the pit cottage and waved goodbye to the woman in her best day frock and pinny. "I think there is something else she's not telling us."

"I'm afraid, Mrs Rolandson, I agree with you," Alice admitted. "I shall drop by again tomorrow. Perhaps without you here, she might be more willing to talk."

"Thank you Mrs Denby; that would be most appreciated. Meanwhile, your daughter and I have a lot to do back in Newcastle. The information about the baby is very useful. Very useful indeed. Poppy, do you think you can look into that when we get back?"

"I can, yes. But before we go, do you mind if we stop in at the sweet shop, please?"

Yasmin chuckled. "Are you feeling peckish?"

"No, but there's something I want to ask Edna's mam."

Poppy pushed open the door of the shop and set off the bell. She remembered this shop from when she was young and her parents visited Ashington on the train. She and Christopher would be allowed a penny-bag of sweets – if they'd been good – to eat on the train back to Morpeth. Back then the shop had been more of a general goods store which sold sweets; now, twenty years later, the pots and pans and balls of string were gone, and the sweets and confectionery expanded. But there, on the shelves behind the counter, were the same jars of fizz balls and bonbons, as well as Poppy's personal favourite: mint humbugs.

They were greeted by a smiling woman in a red and white striped apron and mop cap, whose smile faded when she recognised who her customers were.

"Hello, Mrs Storey."

"Miss Denby. Mrs Denby," said Mrs Storey flatly.

"And this is Mrs Rolandson. I don't think you've met."

"We haven't. Good day to you, Mrs Storey."

Mrs Storey pursed her lips and looked to the door. "What can I do for you ladies? It's nearly dinnertime and the shop'll be busy soon."

"We won't keep you long. We've just been to Mrs Robson's house to offer our condolences," said Poppy.

"Aye, it's a terrible thing that happened. Our Edna's having nightmares."

"I'm sure she is," answered Poppy. "It was a horrible thing to see. And a child should never have to be subjected to it. But if you don't mind, I have a few questions for you. You see, they haven't yet caught Agnes' killer –"

"I thought they'd got that Wilson woman. That's what it said in the paper."

"She's been released on bail and the police admit that the case against her isn't watertight. They are looking at other suspects."

"Oh aye, who might that be?"

"I'm afraid I can't say. But I'm sure we'll all find out in a few days. For now, we – Mrs Rolandson and I – are talking to as many people as possible who might have seen something at the exhibition. Mrs Rolandson here is a barrister."

Mrs Storey looked at Yasmin as if Poppy had just announced that she was a two-headed horse, then crossed her arms across her chest. "I've already told the police what I'd seen and didn't see."

Poppy smiled, but not too widely. Mrs Storey seemed like the type of woman who would be suspicious of pleasantries. "I'm sure you have. We've all been interviewed. But, in mine and Mrs Rolandson's line of work, we've noticed that people often remember things *after* they've been interviewed. Or perhaps don't even realise the significance of something that has happened or that they've seen."

"Oh aye? Like what?"

"Well, for instance, I noticed you talking to Mr Dante Sherman at the gallery on Thursday night – the man in charge of putting the exhibition on."

"There's no law about talking to someone, is there?"

"Of course not. But I couldn't help noticing that you and he seemed already familiar with one another. And I was wondering where you had met him before?"

Yasmin shot Poppy a quick glance, her eyes approving.

"Well, what if I have? Nowt wrong with that, is there?"

"Well no, obviously not. I was just wondering where it was you had met him."

Mrs Storey's eyes narrowed and she looked up at the clock on the wall. "Why do you want to know?"

"Because," said Yasmin, stepping forward, "we need to eliminate people from our inquiries. We don't want innocent people to be arrested now, do we? Innocent people such as yourself, who may know something that could help the case but might be understood – wrongly I'm sure – to be hiding evidence."

Mrs Storey's eyes opened wide. "I ain't done nothing wrong."

"We're sure you haven't," chipped in Poppy soothingly. "And if you tell us what you know, we can ensure that the police know that too."

Mrs Storey's lips pursed, then relaxed. "All right. But there's nowt in it. He came into the shop about a month ago. He was asking questions."

"About what?" asked Yasmin.

"Old history. He wanted to know if I was one of the bairns that Brownley fella taught." She looked at Alice Denby pointedly. "You know the one."

"And were you?" asked Poppy.

Mrs Storey's eyes flicked to the door and back. No one was coming in. "I was. I was one of the younger students. I was about eight or nine. I don't remember much."

Poppy wondered if she should ask whether or not Mrs Storey had posed naked, but she decided against it. She didn't want the woman to clam up in shame. "I see," she said instead. "And what else did he ask?"

Mrs Storey shrugged. "Oh, this and that. He wanted to know if I remembered what had happened the day and the night when Brownley died. I told him I didn't remember much personally, but told him what people had said had happened. They talked about it for years after, they did."

"And what did they talk about?" asked Poppy.

Mrs Storey lowered her eyes. "I can't remember now."

"Come on, woman," said Yasmin, as if she were addressing a witness at the Old Bailey, "we already know there'd been talk about Agnes pushing Brownley down the shaft and that she was pregnant and had an abortion. Was that what you told Sherman?"

"What if it was?" asked the shopkeeper, her eyes defiant. "It's no crime to pass on a bit of gossip, is there?"

Yasmin took a short, controlled breath, then released it. "Unfortunately not."

Just then, the doorbell rang, and two customers walked in.

Mrs Storey smirked. "Well, that's all the time I've got for you. So unless there's anything else, I'll ask you to leave."

Yasmin and Poppy turned to walk away, but Alice Denby stood her ground.

"Mother," said Poppy quietly, "we should probably go."

"I'll be out in a minute, Poppy. You go without me." Poppy and Yasmin looked at one another. Yasmin shrugged.

"All right, Mam."

A few minutes later – during which Yasmin and Poppy assessed the information they'd just received about Sherman – Alice emerged from the shop and handed something to her daughter. It was a penny-bag of mint humbugs.

"You did a grand job in there, pet. I'm proud of you."

Poppy bit back her tears.

Chapter 24

Poppy and Delilah pulled up outside the large Victorian building on Salters Lane, Gosforth, brooding behind a line of fir trees. Gosforth, one of the more well-to-do parts of Newcastle, was a surprising location for a home for poor and despairing women. It was run by the Anglican Diocese of Newcastle, taken over from the Ladies' Association for the Care of Friendless Girls. According to Poppy's mother, this is where Agnes had spent much of her pregnancy as well as a few months post-natally before she got a job as a domestic servant in Durham.

"Golly," said Delilah, "so this is where they lock the bad girls up."

Poppy frowned at her. She knew her friend was being deliberately facetious, but she also knew that if Delilah herself hadn't been born into money and had the support of a loving family, as well as having more than a bit of contraceptive know-how, her Bohemian ways might quite easily have landed her in a place like this.

"Firstly, I don't think they 'lock 'em up'. This is a place to help girls who are in trouble, not to punish them. And secondly, how do you know they are 'bad girls'? Agnes, for instance, was taken advantage of by her art teacher. You don't know the stories behind these girls and how they ended up in here, do you?"

Delilah raised her eyebrows in surprise. "Steady on, old girl; I was just joking. You know me. Why are you taking it so seriously?"

Poppy sighed. "I'm sorry. Yes, I know you were just joking. But what you were saying is pretty much what lots of people think. And it just makes me sad, that's all: all judgment, no compassion. And no sense of 'there but for the grace of God go I'. Sorry I snapped at you, old bean."

Delilah smiled her forgiveness.

A few minutes later the doorbell was answered by a young woman wearing a grey dress and a navy blue pinafore. She asked the ladies' business and then asked them to wait while she went to call Sister Henrietta. Poppy had heard stories that some of these homes, schools and training facilities were horrible places to live where the women were subject to abuse and forced labour. Her mother had assured her that St Hilda's was not one of those places. Poppy hoped she was right – both for the girls who lived here now and those who had lived here twenty-seven years ago. It didn't take long for a tiny, elderly woman, not much taller than Rollo and as slight as a ten-year-old child, to greet them at the door. She wore a dark grey skirt and light grey blouse, with an unbuttoned black cardigan and a large cross on a chain. Her wispy grey hair was uncovered but pulled back from a round, wrinkly face, creased on the cusp of laughter.

"Good afternoon ladies. May I help you?"

Poppy explained who they were and asked if she was speaking to Sister Henrietta.

"You are indeed. And how lovely to see you all grown up, Poppy Denby. You probably don't remember but your mother brought you and your brother to see me once when you were very little."

Poppy smiled, curiously. "I'm afraid I don't, Sister."

"I'm not surprised; you were just a tiddler at the time." She smiled, her lips widening like a drawstringed bag, to reveal a sparsely toothed mouth.

"Well, Miss Denby, what can I do for you?"

"I was wondering if I could talk to you about Agnes Robson. I'm sure you've heard by now about her tragic death."

A cloud fell over the old nun's face. "Yes, I have. I read about it in the *Journal*." She shook her head. "What a waste. What a terrible waste."

"It is. A tragedy and a waste. So we're trying to get to the bottom of it. I'm working with a barrister involved in the case. My mother told us what happened to Agnes twenty-seven years ago and that she came to live with you here. Do you remember that?"

"I do. Please, come in ladies. I think we need some tea."

* * *

Poppy stared in astonishment as Sister Henrietta served them all tea. On the wall behind the nun's desk was a painting of a vase of lilies, almost identical to the one on display at the Laing Art Gallery. "May I ask where you got that painting?" asked Poppy.

Sister Henrietta put down the teapot and turned to look at the painting. She sighed. "Agnes gave it to me. She came to visit back in 1916 when she was up this way for her father's funeral. I was hoping she would come visit again when I heard she was here for the exhibition. I was planning on going to that, you know."

Poppy reached into her satchel, took out the photograph of the painting in the Laing and passed it to Sister Henrietta. "Did you know that there is an almost identical picture in the Laing? One that has only recently been painted?"

Sister Henrietta took the black and white photo and looked from it to the coloured original on the wall. "Yes, I see the vase is the same. But that doesn't surprise me. Excuse me a moment..." She left the office and came back a few moments later with a blue glazed vase. It was identical to the one in both the painting and the photograph.

"Well I'll be!" exclaimed Delilah.

"I've had this vase for many years. Agnes told me that she remembers it – and the lilies that I keep in it in summer – from when she lived here. She said that she returns to that image time and again in her paintings. She said it reminded her of the kindness which she received here. And so she gave us this painting as a way of saying thank you. I think it's beautiful."

"And worth a lot of money now that she's dead?"

Poppy gave Delilah a warning stare.

"I have no idea how much it's worth, Miss Marconi. For me it has sentimental value. And now that Agnes has gone, even more so."

Delilah had the decency to look repentant. "Of course. I'm sorry, sister. I should think before I speak."

Sister Henrietta smiled. "As should we all, Miss Marconi."

She then went on to give Delilah a mini-sermon on what the Bible had to say about the wisdom of taming the tongue. Poppy was amused at Delilah's obvious embarrassment and allowed the sermon to continue as she considered the new information she had received.

It explained why Agnes had painted the painting, but, she wondered, why had Gus and Gerald not told her and Rollo that it was something Agnes did? She also wondered if there was some significance in that *this* painting, along with the one of the railway line, were the ones that Dante Sherman insisted Gus and Gerald bring up with them. That, as she now knew, they (possibly) referenced the same period in Agnes' life surely had to have some pertinence to the case. Without a doubt she would be telling Yasmin *and* DI Hawkes about it. Although she still did not know what the mother and child meant. What was it her mother had said? *Perhaps it was a wish of something that could have been . . .* But if Agnes herself had not painted it, who might have wished what could have been? Or – and Poppy suppressed a shudder at the thought of it – perhaps it was painted by someone taunting Agnes about what could have been – her baby alive and growing up. But why were they leaving . . . ?

"It's actually very curious," Sister Henrietta said, now finished with her moral lecture and addressing Poppy again, "but you are the second person to ask about this painting in the last few months."

"Really?"

"Yes. A gentleman from the gallery was here – oh, sometime in August. He was asking about Agnes' association with us. He said it was in order to write some biographical notes for the exhibition programme. I told him that her time here was confidential and if he had anything to ask he should ask her."

"Good for you. Agnes was very private about her life. The only reason I am asking today is that we are trying to find out what happened to her, to bring her killer to justice. My mother wouldn't have said anything, otherwise."

Sister Henrietta nodded and offered the two younger women a plate of jammy dodgers. Both Poppy and Delilah took one and had a little nibble.

"So," continued Poppy, "you said the man from the gallery was asking about the painting too?"

"Yes, he recognised it as an Agnes Robson. I told him what I'd told you – that she gave it to us as a gift in 1916. The fact that she spent time here I don't think is a secret. He seemed to know that already. Anyway, he offered to buy the painting from me." She looked at Delilah and winked. "But not for a huge amount of money, Miss Marconi. Nonetheless, I declined to sell it. He then upped the price to something that might actually have been useful." She raised her eyes to the ceiling. "We need our roof repaired. But still, I didn't think I could actually sell a gift. So he left empty-handed."

Not totally empty-handed, thought Poppy. *He now knew about the painting . . .*

"Can you remember the name of this man?" asked Poppy.

"I'm afraid I can't. But he was young, late twenties perhaps. He said he was curating Agnes' exhibition."

"His name is Dante Sherman." Poppy decided not to add the further information that he was the son of Michael Brownley, who was also the father of Agnes' baby. She was here to get information, not to give it. "So," she said, finally bringing the conversation around to the point of their visit. "My mother – and Agnes' mother – told me she came to live here when she was pregnant. Then after the baby was born you got her a place as a domestic servant in Durham."

"That's correct. Agnes was a very clever girl and could have done much better for herself, given half the chance, but at least a position in service was a start. It was the best we could do for her."

Poppy nodded at the painting. "I'm sure it was. And by the sound of it, Agnes was grateful. However, what we really need to know is about the baby. My mother said you arranged for an adoption."

Sister Henrietta put down her teacup and clasped both hands together. "We did."

"And are you able to tell us who the adoptive parents were?"

"Why do you need to know that?"

Poppy pursed her lips. "I don't really know, to be honest, but I just have an instinct about these things sometimes. And something tells me that it might help us find out what happened to Agnes."

Sister Henrietta nodded, then closed her eyes. After about a minute, Delilah looked across at Poppy and mouthed, "Has she fallen asleep?"

Poppy shook her heads and gestured with her hands: *praying.*

A moment later, the nun opened her eyes and said: "Yes, I think the Lord wants me to tell you. It's not just instinct, you know, Poppy; don't forget to give God the glory."

Poppy nodded. "I won't. Thank you. So, can you tell us who the parents were?"

Sister Henrietta got up and went to a wooden cabinet in the corner of the room. She pulled open a drawer and riffled through some leather-bound books. Eventually she pulled one out and returned to her desk. She paged through it until she found the entry she was looking for. "Here. Mr and Mrs Matthew Northanger, Lindisfarne Road, Jesmond."

"Jesmond?" said Poppy, surprised. "They're here in Newcastle?"

"Well they were, in 1898. And I believe a few years after this. There's a note here that sadly the baby died two years later. Measles. They sent a note to tell us in case we wanted to let the birth mother know. It was very kind of them to do so. They were under no obligation to tell us anything. Once a baby is adopted that's it."

"And did you let the birth mother know?"

Henrietta nodded. "I told *your* mother, Poppy. I allowed her to decide whether or not to do so."

Poppy shook her head. "She didn't. She decided not to. Agnes was already in France and she felt it would not do anyone any good to scrape open an old wound."

"She was probably right. She's a wise woman, your mother."

"So," chipped in Delilah, "does that mean Agnes still thought her baby was alive?"

"I imagine it did," said Poppy. "What are you thinking?"

"I'm thinking that if Agnes thought her baby was still alive she might have gone looking for him. Or, perhaps, someone could have pretended to be the boy . . ."

Sister Henrietta smiled. "You've got quite the imagination there, Miss Marconi."

Delilah looked put out. "Well, I was just mulling over some ideas, that's all."

Poppy nodded to her encouragingly. "Actually Delilah, I think those are some very good ideas. Very good ideas indeed. And," she added, hoping Sister Henrietta would not be too offended, "I think imagination is a strength, not a weakness."

The old nun chuckled. "And you are right, Poppy. You take after your mother for that. She was never scared to say things as she saw them, and neither are you. I'm sorry Delilah, go ahead."

Delilah shrugged. "Well, that's all I've got so far. Just a thought. You see, I'm in a play at the moment, and it's all about a baby that was lost at birth and everyone thought he was dead. But he wasn't. And he comes back years later, under another name. But there are two people pretending to have the same name, and it's very complicated – and funny, and of course this real story isn't – but it just got me thinking about missing babies who may or may not be dead."

"But this baby *is* dead. Unfortunately," said Sister Henrietta.

"Yes," agreed Poppy, "but Agnes didn't know that. And I think Delilah's right; that may have something to do with what happened to her. So with your permission, Sister, I think we should try to see if the Northangers are still living at that address. And whether or not anyone else has been asking about the baby after all these years."

Chapter 25

Unfortunately the Northangers of Jesmond were not home. The neighbours to the left confirmed that they still lived there but that Mr Northanger only got back from work after six and they didn't know where Mrs Northanger was. Possibly shopping. Possibly visiting an elderly relative . . . Poppy wrote a note and slipped it through the letterbox, asking Mr and Mrs Northanger to contact her as soon as they could. She left both Aunt Dot's telephone number and address. Then Delilah drove them back to Heaton.

As they pulled up, they noticed DI Sandy Hawkes sitting in his car.

"Ooooh, there's your tennis partner, Popsicle. Wonder what he wants?"

"I don't know. But go in; I'll join you in a minute. Pop the kettle on, will you? I'm dying for a cuppa."

Delilah agreed, gave a flirtatious wave to the detective inspector and went into the house. Poppy waited on the pavement while Sandy got out of the car.

"Good afternoon, Poppy. I'm glad I caught you. I have some news for Mrs Rolandson and Mrs Wilson. But I wanted to talk to you first. And – well – to thank you for –" Sandy stopped talking and raised his hat as Maddie Sherman crossed the road from the park with her two poodles. Poppy smiled and waved at the woman, who nodded a greeting in return.

"She's going to be in for a shock today, I'm afraid," said Sandy, quietly.

"Oh, why's that?"

"Because as we speak my men are arresting her son."

"Good heavens!"

Poppy's heart wrenched as she watched Maddie open the door and take her dogs in. But then the implications of Sandy's statement hit home. "Does that mean you no longer consider Grace a suspect? Is that why you're here?"

"I'm afraid not. We have found no further evidence to tie Mrs Wilson to Agnes' death, but the Stanley knife that was left in this house and then used to attack Agnes is still unexplained. As is Mrs Wilson being seen wandering around the back entrance of the gallery on the night of the murder."

"I was wandering around the back entrance of the gallery on the night of the murder, and I was on the roof! But you haven't arrested me. And as for the knife, lots of people could have taken it. This house is like King's Cross Station. There have been workmen and decorators in and out of here for weeks. And then all of Aunt Dot's, Grace's and Delilah's visitors, not to mention me! If the only thing linking Grace to Agnes' death is that she had access to the Stanley knife – and was seen on the back staircase – then I should be just as much a suspect as she is. But I'm not."

Sandy pushed his hat back from his forehead, and with a quirky smile asked: "Do you want me to arrest you, Poppy?"

Poppy was not in the mood for flirtation. "Of course not," she snapped. "I'm just pointing out the lack of logic in your case, which I believe Yasmin already did at the bail hearing yesterday."

Sandy sighed. "Yes, she did. And I would have expected nothing less from a professional like Mrs Rolandson. But I wish you would see that I'm just being professional too. You know it's nothing personal against Mrs Wilson. And you know I was just doing my job. We've been over this before, Poppy. I thought you understood. Grace and Agnes were known to have bad blood. Grace had done prison time before, linked to the death of Delilah's mother."

"But she didn't kill her – Delilah's mother, or Agnes! She was charged with withholding evidence linked to a death, not the death itself. And if you'd done your homework properly, DI Hawkes, you would know that!"

Sandy raised his hands and took a step back. "Whoa, hold your horses Miss Denby. Don't forget I'm actually here to tell you that we have no further evidence linking Grace to Agnes' death. And that we've arrested someone else."

"But if you've arrested someone else then you need to drop the charges against Grace!"

"I'm afraid that's not my decision to make. I'm sure Mrs Rolandson will tell you the same thing." The handsome detective cocked his head, waiting for Poppy's response.

Poppy took a deep, calming breath. "Yes, I'm sorry. It's been a long day. And when I left here this morning, poor Grace was nearly comatose with misery. I had just hoped you were here to tell us she had now been exonerated."

"She might be, in time, but I'm afraid we're not there yet. We are, though, able to declare Dante Sherman a formal suspect. And that's all thanks to you. I wrote up a report of what you told me yesterday about your conversations with the professor at the art school. I then formally interviewed him myself. That, and some information given to me by Gerald Farmer – Agnes' manager – led me to believe that Sherman might have been blackmailing Agnes. I contacted the Met and spoke to our mutual friend DCI Jasper Martin. Then this morning he managed to get a search warrant for Agnes' flat and studio. He telephoned me at lunchtime to tell me what he had found."

"Which is?"

"I'm afraid I can't tell you, yet. I am waiting for the evidence to arrive by special delivery tomorrow. But DCI Martin has given me the gist of it, and we believe there is enough to justify arresting Sherman on blackmail charges, if not – quite yet – murder."

"Does it have to do with the paintings Gus and Gerald brought up with them? Can you tell me that much?"

"I can and it does."

"I thought it would." Poppy then went on to tell Sandy what she and Delilah had learned that afternoon from Sister Henrietta about the *Lilies in the Vase* painting and Dante Sherman's attempts to buy it from her. And also about him trying to dig up dirt on Agnes from Mrs Storey in the sweet shop in Ashington, and, finally, about the threatening letter sent to her mother. "So you see, I really believe that Dante was gathering information on Agnes to use against her. And that bringing those two paintings up here – one that linked to her time in Ashington and the other to her time at the home for unwed mothers – was a way of reminding her about it all."

"To what end?" asked Sandy.

Poppy shrugged. She had been thinking about that all the way home from the Northangers' house. "I'm not sure, but I've got some ideas. Revenge? For what happened to his father? Perhaps he truly believes that Agnes killed his father like the rumours suggest. His mother, yesterday, told me he had been a very angry young man when he first heard about his father's death. Perhaps that rage is still there. And bubbled over. The letter to my mother was threatening – very threatening. He didn't want her talking about what happened with Agnes and his father. And perhaps more than that: talking about his father being a pervert, sexually molesting other children. This could all have been done to protect his family reputation."

Sandy listened carefully and nodded. "Yes, I believe that's a very good theory. But as I said, we may have evidence of blackmail but not, as yet, of murder."

"Sherman was seen in the tower looking down to the pavement."

"He works at the gallery. He had every right to be there. Perhaps he was just going out for a cigarette, just like the stable boy."

Poppy nodded. She noticed the curtains twitch in Aunt Dot's front parlour. It was Delilah, checking up on her.

"Then what's the blackmail all about?" she asked.

"I told you I can't give you any more details about that at the moment."

"But it suggests that Sherman was putting pressure on Agnes about something?"

"It does."

"Was he asking for money? Or putting pressure on her in other ways?"

"I told you, I can't –"

"Yes, yes, I know. You can't give me more details about that. But do you think the exhibition was merely a ruse to bring Agnes up to Newcastle?"

Sandy nodded. "Yes, I can give you that. The evidence suggests that the exhibition was part of a bigger plan on Sherman's part. But what that is, I can't tell you. In fact, I don't properly know myself. The evidence is strongly suggestive but not conclusive. However," and he smiled, "I would like to ask you and Mrs Rolandson to come into the station and listen in to my interview with Sherman. There might be something he says that you pick up on that I don't."

"You want *me* to come too?"

Sandy grinned. "In your capacity as assistant to Mrs Wilson's barrister, of course."

Poppy felt chastised. Here she had been giving Sandy a hard time, when actually he *really* was trying to help.

"Thank you Sandy, thank you. I would love to. But . . . will Sherman be prepared to talk in front of me?"

"He won't see you. We're not a total backwater here in Newcastle. We've recently had one of those newfangled two-way mirrors installed in one of our interview rooms. You and Mrs Rolandson will be able to hear the interview, but you will not be able to be seen."

Golly, thought Poppy, *that is exciting!* "Then I'd love to." She saw the curtain twitch again. "But would you like to come in first for a cup of tea?"

Chapter 26

Delilah dropped Yasmin and Poppy outside the Pilgrim Street police station, then drove off to meet Peter MacMahon for afternoon tea at Fenwick's. Rollo had been disgruntled to hear that he had not been invited along to the police interview too, but offered instead to "have another pop" at Gerald Farmer – and, hopefully, Gus. The women dropped him off at the Grand Hotel on their way to the police station.

Sandy signed the two women in and then ushered them down the stairs to the interview room. It was the same room that Poppy had met Grace in on Friday after she had just been arrested. She had not been aware then that the mirror on the wall behind her was in fact a spying device. She looked at Sandy. Had he been behind there, listening in to her conversation with Grace? She felt a chill go down her spine. There was a lot she didn't know about Sandy Hawkes – like, for instance, if she could really trust him. What was really behind his offer to allow her to listen in to his interrogation of Dante Sherman? But all she got from him was a warm smile and a gentlemanly flourish as he gestured for her and Yazzie to enter a small cupboard-sized room adjacent to the interview room.

Inside the room were two chairs and a small table. And on the wall, above the window overlooking the interview room, a loudspeaker. Sandy gestured for the two women to sit, then stuck his head out and called: "Brown! Test please."

Poppy watched as one of the constables from the Laing Gallery, who had been so dismissive of her and women in professional roles in general, walked into the room and recited a monotone version of "Mary Had a Little Lamb". They could hear him loud and clear.

Satisfied, Sherman closed the door behind him, leaving Yazzie and Poppy to take out their notebooks.

"Have you ever sat in on an interrogation, Poppy?" asked Yasmin.

"No, it's my first. But I was wondering why DI Hawkes has asked me."

"I was wondering that too. Perhaps though it might just be as he said: you could pick up on something he misses. You've done a lot already to gather evidence on this case." She laughed. "You should probably send the police a bill."

Poppy smiled at her. "And if they don't pay, I know who to set on them."

The two women settled back in their chairs enjoying the sense of mutual respect between them. A few moments later the window, like a screen in a moving picture show, filled with the main players: DI Sandy Hawkes, Dante Sherman, a man in a very expensive-looking pinstriped three-piece suit whom Poppy assumed was Sherman's solicitor and a woman stenographer. The door behind them shut, guarded by the artistically talentless Constable Brown. The table over which Sandy and Sherman conversed was set perpendicular to the window, so Poppy and Yasmin could see and hear exactly what was going on.

DI Hawkes opened the interview by confirming Sherman's identity, address and date of birth. He then read out the reason for the interview as "suspicion to commit blackmail". The solicitor countered this by asking whether or not formal charges were going to be laid.

"We'll determine that after this interview," answered Sandy, who reminded both the solicitor and Sherman that he was being questioned under an official police caution. He then proceeded to open a file and produced two photographs – of the two questionable paintings at the Laing – plus the letter from the Tate that Poppy had seen on the curator's desk at the Laing.

"Mr Sherman, can you tell us how much you paid for these two paintings please?"

Sherman cast a glance at his solicitor. His solicitor nodded. "Not off the top of my head, no. But the amount will be in the ledger at the gallery."

Sandy nodded. "That's good, because we currently have a police accountant going through the ledger."

"Well, be aware that he might not find anything. I normally pass on receipts to our bookkeeper, who writes it up. He might not have got around to it yet. In fact, I'm not sure the money has yet been handed over. Although it will be, of course."

"Not a problem," said Sandy, coolly, making a note. "I shall get our man to search all pending receipts too. It shouldn't take long. I don't believe you buy *that* much art at the gallery."

Sherman gave an equally cool stare. "We buy enough."

"Do you often buy artworks whose legitimacy is in question?" He pushed the letter from the Tate across the table.

Sherman glanced at it and curled his lip, as if he had been presented with a menu for tripe and trotters. "I only received that the day of Agnes' exhibition. And only opened it the following morning – after the poor woman had died. If I had known this beforehand, I would have cancelled the sale."

"The sale for which we will find a receipt when we search your bookkeeper's office?"

Sherman smirked. "Yes, that one."

"And will we also find evidence to support your assertion that you only read this letter the day after Agnes died?"

"I doubt that. Unless there is some kind of cinemagraphic or photographic equipment in my office, and the camera operator was hiding behind a curtain, I'm afraid you are going to have to take my word for that."

"Hmmmm." Sandy made a note. "And what about the word of Professor Reid?"

"Who?"

"Professor Reid from the art school. I believe he was your lecturer."

"He was. What's he got to say about it?"

Sandy made a show of flicking through the file in front of him and pausing to read some notes. "Well, he's got a lot to say actually. And one of the things he said was that you and he had a conversation about this very painting three weeks ago. And that he had told you he had been at the meeting at the Tate where questions about its authenticity were first raised."

Sherman smirked. "Yes, I remember that conversation. And did the good professor also tell you that at the time the official opinion was inconclusive? That it was just at that time an accusation?"

Sandy nodded. "He did. But why would you still go ahead and – assuming these elusive receipts can be found – buy the painting? Surely it puts the gallery's reputation in a bad light?"

"Does it? Why do you say that?"

"I am asking the questions here, Mr Sherman, not you. Why did you buy this painting?"

"Because I thought it would be a good acquisition for the gallery. Agnes Robson is – was – a world-renowned artist."

"But why *this* one? And *this* one?" Sandy pushed both photographs towards Sherman.

"Why not these ones? They are both high-quality Agnes Robsons."

"Except one of them is not *entirely* by Agnes Robson, though," Sandy countered.

"Apparently not. But I did not know it wasn't when I first purchased it. Now that I do, I shall be returning it to Gerald Farmer and asking him to reimburse the gallery."

"Are you sure you actually *bought* the paintings?"

"Of course I am."

"Really? You didn't demand Gus North give them to you in return for keeping something quiet?"

Sherman jutted out his chin. "Of course not! Who has been telling you that?"

"I will remind you, Mr Sherman, that I am the one asking the questions." He again perused the file, then after a few moments asked: "Is it correct that you first saw these paintings when you were down in London in August?"

Sherman gave a cool smile. "Ah, so it is Gus North you've been talking to. I wouldn't believe a word that boy says. He's got a drinking problem, you know."

"Really? Well, it was Gerald Farmer, actually. I still have to interview Mr North. But not to worry, he is on the list." Sandy flicked through the file again and stopped at a particular page. He took even longer than usual to read. In the silence, empty of the tick-tack of the stenography machine, Poppy could hear the ticking of the clock on the wall. Sherman looked to his solicitor. The solicitor nodded to him encouragingly. *Stay calm*, he appeared to say.

Eventually, Sandy spoke. "Mr Farmer told me he had not been aware of the purchase of these paintings until the morning of his departure for Newcastle. That is, last Thursday morning. He said Mr North had told him 'at the last minute' that you had requested the paintings be brought up to the exhibition when you dropped in to see Agnes back in August. But Agnes wasn't there and you asked Gus if you could buy the paintings. Why didn't you wait to speak to Agnes? Gus is merely her studio assistant, is he not?"

Sherman leaned back in his seat. He adopted a weary air. "You know he is. But why shouldn't I speak to him? Agnes wasn't there and I didn't have time on my London trip to drop by again. My train was leaving two hours later."

"Didn't you telephone ahead to see if she were in and prepared to receive visitors?"

Sherman shrugged. "I didn't think to. It was a spur of the moment thing."

"And was buying the paintings spur of the moment?"

"It was. But I had been wanting to buy some anyway. So I took the chance when I saw them."

"And you still contend that you paid money for these paintings?"

"I do."

"What if I were to tell you that the Metropolitan Police have found evidence in Agnes' studio to suggest that you were attempting to blackmail Gus North? That you demanded he bring these paintings in return for your silence?"

"I would say you should produce this evidence," said Sherman's solicitor.

Sandy flattened his lips into an approximation of a smile. "Oh I shall, at the right time. Come, Mr Sherman, I asked you a question: did you or did you not demand these paintings in return for your silence about some unlawful activity you believed Mr North to be involved in?"

"I did not. As I said, I bought these paintings in good faith as valuable additions to the Laing's collection. I don't know what 'unlawful activity' Gus was involved in. That's all news to me. But it doesn't surprise me. As I said, he's a heavy drinker and is known for getting into scrapes. He's also run up a lot of gambling debts . . ."

Sandy did not respond to the accusations about Gus and allowed silence to fall again. Then he pushed the *Lilies in a Vase* photo closer to Sherman. "So, to clarify – you bought this very painting?"

A slight smile played on Sherman's lips. "You know I did. That's the painting that's hanging in the gallery. And this is a photograph of it."

"But I've been told by someone who attended the exhibition that the paint is still tacky. I'm no expert, but that suggests to me that it's only recently been painted. Professor Reid and Gerald Farmer both confirmed my observation. This picture could only have been painted early September at the earliest. But more likely, according to Professor Reid, the second or third week in September. Only two weeks ago . . . and you were in London when . . ."

"You know when I was in London," Sherman snapped.

"I do indeed. The thirteenth of August. So this *isn't* the exact painting you saw when you visited Agnes' studio, is it?"

Sherman's solicitor flicked a warning glance at his client.

But Sherman remained calm.

"DI Hawkes, if you had truly done your homework you would know that Agnes painted a number of versions of that painting. It was one of her recurring themes. As it turned out, the one I saw in August was sold to someone else. This one was painted as a replacement."

Sandy raised an eyebrow. "Well, I'm glad you finally got one of them, after all these months of trying to buy one and being turned down."

"Turned down? No one turned me down. There was just a short delay, that's all."

"Are you telling me a nun is lying?"

A look of shock came over Sherman's face but was swiftly subdued. He leaned forward and answered in an admirably calm voice: "A nun? Whatever are you talking about, Inspector?"

"Sister Henrietta. She runs a home for young women in distress in Gosforth. St Hilda's. But you know that already. You visited her over the summer, wanted to know about Agnes' time there when she was pregnant and then tried to buy a version of this painting from her. Now why would you do that?"

The solicitor cleared his throat. "This has nothing to do with the charge at hand, Inspector."

"Doesn't it? It shows your client had been trying to buy this painting – or a version of it – for some time before he procured it from Gus North under what the Metropolitan Police tell me were potentially extortionate means. I – and no doubt the King's Counsel if this goes to trial – will see it as an indication that Mr Sherman was interested in more than just any old Agnes Robson painting. He was interested in paintings that reflected a difficult period in her life – when she became pregnant and had to leave her home. Now why would you be interested in that, Mr Sherman?"

"I've told you, *Lilies in a Vase* is a quintessential Agnes Robson theme. I would be remiss not to get one for the gallery. It would be like me not getting a Constable depicting a pastoral scene." He smirked, challenging Sandy to contradict him.

"Well, I don't know much about art, but I do know that you appear to have been doing the rounds, trying to dig up dirt on Agnes Robson."

Sherman laughed disdainfully. "Digging up dirt? Asking to buy a painting from a nun and trying to get a bit of background information from her for our exhibition programme notes is hardly digging up dirt."

"No? Then what about travelling to Ashington to visit the sweet shop right next to the railway line where this second picture was painted? Why would you do that, Mr Sherman, and why would you ask the shopkeeper to share any gossip she had on Agnes? Particularly about the time she became pregnant? And what about the rumours that the baby was sired by your father, Michael Brownley? Who, according to Professor Reid, also painted naked children."

Into the stunned silence, Sandy produced the photograph of the nude painting of Agnes at fourteen and slapped it on the desk between them. "Do you recognise this painting, Mr Sherman? I am reliably informed it is one of your father's."

Sherman paled. "I – well – I –"

"You do not have to answer that, Dante."

"If he doesn't," Sandy nodded to the stenographer, "then it will go down that the subject refused to answer."

"May I remind you, DI Hawkes, that my client does not have to answer any questions that might lead to self-incrimination."

"Oh aye? So you're admitting there is something to incriminate then?"

The solicitor leaned over the table. "No Hawkes, I am not. I am just doing my job and preventing my client from saying anything that might be twisted and used against him unfairly."

"In that case, then, you should not object to providing a writing sample. We asked your client for one a few days ago but he has not yet complied. Now why is that?"

"Because, DI Hawkes, as we told Mrs Rolandson, providing it would suggest that our client was under suspicion of something."

"He *is* under suspicion of something." Sandy pushed a sheet of paper and a fountain pen across the table. "So, Mr Sherman, in order to clear your name of all this suspicion, why don't you write us a little note. 'Mary had a little lamb' should do it. Or something more highbrow if you prefer. Oh, and please also write 'Stay away.'"

"Stay away? Why should he write that?" demanded the solicitor.

"Will you write it or will you not, Mr Sherman? Be assured that refusing to do so will go down in the interview record."

"You don't have to do it, Dante."

Sherman shook his head. "That's all right, James. I will." He picked up the pen, leaned over and wrote for a few moments. When he'd finished he passed the sheet to Sandy.

Sandy picked it up, read it, then opened his file again, raising the cover so neither Sherman and his solicitor, nor for that matter Poppy and Yasmin, could see what he was looking at. He eventually closed the file and straightened it on the table in front of him.

"Thank you, Mr Sherman. That was not hard to do, was it? You are free to go for now, but do not leave town. I will need to talk to you again."

Sherman looked at his solicitor, who nodded. "That's fine. But make sure you have proper reason to do so – backed up by evidence a judge considers pertinent, not hearsay and gossip – or I shall be laying a charge of police harassment."

Sandy smiled, the conviviality not reflected in his eyes. "You do that."

Sherman and his solicitor left the room. Sandy looked towards the two-way mirror and nodded. A few moments later he was at the door of the viewing room.

"Good job, DI Hawkes," said Yasmin.

"Thank you, Mrs Rolandson, but we have a way to go yet."

"How's that?" asked Poppy.

Sandy looked at the two women ruefully. "Because, unfortunately, Sherman's handwriting did not match that of the person who wrote the threatening note to Poppy's mother. Nor who inscribed the message on the back of the photograph of Agnes as a girl."

"Oh bother," said Poppy.

"Quite," said Yazzie.

Chapter 27

Rollo Rolandson walked into the foyer of the Grand Hotel and consciously deposited his domestic cares along with his coat and hat in the cloakroom. He adored being a father, but by Jove, it was harder work than he'd ever imagined. Being a first-time father at fifty was not for the faint-hearted. He had to admit that when Yazzie had announced she was pregnant, he had assumed she was joking. He had married her when she was forty-two when she was an already well-established career woman. They had been sleeping together on and off for years, so all that happened after the wedding was that Rollo moved into her luxurious flat in Mayfair on a more permanent basis. But their lives continued much as they had done before. They both worked and loved their jobs, and he had kept his rooms near Fleet Street for when he was doing an all-nighter at the paper – or having a lucky run of poker at the club. But when she had convinced him that she was not, in fact, in jest, and after he had digested the news with a large whisky, he had warmed to the idea, imagining the fun he could have with the kid on his days off.

Yazzie announced early on that she would be going back to work after her confinement – he expected nothing else – and they agreed that on their substantial joint income they could more than afford a nanny or two to help out. His fantasy was only slightly disturbed when it was announced that there would be two little Rolandsons, and only just a bit more when his wife almost doubled in size. His fantasy also survived Yazzie's mood swings – so uncharacteristic of the woman he had married – although it took a bit more of a knock with her new-found aversion to sex.

But then reality hit with a bang. A double bang. Despite having two full-time nannies, a cook, a butler and a maid, the Rolandson household had been chaos for the last fourteen months. Sometimes joyful chaos, sometimes scream-into-the-pillow-at-night chaos, but always chaos. And Rollo, if he were perfectly honest, wasn't quite sure how he'd survive it. So he took every opportunity he could to escape – just for a while. And this was one of those opportunities. He had hoped he would be much busier than he had been following the story of Agnes Robson's murder, which was why he had insisted on coming up to Newcastle instead of staying home in London with the children. But there wasn't actually that much to do here. Yasmin was taking centre stage. He realised that that was as it should be – she was Grace's lawyer – but it still irked him. He was a newshound and if he didn't have the chance to follow a scent he would soon start howling at the moon.

So he crossed the foyer of the Grand Hotel with a self-confident swagger, ignoring, as he always did, the stares of people who weren't used to seeing dwarfs outside of the circus. At the reception desk he asked if Gerald Farmer and Gus North were in and was told the gentlemen were in the bar having a drink. Dandy! He would be glad of a stiff whisky.

Rollo spotted Gus and Gerald in a high-backed booth at the far end of the room. He ordered his whisky – a double – and made his way towards them. One of the advantages to being only four-and-a-half feet tall was that he was not easily spotted above the clutter of tall chair backs. Of course, sometimes this was a *dis*advantage, but not today. Gus and Gerald, their heads bowed, did not see him approach, and as he got into earshot he heard Gerald say: "For heaven's sake, Gus, you can't just run. They'll think you're guilty."

Then Gus answering with his not-properly-formed, but still recognisable, words: "But I am guilty. We both are."

Rollo, stunned at what he was hearing, slipped into a nearby booth, not wanting to interrupt the confessional flow. He noted that there were no other customers at this side of the room – no doubt why the two men felt able to talk so freely.

"Look Gerald, the only reason I came back was to convince you to come with me. Will you?"

"I don't think it's wise, my boy, I really don't."

"They will arrest us!"

"They haven't yet . . ."

"Then that's our chance to leave. I've been checking out the ferries to Amsterdam. There's one leaving tomorrow morning. We can check out of here, book in somewhere near the Port of Tyne under assumed names and be at the ferry first thing."

"I am *not* going with you to Amsterdam, Gus."

"For Pete's sake, why?"

"Because I think we have a chance to clear our names. What we did wasn't so bad, was it? In fact, I don't think charges can even be laid against us, now that Agnes is dead."

"We committed fraud, Gerald. I produced paintings, pretending to be Agnes, and you sold them under her name."

"I only suggested doing it that time when we had the order from Buenos Aires and Agnes was in one of her moods, unable to work, unable to deliver. How I hated those moods of hers. It was so hard to run a business like that – when you couldn't guarantee to buyers they'd get what they ordered."

"She was an artist, not a production line, Gerald."

Rollo took a sip of his whisky and swilled it round in his mouth. He would have lit a cigar, but the smell would alert Gus and Gerald to his presence. This was interesting, very interesting . . .

Gus continued: "Besides, it wasn't just that one time. You know it wasn't. And you said yourself, that copper has been asking you about *Lilies* and *The Railway Family*."

"Oh my boy, it was *those* paintings that got us into trouble in the first place! Why, for heaven's sake, did you let Sherman pressure you into bringing them up? And why, now that I think of it, did you try to slip *The Railway Family* into the Tate exhibition?"

"I didn't try to slip it in. Agnes chose it."

"So you say."

"Are you calling me a liar, Gerald?"

Rollo heard Gerald take a deep breath, then emit a rattling sigh. He imagined the large man's chins wobbling as he did so. "No Gus, I'm not. I just think perhaps you might have made an error of judgment, that's all."

"An error of judgment? And that from the man who asked me to forge his client's paintings?"

"Touché, Gus, touché. But I still can't believe Agnes submitted that painting herself, knowing that only half of it was hers. Did she tell you why she'd done it?"

It was Gus' turn to sigh. "She did, yes. She came in one day when I was doing some of my own painting. The railway line was one of her abandoned canvases. You know how she would do that. Start something then change her mind. She'd asked me to get rid of it. But I didn't. There was something that drew me into that painting. So I decided to finish it."

"Why the mother and child?"

There was silence. Then Gerald replied: "Oh I see."

Damn. Rollo wondered if Gus had slipped into sign language. If he had, that would be pretty much the end of his eavesdropping. But to his relief, after a few moments, he heard Gus speak again. "She said she loved it. She wasn't angry with me at all. She said that I had finished the sentence she had started. That she hadn't known how to complete it. She was . . . well . . . she started crying, Gerald."

"Really? Why?"

"I don't know. But it was her decision to submit it for the Tate exhibition. I told her then that if she did she should acknowledge that it was only partly hers."

"I wish she'd listened to you."

"So do I. And I wish I'd insisted. But she told me that she didn't want to muddy my name with hers. She told me that she believed in my talent and wanted to help me launch my own career. She said I should produce a couple of dozen originals and when I was ready to let her know she'd see about helping me get my own exhibition. Or joining in with one of those 'new talent' shows her friend Roger Fry arranged. So I backed down."

"Yes, Roger would do wonders for you. I hope he still will. He helped launch Agnes' career, you know."

"Yes, she told me."

There was silence again. Rollo drummed his fingers against the whisky tumbler. How he wished he could nudge the conversation in the direction he needed it to go.

"So . . ." said Gerald eventually. "Have you changed your mind about leaving? I really think we could explain all this, you know. The police don't know anything about the Buenos Aires painting. It's just the lilies and the railway one. And you have an explanation for that."

"But not for the lilies. I painted that one for Sherman when he asked for it because I knew Agnes wouldn't be up to it."

"You still haven't explained why he asked for it."

"No, I haven't."

"Don't you think you should? Particularly if you want me to leave the country with you. What is it you're running from, Gus?"

Another deep sigh from the younger man. "Sherman knows about the Buenos Aires painting. And the other one I did for that dealer in Leeds."

"Oh Lordy! I'd forgotten about the Leeds one." A bang on the table clattered glasses and startled Rollo.

"You're not telling me he knows about both those paintings?"

Silence.

"Oh dear God. How?"

Silence.

"What the hell was he doing searching my office? How did he get in?"

Silence.

"All right, so he has threatened to expose us? Why didn't you tell me, Gus?"

Silence.

"Oh my boy, bless you. Bless your kind and loving heart. But you really should have told me. We could have dealt with Sherman together, instead of you having to suffer under his blackmail. What did the swine want with those two paintings anyway?"

Silence.

"All right, all right. So that's why you want to leave the country? To get away from Sherman?"

"Yes." To Rollo's relief Gus spoke again.

"Is that the only reason?"

"Of course. What other reason could there be?"

"Well . . . now Gus, I don't want you to get upset now. And I hope you know that I will do anything for you. Anything to protect you. You know that, don't you?"

Silence.

"Well I do. And it's true. And that's why I never told the police what I really saw the night Agnes died."

Rollo's jaw dropped. *Surely it can't be . . .*

"What did you see?" Gus' voice was defensive.

"Oh my boy, don't make me say it. You know what it is. You and Agnes leaving together. Out the back door. But then, only you returned – later. Before Poppy came back and told us Agnes was dead. I didn't mention it to the police, of course, but – oh Gus – did you? Did you kill Agnes?"

There was silence. A deathly silence. Rollo's hand gripped the tumbler until his knuckles turned white.

Then, eventually, Gus spoke, his voice quivering on the verge of tears.

"I cannot believe you asked me that. I just can't."

Then he stood, catching Rollo off guard. The little editor slipped off his seat and under the table, praying to the God he didn't believe in that he wouldn't be seen.

"I'm checking out now, Gerald. You can come with me if you like. Or you can go to the police and tell them what you know. I don't care. I don't care at all."

Rollo, under the table, now had a clear view under the bench between his and the next booth, and saw Gerald struggling to get up. But his large frame would not shift easily.

"Gus! Please! Don't be like that. Talk to me – please! I'm sorry if it's upset you, but I need to know. I promise I'll stand by you either way."

"Goodbye Gerald."

Rollo watched the younger man's legs stride away, then waited to see what Gerald would do. But all he did was weep.

Chapter 28

Delilah dropped Poppy on Osborne Road, Jesmond. She needed to get to the theatre so couldn't accompany her friend on her mission. However, there were plenty of buses that could get Poppy back from Jesmond, and at a push, she could walk the half-hour or so back to Heaton Road. Yasmin, who had plenty to work on after the sensational interview with Dante Sherman, asked to be dropped off at Aunt Dot's house. And Rollo, who had not been at the Grand Hotel when they went to pick him up, would just have to make his way back alone.

"He's a big boy," said Yasmin without irony. And both Poppy and Delilah agreed.

Poppy's note to the Northangers had borne fruit. Mrs Northanger had called Aunt Dot's and left a message. She would be in this evening if Poppy would like to call on her. Mr Northanger, however, would not be able to join them as he was working late. Poppy managed to shovel down a ham and pease pudding sandwich and half a glass of milk before she jumped in the Rolls with Delilah and headed off to Jesmond.

And now here she was. Delilah dropped her off outside the beautiful St George's Church, which Poppy's father had attended as a child. Lindisfarne Road – where the Northangers lived – was just a short walk away, down a tree-lined avenue that met up, finally, with the genteel Jesmond Dene. It was an area rich in lawyers, accountants and prosperous medium-sized industrialists. In fact, Poppy's paternal grandparents had lived not far from here. They had both died a few years ago, within a few short months of one another. Poppy wondered if they had known the Northangers, the couple who had adopted Agnes' baby all those years ago. And if they had, had they known that her mother, Alice, the woman whom they considered so far below their son, had been instrumental in paving the way for the adoption? It's something she might ask her father the next time she saw him.

Poppy was very sorry that she had not been able to spend more time with him on his birthday, and vowed to correct that once all this hullaballoo had died down. Poppy still could not believe, however, that her very own mother – the woman who for so many years had been critical of her daughter's life choices – was actually now supporting her in this "hullaballoo". Along with the message from Mrs Northanger was another one from Alice Denby, asking Poppy and Yasmin to come back through to Ashington in the morning. She had spoken to Sadie Robson – Agnes' mother – and there was indeed more to tell. Poppy was intrigued to know what.

But first, she needed to find out what, if anything, Mrs Northanger could add to the story. The Northanger house was set back from the road along a gravel drive and hemmed in by a row of pine trees. The wrought-iron gates were closed though not locked, and creaked in protest as she opened them. It was now approaching half past six and Poppy felt uneasy leaving the safety of the streetlights and heading into the shadow of the pines. She could see beyond them and, through a garden plump with shrubbery, the lights of the house. She knew she was being silly, but she was in the middle of a murder investigation and, she couldn't help noting, the killer had not yet been caught. A rustle to her left brought a gasp from her mouth, forming a cloud of white in the chill autumn air. She squinted through the gloom, readying herself to run if necessary, but was relieved – and amused – to see a podgy hedgehog shuffling out of the undergrowth to hunt for slugs on the lawn. Yes, it was a killer, but a delightful one.

Nonetheless, Poppy hurried on and was soon on the front step ringing the bell. It didn't take long for the door to be answered by a maid in a uniform worthy of a country estate. *Old school*, thought Poppy. The maid said Mrs Northanger was expecting the lady, and took Poppy's hat and coat. When the maid opened the cloakroom door off the hall, Poppy noticed small mackintoshes and three pairs of children's wellington boots. But there was no sound or sign of children in the well-appointed reception room where Mrs Northanger waited to greet her.

She was an elegant woman, approaching seventy. She had the long sinewy neck and erect posture of someone who had done ballet in their youth, perhaps as part of the curriculum of a girls' finishing school. She stood, easily, not showing any signs in her body of the age Poppy could see in the lines on her face.

"Miss Denby," she said, her voice cultured but still unmistakably Northumbrian. "Thank you for coming to see me on such a chill night. Would you like some tea to warm you?" She cocked her head and smiled, charmingly, looking more like the grandmother Poppy suspected she was. "Or perhaps some cocoa?"

Poppy said she would love some cocoa and the maid was dispatched to get some.

Mrs Northanger gestured to the armchair next to her, near the fire, shooing away a white cat that had already claimed it. Poppy sat down, resisting the urge to brush the seat first to remove any pet hair. The two women engaged in small talk: the weather, Poppy's grandparents (yes, Mrs Northanger *had* known them) and the antics of George the cat, who did not take too kindly to being usurped and decided to lie along the top of Poppy's armchair and flick at her hair with his paw. He was eventually sent away with the maid when she returned with the cocoa.

Finally, all distractions aside, they got down to business. "So, you've come about my boy."

"The child you adopted in 1898, yes."

"I was wondering when you would."

"Oh? Why's that?"

"Oh, not you. But someone. Anyone. Possibly the police . . . I have spent the last twenty-five years waiting for someone and then two of you come along in one week. Actually, that's not quite correct. She came for the first time ten years ago – or was it nine?"

"She? You mean Agnes?"

"That's right. Agnes. Agnes Robson. I think it might have been 1916 . . . Yes, definitely 1916, because my Claudia had just had her sixteenth birthday."

"Claudia is your daughter?"

"Yes. I had three children. But now I just have two. Claudia and Julius."

Poppy smiled. "Lovely, classical names."

Mrs Northanger smiled too. "I'm glad you picked up on that. I went to Girton College you know; read History and Classics. That was before the days when women could actually be awarded a degree, of course, but I went up, nonetheless."

"So," said Poppy, not wanting to go down a side road of the rights of women to an education, "you had two other children, besides the one you adopted."

"That's right. But all three were adopted. We got Claudia and Julius after . . . after . . ."

"After your first son died?"

Mrs Northanger bit her lip and shook her head. "No, not after he died. After we – after my husband, Mr Northanger – sent him away." She looked up, her sea-green eyes awash with tears. "You see, Miss Denby, Agnes Robson's baby didn't die."

Poppy felt the blood drain from her face. "But the records at the women's home –"

"Were false. Although Sister Henrietta didn't know. Please, I don't want you to think that. My husband . . ." She looked to a cluster of gilt-framed photographs on the polished grand piano. ". . . my husband told them the baby had died. He said it was for the best. He said if it was known that the child was alive there would be all sorts of complications: people pressuring us to keep him, blaming us for giving him away and so forth."

Poppy shook her head in confusion. "What are you telling me, Mrs Northanger? That the baby got measles but didn't die and you – you – *gave him away*?"

The older woman hunched her shoulders and shivered, then in a voice as brittle as an autumn leaf: "Please, Miss Denby, don't judge me until you hear the full story. Then you may think of me as you like. That's what I told Agnes too when she first came to see me."

"Back in 1916 . . ." Mrs Northanger began.

1916 . . . Of course! Poppy remembered Agnes had visited Sister

Henrietta that same year. Had she too asked to see information about her child's adoption? She must have. Why didn't Sister Henrietta say?

Mrs Northanger, her cocoa untouched, saw the distracted look on Poppy's face and waited for her to return her attention to the conversation. When Poppy nodded her assent, she continued her tale.

"My husband, you must understand, could be a very – well, a very *forceful* man. He worked hard. He had – in fact still has – a pickle factory down by the quayside. But he was a self-made man and married 'up'. I loved him for exactly who he was, but my family weren't always so kind. As a result he felt he had to always prove himself worthy. He had a dream of having a son whom he could leave the business to. But I – unfortunately – was unable to produce a child. I was forty-two when we realised a baby would never come by natural means, so we decided to adopt.

"That's how Augustus came to live with us – another classical name, you might note. He was a beautiful boy. He had a mop of black curls and looked, I thought, like a young Roman emperor. We had him for two years before – well, before he became ill. As you already know, I believe, it was the measles. Other children in the neighbourhood got it and made a full recovery, but Augustus didn't. We thought for a while we were going to lose him. He survived, thank God, but not without impairment.

"You see, the illness had left him deaf. We hoped for a while it was just temporary, and that his hearing would return, but after a few weeks the doctor told us that it was likely to be permanent, and that it would affect his ability to speak and learn. We were told that he would most likely end up an imbecile. Now, an imbecile was not the type of child one could leave a thriving business to. I didn't care; he was my son and I loved him. But my husband saw things very differently. As I said, Miss Denby, he could be a very forceful man, and I dared not defy him."

Poppy nodded her understanding and waited for Mrs Northanger to continue with her tale.

"So, he paid the doctor to falsify a death certificate, and arranged for the lad to go to an institution on the outskirts of London. I begged him not to, but he wouldn't listen to me. He did, however, allow me to accompany Augustus down to the institution and I was able to see the place for myself. It appeared to be well run and the children clean and as happy as they could be with their various handicaps. We would pay for his upkeep until he was eighteen. It was agreed that he would be told when – or if – he was ever able to understand, that his parents had died. We all agreed that it was the kindest thing to do. Better that than to know . . . to know that . . ." Mrs Northanger wiped away a tear from her cheek, ". . . to know that he'd been rejected. That he'd been considered *defective* and returned like used goods."

Poppy swallowed hard. Augustus Northanger. Gus North. It had to be. Agnes' son was not only alive but had been working for her for the last four years. Had she known? She cleared her throat and, making every effort to keep any note of condemnation out of her voice, said: "That must have been a very difficult thing for you to do, Mrs Northanger."

The older woman, perhaps hoping for vindication, answered: "Oh it was, Miss Denby; you need to believe that. I would *never* have given my boy away if I had another choice."

Poppy nodded. "Yes, I can see with your husband being, as you say, so *forceful*, that your options were limited. However, there's something you said earlier that I would like to clarify. You said Agnes Robson came to see you – twice. Once in 1916 and then again, just recently. Is that correct?"

Mrs Northanger took a moment to blow her nose and dab at her eyes. "Yes, that's right. I had no idea who she was at first. She was a very elegant lady, as you know. Nothing – of her appearance – suggested to me that she was the poor daughter of a coal miner who had a baby out of wedlock. She told me that she was hoping to do a fundraising event for the women's sanctuary. That's how she got into the house. But it didn't take long for her to reveal her true purpose. She wanted to know about the baby. What happened to him. Where he was buried. She wanted to visit his grave . . ."

At this, Mrs Northanger's voice cracked and she lowered her chin to her chest and sobbed, her bony shoulders jerking up and down. Poppy could not take it anymore. She jumped out of her chair and kneeled in front of the weeping woman, taking hold of her hands.

"It's all right, Mrs Northanger, it's all right. It's a terrible tale, but you need to finish it. I assume you know that Agnes Robson is dead. That she was murdered last Thursday at the Laing?"

Mrs Northanger nodded through her sobs.

"Well, I need to hear the rest of the story. Because I think that it's got something to do with why she was killed, and who did it."

Mrs Northanger nodded again. Poppy stayed on her knees until Mrs Northanger had composed herself, and then sat back up and waited to hear the rest of the woman's story. She told it, quietly, with her emotions contained.

"When Agnes asked to see the grave I could not lie to her any longer. I told her everything I have told you. She was shocked, yes, but said she didn't judge me. She said she too had been forced to give the baby away. She said we were both guilty of not being good enough mothers. So I told her where Augustus was. She wrote to me, a while later, and told me that she had gone to the school but that he had already left. He was eighteen then and a man. She told me, though, that apparently the school told her that he was a bright boy and that his deafness had not prevented him from getting an education. She went to the address they gave her, but he no longer lived there. They had no forwarding address. She told me that she would, however, keep on looking for him, and when she found him she would let me know."

A lump of coal fell off the grate and sizzled. Without asking permission, Poppy got up and took a pair of tongs, replacing the coal on the fire. She returned to her seat. "And did she find him?"

Mrs Northanger attempted a brief smile. It lit her lips for a moment then faded away.

"She did. Four years ago, I think it was, I got a letter from Agnes saying she had found him. And she had offered him a job, working for her in the studio. Not surprisingly, considering who both his natural parents were, he was a gifted young artist. So she took him on as an apprentice."

"Did he know who she was?"

Mrs Northanger shook her head. "No, she didn't tell him. She said she was too ashamed. She worried that if he found out he would blame her for giving him away. She wanted to tell him, so many times she said, but each time couldn't summon up the courage. Until last week..."

Poppy felt an icy hand clutch her heart. *Dear God, don't let it be...*" What happened last week, Mrs Northanger?"

"Agnes came to see me. Last Thursday. The morning before... before... she died. She said she had decided to tell Augustus that she was his mother. She said she had hoped he was going to be up in Newcastle for the exhibition, but apparently Agnes' manager was poorly, and they didn't come up. So she said that she planned to tell him as soon as she got back to London." Poppy absorbed this information, realising that Mrs Northanger must not have known that Gus actually did come up – that he was at the exhibition. So, did Agnes tell him after all? And if she did, what did he do when he found out?

Chapter 29

Poppy got off the bus opposite Aunt Dot's house at the entrance to Armstrong Park. She was exhausted. It had been an emotionally draining meeting with Mrs Northanger and a long wait for a bus to bring her home. It was now nine o'clock, but she knew the night was far from over. She could see the lights blazing in the town house, and was looking forward to a bite to eat and a warming cup of tea before hunkering down to tell everyone what she had learned in Jesmond. She waited for a motor car to pass before stepping into the road. But as she did, she felt someone grab her around the neck and pull her backwards towards the park. She tried to scream but her air was cut off by a forearm across her throat. She clawed at the arm and kicked at the legs of her assailant.

Think! Think!

Images of a self-defence course that she and Delilah had attended after they had both been abducted during a previous murder investigation flashed across her mind: a knee to the groin, forked fingers to the eyes . . . impossible from this angle. She felt a sickening pressure against her buttocks and to her horror realised what it was. But . . . she also now knew where it was.

She stamped as hard as she could on his foot, resulting in a slight loosening of pressure around her neck, enough to give her some wriggle room, enough for her to aim a sharp blow of her elbow to the approximate area of her assailant's genitals.

"Whoomph!"

He buckled.

She twisted away from him as he doubled over. Then she raised her foot and gave him a kick, not quite sure with which part of his body she had connected. It knocked him to his knees, groaning in pain. In the dark she could not see his face. He was youngish, definitely male, but beyond that she couldn't see.

A flash of headlights.

A car slowed down. It was a taxi. Poppy turned and ran towards it.

A moment later, Rollo and Gerald Farmer got out.

"Good grief Poppy! What's wrong?" asked Rollo.

"A man! He attacked me! He –" Poppy turned to point, but the assailant had gone. With the entrance to the park behind him, it was no surprise where.

As the taxi pulled off, Rollo ran across the road, followed by a puffing Gerald, whose excess weight reduced his efforts to a merely lukewarm pursuit. By the time the two men and Poppy got to the entrance to the park the assailant was nowhere to be seen. Even with the blows Poppy had managed to inflict, he had had too much of a head start. The park was large with plenty of places to hide – not least the lurking ruin of King John's Palace. Rollo looked ready to head in though, so Poppy put her hand on his arm. "Let's leave it. I doubt we'll be able to catch him."

"I'll kill the bastard when I do!" fumed Rollo.

"I know you would, thank you. But I think we'd better leave it to the police. And if my suspicions are correct, this no doubt has something to do with me investigating Agnes' murder."

Rollo was still fuming but managed to rein his temper in. "All right. Let's leave it. But until the killer is caught, I don't want you – or any of us – going out on our own. Is that agreed?"

"It is."

Gerald, his shoulders hunched, peered anxiously at Poppy. "Did he hurt you? Did you see who it was?"

"No and no. It was a young man. Not too strongly built. But no softy either. I didn't see his face and he didn't say anything."

"Could it have been Gus?"

Poppy looked at the large man in shock. "Why on earth do you ask that?"

Rollo took Poppy by the arm. "We'll tell you inside."

***

Poppy declined a second glass of sherry to calm her nerves. She needed to keep her wits about her, as she and her fellow investigators had a lot of work to do. Yasmin had called the police as soon as she heard what had happened to Poppy, and was told someone would be sent over – eventually. As the lady was not injured, there was no immediate urgency. Yasmin insisted word be sent to DI Hawkes, but was not assured that her request would be honoured. So, with the children in bed, and Delilah still at the theatre, Yasmin, Poppy, Aunt Dot, Grace, Rollo and Gerald settled around the dining room table to thrash out their next moves. Betty had made some stottie cake, and they all tucked into slices of the sweet fruit bread with lashings of butter and jam.

Firstly, Yasmin went through the details of the interview with Dante Sherman at the police station, ending with the news that his handwriting didn't match that of the person who wrote the threatening letter to Poppy's mother, nor the note on the back of the photograph of Agnes.

"Does that mean he's completely off the hook?" asked Grace, her face awash with disappointment.

"No, it doesn't. I spoke to DI Hawkes afterwards and he told me Sherman is still a person of interest, in light of the information he received from the Met Police when they searched Agnes' studio."

"And do we have any more information on what that is, exactly?" asked Poppy.

"No more than Hawkes has already told us, no."

"I think we know what it is, don't we Gerald?" said Rollo. A morose Gerald nodded.

Rollo then went on to tell the women what he had overheard at the Grand Hotel and how he had revealed himself to Gerald after Gus left.

Rollo looked at his wife. "And Yazzie, the only reason Gerald agreed to come with me is that I said you might be willing to represent him in any legal proceedings."

"And Gus," beseeched Gerald. "Please try to help Gus too."

"Not if it was him who attacked my niece!" declared Dot, reaching out and squeezing Poppy's hand.

"I don't know if it was him, Aunt Dot. I only said to Gerald that it might have been. The right age, the right physique . . ."

"But you said it could also have been Dante Sherman," said Grace. "Which one was it?"

Poppy put down her stottie bread and brushed crumbs from her fingertips. "Either of them – or neither of them. It could just have been a random attack. It's not unheard of around here. Remember the other night when someone tried to snatch my bag at the cinema?"

"That was just an opportunistic snatch and grab by a young scallywag. This seems to be far more serious. More targeted. Don't you all agree?" asked Grace.

There were nods of agreement around the table.

"And thank God Rollo and Gerald came along when they did!" declared Dot.

Rollo grinned. "Oh, I think your niece had already got the measure of him before we arrived, Dot."

Poppy smiled. Yes, she had been shaken up by the whole affair, but she was also very proud of how she had handled herself. She couldn't wait to tell Delilah that those self-defence and jiu-jitsu classes had *not* gone to waste. She hoped that whoever it was who had attacked her was nursing a very sore body part tonight.

"Nonetheless," said Yasmin, "it could easily have turned out differently. So I think – for now – we should go with your initial assessment, Poppy, that it was somehow connected to the investigation, that whoever it was who attacked you was trying to stop you finding out any more. On the current evidence before us, the two most likely suspects are Dante Sherman and Gus North. We need to figure out which one."

Gerald shook his head, tears welling in his eyes. "I know I suggested it might have been Gus, but on reflection, I don't believe I should have. I don't think Gus would hurt anyone. I really don't."

"But you said yourself that you thought he might have killed Agnes – and that that's why you didn't tell the police you saw him go out the back door of the gallery with her," said Rollo.

"I know, I know. But if he did kill Agnes, I can't believe it was on purpose. An accident, perhaps – a tragic accident."

"Slitting her throat with a Stanley knife?" asked Grace. "That's quite an accident."

"But the Gus I know would never do that! Nor hurt Poppy."

"The Gus you know?" asked Poppy. "How well do you really know him? Do you know, for instance, that Gus is Agnes' son?"

Aunt Dot dropped her sherry glass, the amber liquid seeping into the tablecloth like a pool of spreading blood.

"He is *what*?" asked Yasmin.

So Poppy went on to tell her friends what she had learned at the Northanger house, the five of them sitting in stunned silence as she recounted the tragic tale of Agnes' baby boy.

"So," said Yasmin, eventually. "That paints a potentially different picture of events. It now seems very likely the reason Agnes and Gus went out that evening was so that she could tell him she was really his mother. We need to get Gus to confirm that though. Gerald, you said that Gus was planning on leaving tomorrow morning for Amsterdam. We will need to get hold of DI Hawkes to tell him. He *must* be apprehended."

"But what if he didn't do it? I cannot believe he would have killed his own mother," said Gerald, his voice quivering along with his chins.

"Then this is his chance to clear his name. And help us catch the real killer."

"Who is . . . ?" asked Rollo.

The six of them looked at one another around the table, variously shrugging or sighing. Eventually, Grace said: "I still think it's Dante Sherman."

"And so do I," said Poppy.

Yasmin leaned forward, poised as though she were cross-examining a witness in the Old Bailey. "But why? What was his motivation?"

Poppy thought for a moment, her mind racing over the events and conversations of the last week. "I keep coming back to the conversation I had with his mother. When she told me of his anger when he found out about his father, Michael Brownley – his anger and his shame. I still think he might have been trying to avenge his father's death. Bringing Agnes up here, forcing Gus to bring the two paintings associated with her time in Ashington and the birth of his half-brother – whom we now know was Gus."

"Do you think he knew that Gus was – or is – his brother?" asked Rollo, his sharp editor's eyes alight with the possibility of some sensational headlines.

"It's possible," said Poppy. "He was certainly sniffing around the story, visiting Ashington and also Sister Henrietta. And he did seem to take a sadistic pleasure in taunting Gus –"

"But what did he intend to do with the paintings?" asked Gerald. "I can't figure that out."

Poppy again gave it some thought. "What was it the stable boy told us, Rollo? That Sherman said that he needed the paintings to 'show her he meant business.'"

Rollo nodded. "That's right. Is that what you remember him saying, Gerald?"

"Y-yes. I think so. I didn't know what he meant though."

Poppy's mind was whirring. "What if he meant to use them to threaten Agnes?"

"With what?" asked Yasmin. "We know that he was using them to threaten Gus that he would reveal he had forged some of Agnes' paintings, but what – if you are correct – might he have used them for in relation to Agnes?"

"He must have known about the baby. That the baby hadn't died. And he was going to tell Gus – and everyone else – about it, knowing that Agnes had not actually told Gus. That she was too ashamed to. It's the only thing I can think of."

"Did Mrs Northanger say he'd been to visit?"

"No, she didn't, but perhaps he did some investigating of his own. There was a forged death certificate, for instance . . . or perhaps Agnes might even have told him."

Yasmin nodded. "Perhaps. But it's still speculation."

"Yes it is, but surely we can't discount all the circumstantial evidence. The letter to my mother, for instance – threatening her and telling her to not talk about what she knew about Agnes' baby – suggests this had been planned for a while. And don't forget he visited Sister Henrietta, trying to get information about the baby. And then there's the photograph sent to Agnes – of her, naked – and remember that he had access to the paintings in the basement of the art school –"

"But it wasn't his handwriting. Besides, the letter mentioned abortion, but you are now suggesting that Dante actually knew the baby hadn't died. His defence team would have a field day with those contradictions," said Yasmin, who for the first time since the start of the investigation appeared to be showing signs of frustration.

Poppy slumped back in her chair, feeling equally frustrated. And tired, so very tired. She was so sure Dante Sherman was involved in this – call it a gut instinct, intuition, or divine guidance if you will – but she just couldn't figure out how. Perhaps if she had a good night's rest, she would be able to think more clearly about it all in the morning.

"What if he got someone else to write it for him?" It was Dot.

Poppy sat up. "What do you mean, Aunt Dot? That Sherman had an accomplice?"

The older woman's heavily made-up eyes were wide with excitement. "Yes! And I think I know who."

All eyes at the table were on the former actress. She preened, loving the attention. "Excuse me Yasmin, if you don't mind, could you pass me the pathologist's report of Agnes?"

"How do you know I have a pathologist's report?"

Dot flushed charmingly. "Well, I did have a little snoop when you were out . . ."

"Heavens, Dot! Why ever did you do that?"

Poppy raised her hand to calm Yasmin. "It's a *fait accompli*, Yasmin. Aunt Dot, what are you saying? What did you find out?"

"Well, in the report – among all the gruesome details of poor Agnes' injuries – I noted something quite odd. It's been bothering me for a while, but I didn't want to mention it in case – well," she bit her lip like a naughty schoolgirl, "– in case you found out I'd been snooping. But, I'm prepared to fess up to it, because I think I might have solved the case!"

"Well, spit it out woman!" shouted Grace.

Dot, seemingly unoffended by her friend's outburst, continued: "Did you notice, Yasmin, that some short white hairs were found on Agnes' gown?"

"I did, yes. They were just listed as an oddity. Nothing of any forensic interest."

"Ah, but what if they do have forensic interest? What if they give us a clue to the identity of Agnes' real killer?"

Poppy's blue eyes, so like her aunt's, widened as the implication of what Dot was saying sank in. "Good Lord! Mrs Northanger has a white cat. Its hairs were all over me when I left there. Are you suggesting –"

"No! No! Not her. It's –"

"Maddie Sherman and her two little dogs!" blurted out Poppy, before her aunt could finish.

Dot clapped her hands. "Yes! Yes! Yes! And that's not all." She reached for a file in the centre of the table. "Yasmin asked me to go through the guest list from the night of the exhibition and cross-check it with the list of volunteer stewards at the Laing. We were trying to figure out who else might have access to the keys to the back door of the gallery, remember? And guess what?"

"Maddie Sherman is a steward!" said Rollo, flicking open his reporter's notebook and frantically making notes.

"She is! But not just at the Laing. She is also . . ." Dot paused dramatically, ". . . drum roll please, ladies and gentlemen – she is also a volunteer steward at the Hatton Gallery. That's the gallery attached to the art school, whose basement holds the painting of Agnes as a naked girl."

"By Jove! Brilliant work, Dot!" Rollo jumped up and headed for the door.

"Where are you going?" asked Yasmin.

"To write up an article for tomorrow's paper. This will stop the press!"

"Whoa, hold your horses, Rollo, this is just speculation. Very intriguing speculation, I'll admit, but it's not yet a watertight case," chastised Yasmin.

Then, suddenly, Grace got up too, and slipped past Rollo, out of the room.

"Grace! Where are you going?" shouted Dot.

"I'll be back in a minute!" she called down the hall.

A few moments later she returned with a greeting card. On it was a hand-painted picture of some lilies in a vase – similar to, but nowhere near as accomplished as Agnes' version, nor for that matter, Gus'. But it quite clearly was meant to represent it.

"What have you got there?" asked Dot.

Grace sat down and opened the card, laying it on the table. "It's a condolence card. It was dropped off the morning after Agnes' death. I didn't get around to putting it up on the mantelpiece because – well – because I was taken into custody." She cleared her throat.

"Who's it from?" asked Poppy.

"See for yourself."

Poppy picked up the card and read out loud the kind platitude, regretting the death of Agnes and expressing sympathy for her friends and family. It was signed Maddie Sherman. And the writing – as far as she could tell – was exactly the same as on the letter to her mother. Poppy laid it out on the table for all to see.

Yasmin opened her file and extracted the letter and the photograph. Yes, on inspection, it was most definitely Maddie's.

"So," said Dot triumphantly, "I was right! Maddie *did* write the letter. Do you think she did it on her son's behest?"

Poppy nodded. "I think that's a reasonable supposition, don't you, Yasmin? And wasn't it posted in Leeds? I bet if we – or the police – do some digging they will find that either Maddie or Dante, or both of them, were in Leeds the day it was posted. And if you all recall, Gerald told us one of Gus' forged paintings was for a dealer in Leeds. And Dante knew about it. He might very well have been visiting that dealer the day the letter was posted. You know, there is so much tying Dante to this that I'd be loathe to let him off the hook and turn all my attention to his mother."

"I agree," said the barrister. "It looks like they might have been in cahoots to try to keep Agnes' relationship with Michael Brownley firmly in the past, possibly fearing that his predilection for painting young, naked children might come out and taint Dante's career. But it still doesn't prove murder . . . there is still the matter of the Stanley knife . . ."

Grace sat down and folded her arms across her chest. "Yes, there's that."

Poppy's mind was racing. She was recalling the morning after Agnes' death, when they had all been having breakfast. The morning Maddie arrived with her dirty boots, after walking the dogs in the park. And the morning before that . . .

"Grace," she said, "how did that card arrive? Was it delivered by the postman or did Maddie drop it off herself?"

"I assume she brought it with her that morning when she came to visit. I found it on the hall table after she had left."

"And did you see anything else on the hall table?"

Grace's eyes flicked to Poppy and then Yasmin. "You mean, like the Stanley knife?"

"Yes," said Poppy, "like the Stanley knife. That's where the decorator said he had left it. Was it there when you found Maddie's card?"

"No, it wasn't. Come to think of it, I hadn't seen that knife for a while."

"When do you last remember seeing it?"

"I'm not sure. It was definitely there on the Tuesday; that's the day the decorator was here, and I noticed he'd left it. I thought it best to just leave it there in a visible place until he came back. And I asked Betty not to move it when she dusted."

"All right," said Poppy. "That was Tuesday. But what about Wednesday – the morning I was out in Ashington with Agnes opening the community hall? Do you remember seeing it then?"

All eyes at the table were on Grace. No one queried why Poppy was going down this line of questioning; there was a sense that it was important. Very important. Something that had been staring them in the face all along . . .

"No, Poppy, now that you mention it, the knife was not there. The last time I saw it was when I collected the milk that morning. But by lunchtime, when you and Agnes returned, the knife was gone. I thought perhaps the decorator had come to collect it without us knowing. Although on reflection, that wouldn't have happened. He wouldn't have just let himself in. I did think of asking Betty about it, but I didn't get around to it."

"Had anyone come to visit that morning? Aunt Dot, do you remember?"

"Well actually, yes! Oh good heavens! Thank you God!"

Grace smiled at Dot and her friend beamed back. "That's right," said Grace, "it was Maddie. Maddie Sherman popped in to visit. I had asked her to go back into the hall and remove her muddy boots – just like I did the morning she came to offer her condolences – so she had time, alone, on Wednesday to see the knife and pick it up."

Poppy was immensely relieved. "That's exactly what I think happened too. I also don't recall seeing the knife there when I returned from Ashington on Wednesday. And I expect if we ask Betty, who cleaned the house that day, she too will remember it being there and then not. Yasmin? What do you think?"

But Yasmin was already up and heading out of the room. "Where are you going?" asked Poppy.

"If Mohammed won't go to the mountain, the mountain must go to Mohammed. I'm calling a taxi. Actually, I'd better call two. We're all going to the police station. Oh, and Poppy, ask Betty to come with us too."

Chapter 30

Wednesday, 9 October 1924

Ashington Colliery, Northumberland

Poppy and Sandy sat together in his police-issue Model T Ford, sharing a flask of tea.

"So Gus was exactly where Gerald said he would be, waiting to get on the ferry. He tried to run – poor blighter – but we caught him. Took him into the harbour police office and told him that we knew he was Agnes' son. And then we told him that we thought we knew who killed her. But we needed his help to find out – conclusively – once and for all."

"And he agreed?"

"Well, he didn't have much of a choice. I threatened to charge him with forgery and fraud if he didn't. But I think he would have agreed anyway, once I laid out our . . ." he smiled at Poppy, ". . . *your* theory of what happened."

Poppy flushed. "It wasn't just me, Sandy. It was definitely a team effort."

His smile grew wider and he clicked his tin cup against hers. "And that's one of the things I like about you, Miss Denby – your humility. And," he winked, "your beautiful blue eyes."

Poppy flushed again. "Are you flirting with me, DI Hawkes? Perhaps an eyeballing is not the best place to do that."

"An eyeballing?" He threw back his head and laughed. "Oh Poppy, you've been reading too many detective novels."

Poppy, slightly stung, tried to keep the edge out of her voice when she asked: "Then what would you call this, Sandy?"

"This," he gestured to the industrial landscape in front of them, "is a carefully laid plan to gather the last evidence we need to confirm who killed Agnes Robson."

Poppy looked to the right towards the pit head where Michael Brownley had died so many years ago, and to the left where she expected soon to see her mother and Sadie Robson.

The previous night, after Poppy and her team had finally managed to track down Sandy Hawkes and tell him everything they had discovered, he had driven Poppy through to Morpeth to speak to her mother. It was after midnight when she knocked on the door, and her father, used to parishioners calling him at odd times, had answered in his dressing gown. He had not, however, been prepared to see his daughter and a police detective. But after the initial shock he invited them in and woke up his wife. Sandy and Poppy told Alice their plan and left, an hour later, with her commitment to get Sadie Robson to the pit head at the agreed time the following day.

Meanwhile, earlier that day, under threat of arrest for fraud, but also with the positive incentive of helping to catch his mother's killer, Gus had gone to see Maddie Sherman. As instructed, he told her who he really was and that he knew who had killed Agnes – without actually saying who it was. He also told her that he didn't care that his mother was dead, as she had never been alive to him, and he couldn't forgive her for keeping it a secret from him for so many years. He told Maddie that he would keep quiet about what he knew about Agnes' death, as well as Michael Brownley's perversion, if she brought £1,000 to the pit head in Ashington by six o'clock that evening. The police had already checked the Sherman bank account and knew that she did in fact have that amount of money available. After an initial denial that she knew anything about it, Gus, as instructed, said that he had evidence that her son, Dante, was Agnes' murderer and he would give the evidence to the police if she didn't comply. She had then, tearfully, agreed. After that he went to visit Dante Sherman at the gallery and told him the same thing. But this time he said he had evidence that Dante's mother was the murderer.

"But what if Dante and Maddie compare notes and find out Gus has told them two different things?"

Sandy shrugged, then took a sip of tea. "It doesn't matter. What's clear is that Gus knows one of them is the killer, if not both."

"Do you think they'll come? And if they do, will they bring the money?"

Again Sandy shrugged. "I think at least one of them will come. Hopefully both of them. I think they'll want to confront Gus once and for all, now that it's all out in the open who he is. I think they're both emotionally trapped by the death of Brownley and need to free themselves from it. Agnes was a link to that. And so, too, is Gus. Which is another reason I suggested they come here. It's an emotionally charged place. And Brownley's ghost – so to speak – will be here too. They might be prepared to just pay Gus off. Or they might – and this is unfortunately possible as at least one of them has killed before – try to silence him."

Poppy's hand flew to her mouth. "Oh Sandy! Should we be putting Gus in danger like this?"

Sandy smiled at her. "And that's another thing I admire about you, Poppy. Your kindness. But sometimes you have to be cruel to be kind. Don't worry: I've briefed Gus, and he knows that me and my men will be close by and will be there to help if one of them tries anything."

"And Sadie?"

"She'll be fine too. We'll be right there, Poppy, don't worry. I've made arrangements with the mine manager to help us hide in the lift where we'll be able to hear everything. Gus has been instructed to stand as close to the lift as he can. We'll be out of there in a flash if either he – or Sadie – needs us." He turned to look at Poppy, his face earnest. "Trust me, Poppy."

But Poppy, as before, was not entirely sure that she did.

Poppy held her breath as she waited for Gus North to take his position near the lift. They were in a disused mine shaft, which had been closed due to the lowering of demand for coal since the end of the war. But all the equipment – including the lift – was still there, waiting to be called into action if and when it was needed again. The lift was a large cage that would take miners – and ponies – up and down at the beginning and end of their shifts. Even though it was currently not in use, it still smelled of sweat, coal dust and horse manure. At the top of the shaft, the lift was further separated from the wheel house by a wooden gate. This was usually locked with a padlock, but this evening, by Sandy's request, it was just loosely hooked. The gate was made up of horizontal slats of wood, sufficiently rough-hewn and shoddily constructed to leave small gaps here and there between the planks to allow Poppy, Sandy, a sergeant and two constables scope to peer out on whatever transpired outside. At nearly six o'clock in early October there was still enough natural light to create a dusky setting.

Despite Sandy's initial protestations, he had reluctantly agreed to allow her to hide in the lift to witness the final showdown between the family members of the late Michael Brownley: his widow and his two sons. Poppy was aware that two hundred feet below her was the floor of the mine shaft where Brownley's body had been found. Sandy told her that records from the time showed that during the month in which the art teacher died, this particular shaft was again not in use, being shut for repair, and the lift itself had been temporarily removed for upkeep. So, all that had been between Brownley and the hard, dark floor of the mine below was a wooden gate, which, the police inspector at the time had discovered, was rarely locked. In fact it was Brownley's death that had caused the mine management to put more stringent safety measures in place.

Sandy checked his pocket watch. It was five to six. "Where is he?" he muttered. But then, just as Poppy was beginning to stiffen with anxiety, wondering if the whole plan was going to be scuppered, Gus North appeared, silhouetted at the entrance to the wheel house. He looked nervous, flicking his eyes to the lift and back out the door. Sandy had told Poppy that Gus had been brought here earlier and held in the manager's office until the time they had agreed to send him to the wheel house. He could of course have done a runner, but Sandy had spoken with him long enough to know that, although frightened, he was willing to play his part in catching his mother's killer.

Poppy knew too that Sandy had spent some time with Sadie

Robson and her mother, coaching Sadie on what she needed to do. She had been taken to the mine manager's office earlier in the day and introduced to her grandson, Gus. Poppy would have loved to have been there for the emotional meeting, but she would just have to settle for hearing about it from her mother. Would Gus and Sadie now try to forge a relationship? Poppy hoped so. For Agnes' sake. Her heart broke thinking of all the lost years of regret, of the unspent love. Why, oh why, hadn't Agnes told Gus the truth when she first found him four years ago? Why had she not then gone public with the news that he was her son? Yes, Poppy knew that it was not the done thing for a single woman to publicly acknowledge she'd had a child out of wedlock. Children were often raised believing a grandmother or an aunt was their mother, to spare the reputation of the family. But Agnes was not a normal woman, constrained by societal norms.

She had run off to Paris and lived openly with her lover. On her return to London, buoyed into higher social strata by the money she'd inherited, she did not pretend to be a Mrs so-and-so. She was open about who she was and was not. So, worrying about social stigma was not her real concern – although she was grateful her money bought her some respectability and entrance to circles that a poor girl of dubious reputation would not ordinarily have. Poppy had thought long and hard about it, remembering her own conversations with Agnes, and later, Mrs Northanger, and had come to the conclusion that Agnes was most concerned by the fear of rejection by those she loved. What if she told Gus who she – and he – really were and he turned on her? As things stood, she could see her son daily at the studio and was able to watch him develop into a gifted artist and (his forging activities aside) an admirable young man. But, finally, as Mrs Northanger had said, Agnes had summoned up the courage to tell him the truth. And according to Sandy, in his police interview, Gus had confirmed that was what she had done.

Agnes had approached him at the gallery, standing in front of *The Railway Family* painting, and had tried to talk to him about the mother and child, asking him again why he had painted them. He said it was a dream he kept having, of him, as a small child, walking hand in hand with a woman he thought was his mother. It wasn't along a railway line in his dream, but he said when he'd seen the painting he just felt that the woman and child belonged there. So he added them.

She had then tried to speak to him, but he found it difficult to read her lips as she was mumbling and not forming her words properly. So, after noticing Grace Wilson slipping out and then, later, returning through the back door (which finally cleared Grace of any involvement), he suggested they go out to the stables where Agnes could speak more freely. So it was there, not on the roof, that she had told him who she really was. And it was there, not the roof, that he had first shouted at her, blaming her for all the years of pain and hurt he had endured. And there that she had begged him not to leave her. As she sobbed in front of him, his heart had softened. He had told her that he just needed a bit of time to work through it all. He asked her not to tell anyone else just yet. She had agreed, and he had come back in while she spent some time gathering herself. He had slotted back into the party, finding Gerald and pretending that nothing had happened. He and Agnes had arranged to meet the following day – once the hullaballoo of the exhibition had calmed down – to talk about things further.

Poor Gus, thought Poppy. *Poor, poor Gus*. His face was deathly pale, making his dark brown eyes and black curly hair stand out even more in the dusky light. He held his hat in his hands, worrying at the fabric with his beautiful long artist's fingers.

Sandy looked at his watch again. It was ten past six.

"Do you think they're not coming?" whispered Poppy.

"I don't know. Let's give it a bit more time. Sadie won't come until they're here. She's with one of my men who has sight of the wheel house."

Poppy shifted her weight from leg to leg, as Gus paced back and forth in front of the lift. It was pointless speaking to him – he would not be able to hear. But he and Sandy had locked eyes through the gate slats and he knew they were there.

And then, at quarter past six, Maddie and Dante Sherman arrived. She was dressed in her boots and tweeds as though she were just out walking her dogs. He was in one of his less flamboyant suits and a bowler hat. Poppy noted that he was walking with a slight shuffle and limp, confirming to her that it was indeed Dante who had attacked her the night before. Her eyes narrowed as she tried to control the rage that welled inside her.

Dante gestured for his mother to wait in the doorway and shuffled forward, positioning himself directly in front of Gus so the deaf man could read his lips.

"Let's get this over and done with, shall we?"

Gus nodded. "All right. I see you brought your mother."

"Yes. We both want to make sure you're serious about keeping quiet."

"You brought the money?"

"Some of it."

Gus put his hands on his hips. "I told you, I want £1,000 or I'm going to the police."

Dante curled back his lip into an approximation of a smile. "I see they raised you well at that orphanage. No moral backbone."

"How do you know I was raised in an orphanage? I never told you that. Just that I was adopted."

Dante shrugged. "I have done a little digging."

"Why? Why did you need to do any digging?"

Dante paused, then looked over at his mother before returning his cold gaze to Gus. "Because when I first met you it was like looking into the face of my father that I'd once seen in a photograph. The resemblance is remarkable. Do you know that he was only a year or two older than you – than us – when he died?"

Gus did not say anything.

"Isn't that right, Mother?"

Maddie Sherman stepped forward, her body language screaming that she'd rather be anywhere other than where she was now.

"I said, isn't that right, Mother?"

Maddie mumbled something.

"You'll have to speak up! The boy's deaf!"

With an enormous effort, Maddie looked up at Gus. "Yes, you look like him. Far more than his real son does. But Dante takes after me."

Dante laughed. "Oh, you always said that, Mother. But I don't think it's true. I might *look* more like you, but not in personality. Not in *appetites*. Did you know, dear brother, that our father liked fornicating with little children far younger than your mother?"

Gus' eyes widened in shock.

"No? Well, he did. Your mother was almost at a decent age. But others weren't."

"That's a *lie*, Dante, a *lie*. I know that's what people said, but it wasn't true," declared Maddie, wringing her gloved hands.

Dante shook his head, as though pitying the woman. "But it is. You could just never face up to it, saying it was just the drink. But it was more than that. And you knew it. I found his letters, his notebooks in the loft. Don't you remember? When I was twelve?"

"I remember." Maddie's voice was so soft that Poppy barely heard her. But Gus didn't need to hear. He could read her lips and her expression.

But before he could speak, another voice, a female voice, entered the conversation: "And so do I. I remember as well."

Maddie and Dante jerked their heads towards the door where Sadie Robson was standing. She wore her best black coat and best black hat, as though attending a funeral.

"Who are you?" asked Dante.

"Don't be coy, lad. You met me at the gallery. I'm Agnes' mam. And this lad's grandma."

"What are you doing here? How did you get here?"

"I brought her," said Gus.

Dante smirked. "Is she after money too?" Then to Sadie: "All right, how much do you want?"

Sadie Robson spat on the ground in front of Dante. "You can keep your money, you filthy pervert. You've taken me bairn. Nowt'll bring her back."

"Then why are you here?" asked Maddie, stepping in front of her son, as if trying to shield him.

"I've come to make an exchange."

"An exchange?"

"Aye. An exchange of truth. I'll tell you what really happened to your husband, Mrs Brownley, if you tell me what happened to my Agnes."

Dante put his hand on his mother's shoulder and lowered his voice, whispering into her ear: "Don't say a word, Mother."

"Shut up, Dante!" she snapped, to the surprise of everyone listening. Then to Sadie: "All right, I'll tell you. Mother to mother. Because that's what this is all about, isn't it? Mothers trying to protect their children."

"Aye, Mrs Brownley, I believe it is. You go first, then I'll tell you what I know. How did your son kill my Agnes?"

"It wasn't him."

"Of course you'd say that."

"It's true. Dante didn't do it. But I thought he might. Ever since he found his father's notebooks – and read what he'd been up to – some kind of darkness settled on him. He – well – he *interfered* with other children at school, and –"

"Mother, don't you dare!"

"Shut up! Shut up! Shut up! I have tried all my life to protect you. But I could never protect you from *his* blood in *your* veins, could I? Then when I found out you were bringing Agnes up here, that you were *obsessing* over her, I feared the worst. You kept notebooks yourself when you were a boy. And I read them. All your fantasies about what you would do to the girl you believed killed your father. To Agnes. So I decided to warn her. I saw her go out of the gallery with Gus that night and decided to follow. I listened in and heard what they talked about, when she told him that she was his mother. Then Gus went back in. I was hiding up the steps, on the way to the roof. And when Agnes finally gathered herself and was ready to go back into the party, I confronted her.

"I had brought a knife with me – a Stanley knife I'd found – but I didn't intend to use it. Just to frighten her. I wanted to warn her off. I'd already tried before – I'd sent Agnes a letter with a photograph of that disgusting painting Michael had done – and I'd told her to stay away from Newcastle, but she didn't listen. I knew if she came Dante would try to hurt her. And I didn't want her to be hurt. I swear to you. But more than that, I didn't want Dante to do something that could cost him his life. So I needed to warn her. Or to threaten her. Whatever it took to get her to leave.

"I knew that Dante sometimes went onto the roof to have a cigarette. I knew he enjoyed going out there to look over the city. And it seemed like a good place for me and Agnes to have a talk without anyone walking in on us. I had taken a key earlier, just in case the back door was locked. I had intended to ask Agnes to step out with me, but I hadn't accounted for other people finding that the door was open – like Grace Wilson and Poppy Denby. Although, I must admit, having Grace there was useful in terms of diverting the police's attention away from me – as was the knife. That hadn't been my intention when I first picked it up – framing Grace, that is – but it did turn out to be helpful.

"But I digress. So, Agnes and I, we went out onto the roof. And along to the tower. She was frightened, so I offered her a cigarette. And I had one, just to calm us down. I really didn't know what I was going to say to her. I thought I might threaten her, warn her off, act like a madwoman so she'd be scared of what I might do. But I didn't really want to do anything. I just wanted to stop my son from getting himself into trouble – just like my husband had got into trouble. You see, Mrs Robson, your daughter was the stumbling block on which both my boys fell. And she had to be removed."

"So you killed her?" Sadie asked, her voice cracked with emotion.

"Yes, I did. When she told me what Michael had done to her, I knew she couldn't be allowed to tell it to anyone else – not least Dante. So I killed her. I slit her throat. I didn't push her though. But if she hadn't fallen, I would have. Just like she pushed my Michael down this mine shaft. So I suppose justice *was* finally served."

There were tears streaming down Sadie's face. "But Agnes didn't push him."

"She said she did."

"I know. She told me the same thing – right back when it happened. But I didn't believe her. She was never a good liar."

"What are you talking about?" asked Dante. "Of course she killed him. Everyone knew she did. There was just never any proof."

"There was no proof because she didn't do it."

"How do you know?" asked Gus, his eyes on his grandmother's lips.

"Because she was trying to protect someone – her little brother Jeremy. Your uncle. Me other bairn. He'd followed her that night when she slipped out. He saw her meet Brownley. He was drunk. Agnes was upset. He brought her here. He was going to have his filthy way with her again. But Jeremy would have none of it. They were standing here beside the shaft. The gate was open, she told me. He – Brownley – started kissing her, pawing her. And she let him. But Jeremy saw it and ran at them. He pushed Brownley off his sister. But he didn't know the lift wasn't there and there was a dead drop down the shaft. And that's how he died." Sadie gestured to Maddie and her sons. "Your husband. And your – and your – father."

Silence fell in the wheel house. Poppy waited for someone to say something. For Maddie or Dante or even Gus to cry out, to run, to do . . . something. But nothing happened. And then Sandy pushed open the gate of the lift and he and his men stepped out and revealed themselves. Maddie gasped and cowered. Dante laughed, scornfully, turning to face Poppy and the posse of policemen.

He opened his arms wide, as if to show he was unarmed, then said: "I see the game is up. How sneaky of you, Miss Denby. How very sneaky. But as you heard, Inspector, I am *not* guilty of murder. And you shall be hearing from my solicitor."

"I look forward to it, Mr Sherman. Take them away."

Two constables handcuffed Dante, while the sergeant took Maddie by the arm and escorted them out of the wheel house.

Standing side by side, watching them go, were Gus and Sadie.

"Can they have some time alone?" asked Poppy.

"Aye," said Sandy, "they can."

Chapter 31

Monday, 21 October 1924

London

The Flying Scotsman let off a welcoming hoot of steam as it chugged into King's Cross Station, greeted by bundled-up passengers waiting for its return journey north. *Golly*, thought Poppy, *it's good to be home*. She was surprised to find herself thinking that. Since when had she started calling this city home?

She smiled as she thought of her friends and family that she'd just left behind in Newcastle and Morpeth, glad that she could visit them whenever she wanted. But if she were honest, she was relieved that she had a life of her own here in London.

It had been an exciting – although tragic – few weeks up north. She – as well as the Rolandson family who had travelled with her back down to London – would need to go up again in the spring when Dante and Maddie Sherman's trials were scheduled, but for now they were free to go. Aunt Dot, Grace and Delilah would be spending a couple more weeks there. Dot and Grace had the finishing touches to put on the town house before they could turn it over to the housekeeper they had hired to supervise the property when the new lady tenants moved in. Delilah, whose run at the Theatre Royal had finished, had decided to spend a few weeks seeing the sights of Northumberland – and perhaps popping up to Edinburgh – with her latest beau, Peter MacMahon. Whether anything would come of the fledgling romance, Poppy was not quite sure.

As far as her own fledgling romance went, Sandy had seen her off at Central Station. He said he would most definitely be staying in touch – personally and professionally – and looked forward to seeing her again. She had not tried to dissuade him, and was pleasantly surprised to hear him say that he was considering asking for a transfer down to London. His work on the Agnes Robson case had drawn the attention of the powers that be at Scotland Yard, and a promotion to the capital was being touted.

"What do you say about that, Poppy?" he had asked.

"I say let's cross that bridge when we come to it." Then she had kissed him on the cheek.

On the journey down, when the Rolandson twins finally fell asleep, she allowed her thoughts to drift to the possibility of furthering her romance with DI Sandy Hawkes. Oh, he was most definitely attractive, and it was clear that there was a mutual admiration between them, but there was just something, something she couldn't quite put her finger on, that gave her pause for thought. She still wasn't really sure she could trust him, and she didn't know why. Perhaps, though, in time, her concerns would be allayed. They had hardly had much time to spend alone together, without the professional complications of a murder investigation between them. So yes, she would welcome him visiting if he came down to London. And she would see him – and everyone else – again at the trial.

Fortunately, Gus North would only be at the trial as a witness. Yasmin had managed to get Sandy – and the Newcastle Director of Public Prosecutions – to not lay any formal charges against him regarding the fraud, as long as he and Gerald returned the money they'd received for the paintings and gave the collectors real Agnes Robsons in exchange, a deal the collectors were not likely to argue with, as the originals would be worth a lot more now that the famous artist was dead. In fact, her estate would now be worth a fortune. Agnes' solicitor had revealed that she had filed a new will with him the morning before she died – having it signed and witnessed at an office in Newcastle. The will had been read after Agnes' funeral. She was buried in Ashington, next to her father.

She had named Gus North – formally known as Augustus

Northanger – as her majority heir. But she had also left money to her mother and brother Jeremy. Jeremy, it was decided, would also not face legal consequences for the death of Michael Brownley. It was too long ago, he had only been eleven years old, and all the witnesses were dead. On top of that, there were questions about the culpability of the mine owners for not having a secure gate over the lift shaft. Agnes had also left a sum of money to St Hilda's so their roof could be fixed. And then, finally, she had been true to her word and had set aside some money for a bursary fund for gifted young female artists. She had named Dot Denby, Grace Wilson and Alice Denby to be co-trustees. Poppy chuckled to herself. Oh, that was going to be a challenging relationship. However, all three women agreed that they would work together.

Poppy smiled as she thought of her mother. Yes, it had been a distressing few weeks for everyone. But one of the good things that had come out of it was that she and her mother had developed a new respect for one another. Alice had told her she was proud of her and finally, after all these years, given her her blessing to go back to London and work on the newspaper. Perhaps that's why Poppy finally felt free to call London home.

The train had now stopped and Rollo, Yasmin and the nanny were gathering the children and luggage. Little Cleo was niggling. Poppy had discovered she had a knack of soothing the child, although it didn't seem to work quite so well with the other twin.

"Here, give her to me," said Poppy, and she took the child from Yasmin.

Poppy and the family stepped out of the carriage while Rollo called a porter to help them with the luggage.

As he did, a tall man in his early thirties walked towards them, grinning.

"Well, I'll be darned, if it ain't Danny Boy Rokeby!" Rollo strode towards his old photographer and pumped his hand up and down. "What are you doing here, old sport? I thought you were still down in Africa."

Daniel smiled down at his former editor. "Well, I'm back. And I was wondering if you might have a job for me?"

"For the best darned press photographer in London? You bet I do! When do you want to start?"

"Well that depends . . ."

"On what?"

"On whether the best reporter in London wants to have me here."

Rollo, suddenly serious, looked back at Poppy and his family. He cocked his head. "I think you two had better have a conversation. Let me know what happens."

Then he took his daughter from Poppy and ushered his family away.

"Good luck," whispered Yasmin as she left.

Poppy was struggling to hold back her tears. She couldn't believe it. Here, on the platform of King's Cross Station, almost in the very spot they had first met, was the love of her life. All thoughts of Sandy fell away.

Daniel stepped towards her and stopped. She stepped towards him, then stopped too. Between them were four and a half years of love and longing.

"You're back," she whispered.

"I'm back."

"But the children? Your sister?"

"Maggie's had a baby."

"I heard."

"Her own baby. She – well – she doesn't have as much time for Amy and Arthur any more. And Arthur never really settled down there. He missed his London school friends. He's eleven now. He should be going to grammar school. And Amy's eight. She wants to see her grandparents. They were never that happy we left either."

"And you, Daniel, what do you want?"

Daniel pushed his hat away from his forehead so Poppy could see his beautiful warm grey eyes. His skin was tanned – it suited him – although there were a few more wrinkles around his eyes than she'd remembered.

"I want you, Poppy. I always have. I wanted you to come with me to South Africa, but I loved you enough not to make you. I knew you'd never be happy there."

Poppy caught a sob before it escaped her lips. "I would have been happy with you. I know I would have. But you're right; I would have found it hard to leave my life here. My family. My friends. My job. But don't think I didn't lie awake at night, praying and begging God to bring you back to me. Or dreaming of what might happen if I decided to follow you there. I was thinking of doing that. I really was. But then you stopped writing. I haven't heard from you since Easter . . ."

"But I wrote! I did! Something must have happened to the letters. I swear to you, Poppy: I wrote to tell you I was thinking of coming back. That I could no longer live without you. But then you didn't reply and I thought –"

It was Daniel's turn to catch a sob in his throat. Poppy closed the space between them and reached up her hand to touch his cheek. He covered her hand with his own then pulled her towards him. And then, despite the stares and sniggers of passengers on the platform, he kissed her. And she kissed him back.

Yes, thought Poppy, as she softened her lips against his. *This is a man I can trust.*

happy with you. How I would have. But that night I would have found it hard to leave my [illegible] family. My friends. My [illegible]. But the [illegible] I didn't [illegible] at night, [illegible] to me. Or dreaming of what might happen. I decided to follow you there. I was thinking of doing that when I [illegible] was. But then you'd stopped writing. I haven't heard from you since."

"But I never did. Something [illegible] that [illegible] I went to you, Poppy. I wrote it, and I was thinking of coming back. That I could no longer live without you. But then you didn't [illegible] and I thought—"

It was Daniel's turn to catch a sob in his throat. Poppy closed the space between them and reached up her hand to touch his cheek. He covered her hand with his own then pulled her towards him. And then despite the stares and sniggers of passengers on the platform he kissed her. And she kissed him back.

Yes, thought Poppy as she softened her lips against his. This is a man I can trust.

Acknowledgements

Murder at the Art Gallery was first published as *The Art Fiasco.* I remain indebted to the team at Lion Fiction for all the work they put into making the first incarnation such a success. As explained in the historical notes, the idea for the story has roots in my own family's experience in the 1920s. It is set in my home town of Newcastle upon Tyne and there is something really special about walking the streets of Grainger Town or browsing the Laing Art Gallery and seeing it all through Poppy's eyes. Some of the book is also set on the same street as the church I attend, Heaton Baptist, and I was able to plot as I drove or walked past the various locations. I also visited Morpeth and Ashington – places I have known since I was a child – but now saw them through different eyes.

As always, there are many people to thank. Firstly, Dave, Robyn and James Giles at the Laing Art Gallery, who helped me see what the gallery might have looked like in the 1920s. James, particularly, was helpful in guiding me around the "backstage" area of the gallery and pointing out the staircase to the roof that became so important in the plotting of the book.

Thanks too to Rajan Nair, who let the eccentric woman in to look around his town house on Jesmond Vale Terrace, on which I based Aunt Dot's house. It really helped to envisage where my characters would be living for the duration of the story. Thanks too to Lorrie at Morpeth Methodist, who not only showed me around the church but also pointed out the exact house that Poppy's parents would have lived in if they were really ministers there in 1924.

I am also grateful to the archivists at Woodhorn Colliery Museum and the very helpful folk of the Heaton History Group.

Thank you to my agent Sara Keane and the fabulous team at Embla Books, especially Emma Wilson and Martina Arzu, for breathing new life into the book and the series.

And finally, as always, thanks to Rod and Megan.

Characters

1897

Agnes Robson (14) – daughter of a coal miner from Ashington Colliery. Art student.
Jeremy Robson (11) – brother of Agnes.
Mrs Sadie Robson – their mother.
Mrs Alice Denby – mother of our heroine, Poppy Denby (b.1898). Wife of a Methodist minister.
Revd Malcolm Denby – father of Poppy. Methodist minister.
Christopher Denby (2) – brother of Poppy.
Michael Brownley – art teacher.

1900

Claude Moulton – a Parisian artist and Agnes' lover.

1924

Poppy Denby – arts and entertainment editor for *The Daily Globe*. Amateur detective.
Dot Denby – Poppy's aunt. Former suffragette and leading lady on the West End stage.
Grace Wilson – Dot's companion. Former suffragette and bookkeeper to the Women's Suffrage and Political Union (WSPU).
Delilah Marconi – actress, flapper and socialite. Poppy's best friend.

Rollo Rolandson – senior editor and owner of *The Daily Globe.* Poppy's boss.
Yasmin Rolandson (née Reece-Lansdale), KC – barrister. Rollo's wife.
Daniel Rokeby – press photographer. Poppy's former beau.
Agnes Robson (41) – world-famous artist.
Gerald Farmer – Agnes' business manager and publicist.
Gus North – Agnes' studio assistant.
DI Sandy Hawkes – police detective inspector with Newcastle CID.
Peter MacMahon – journalist with the *Newcastle Daily Journal.*
Walter Foster – journalist with the *Morpeth Herald.*
Dante Sherman – curator at the Laing Art Gallery.
Maddie Sherman – Dante's mother and Aunt Dot's neighbour in Newcastle.
Mr Helsdon – caretaker at the Laing Art Gallery.
Jimmy Jackson – stable boy at the Laing Art Gallery.
Professor Reid – head of Newcastle Art School, Armstrong College.
Edna Storey (12) – art student in Ashington.
Mrs Storey – Edna's mother. Owns a sweet shop in Ashington.
Betty – Aunt Dot's char.
Sister Henrietta – runs St Hilda's home for unwed mothers and women in distress.
Mrs Northanger – patron of St Hilda's.

The World of Poppy Denby

A Historical Note

In 1920 my great-grandfather, Matthew Gill, was attacked and killed in a working men's club in the mining village of Crawcrook, County Durham. His assailant (a fellow coal miner) was arrested and charged with murder, but at the trial this was commuted to manslaughter. Matthew left behind his wife, Mary Jane, and five children, including my grandma, Betty, who was fifteen at the time. The story of the "murder" is something I have grown up with, and I have long wanted to write a murder mystery set in a mining village in the North East of England in the 1920s. However, although tragic for my family, there was nothing very exciting about my great-grandfather's death. It was a cut-and-dried case. It happened in front of a dozen or so witnesses and the killer was arrested almost immediately. So it was not really an option to fictionalise that story. But the core idea of a murder in a mining village stuck with me.

Another thing that has stuck with me is the memory of my grandfather, the man Betty Gill was to marry. Fred Veitch came from a working-class family in Newcastle. He made a living out of painting and decorating, but in his spare time was a very gifted artist. I never met Fred – he died in his early forties when my dad was only eleven – but I grew up looking at and dreaming about the beautiful landscapes that hung in my childhood home. Fred's sister once told me that her brother had always wanted to be a professional artist but never had the opportunity, in her words, to "better himself". His great-granddaughter, my daughter Megan, is also a gifted artist. She was fourteen at the time I started writing this book, the same age as Agnes Robson when the story begins.

So art, mining and the limited opportunities of gifted working-class people to pursue their dreams became the kernel of this book. Readers will know that Poppy Denby comes from the Northumbrian market town of Morpeth, just up the Great North Road from Newcastle. Morpeth is only a few miles from the mining village of Ashington Colliery. In the 1930s and '40s Ashington became famous for a group of amateur artists who either were or had been miners. They initially worked with a tutor from Durham University called Robert Lyon, but they soon outgrew the course material and he suggested they start producing their own work. In 1936 they put on an exhibition at the Hatton Gallery in Armstrong College, which now forms part of the modern Newcastle University.

Paintings by members of the Ashington Group (also known as the Pitmen Painters) are still highly acclaimed and widely exhibited to this day. This gave me the idea to have a tutor from Armstrong College travel to Ashington in 1897, and start art courses for the children of miners. This is entirely fictional, but historically plausible, as the managers of Ashington Colliery encouraged and funded a host of recreational and educational activities for the miners and their families. Ashington was set up as a "model mining village" and the welfare of the workers was prioritised. However, two years after this book is set, the 1926 General Strike was to have a devastating effect on the community of Ashington and coal miners across the country.

But in 1924, the North East of England, with its regional capital of Newcastle upon Tyne, was still enjoying the last rays of economic prosperity from the profits of its ship building and armaments factories which thrived during the Great War. The side of Newcastle shown in *Murder at the Art Gallery* is that of the art-, cinema- and theatre-loving middle class, centred on the gorgeous Georgian heart of the city known as Grainger Town. Aunt Dot's row of splendid town houses overlooking Armstrong Park in Heaton, with its bowling greens and tennis courts, was and still is a real place – and yes, the pavilion really was firebombed by suffragettes in 1913.

The Laing Art Gallery is still a cultural hub in the city today.

The paintings mentioned in this book (apart from Agnes' fictional works) were in fact part of the Laing's collection in the 1920s, when my grandma Betty and her sister Emma would sometimes visit. The curator, Dante Sherman, is an entirely made-up character, and there is no suggestion whatsoever that any of the Laing staff at the time (or since) were involved in procuring dodgy artwork. The layout of the building, with its intersecting galleries and the tower that can only be reached from a staircase onto the roof, is historically accurate. The stables are now part of the gallery's workrooms, and the staircase – and the tower – are still there.

The only historical tweak I have made in this novel is to bring forward the UK release of *The Humming Bird* film to autumn 1924 from February 1925. Otherwise, to the best of my knowledge, all historical references in this book are accurate. However, errors are still sometimes made: to err is human, to forgive divine.

About the Author

Fiona Veitch Smith is a lover of Golden Age mysteries and historical fiction and has been shortlisted for the CWA Historical Dagger. She has worked as a journalist, a university lecturer and a communications manager, and mentors new novelists. She grew up in Northumberland, then spent her teens and twenties in South Africa. She now lives in Newcastle upon Tyne.

Visit http://www.poppydenby.com/ for more information about the author, and about the world of Poppy Denby.

Visit http://www.claravalemysteries.com/ for information about the world of Miss Clara Vale.

About Embla Books

Embla Books is a digital-first publisher of standout commercial adult fiction. Passionate about storytelling, the team at Embla publish books that will make you 'laugh, love, look over your shoulder and lose sleep'. Launched by Bonnier Books UK in 2021, the imprint is named after the first woman from the creation myth in Norse mythology, who was carved by the gods from a tree trunk found on the seashore – an image of the kind of creative work and crafting that writers do, and a symbol of how stories shape our lives.

Find out about some of our other books and stay in touch:

X, Facebook, Instagram: @emblabooks
Newsletter: https://bit.ly/emblanewsletter